AZURE BLUE

A. L. HAWKE

PHANTOM HEART, LLC

ISBN: 978-1-953919-07-6 (ebook)

ISBN: 978-1-953919-08-3 (paperback)

ISBN: 9781953919397 (hardcover)

Library of Congress Control Number: 2021924350

Line edited by Stephanie Ward

Proofread by Alexa B., alexabooks.wixsite.com/authors

Cover & Map Design © 2021 by Sean Counley

Published by Phantom Heart, LLC

27702 Crown Valley Pkwy D-4, #201

Ladera Ranch, CA 92694, USA

Printed and bound in the United States of America

First printing December, 2021

Learn more about A.L. Hawke at www.alhawke.com

Correspondence: contact@alhawke.com

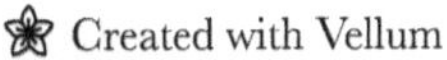 Created with Vellum

MOUNT AMBITUS
THE STRATOS RIVER
Napea
AZUR
THE CRYSTAL PALACE
Tartarus
Elysium
River
THE UN

The Hinterland
RE BLUE
THE STYGIAN HOLE
STRAIT OF AZURE
THE LANDS OF ATALA
Mangorilla
Mount Ambirys
Plum Caves
Styx
UNDERWORLD

Crete
MOUNT AMBITUS
NAPEA
Azure Blue
CRESCENT
SHADOW FOREST
NZERBAN
SUN KING
CRYSTA
KEI
THE CONTINENT OF ATALA

ADELAIN
BLUE
MOON DESERT
KINGDOM
FOX KINGDOM
CALAVIA
L. LAKE
KINGDOM
RIVER OF TRINIZ
IOGENAS
CLIFFS OF ZONOGH
THERIA
STATERIA
TELERIA
OR DUNN
HARKIST
ROITHIAN
Strait of Aethiopia
Egypt

1

AVVA

"Let's get away from here, Antilus," Avva said. "Hmm? Far away." She gripped her white winged unicorn's neck tightly and tugged it upward. They soared higher, leaping over a spire of a crystal tower then leveling off, bobbing up and down as wind passed over her long dark hair. The palace walls below reflected blue-green from the surrounding forests. The glass towers were over seven stories tall reaching up toward a chartreuse sky. And the front of the castle was violet grass, and ivy grew with some of the vines climbing the walls. She passed over the ancient wooden drawbridge. Its worn deck and railing designed for battle contrasted with the crystalline beauty of her home. And, fittingly, a depressing procession of black-robed nymphs slowly walked over the bridge into the castle. A few looked up. They waved.

"Far away, Antilus," she said, ignoring the nymphs. "Far. Okay, girl?"

Antilus whinnied.

Soon the blue-green branches and leaves of the coastal forest sped under Avva's sandals. The green sun set to her right, along the horizon over Mount Ambitus. Usually her route headed to Mount Ambitus by the Stratos—Mount Ambitus, more like a great earthen wall covering the view to her right in the Isle of Napea. But today, she headed toward the sea.

Avva descended near the water and jumped off her unicorn onto purple-and-white sand. She petted her soft, feathery hide. "Oh Antilus, tired, girl? Too much flying? And now the sun's setting." Antilus snuggled her head under Avva's arm.

As they walked close to the shore, she allowed waves to break over her feet. She took off her sandals, and her blue toes touched the wet violet sand. Her nymph skin was faint blue over her body, but very dark on her palms and the soles of her feet.

"There he was laid to rest," she said, more to herself than her unicorn, pointing to the lands beyond the sea. The cool water washed over her ankles. "Oh, what I'd do to visit there."

"You're not allowed."

Avva whirled around. It was her best friend, Hanna. And Avva spotted Maythra, Hanna's brown winged unicorn, on a sandy slope toward the trees.

"What are you doing here?"

"Following you," Hanna said. "Must you always look for trouble, Blue? Do you know what your mother's going to do to you when she doesn't see you in the evening procession?"

"I don't care. It's so depressing. Why'd you follow me?"

"To be with my friend." Hanna smiled and hugged her. "But it's your father's funeral. You must attend."

"I never knew—"

"You never knew your father. I know. We all know. All Azure knows. You made it quite clear, shouting it in Court. Do you have any idea how worried Engel is?"

"He worries about everything."

They laughed. They walked together as a purplish black hue fell over the land with the setting sun. Avva could only see shadows of trees surrounding the beach now.

"We could honor him," Avva said. "We could prepare a ceremony in the Crescent Kingdom for Father's journey to Hades and Persephone in the Underworld."

"Only if you want to join him there."

"Who's to say anyone'll know?" She flashed her friend a sly smile. Hanna laughed but, deep inside, Avva was quite serious.

"It's getting dark." Hanna gazed up at the moon. "Whether you're going to attend or not, princess, we should make our way back."

"How come you came after me?"

"I told you. My friend needed company."

"Hmm." Then Avva searched her friend's eyes. "I bet Engel sent you. Didn't he?"

Hanna turned from her.

"He did!"

"Oh Avva, he told me that you flew off with the queen's unicorn. He's very worried. He figured I'd know where you'd go. You know you're in so much trouble. The queen won't get out of her room, except for the ceremony—the ceremony you came late to and caused a scene."

"I caused a scene? What about her? And when is she not angry, Hanna?"

Avva stopped walking and turned toward the sea once more. She folded her arms and enjoyed the mist as it blew along her face, and the sounds of the waves touching the shore.

"We'll cross the sea to my father's lands tomorrow."

"What!" said Hanna. Avva laughed at her wide-eyed look.

"Across the Strait. We'll go to the Hinterlands tomorrow. In honor of my father."

"I heard what you said, but you're obviously not well. Are you crazy?"

"Aha, you know I am."

Hanna searched Avva's eyes again. Avva shrugged. But as she turned back to the sea, she felt a choking sensation in her throat. She felt so mad. She hated her mother.

"Now's the perfect time," Avva said with a shrug. "I'm in trouble anyway. Mother thinks I don't care about my father, but I adored him, probably far more than she ever did. He was so kind to me at the games. Then she sent him away. I hate her. Oh, you don't know how much I hate her, Hanna. But ... I love him."

"Avva." Hanna gently touched Avva's cheek. But that was the cheek that still hurt from her mother's strike. "You embarrassed her. You accused her in public."

"Sard all her rules!" Avva shook her head violently. "I only saw my father for a handful of days. She might have struck me in the face, but I've wanted to do far worse to her. Hitting me was only showing what a wicked witch she is. It's her fault that I never saw Father. I will never forgive her."

Avva felt the sting on her cheek, partly from humiliation, partly from her skin still burning. She had come to the throne room that morning late wearing the same lovely white dress she wore now. A formal white lace peplos. That was already an insult, for it was white and not black: the traditional color of mourning. Then, after she embarrassed her mother in the throne room, shouting about not ever seeing her father, the queen rushed down the three steps from her throne and struck Avva squarely across her cheek in front of a hundred nymphs.

"Just come back to the palace."

"But on the morrow." Avva gestured toward the sea. "We cross the sea." Avva turned and almost laughed at the terror on Hanna's face. "Serves her right. I won't cower over fake edicts. After all, I'm not only a queen's daughter but a king's—a human king's. I need to honor my father on his soil."

"Then you'll die." Hanna shook her head, befuddled.

"Whatever. You coming with me?"

2

CRESCENT BLUE

Avva flew with trepidation but determination to make it to the other side. She had never traveled beyond her shore. No nymph she had known ever had. But she had longed for the Hinterlands beyond the Strait all her life, staring at her father's distant yellow and brown lands from the glass towers of her palace.

She gasped as the sky changed from green to blue and the green sun turned yellow. The air thickened and weighed down on her. It became harder to breathe, and it seemed to become harder for Antilus to fly. But the great steed pushed forward, charging through the wind. Colors continued to change. The sea's waves turned as bright a blue as the sky. The Hinterlands grew browner. Greener. She could see green-leafed forests beyond a yellow sandy shore. It was absolutely lovely.

"This is it, Antilus." She ran her blue fingers along the white feathers of her unicorn's hide. "Legend says you were here with Queen Harmonia centuries ago, weren't you, girl? Hmm? Now you return."

But the unicorn objected. Avva dipped her head down, but the unicorn bucked up refusing to land.

Avva swooped over the yellow shore, similar in shape to the

beach back home. She looked down in awe at the white and yellow sand. Then she flew over brown and green trees and a hillside.

Avva dipped Antilus's head down again. "What's the matter? I order you to touch down." Avva hit the unicorn's glistening rainbow horn. This was a rare action by Amazons when forcing steeds to obey, and Antilus shook her head violently and neighed.

She finally swooped close to the beach. With some hesitation and further coaxing, Antilus touched the sand, falling into a gallop, then a trot. As soon as Antilus was steady enough, Avva jumped off, landing crouched on her knees in an Amazon fighting stance as she'd been trained. She froze and looked around, thinking something like a bolt of lightning from Zeus would fall from the sky. But nothing happened. Remaining low on the ground, she ran her hands along the white-yellow sand, letting the strange, warm, soft kernels flow between her blue-tinged fingers.

She stood up straight. Then she walked to Antilus and stroked her mane. Antilus was shaking.

"It's all right, girl. Nothing happened. You're okay." Avva pointed to a nearby cliff covered by a canopy of yellow and green trees. "Crescent Blue, hmm? Doesn't appear blue. I don't get it." She turned and looked at where she had come from. Just as at home, she could see the distant lands across the sea. But here, Azure Blue was visible on the horizon. And it was bright blue, like a glowing sapphire. "Oh, how stupid. It's Crescent Blue with the view of Azure."

Antilus shook her head violently again and stomped her feet.

"It's okay, girl," Avva said, petting the soft, feathery wings. "It's all right. Calm down." Avva searched her surroundings. It was desolate. Just sand and a cliff wall for as far as the eye could see. "I'll be back, okay? You stay here. If anything happens, fly home."

The horse whinnied, jerking her head back and forth again. Avva petted her head one last time; then she walked up the hillside toward the trees alone.

As she walked, she saw grass, not purple grass but green grass. She dipped her hand down and pulled some blades of grass from the wet mud. Then she touched brown soil, not purple, but dark brown dirt.

Her eyes fell on a stone settlement further up the shore. It was a simple stone building with ramparts. A fortress? It was small. She walked in that direction.

Then she discovered a dirt path veering deeper into the woods. She followed a trail of footprints. She could head back to the beach and continue toward the castle, but this walkway interested her—so did the footprints.

She labored as she walked. The air felt heavy.

After a long hike, she looked back toward her home through an opening in the trees. She could still make out the outline of her blue land shining like a jewel. Beautiful. Crescent Blue, indeed. Then up higher in the blue sky, she spotted a faint silhouette of an object circling in the clouds. At first, she thought it was a bird, but then she recognized great white wings. She smiled. It was Antilus. Her unicorn had taken flight and was now watching her from above.

Green foliage grew thickly as she walked deeper into the woods.

She came upon a lovely stream. The water trickled among trees and bushes and down granite rocks beside thick foliage. She found another clearing between trees where a waterfall flowed over stones. It all reminded her of the streams and brooks along the Stratos back home, but here it was not glowing blue; it was vibrant brown and green.

The yellow sun shone directly above, and she was getting hungry. She shrugged, sat down on a large white boulder, and untied a brown leather knapsack strapped to her shoulder. She took out some dried meat and chewed it. Then she removed her boots and dipped her blue feet in the water.

It was quiet. A squirrel leaped from a tree and made her jump. Then she giggled at its brown color.

She had been afraid to touch down in the Hinterlands. Now

she wondered why she hadn't before. What were her people so afraid of?

As she ate her midday snack, she heard another sound in the bushes. Another squirrel? No, this sounded bigger. Her feet splashed as she jumped up and pulled a camping knife from her belt, searching around the bushes and trees.

"Who's there!"

Nothing. It was quiet.

She slowly sat back down on the rock. But then more leaves and sticks rustled.

"Who's there?" Her voice sounded scared. There was movement in the bushes. Then the leaves and sticks on the shrubs cleared.

A man emerged. Or a boy? He was a little older than she was, but not by much. He had a boy's face, perhaps eighteen years old. But he was strong with huge broad shoulders and a chiseled face. He had a dark, thin beard, his face was worn and, though youthful, his features were rough. He wore armor, similar to the hoplite armor her guards wore, but while her guards wore scarlet, his armor was splashed with sky-blue paint. His dark hair was in a ponytail. But in all his fierceness, there was kindness in his dark eyes. The kindness turned warmer as he smiled.

"My lady, are you all alone in my woods? Or … are you a wood nymph, perhaps? Perhaps they are your woods?" He looked down at her blue feet under the water as she stood in the stream. He nodded. "I've found a lovely wood nymph in my forest."

She stared at him. Then she realized her mouth was gaping open. Reflexively, Avva dropped her knife and pulled a short sword from her belt. Then she positioned herself in the Amazon stance as she had been trained to: sword above her head, legs crouched down, head dipped, ready to strike. The man put a hand out. "I mean you no harm."

Avva squinted, waving the sword at him.

"Do you speak, wood nymph?"

"I'm not a wood nymph. I am Princess Avivae. I live across the sea."

"Princess?"

"Yes. Who are you?"

"Nobody." And he gave a smug grin as if that answered the question. Then, for a moment, he turned toward the waterfall, revealing a fierce, profoundly sad look. His demeanor did not fit his boyish face. He acted like a man.

She remained in the fighter stance. She knew how to use her sword. She had competed with men in the games, a few years ago, back home and had learned how to fight like all Amazon did since she was a little girl. This man had a sword too, a very large menacing one, hanging from his belt. And it looked worn. But he didn't touch it. Instead, he backed up to a tree and leaned against the trunk. He folded his arms and smiled.

Avva smiled despite herself. "If you stand back, I'll stand at ease."

"I wouldn't dare lay a finger on you."

"What's so amusing?"

"Your forward knee needs to shift closer to your body. You need to dip your chin down further to protect your lovely blue throat. Your sword is shaking. I'm afraid, though you're menacing, you're unbalanced. That is a disadvantage. It would be my advantage."

"Come closer and we shall see."

"I wouldn't dare."

"Then … perhaps you'd care for something to eat, boy?"

"Boy?" he asked, amused, shaking his head. "I'm not a boy, princess."

"All right, *sir*." She smiled again. "What is your name, *sir*?"

"Nobody. I am nobody. But you, princess, you come from across the Strait? You are far from no one. You are the princess from Azure Blue in Napea?"

She nodded.

"You are an Amazon. Put the blade down, princess. Please."

Then he opened his arms wide and said, "Why, I welcome you. Welcome to my kingdom."

"Your kingdom, *Nobody*?"

"Crescent Blue," he said with a smile and a nod. "Aye. My kingdom."

"What is your real name, *Nobody*?"

"Does it matter?"

"If you want me to drop the sword, it does."

"I am Prince Solinair Solinaray of Crescent Blue. Named Sol by King Darius." She relaxed at the sound of her father's name. "Perhaps, instead of Nobody, you can call me Sol." He pushed himself up from the trunk. She threatened him again by slashing the sword in the air before him. He smiled more widely and walked slowly toward her. Then he gently touched the tip of the blade with his finger. He lost his smile.

"Mandrigelian," he said with a nod. "Sharp—almost enough to cut my finger with a touch." Then he examined it from the side. It shone red and blue, depending on the direction of the light. She moved the blade close to his neck. He laughed. "But this is unfair. You are the one trespassing. I can, of course, look away from the offense and enjoy your pretty face as payment. Anyway, killing me after seeing such a vision would hardly count as a bad day."

"Don't think I can't cut you." But then she smiled and relaxed her stance. "Humph. You hardly look like a king."

"I'm nobody. I already told you that. But your face is white. Except for your neck. And your hands and feet. You don't look like a nymph. Well, I've never seen a nymph this close. Maybe your ears … are a little pointy. But legend says your people have a tinge of blue on your faces. Your features are pale. But your hands and feet are—"

"I colored it," she said, finally sheathing her sword. Then she flashed him a fake smile and showed him her blue palm and pointed at her bare blue feet. She threw her long black hair back and said, "Don't get any closer. I can take my sword out just as fast as before and cut you."

"I see that. Is it a Mandrigel blade?"

"Yes, it is."

"Incredible. I've heard of your people, but only saw you once. I saw your archers burn King Morteus's naval fleet and defend Castle Cove with your flying horses, helping my father when we were trapped in a tower. Your mother is Queen Delia, I suppose? She fought and helped free us that day."

"Impossible. Mother's never helped men. She's never helped anyone."

"I saw her and her people at the tower. She did, Avivae."

"Liar. My mother doesn't help anyone. Particularly men."

She sat at the edge of the stream and submerged her feet in the water again. She decided he wasn't a threat to her. She would just go back to what she had been doing. But she cocked her head back and looked at him.

He smiled. And that made her smile.

She liked his smile. And those eyes. Onyx eyes, sharp and intelligent, but kind. A handsome face. What a strange mix of strength and care. He seemed like a great warrior—no—a great man. Hardly a boy. A man. But young.

"I've always wanted to travel to Azure Blue," Sol said. "Darius spoke so fondly of you. But he said your queen forbids contact outside of the island. What are you doing here?"

"Well, the king was my father," Avva added with a shrug. "That's why I'm here."

"Really?" Sol opened his eyes wide. "Of course. You said you were a princess and Delia's daughter."

"Yes. Why?"

"Then…" He paused. He looked sad. "I'm sorry, princess, but you've arrived too late."

"I know. He's dead."

Sol seemed taken aback by her frank words. Even more when she laughed.

"I met him only once when I was a child," she added.

"You're a strange girl," he said, furrowing his brow and

nodding slowly. "It seems we're quite a pair. If Darius was your father, you realize you're my sister. He adopted me as his son."

Well, that was too bad. He was strikingly handsome. A very attractive *brother*. She patted a space beside her on the rock. "Are you hungry, King Nobody? Sit beside me. I brought some food and I'd love no one's company right now."

He leaped over and jumped on the rock beside her. She was startled at how fast he moved. She chuckled again but then lost her smile when she looked deep into his dark eyes. He took her hand gently and ran a finger along it, examining it.

"Blue," he said with a nod.

Yes, Blue. How does he know my nickname? … He's talking about your hand, you idiot. Are you getting smitten by this "nobody," stupid girl? Oh, but I like it when he touches my fingers.

She jerked her hand back.

"Why would you cover your lovely face by painting it white?"

If she hadn't, he would have seen her blush then. She felt the warmth on her cheeks. She just shrugged. She rummaged through her bag, took out some bread, and placed it in his hand. Then she touched his palm just like he had touched hers. His fingers were worn with cuts and dirty. Worn hands. But such gentle eyes.

"Thank you, Avivae."

"Are you hungry?"

"Yes."

"Call me Avva. Or Blue. My friends call me Blue."

"Thank you, Blue."

They ate quietly, but she enjoyed just sitting near him. He went through all the food in her sack. Then they talked about all sorts of nonsense like the kinds of plants and flowers growing near the stream. Or what animals roamed about in these parts. But none of it mattered. The only thing that really mattered now was *Nobody*.

"You met Darius?" he asked. "Or your father. When? Where?"

"Oh," she said with her mouth full of dry jerky. "The games. You know the games we hold. Just for a day or two."

"That was before the war," Sol said solemnly with a nod. "Many men do love the festivals with your people. Did he speak of me? His adopted prince?"

She shook her head.

"I see," he said contemplatively. "Princess, my father was the best man I've ever known. He devoted his life to the lives of others. He cared little for himself. He was just and strong. His courage had no bounds. He raised me like a son. In fact, he called me his son—to my brothers' dismay. He raised me. I'll miss him dearly."

She thought perhaps he'd cry. But could such a tough man cry?

"Why did you come here?" he asked.

"I told you. It was in honor of him. In honor of his passing."

"Did you bring libations to the gods?"

"No."

"Choai?"

She shook her head.

"So … you just flew across the Strait?"

She nodded.

"Hmm. You are a very strange girl."

"It's funny, Sol. You said you didn't know your real father but lived with mine. And I never knew mine. I only spoke with him a few days. Was he truly so great?"

"Darius was the best man I've ever known."

"I thought so. I knew that. Even the little I saw of him. He's better than my mother, anyway."

He looked straight into her eyes. His eyes were so piercing. "You don't like your mother?"

Avva nodded. Then she shook her head. "She's a witch."

"Really? A witch?" he asked with his eyes wide. "Is she really a witch?"

"Not a real witch, silly. An evil woman."

"Avva, your mother can't be so bad."

"Why?"

"If she were a witch, then you'd be a witch. And you seem far from that."

"Do you talk like honey to all the ladies in your kingdom?" she asked with a laugh, pushing his shoulder.

"No, I don't."

She lost her smile.

"Do you like my kingdom?"

"I'm still not sure I believe it's really yours."

He bit into an apple and shrugged. "I was given a small parcel of land. My brothers mock me and call me the Crescent king. I hold the Crescent Kingdom. Crescent Blue, as it was called before being handed to me. But I shrug at my brothers' disrespect. I am, in fact, no one. I'm proud of that. Considering my upbringing, I'm lucky I didn't end up a slave … Or remain one.

"The problem now, Avva, is not the death of our father, it is what will become of his lands. I don't know if you know, but King Darius kept the peace. By breaking his land into pieces and dividing it among my brothers, we're now at war. That was the other reason I traveled alone. I came to think. To mourn, but also think. I really don't know what I'm going to do."

Avva just nodded.

"There's war brewing. Your father should never have split the lands. He was a great king, but he had too great a heart. We shall fight each other, or be vulnerable to an outside invasion. That is why I walk alone today. To think. Honestly, I am nobody. But my brothers want to take my life. That I won't allow." She believed that. This was not a weak man. Then he laughed. "I don't know why I'm telling you all this. But you make me feel comfortable."

"You make me feel comfortable too, Sol." She tied her leather bag closed. Then she stood up. "But our meal's over."

"Don't tell me you're leaving already?"

"Sol, my mother is going to kill me when I return." She laughed when he smiled more widely. "It's not funny. She's *really* going to kill me. I'm only here for the afternoon, and I don't even want to think about what will happen when I come back."

"She doesn't know you came?"

"No."

"I like that. I like your spirit." He took her hand and gently turned her toward him. She looked up into his eyes and her hand trembled a little and her heart raced again.

"Just the afternoon?"

"Huh?"

He furrowed his brow. "Just today?" he asked.

She nodded.

He reached down and touched his lips gently to hers. She moved back for a moment, but slowly, because she wasn't sure she wanted to escape.

"I'm sorry," he said. "Was that wrong?"

She shook her head.

"You're not going to reach for your sword?"

"No," she said with a laugh. "It's just, oh, there's so much happening to me right now."

"Life is hard." And that seemed to answer everything. Then he said with a boyish energy, "Would you like for me to show you my forest? I know every inch. We must make the most of your time before your mother kills you. I enjoy the peace of walking alone among the trees and sleeping outside under the moon. Or riding across the sand. It's so peaceful in Crescent Blue. It always has been. The view of your lands puts me at ease. Just as you do now. This is my home. And it's funny, Avva, because I was given so little, but I love every inch of it. It was your father's gift. When I was younger, he lived with me in the summers, at the castle there beyond the hill, and truly cared for me. Now that castle, since his passing, has been bequeathed to me. It's paltry and nothing. Fit for a nothing king, but I am forever in his debt."

"I see your lands every day, Sol. Every day when I gaze with longing across the Strait. Now I know who this land belongs to. You find ease when you view our blue world, while I'm at ease gazing at your yellow one. It appears we both long for each other … I mean, each other's lands, you know."

What is it about him? He's just a boy. Well, I haven't seen one in so long … That's it. No. It's more.

Sol smiled and touched her hand again. She loved that. He raised it and ran his fingers along hers, and she felt a tingle all along her body. He seemed to be in awe of her blue palm. Then he kissed it gently, and she felt the stubble of his beard along her skin.

She giggled and pulled away. "Really, Sol, you act as if you've never touched a woman."

"I've never seen a nymph, Avva, up close. And certainly, never, never a woman as beautiful as you."

They touched lips again. There was something wrong about that—something very wrong. But everything was wrong about this afternoon, yet it felt right. Why? The mere fact that she was standing on brown soil was wrong. Every labored breath she took outside her home was wrong. And this man whose tongue now danced by hers, this *nobody* who was her "*brother*," that was wrong too.

But the water trickled along the stones. The birds chirped. And there was a breeze, no, his fingers, now running along her hair, touching her ear as they kissed. And she felt his breath. And his hand running along her back and side. And it was more right than anything was ever wrong before.

He cradled her head in his hand.

"I will savor every moment of this day," he said quietly, almost breathless.

"Do you always speak … like this to girls?" she asked.

"No. I told you, I don't, Blue."

"Your land is magical," she said almost breathlessly. "I wish this day would last forever." She said it more to herself than to him, but he answered by embracing her more closely. His arms were so welcoming.

They walked hand in hand on paths between trees. Indeed, Sol knew his forest. He pointed at waterfalls, many far greater than their shelter. He showed her views from atop the hills. Many were of her home beyond the Strait. He knew of all the beauty in the surrounding trees. All the right spots. And he loved sharing it with her.

They talked for hours. She asked him to talk about Darius. At first she hesitated, for it seemed to hurt him. She had been affected by her father's death, but she had never really known him. Sol had known him. Indeed, it seemed he had known him better than anyone. Then, in return, he asked her of her home, listening in disbelief to her description of Azure Blue's wonders.

The walk was physically difficult for her. She wasn't used to the heavy air. They stopped often so she could rest.

She was surprised at his chivalrous care for her. He could be so sweet, but then, if they heard something among the bushes, he could suddenly become fierce and focused. One time he even drew his large sword. Although she was trained, she jumped, afraid, just watching the ease with which he wielded it.

Time flew by. They enjoyed each other's company. Avva's only complaint was that it would soon be over. She tried to avoid thinking about it, but couldn't.

She remembered her promise to Hanna. She would return home, though she wanted to stay in this strange world forever. If she could be with *Nobody*.

As the yellow sun began to set, she had to go.

He walked with her all the way back to the beach. He took her hand again, looked closely into her eyes, then softly kissed her lips, so gently. "I shall never forget this day, Blue."

"Neither will I, Sol."

"When will I see you again?"

Avva gave a whistle. Antilus fell from the sky. Sol fell back in amazement at the strange white creature as she flapped her great wings and landed.

"I've never seen such an animal up close!"

"Her name is Antilus. She was Queen Harmonia's unicorn. And then Nefertiti's. Then Dainya's. All the way down the line, and finally my mother's."

"Hello and goodbye, Antilus," he said, petting her feathers in awe. "Please take care of your beautiful princess."

Avva quickly mounted the unicorn and looked down at him. He gazed into her eyes. He looked so sad that it made her laugh.

"Don't be sad."

He nodded and tried to force a smile.

"Thank you, Sol. I got what I was looking for. You reminded me of my father, the little I saw of him. That helped."

"You gave me what I was searching for too. Know, princess, that you have a home here as long as I am king."

Avva slowly rose as the unicorn flapped its wings.

"You didn't answer me," Sol hollered. "When will I see you again?"

"What if you won't?"

Sol shook his head. "I shall sail across the Strait. I shall climb your legendary Mount Ambitus to Olympus and speak of it to the gods. I shall approach Queen Delia and ask for audience. I shall—"

"My mother will kill you," she said with a laugh.

"Strike me down, Queen Delia," he said, tapping his chest hard. "I will see you again, my lady. I swear it. Whatever the cost. You've touched my heart."

She lost her smile and nodded. "In time, Sol. Perhaps. I hope so."

"Please don't make me wait too long."

She blew him a kiss and rose into the sky.

As she flew above the waters in twilight, she glanced back. Sol still stood by the shore, never moving. She watched him until she could not see the yellow shore anymore.

3

THE DUNGEON

"*Kneel before me, Avivae?*" her mother snapped, with her voice echoing about the throne room. *"But you have no respect for your queen!"*

Avva kept her head low as she knelt at the foot of the three stairs leading up to the throne. Her mother stood over her, waving her fists. Avva tried not to shake, but she couldn't help herself. Her mother was notorious for her wrath. She knew she was going to go crazy.

"Kneel before me, Avivae, but you have no care for my wishes?"

Avva said nothing.

"You kneel before me, Avivae!" she shouted. *"Idiot!"* She leaned down and grabbed her golden scepter and spat out her words. "Kneel? You've no understanding of our world! *Do you think because you are the queen's daughter, you don't have to obey the law! The law given by the gods!"*

Silence. But the silence seemed to bother the queen more. Avva permitted another quick glance up.

A black cloth was wrapped around her mother's head, and she wore a long draping blue peplos. Her face, covered in blue makeup, was shining and red with rage as she glared down in hatred.

Avva turned from her glare.

The throne room was oddly lovely in the midst of her mother's fury. It was a spacious room surrounded by large glass windows looking over the blue-green palace gardens. Glass was an invention only seen in her realm. So were chairs. The barbarians across the Strait, apparently, lay on their sides on rugs. Here, rows of wooden chairs lined both sides of a central aisle. Vines were permitted to grow along the rows of chairs, and red and purple branches filled large marble vases. A great glass dome rose high above her.

The queen kept seething with rage. After more silence, she rushed down the three steps from her throne and hurled her gold scepter at Avva. Avva winced as it hit her head. A guard, an Amazon nymph in scarlet metal armor—Cambria was her name —ran to them from the two doors at the entrance as the golden staff bounced on the stone floor, the sound echoing throughout the room.

"Kneel before me! Do you? Why not spit on me, you sarding brat! You've broken the most sacred law of our land and destroyed everything! Too bad I didn't break the scepter over your head! You think that this is an act of simple defiance? You broke everything in Azure, you imbecile!"

Avva said nothing, remaining on her knees.

"Guards, call forth Engel!"

To this, the princess raised her head, but she did not stand.

Engel hobbled into the throne room wearing a simple white linen tunic, pants, and sandals. He stood beside Avva, cocked his head, and scowled at her. She imagined if he'd had a golden rod to toss, he would have.

"Engel, why didn't you stop my daughter?"

Engel bowed deeply. He was about to speak, but—

"Engel, why didn't you tell me where Avivae was going?"

"Your Majesty," Engel said. "I tried. It was too late."

"Why was it too late?"

"I thought she was in jest. And when I called for Cambria and Falena, she was gone. Please try to forgive her. You're right to be upset, but—"

"Forgive her? Of course, I'm right!" Delia leaned over Avva, who was still kneeling. "Did you think that your scheme would not get others in trouble? How selfish."

"Sorry."

"*Sorry!* Guards! Call in Hanna! Stupid fool. I will hurt you. You want to hurt me, daughter? Watch what I do to you. I will hurt you, so help me!"

Hanna walked forward. Her friend was shaking as she approached the queen. Poor Hanna. Avva had promised that she'd protect her, and now she wasn't sure how. Hanna kneeled down beside Avva and lowered her head. All three kneeled before Delia, who anxiously paced.

"Hanna, why did you not tell me of Avivae's intentions this morning?"

"Avva's very strong willed, Your Majesty. She sometimes moves me to—"

"Shut up!" Delia raised her hand and closed her eyes. Avva could hear her mother panting. She was probably thinking of throwing a shoe or some other object.

"You should see you three groveling." Then the queen sighed and ran her hand over her forehead. She clapped her hands and Cambria, who had been standing by the double wooden doors, walked over with a feather and a rolled parchment.

"Avivae, it is decisions such as these that only prove your unworthiness as the princess of Azure—but, more so, your unworthiness as my daughter."

"I don't care about being princess!" Avva finally stormed, forcing herself to look up at her mother in defiance. "Why would I care about anything under you!"

Delia's tone seemed to strangely soften, "I'll ask once. Only once. And then you will see what shall be done. Why, daughter, did you travel to the Hinterlands?"

"I had to leave."

"Explain."

"I can't stay here." She shook her head and looked at her poor friend again. Hanna was crying now, whimpering as quietly as she could. "I, I can't stay here forever. I hate Azure. I … I hate you. I have to free myself."

"Princess, why would I allow you to do what no other nymph in the realm is permitted to do?"

"But I can't stay here."

"You're confused. You don't understand that our lot has nothing to do with what you like or don't like." Delia turned to Engel and snapped, "Why didn't you warn her? If you couldn't come to me in time, why didn't you stop her? You of all people."

"I thought she wasn't in earnest," he said again. Avva looked over and his gaze broke her heart. The little blue man wasn't scowling anymore; he looked sad. Sad for her?

Delia gasped and turned to her daughter again. "You didn't consider your friends. Or Azure Blue. Thank the gods Hanna didn't touch ground. Then you would've cursed her and owed her life too."

"Mother, I didn't," Avva said, rising. "It's not her fault."

"*Kneel! I don't care!*"

Delia grabbed her feather and began scribbling on the scroll on the ground. "Shall we write your fates? Let us see. Engel, you are now to be confined to the basement dungeon a fortnight."

"No!" Avva screamed, jumping up. "No!"

Cambria ran and bound Avva's arms behind her back, pushing her back onto her knees. Avva squirmed to break free with tears now rushing down her face. "But Engel didn't know! Please! And he never wanted me to leave. You can't punish him, Mother!"

"Oh, I'm not finished."

"I accept my fate," Engel said, turning to Avva solemnly. Then he looked down and shook his head. "I should be given far worse. I failed you, Blue. I'm so sorry."

"You didn't." Avva shook her head. "You didn't."

"Indeed," Delia said, opening her eyes wide. Then she added, "Now, Hanna, you shall be confined to the north tower for a fortnight."

"*No!*" Avva screamed again. But Hanna bowed deeply before the queen.

"Your punishment, both your punishments, are for not confiding in me that my daughter was in danger." And Delia shook her head. "May the gods help us for that."

"Hanna was sent back to the shore by me," Avva continued, shaking her head, "You can't punish her. She came back. It's unfair!"

"I haven't gotten to you yet," Delia said with venom. "Hanna, Engel, you are dismissed. Get out of my sight."

"I'm … so sorry, my queen," Engel said with a broken voice. "I am so sorry for this." Then he quickly hobbled out with Hanna. Guards by the door took hold of them.

Delia turned to Avva, squinting.

"Cross out the order!" cried Avva. "Cross it out!"

"*Kneel!*" her mother shouted, "or so help me, I'll punish you like my mother did. It was enough that you embarrassed me at the funeral. My mother would have beaten me for doing that."

"You struck me in the face!"

"I said she would have beaten me, Avivae, not slapped me."

Cambria forced Avva back on the ground again.

"You've committed the worst crime." Delia paused, as if collecting her thoughts. Or perhaps she was catching her breath. "You stepped foot on their shore. Are you aware of the edict given by Hades?"

Avva nodded.

"No, you're not. We recite it every day. Now you pretend not to know it. You see, I have no edict that I can write on a scroll for you. Your punishment is sealed. Not by me this time. Allow me to repeat the god of the Underworld's edict: *Any Outworlder who steps foot on Gaia will come to me.* Avivae, my daughter, you will be taken to Hades. You will die. You are now mortal and shall live only a handful of years like man. This punishment is enough. The edict you broke was not mine."

She threw the roll of parchment down at her.

"It's a myth!" cried Avva. "I won't die. You're all afraid over a stupid myth! You are all cowards to not face the gods."

Delia rushed to one of the windows. She leaned on the glass, took a deep breath, and pressed her hands on the window. Then she leaned her forehead on the glass and shook her head.

"Cambria, leave us," Delia said quietly.

After Cambria bowed, she walked down the main aisle and closed the double doors.

They were alone.

"Why?" Delia continued to stare outside at the garden and repeated quietly, almost docile, "Why? Avivae, why? Why did you do this to me now? I'm still grieving."

"You've been there too, mother!" Avva snapped. "You never told me. You always lie. You were there to help men. I heard it. You were there to help Dad."

Delia shook her head.

"You attacked King Morteus on the shores near Castle Cove. You want to know why I did what I did, well, why'd you do that?"

Delia furrowed her brow. But she did not turn from the window.

"I loved your father," Delia said, still staring outside. "I would have died for him, Avva. Yes, I sacrificed and risked my life for him once."

"So you were there. Why should it be different for me?"

"I never touched down. I fought from above by monokera." She shook her head and said in a broken voice, "It's unfair. You're too young. It's so unfair for this law to—"

"You didn't love Father! You never mentioned him. Only on his death."

"*'Any Outworlder who steps foot on Gaia will come to me,'*" she repeated with a nod. "The edict applies to me. It applies to you. Set by our great ancestor, Nefertiti. It was followed for centuries by my mother, Dainya, and remains with us. It can't be ignored." She turned to Avva. Avva was surprised to see tears streaming from her mother's eyes. Delia was the hardest woman Avva knew.

She had never seen her mother cry. "I can only guide you. I can't change your foolish nature. Now I must petition Hades himself on your behalf."

"All will be all right," Delia said, seemingly more to herself, turning to the window overseeing the garden again. "All will be all right. I will find a way out of this."

"I am to go to Tartarus? But that's upon death? So? I will die like Father. So what? Living like a woman instead of living my days forever as a stupid nymph in Azure Blue is what I want. I like that. That's what I want. I just want to be a woman."

"You hide your blueness with makeup," Delia said with a tinge of anger again in her voice. "You've been clear enough about what you want." Then Delia shook her head. "But you don't understand. This is what the gods need to destroy us. Daughter, you're the princess of Azure Blue. The gods will take you to the depths *now*. If they finish you *now*, they can destroy our kingdom. Everything I do is not for me, it is for our people. That is our lot in life as Ambrosia.

"You complain so strongly that you never saw your father? You never saw him out of duty. I missed him every day of my life." Delia walked over and picked up the parchment from the ground. "No, it is I who am sorry, Avivae. You've thought me so cruel. I tried to prepare you for this world and now I failed you. Now this world comes for you too." She placed the parchment on the floor and wrote under her other edicts, while speaking aloud. "Avivae is to be confined to the first-floor dungeon of the north tower until I am taken from this world and she is crowned queen."

"What! The dungeon? You put your own daughter in a dungeon?"

"To protect you."

"*Protect me?*" Avva shouted. She prepared to charge her mother. The double doors swung open, and Avva heard Cambria rush back into the room. "Save me from the gods? By imprisoning me? This is the life you want your daughter to have?"

"Get out," replied Delia. "One day you'll understand. If

you're not confined until my death, you shall be taken by the Lord of the Underworld just as his wife, Persephone, was taken from Nefertiti. At least within my walls, the demon must go through me first."

Cambria and another guard grabbed Avva. Then her mother said, "Goodbye. Perhaps one day you'll forgive an old, tired queen. I love you."

"Love? You love me? How dare you. You imprison me, but love me? *I hate you!*"

THE HOURS STRETCHED LIKE DAYS. The days like weeks. Time slowed to a crawl. Avva was caged in a cell, but it was furnished, made comfortable for a princess with a large soft mattress and a chair to sit on while staring through a tiny window and doing nothing. The window was the size of her head and had metal bars.

For meals, she was allowed to eat alone in a large empty hall with columns that looked out upon a private garden. Occasionally passersby sneaked by a fence, slid open a window, and talked to her. But most of her time was spent in her small, dusty stone-walled room. Her window faced the northern hills, and she gazed out at them when bored. She did that a lot.

But her friends visited often. Engel practically lived there. He couldn't stay mad for long. Even in a prison cell, the little man remained jovial. She loved him. Dimitria and Rania came by and played a card game that was popular around the Court called Spades. But she missed Hanna. Hanna was confined too.

One day her best friend finally visited.

"A fortnight!" Avva said, running into her friend's arms. "A fortnight! That sarding witch! How could she be so wicked as to sentence you to a fortnight?"

"It wasn't that long, Blue. I'm free now. But what of you? You're still here, and I don't hear any plan of letting you out. Why, Avva?"

"Engel said the witch is protecting me," Avva said with a shrug. "Humph! When I got mad and insisted he explain, he got upset. It reminded him of why I'm in this predicament in the first place. I didn't pry. But Engel never lies, you know. He claims Queen *Huaina* is protecting me."

Avva sat on her bed and put her head in her hands. Hanna walked over, sat down, and hugged her.

"Really, Avva," Hanna said with a laugh. "*Huaina?* Don't cuss."

"Why? Afraid she's gonna put us in the dungeon?" Avva looked up and cocked her head sarcastically. Then she threw her hair back and leaned her head in her hands in a huff. Hanna put an arm around her.

"Avva, I know something that might please you."

"What?"

"A man," Hanna said with a giggle.

"Hmm?"

"A *handsome* young man." But then she just clammed up with a huge grin.

"What are you talking about?"

"Well," said Hanna, patting Avva's knee, "a handsome young man crossed the Strait. He came on a small rowboat alone. The queen's guard, under Cambria, rushed down from the stable tower. Then ... well, I was so curious, I flew down too. We met him by the beach. We asked him why he had come. He insisted on approaching the palace—insisted on speaking to the queen you call a *pig of a mother*, Queen *Huaina*."

"She is one."

"Yeah. Cambria assumed the man was crazy, of course, and brandished her sword, but he insisted. When he refused to get back in the boat and even fended the guards off with a sword of his own, an entourage escorted the human over to the palace. The queen was so surprised she rode over the drawbridge on Antilus. Of course, by now, a crowd of over a hundred people was gathered over the walls and ramparts looking down at this stranger. She met him in the purple fields.

"The queen dismissed us and Cambria forced us to ride back into the castle, but I was still within earshot. Your pig mother asked him what his business was. He said he was a king who came from Crescent Blue to see the princess. *You.*" Hanna paused and looked at Avva. Then she put her hand over her mouth and giggled. "Your mother, of course, went crazy. She even pulled out the scepter. But this man was crazier. He kneeled as your mother held the scepter over his head. Then all of us, even all the girls above the castle walls, were completely quiet as he went on to say that striking him down would be more merciful than keeping him alive living apart from you. Oh, Avva, you should have heard the laughter. But, of course, the pig on Antilus with Azure's scepter didn't smile. She kept her usual stern look. I thought she was going to freeze him solid. Then …"

Hanna paused and looked out the window. She turned back with her stupid smile and Avva wanted to throw her off the bed for not finishing.

"What? Get on with it."

"Avva, your mother got off her unicorn and put her hand out. She asked him to rise. His bow seemed to have softened her heart. Then—and this is the strangest part—she said, "Return when winter comes. When winter comes, she can see you." None of us understood. We've been told that you're to remain in the tower for good. As she turned and looked out toward the Hinterlands across the Strait, some of the guards by the gates claimed that your mother was crying.

"Well, this man promptly turned around and walked back to his boat and left. When your mother said farewell, she called him by his name. She said—"

"Solinair," Avva said. "King Solinair of Crescent Blue."

"Yes, Avva. Yes. That's it. Solinair. You do know him! Who is Solinair?"

Avva stood up from her bed and walked over to the window. Her eyes gazed out dreamily. "He's so sweet, Hanna. So gallant, brave, and strong."

"Ha, you're in love!"

She whirled around, annoyed, but she couldn't hold back a smile. "Come on, Hanna." Then they laughed some more. "I only saw him for an afternoon."

"So that's why you wanted to go there. Now I understand. He was so handsome, all of us wanted him too."

"Don't be an idiot. I didn't even know he'd be there. But he was ... well, yes, he is very good looking."

"Well, Avva, I saw him. I see what you mean." And they giggled again.

Avva sat back on the bed.

Then she turned to Hanna. "Do you think I can visit him again? Maybe ... if you bring Antilus, I can escape here?"

"No, Avva! No!"

"Just for the morning. You could have Antilus materialize inside the prison cell, using her horn."

"Avva, the queen will kill you if you leave. Or have you banished this time."

"So what," Avva said with a shrug. "Better than staying here."

"I just told you that you're going to be free come winter. That's in only another moon. Just wait. If what the queen says is true, she's freeing you in four weeks, when the snow falls. Somehow, she said, Imada told her this. I don't understand how, perhaps by prophecy from Demeter or Persephone."

"He came to me," Avva said dreamily. Then she looked out through the bars of her window. "He said he would. He said if he didn't see me, he'd come to me. To me. And he did."

"Avva, your mother almost killed him."

"But he came to me." Avva plopped back on her bed. "I think I'm in love."

Hanna laughed and put an arm around her again. "Don't be crazy. You just said you only saw him for a day."

"Yeah. Out there, it was the best day of my life." She pointed at her window. "I love him. I really do, Hanna. I do."

"Okay, princess," Hanna said, rolling her eyes. "How can I

not believe every crazy thing you say? Coming from someone who landed in the Hinterlands, I believe you."

"I'm so sorry, Hanna," Avva said, quickly turning and gazing into her eyes. "I'm sorry I got you into so much trouble."

"It's okay," Hanna said, turning serious. "Forget it. It's … worth hanging with you."

"But I am sorry."

Then Avva sighed and said, "You know, Hanna, all this time spent here has made me realize something. This prison cell is not the first time I've been jailed. All of us in the whole kingdom have been jailed ever since Nefertiti laid down that edict centuries ago."

4

MANDRIGELIAN TEARS

"How much longer, Engel?"

Queen Delia sat on her throne with her chin leaning against her hand, her other hand holding her scepter. A black cloth was wrapped around her head. Engel sat at her feet, almost like a pet, writing on a parchment on the bottom step. But Engel was not a pet—far from it. Delia had learned that this little man had a golden heart, immense courage, and wisdom far greater than any man she had ever known. The guards had been dismissed. Only Engel and the queen remained in the throne chamber.

Engel stopped writing on the parchment and raised his head. "Imada have seen Eruboi riding through the northern regions by the border of Shadow Forest, my queen. Then across the border of the Crescent Kingdom. I don't even think the child king knows they travel through his lands."

"He is not a child. He is a man."

"Are you fond of him?"

"He's Darius's adopted son. He's my son."

"Apparently stricken by love for your naughty daughter."

"They aren't related by blood. And they haven't known each other."

"Sounds like they knew each other enough for him to cross

the Strait alone in a rowboat. You know Poseidon rages along those waters. Are you favorable toward the two of them being together?"

"Aye," Delia said. She smiled using the same expression that her husband, Darius, had shown her so many times in the past. *Aye.* But its pleasantness made her bitter again. "Oh, how can I not be? He reminds me so much of Darius."

She jumped up, startling Engel a little, and walked down the steps from her throne in sandals, rearranging her long trailing violet peplos, and walked to one of the giant side windows overlooking her outdoor garden. The walls were huge glass windows spanning the distance between Doric marble columns. They overlooked a garden, creating the effect of being outdoors. She ran her hand along the glass. It was cold and moist from the morning mist. It would snow soon. Winter was approaching. And then it would all be over.

Of all the windows, she preferred this one because it afforded the loveliest view. She could make out Mount Ambitus towering to the clouds, bordering her blue lands on one side and, on the other, she could make out the sea. And beyond the sea lay Darius's golden lands. She wondered if his son, now a king, was looking back at her from across the sea right now.

Oh Avva, if you only knew. I long for those lands more than you do. But now that your father died, how is it that I long for them even more?

"This young king reminds me of Darius, Engel," Delia said again, still staring at the horizon. "Aye, I like him. I like him a lot. He is a better king than his spoiled brothers. Far from a Crescent. He is the strongest of all of them."

"You think Avva flew over because she already knew him?"

"Impossible," Delia said, shaking her head. "He hadn't attended the games. Too busy. I was told in letters that he was used as a spy. He was raised in the forest like an animal, Darius said. Then at only thirteen, he was used by the Sun Kingdom to gather surveillance regarding the Caravians. He lived alone in Shadow Forest, for many moons, in secret."

"Incredible."

"Yes." Delia nodded. Then she smiled. "I predict this Crescent king shall be quite a surprise for his arrogant brothers—Ansel, Balen, and Torinth. They're fools if they don't take him seriously."

"Perhaps Sol can restore order."

Delia nodded with a smile. But then she shook her head. Her grin vanished as quickly as it had come. "Avva's not ready, Engel. She's smart, daring—a stubborn, fierce Amazon—but she doesn't understand the world. She's too young. And my strongest son holds the weakest lands. The continent is in peril. And now Avva pulled this stunt. Well … let her blame me if it pleases her. I should have taught her better. I should have shown—"

"Her the land across the Strait?"

Delia turned. Engel had a smug smile, the expression he always gave when offering advice. Such a wise man. But then, as he often did, he quickly bowed to show respect.

She shook her head. "Shown her the world, I was going to say. But never threatened her mortality and her people."

"There must be a way for both of you to stay."

"There isn't. Goodbye, Engel. You've been such a dear friend."

"Don't say that." Engel's voice cracked. He hobbled over. Then, as she turned back to the window, she felt his stubby fingers touch her back.

"Is there anything different I could have done?" Delia asked. "Could I have averted this fight with the gods? With Hades?"

"My people warred with Hades my whole childhood. He butchered and enslaved my people. Not even you, my queen, with your wisdom, can get out of this. But if anyone is to blame, it would be Nefertiti. But Nephree—"

"Your beloved queen?" Delia said with a nod and a faint smile. "What wrong could she have possibly done to you?"

Whenever Engel mentioned the fabled queen, she could see his reverence. It was no different now.

"Nephrea saved everyone. She made that deal because she

had to. And she would do exactly what you're doing now for Avva. I know she would."

Delia nodded morosely, still staring at the Strait.

The two of them stood together in silence for a while, both just staring out to the horizon over a forbidden sea. She wondered if Hades had crossed the waters yet.

"I'm afraid, Engel."

She felt his hand on her back shake. Crying? Probably. But she didn't turn. Then she felt his head lean on her side as they looked outside together.

"You will take care of her when I'm gone?"

"As much as I cared for you," he said with broken words. "But, why? Why must you go?"

"It's the only way. Tell me about Nefertiti. What happened to her when she died? It's strange, legend says that Harmonia and my mother went to Elysium, but not her. What happened to this Egyptian pharaoh? Where did she end up after Egypt?"

"No one knows. Some say she went the way of their gods in the South: to Osiris. Others say she was not meant for the Underworld, but for the clouds. But…" Engel actually chuckled. "Not the clouds in Mount Olympus. You see, she didn't believe in gods. She faced the gods as equals. I believe she went to Aten, her one god. But she suffered more than anyone I have ever known. Even more than you."

"So you've said. I wish she could help me now. I wish all our revered queens could come back and help me. I could so use their guidance. But Engel…" She turned and touched his shoulder, looking down at him. He brushed his eyes with the sleeve of his tunic. His eyes were bloodshot and full of tears. "You've been here for me, haven't you? You've always been here."

"Don't go."

"Perhaps I sheltered my daughter too much." She turned back with a shrug. "Perhaps you're right. Perhaps this is why she erred. The gods want to harm me. Maybe I should have taught her that too. Ah, I can only hope that they will sacrifice me instead of my beloved Avivae. I will die before Hades, protecting her, if he refuses the trade."

"There must be another way? Why can't—"

"I give everything for her. I always have. And you know the edict better than anyone."

Engel nodded. But after a while, as he cried, he said again, almost in a whisper, "Why?"

"Shall I comfort the man who fed me milk? Shall I tell what Engel the wise, the Mandrigel, told me when my mother passed away?" There was no answer. So she said the words, more to herself, "You might as well ask why the sun sets. Or why there are stars in the sky. Or why clouds form."

"Why?" he asked with a broken voice.

"Because the sun rises, the stars fade, and the clouds disperse."

"Why, Your Majesty?"

He wept in her arms.

"Not even the gods know, do they? Maybe your Queen Nefertiti knows. But that great man, Engel the Mandrigel, once told a little girl this: "The sun sets, stars fill the sky, and clouds form." Then the queen whispered to herself, as she held Engel tightly, "Because the sun rises, the stars fade, and the clouds disperse."

"I love you, Delia," Engel said.

Delia said nothing. Nor did she shed a tear. But she would hold and comfort Engel until he stopped crying.

5

THE DARK LORD

THE QUEEN'S WAIT WAS SOON OVER. IT WAS A COLD DAY, BUT THE sky was clear. The bright green sun shone through the glass dome of the ceiling. Green rays pierced through the glass into the throne room. But a light frost had fallen around the glass during the night.

Again, Delia wore a long violet peplos with a black cloth wrap over her head. But, expecting guests, she had ceremonially adorned her face with very thick blue makeup and placed a thin gold crown on her head. She carried her scepter in her right hand and clutched the arm of her golden throne with the other as she heard the steps of her infernal guests approaching the great throne room.

The queen had been notified the minute the Eruboi washed ashore. There were some twenty Eruboi—not a lot. But as they filed into the throne room, it seemed like many more. The huge pitch-black-armored hoplites walked single file down the central aisle and surrounded one tall man, in the center, wearing a black-hooded robe.

The leader walked forth, dropped his hood, and gave a regal bow to the queen, almost too low, as if in mockery. He wore a silver breastplate under his black cloth robe, and he had a bald head and bright blue eyes. His beard was short, ears a little pointy like hers, and he had a pointy nose.

He gave a wicked smile.

"Delia," Hades said. "Queen Delia Ambrosia, Amazon nymph queen of Azure Blue. Why, you've aged well. Still with beauty that would rival even lovely Persephone. It's been too long."

"I'm sure your wife would object to that."

Hades shrugged.

He was tall, over seven feet tall. Menacing. He had inhuman musculature. His entourage stood behind him, quiet and still. Of course, they were not alone. The queen had almost twenty armed guards, in red Amazon armor, standing at the doors behind them.

"To what do I owe the pleasure of this visit?" Delia asked.

Hades looked out through the large glass walls and took a deep breath.

"Your land has always been my favorite." He removed his black leather gloves. "Ah, if only you could see the way the barbarians live. Perhaps then, madam, you would appreciate your lot. Then again, you did once visit the Hinterland clouds, didn't you? Anyway…" He returned to his spot at the foot of the throne—"I wonder where your subjects sit? Would you like me to squat on the floor like the barbarians?"

"Guards, provide chairs for the god of the Underworld and his guests."

In a moment, many more nymphs rushed in, moving the wooden chairs from the aisle closer to the throne. They offered refreshments on silver trays.

After a long, painful wait, and after the leader had grabbed a leg of meat from the tray, he said with his mouth full, "So … where's your daughter?"

"Hmm?"

"Your daughter. Princess Avivae? Where is she? I'd so like to see her again."

"Imprisoned."

"Ah," he said with a nod.

Hades took a fig served by another nymph and took a large bite. Then he spit some of it back onto the tray, smiled at the server, and said, with his mouth full again, "Tell me, great Azure Queen, why are you imprisoning your daughter? Did she do something wrong?"

"That's none of your business."

He laughed. He did not stop laughing. He turned to his men and they laughed too, almost as if out of duty. The queen's guards looked at each other, nervously tightening their hands around the hilts of their swords.

"How, my dear queen, is it not my business? When you eat, sleep, or fart, it is my business. Indeed, everything that happens on this isle is my business. I laid claim."

"She's in prison in order to be protected from you. I rule here. You're my guest. This is my kingdom."

"*This is not your kingdom!*" shouted Hades, opening his eyes wide. But he still sat. Then he slowly raised a single finger. "This is not your kingdom. This is *my* kingdom. This is *my* palace created by my hands. Do I need to remind you of this?"

He glared at her. Delia looked down at the fingers of her left hand, which shook over the arm of her throne.

He sighed and cracked a very fake smile. He tore more meat from the leg with his teeth and threw the bone on the floor. Then he wagged another filthy finger at her. "I'll allow you to remain above me and not bow, for it reminds me of my beloved Harmonia. In reverence for her, and your resemblance, I ignore this transgression. But I won't allow you to call Azure or Napea yours. The kingdom is rightfully mine. Azure Blue is not yours, Delia." He stood up and walked closer to the steps. "But if you don't believe me, I can show you. I can overrun your kingdom in a few hours. Your army's become weak. Too accustomed to centuries of peace. Only your guards…" He pointed to them by the door. "Still wear armor. *My* armor, now rusted and in decay. The armor I also bequeathed to your people with my own hands."

"I meant no disrespect, Hades."

"Hmm." Hades looked around the throne room. "Where is your daughter? I'd so like to see her again. I've heard she's grown." Then he gestured to his chest with both hands as if holding breasts. "Filled out into adulthood, so I hear. Oh, how I'd like to gaze upon her body. You know, I've always fancied your beautiful people and your figures." Then he turned back to his black-clad soldiers. "Beautiful sarding nymphs, aye, men?"

"Aye!" And the Eruboi laughed. "Aye!"

"I told you. She's—"

"Prison, aye? You do remember my edict, don't you?" And he cocked his head and smiled a nasty smile. "*Any Outworlder who steps foot on Gaia will come to me.* Surely, oh Queen, you remember? The gods demand punishment. I told Lord Zeus that your people are my business. Told him I'd deal with you personally. We have eyes everywhere. And we saw her, not only *above* Crescent Blue, like you, but *landing*, Delia. Landing on the ground."

"We live imprisoned by your edict every day. How can I forget?"

"Perhaps *you* didn't. Perhaps your daughter did."

"She knew the curse. She lives as a mortal now. Isn't that punishment enough? But the edict doesn't mean you can take her life. I'm protecting her from going down to the Underworld."

"Hmm, sounds familiar. A nymph once protected someone I desired very much. But even Nephrea didn't imprison Cora. That's cruel. I ... well ... I kind of like that."

"Perhaps she should have. It would have been better than ending up with—"

"Ah!" Hades warned, raising a finger and shaking his head. "Don't. Don't provoke me." He shook his head again and walked back to his chair. Then he sat down. "Zeus believes the edict was too lenient. He says even a human lifespan is enough time for your people to cause mischief again. He doesn't want to see any nymphs living outside the island. He is concerned that your daughter could become as lovely and vicious as your great-grandmother. I told her, impossible. No one could be as resplendent and wonderful as the founding Amazon queen."

"We have no interest in conquest."

"You don't, but what about your daughter? Let me talk to her. Let me see. I'm an excellent judge of character. Perhaps you're right. Let me see for myself."

"Why are we even of any concern to Lord Zeus?"

"Because…" He spoke more softly and put a finger to his lips. "He fears you." He nodded with another one of those infernal sardonic grins. "I take your daughter's life or I violate the wishes of my brother. I'm not here for me. I'm here as a messenger for my brother."

"You loathe Zeus."

"True." He laughed and folded his arms. "That's true. But I warn you, if I play along with your charade, he'll bring my sister. And if I don't punish Avivae, Sara will. And she'll be far crueler."

"Are you gods that forgetful? Why would Sara do anything for him? Didn't she rage after Zeus allowed you to take your wife, Persephone?"

"*Call us forgetful!*" Hades thundered, opening his eyes wide. But his anger passed quickly, and he gave a stupid smile again. "Harmonia's blood." He closed his eyes as if relishing her insult. "I forgot. Of course. I relish it. Carry on. Oh, how I miss a nymph's disrespect."

Delia impudently stared down into his eyes.

Hades broke eye contact with her. "Prison, huh? How droll. Do me a favor and release her. I will take her to the ferryman now."

Delia looked at her guards and said, "Leave us. All of you, leave the hall."

Hades turned back and watched the red-armored guards bow and leave. Then he looked back, furrowing his brow.

"Leave us," she repeated to a few stragglers by the door. "I speak with Lord Hades alone."

Her guards hesitated, staring at the Eruboi forces. But after

Delia nodded again, they bowed and walked out. Hades smiled again, seemingly loving any possible scheming. He said, twirling his fingers in the air, to his guards. "You're all dismissed too. Get out."

When the two great wooden doors of the throne room were shut and only the two of them remained in the Court, Hades looked up at Delia, folding his arms and waiting.

"There is only one solution," she said quietly.

"Go on."

"Take me."

"Huh?" He chuckled, putting a hand to his ear. "What did you just say? I didn't quite hear that."

"Take me."

He paused. Then he ran his fingers along his goatee.

"How touching. You offer sacrifice? Another Ambrosia sacrifice. I like that. I tell you that such sacrifices are worth a million temple offerings to my pernicious family. But tell me, Delia, does she really deserve it? I've heard rumors that the two of you don't get along. You are not close to your daughter like Harmony was close to Nephrea. And I am one who loathed their exchange more than anyone. I think you're still young yet, Delia. No, I strongly advise against it."

"Take me," she repeated. "Olympus shall have their victory if I leave. Tell Zeus. They'll have Queen Avivae, a young, inexperienced ruler the surrounding kingdoms can take advantage of. You know war is on the horizon. What a perfect time for Zeus to disrupt my lands."

"Very true … Hmm." He stroked his beard some more and nodded. "I shall deliberate upon this on the Mount. Perhaps. But now you're making me feel a little bad for you."

"Liar."

"Am I so bad, Delia?" he said with a chuckle. "Once I loved your race, you know. Why not just give her to me? You can grieve for a day, then go back to ruling your beautiful kingdom. You don't really care about her."

"*Take me!*" she demanded and stood up for the first time,

slamming her scepter against the stone floor. Her voice echoed through the Court and one of entry doors cracked open. It was likely one of her guards.

Hades wagged his finger in warning, but then he smiled.

"Done. But I don't understand it. You Ambrosia hold such odd maternal sentimentalities."

Delia fell back into her throne. She had a strange sense of relief. Her decision and this final meeting had been weighing heavily on her. Now it was over. Her words finalized the decision not only for Hades, but for herself. But what a terrible cost.

Hades sighed and got up.

He walked to the window and looked at the view of the outside garden. She walked down the steps from her throne and stood beside him. Then he picked up a flower from a vine, inter-twined with a branch, by a wooden chair.

"I advise you to speak with Avva about our rules before you go," he said. "It seems she's wilder than you. Such rebellion passed down to the next generation might just cost the life of her daughter."

"Are you whispering prophecy? Are you trying to cause me more pain than I already have?"

"No. I delight in watching you *deal* with pain. Don't blame me for it. And don't think you're the only one suffering. My pain is far worse than you will ever have. If it were up to me, you'd never have existed and I would be ruling Gaia with your great-grandmother."

He stared at the beautiful blue flower in his hand. The blue reminded Delia of her Azure lands. He broke it from the vine, and it wilted in his palm. He dropped it on the ground.

"A life for a life. It is done."

Delia crouched over the flower and picked it up. "This is why you walk the Earth, viper. To destroy all you touch." She touched the flower with the tip of her finger, and it bloomed again. She laid it on a windowsill and walked back to her throne.

He laughed. "Oh, there's one more thing."

She quickly turned.

"'*Any Outworlder who steps foot on Gaia will come to me.*' My edict can't be violated. It was signed in Nephrea's blood. All you've done is delay the inevitable with this sacrifice. I won't kill her but I will have her. You know that. And it will not be centuries from now. She lives a mortal life."

"When do I leave?"

"I shall return with my flying chariot in one week. Meet me on your beaches, at the edge of the sand, where the land meets the wall of Mount Ambitus. There, at dawn, I shall take you. I will bring your body straight to Charon personally. You will be honored in Elysium, like your mother, Dainya, and Harmonia before her."

"Olympus will stay their hand on Azure?"

"I will discuss it with Zeus. But don't worry. They will. I know they will. This is quite a sacrifice, and my sadistic brother and sister adore the sport of suffering more than I do."

"And Avivae?"

"Believe it or not, Delia, I care more about your Ambrosia family than any god, aside from my wife. But Avva is Zeus's concern, not mine. Cora has made it clear to me that Avva's daughter is the one who holds promise for me. I shall protect Avva for the benefit of her daughter alone."

"I have your word that Avva will not be taken swiftly after I go?"

"No. I do as I please. I am a god. And you're in no position to ask anything further from this agreement."

6

SHIVER

AVVA OPENED HER EYES, STRETCHED, AND SLUGGISHLY ORIENTED herself to the same small dull room: a prison cell of sorts that she had now slept in for three moons. The same soft royal bed taking up half the space with a tiny wooden dresser and two chairs: one chair for company. And the same small glass window. But as she reoriented herself to her misery, she noticed something new—and anything new in her boredom was a great relief. There was snow along the ledge of her window. Although warm inside her tower, it was cold outside.

She got up, yawned, and stretched in her soft saffron linen nightgown. Then she walked to the window. Outside, the view, which had been blue, had changed. The reflection of the rising green sun had created a layer of faint green everywhere, over icy surfaces. The snow covered the tops of the trees, turning them white. And another crystal tower close by no longer shone blue, but emerald green.

Avva liked snow. She had loved to play in it as a child, running along the Court maze. But now her melancholy returned, for she remembered that she was still forced to remain in her room.

She gazed further, over an icy horizon, to the sea. There she was surprised to see a second great change. Foreign naval ships were crossing the Strait. Invaders? Many years ago, when Avva had attended the festival for the games, the same sort of ships had crossed the sea to Azure. But these were not warships. She recognized Hinterland ships—Caravians and Kitherians. But she knew of no festival, particularly on the first day of winter. She watched as a hundred ships docked along the shore.

Then, with even more surprise, she recognized a Trireme, one of the Greek battleships. This was a battleship with over thirty rowers along a hull manned by hoplites. But a few did not have the flags of Hellena. Some warships had flags from Egypt. Perhaps it was an invasion? Impossible. Not from so many different lands. And she caught some of her subjects scouting, with unicorns, in the sky. Most weren't wearing war armor. And many had smiles on their faces. The last time Avva had seen her people so excited was at the festival.

But, oddly, some were crying. Many of the guards stationed at watchtowers were wiping tears. Why were some happy while others were sad? And what sort of festival had been arranged for the first day of winter?

For the rest of the morning, having nothing better to do, Avva watched as her subjects ran about, busy preparing for the hundreds of foreigners, as the strangers made their way, on horseback and chariot, across the woods by the beaches and up through the snowy fields to the front of the palace.

The spectacle was interrupted when her cell door was opened. She supposed it was around midday and time for lunch. But a guard dressed in red Azure armor was accompanying a very short man. Engel.

Avva ran to her favorite dwarf and scooped him into her arms. But Engel seemed weak, and his blue eyes were bloodshot. When Avva put him down, he fell to his knee and bowed before her. Engel was shaking on the ground.

"My queen."

"What's the matter? What's going on around the palace?"

He remained silent with his head to the ground.

"What is it, Engel? Get up and tell me."

"I thought I'd bring you news in person," he said, wiping tears from his eyes. His voice cracked. "I had hoped I could contain myself."

"What? What's going on? I've never seen—"

"Your mother's abdicated."

"What do you mean, abdicated?"

But Engel could not speak. Avva felt a mix of emotions and confusion. Engel brushed his teary eyes with the sleeve of his simple brown tunic again. Then he shook his head, as if trying to shake off his sadness, and hobbled over to a chair. Avva sat on her bed close by.

"I'm sorry, Blue."

"What's going on?"

"The queen abdicated her throne. This festival marks the change. Poseidon allows ships to cross freely for this one occasion. Most joyously, you're free." And he finally forced a smile. "Your prison door is open. You no longer need protection. The gods, and now thousands, bear witness. All of us are now under your rule. You are queen, Avivae. The Azure queen."

"Why would she abdicate?" asked Avva with a laugh. "I don't want to be queen." She looked outside at the raucous gathering and understood. It was a coronation. But she lost her smile as soon as she looked back at Engel. "I'm free? Then … why are you so sad?"

Engel took Avva's blue fingers into his. Then he looked up into her eyes. He stood up, ran his stubby fingers along Avva's bangs, and said, "Avva, your mother passed. She died. She's been taken to the Underworld."

Avva laughed because she didn't believe him. Engel wasn't laughing. He looked pained. Avva looked deeply into Engel's eyes.

"No." Avva quickly grabbed her hand back. "No."

Engel nodded again.

"But I don't want to be queen." Avva jumped up. "What are you talking about?"

She rushed to the window. She saw so many outside now. Tents were being set up, and nymphs were bringing out silver trays as if preparing for a festival. It was cold and many wore heavy coats, but few seemed to mind the cold in all the excitement. She caught some of her sisters' faces. They looked so sad. It was such an odd contrast to the foreigners walking through the icy purple grass as if it were a holiday.

"You're queen," Engel said gently, taking her hand again. She turned back and he was still looking up at her. "You, Avivae. You are now the queen of Azure Blue. Our nymph queen for all of Napea. And thousands have come to welcome you and recognize your power."

The words seemed foreign. Her companion ever since childhood seemed to say them as if they were being read off a parchment. Engel was sad, but so serious. Then he took a knee and bowed below her again.

"Stop it!" Avva cried. "No! Get up!"

"Do not dishonor your mother, Avva," Engel said sharply, shaking his head. "Not this time. Put aside your differences. More importantly, do not dishonor the Ambrosia family."

"But I don't want to be queen, Engel. You know that."

"We don't want a lot of things. I came here centuries ago with a nymph who didn't want to be queen either. She was forced to care for a young girl as ruler. At first, she didn't want her, but then she found the girl to be her closest friend. And that is how I became part of your family." He looked back. "Queen Delia has abdicated, and you are queen. You must do what you must do now. Your mother is dead."

"Then we will mourn her, not have a coronation."

"We won't. Your mother was strict but never proud. She's asked the people not to mourn, but to welcome you. This is her gift to you. She asks that all shall respect their new queen. For you."

"Mother never respected me, Engel. She laid down that edict for order, never for me. Nothing she ever did—"

"Enough, Avva!" snapped Engel, violently shaking his head. "Put away your bickering. This is for the kingdom."

"Get out." Avva looked back at the window.

"Yes, my queen."

"Shut up. Stop saying that. Just leave me alone."

"I will never leave you alone, Blue," he said quietly. "I won't. I won't ever do that." Then Engel did, in fact, walk out. But he left the cell door ajar.

It seemed to take forever for her to get dressed. In her defiance, she did not adorn herself with makeup. She put on a simple brown tunic and sandals—as far from royalty as she could look. Of course, a true Ambrosia queen wore ceremonial blue makeup. It was said that the great Queen Harmonia wore a darker blue every day of her life to accentuate her differences from their human neighbors. Avva would never do that.

She moved almost in a dream state from her prison cell, as if in a fog. She had spent many moons wanting to escape. Now, when the door was unlocked and the guards gone, she didn't want to leave. But when her legs were strong enough, she walked out the door.

There wasn't even a guard in the hallway. There wasn't anybody. Only occasionally she'd see someone run frantically through a hallway back toward the main palace.

She went to the grand hall with two spiral staircases and a magnificent three-story window facing the fields and shores of the Strait. This was her favorite spot in the palace. Then she headed down another hallway to the throne room.

Many nodded and greeted her. It was as if they had been expecting her. They were quiet but reverent, bowing deeply and congratulating her on her way to the double doors, where they stood solemnly. Her mother might have planned a coronation, but her people still mourned.

For her father, King Darius, her mother had ordered all her people to mourn. But for her own death, she had asked them to ignore her. She had ordered all the nymphs to wear formal blue, green or, yes, even white peploi. No one had put on a veil or dressed in black for her funeral.

Avva found Engel and Cambria standing beside the great wooden double doors of the Court. How had Engel known he'd find her here? He was so wise. But he didn't say a thing. He just bowed like everyone else. Cambria wore sparkling scarlet armor, leather pteruges, and crimson breastplates. But her eyes were as bloodshot as Engel's. Avva approached her guard in her simple brown leather tunic and nodded. Then Cambria opened the double doors.

The crystal throne room was empty. Avva walked alone down the central aisle, hearing the two doors shut behind her. Outside, through the side window, it was dark and misty. It might snow again. Little light could be seen through the side windows or above the glass dome. It was approaching evening. But she spotted campfires, likely from all the foreigners joining the festivities. And many torches had been lit throughout the throne room to prepare for darkness.

She climbed the three stone steps and sat on the great throne for the first time in her life. Her mother's crown and scepter lay on the step below her.

She sat there for a long while. She had dreamed about this, knowing that one day it would come, but before, she had desired it.

She reached down and picked up the thin gold crown and scepter. She ran her blue fingers along the gold of the crown and tried it on.

Imprison me? Then crown me? I will never understand you, mother.

Tears ran down her cheeks. They surprised her. Bereavement? Or hatred? Or sadness in a final realization that she had never really known her mother. Now she never would.

She lost control and her sobbing echoed throughout the great empty hall. No one opened the door. But faintly she heard a snort from Engel from outside the throne room. Snorts between sobs. He was crying with her.

7

———

QUEEN

Queen Avivae Ambrosia sat atop her gilded throne, raised above three marble steps on a stage at the end of the crystal throne room, wearing the black cloth wrap over her head like her mother, with the golden scepter in her right hand and a thin golden crown upon her head. Many cried. She wondered if it was because she looked like her mother, except that she refused the heavy blue makeup.

All the seats in the throne room were filled, with some sitting on the stone floor in the central aisle. And many were foreigners. Many were men. Another hundred stood outside, in the palace gardens, witnessing the ceremony through the windows. And even though snowflakes were falling, it did not stop them from standing in the cold.

Avva searched the crowd looking for Sol. She had asked Hanna to arrange lodging for him. She didn't spot him and she wasn't sure if he'd even come. She hoped he had.

Hanna sat in the front row with a ridiculously large grin. She didn't mourn Delia. And there was more hidden in that smile. She knew Avva hated public speaking.

Hanna wore a lovely flowing lavender peplos. The redhead Iris sat grinning beside her, wearing a fluffy turquoise dress.

Their faces were coated with the ceremonial blue makeup. Every one of her subjects wore the ceremonial makeup, which only enhanced Avva's rebellion. And she caught many elders casting disapproving glances at her face and murmuring to one another. Some she knew were members of Milda's secret Imada. The elders were easy to make out as they, and the horrible hag Milda, were the only ones who had disobeyed her mother and worn black.

Sitting not far from the witch Milda, with her curly white hair, was another elder with a similar name, but of a completely opposing heart: Maina. Maina was the oldest nymph in the kingdom. It was claimed that this sweet white-haired woman had even cared for the ancient Queen Harmonia as a baby. Avva loved Maina. And next to her were many other ancient women, old and frail, along the front row.

Avva's guards Cambria and Falena stood stiffly on either side of the throne, wearing bright scarlet hoplite armor, now shined for the ceremony. Cambria kept turning to Avva with a reassuring smile, but she seemed impatient to start the ceremony. They waited for the scowling black-robed Imada witches. Milda surveyed the crowd. What she waited for, Avva didn't know. When Milda finally turned back and nodded, Cambria hammered her spear on the stone ground.

Avva rose.

"All rise for our blessed Princess Avivae Ambrosia!" thundered Cambria.

Then, as Avva's heart raced with so many eyes staring, she cleared her throat and said what she had planned for days.

"Welcome to our visitors from the farthest reaches of the Hinterlands, and even from beyond Atala. Welcome. I am so honored that you have come so far to join us. I look forward to meeting each and every one of you in person to share stories of my mother when the ceremony is over." She cleared her throat and took a deep breath. Then she tightened her fists and gazed up at the glass dome in the ceiling, the only direction where a hundred eyes weren't staring at her. "When I saw you on our shores, I must admit, I thought you were here to pay respects to my mother. Queen Delia was so well respected and revered throughout the kingdom and the whole world." There were cheers from some men near the exit. Avva paused and squinted, spotting the group of men applauding her. They wore light-blue leather armor—the soldiers from the Crescent Kingdom. "Then I was very surprised to learn that you came not to mourn her, but to acknowledge my right to the throne." And those words made the men in the back cheer even louder.

"To my sisters." And she forced herself to gaze at the nymphs. "I'm so sorry for your loss. My mother was such a strong force for peace. I only hope to work hard to earn your trust, but I cannot hope to achieve her greatness."

She paused. Then she felt strange. It was quiet. Not one person stirred. She could even hear chirping from the gardens outside.

It was a lovely day. The green sun shone through the glass dome above, permitting the dust in the air to reflect a faint turquoise. The flowers bloomed red, amber and white. She permitted herself a smile when she watched a warrior in brown leather pteruges and a polished silver breastplate jump as a glowing azure butterfly with rainbow wings landed on his hand. Their land was wondrous to the outsiders, indeed.

"Well … anyway, I humbly accept the crown."

Silence turned into a roar of applause. The men in blue armor at the back of the room shouted in triumph. Then Cambria hammered her spear on the ground for order again. When she didn't get order, Cambria cried, "There will be silence in the hall of Azure!"

"I ask for patience," Avva said, raising her hand. "I'm young. Do not doubt that I'll make mistakes. Our kingdom is so special. It's been preserved by my great mother, a brave and caring—"

"You never liked your mother."

The words had come from the wooden double doors. There were gasps and then a scuffle as a group of black-armored soldiers rubbed shoulders with Hinterland men.

Slowly, maneuvering around the crowd at the entrance, came ten Eruboi, Hades' mercenaries, wearing black hoplite armor. They accompanied a very tall man, in the center of the group, wearing a black-hooded cloak. Rushing behind were another twenty blue-armored Hinterland knights, seeming ready to stop them.

That's when Avva saw him. Sol. King Solinair. He was not the same "boy" she had met across the Strait. No, this *man* was adorned in the finest jewelry, his long ponytail was straight and the rest of his hair slicked back, and his armor, painted cerulean blue, was decorated with silver and gold. He and his soldiers rushed the black hoplites drawing their swords.

"Go no further!" shouted the nymph guard Falena, hammering the floor hard with her staff. Both Falena and Cambria brandished their spears, weapons that Avva had always viewed as ceremonial ornamentation. And with that, some Azure women throughout the chamber, not wearing any armor at all, drew knives of their own.

"There will be no fighting in the Azure Palace!" cried Cambria.

But some of the soldiers ignored the order and charged with their swords drawn against the black-clad Eruboans. People backed up and the small group of soldiers fought along the central aisle, between the chairs.

"*Stop at once!*" repeated Falena.

Nymphs who had been sitting in the central aisle jumped over each other to get out of the way. Cambria and Falena ran down the aisle and started hacking at swords with the tips of their spears to stop the violence. But during all the commotion, Avva's eyes turned from Sol to stare at the hooded-cloaked man. How could she not? He gazed at her now with a wicked grin. Under his hood, he had a goatee and bright blue eyes. She had seen this man visit her mother. He was not mortal. He was the Dark Lord of the Underworld. The god Hades.

Hades dropped his gaze from Avva and looked at the fighting around him. He lost his smile.

"*Enough!*" Hades raged. And with his shout, air seemed to blow as if from a vortex within the palace walls, and the combatants were hurled against the aisles of chairs. Avva's guards fell over too. Then Hades spun his cloak around his body and charged up to the throne. Avva jumped up, thinking she'd have to fight the beast herself, but he fell on a knee at the bottom of the steps. That spectacle stopped the fighting. But even now, both the Eruboi and Sol's blue soldiers brandished their swords.

Cambria and Falena ran past them to the throne to protect Avva. That's when Avva got what she had dreamed of all morning. Sol looked at her and smiled.

"Lustrous," Hades said while gazing at her guards. He gave a broad sweeping gesture toward Cambria. "Polished."

"Back away from the throne!" cried Cambria.

"But not well used like my men, Cambria." He looked back at his soldiers. "Eh, men?"

"Aye! Aye!"

"Don't step any closer," Cambria warned again, shaking her spear at him. But there was uncertainty in her voice.

"When is the last time you saw battle, Cambria?" Hades asked her. Then he removed his hood. "Hmm?" He gestured back at his Eruboi behind him. "Our armor is bent and worn, wood nymph. Unlike yours."

"Stand back from the princess," Cambria repeated. "You're close enough, sir."

"But I'm here to congratulate her." And he gestured with wide open arms again. "Blessed be the day! A blessed, blessed day. And…" He faked a sad smile at Avva. "Sad." Then he wagged a finger at her. "You've been a naughty girl, Avivae Ambrosia. Decorative fake pride and power, wielding a scepter, but all this nonsense won't hide what you did. Or who you are."

"Back away!" cried another voice. This time it wasn't Cambria. And when Avva saw who it was, she nearly fell off her throne. It was Sol.

"Calm yourself, barbarian," Hades said. "I'm not threatening her. I'm congratulating her."

"Liar!" Solinair said with his sword still drawn. He pointed it at the god, and his hand was the only one that did not shake before him. Everyone rose from their seats.

Avva feared that Hades would turn and kill Sol. Even poor old Maina was standing by in the front row. Avva sat back down out of duty, but her heart was pounding.

"But *your* weapons are well worn, aren't they, bastard king?" Hades said, addressing Sol again. "Interesting the tide of change when not only Amazon nymphs but Hinterland warlords do not mind a bit of hubris when addressing me."

"I know well who you are!"

"Then you'd be wise to drop your sword. Or must I snap my fingers and break your neck?"

"Lower your sword, King Solinair," Avva said.

Both Hades and Sol turned and looked up at Avva in surprise. Hades nodded and, not waiting for Sol to obey, batted Sol's longsword down with a quick strike from his palm. Sol nearly raised it to the god again, but then he looked at Avva. He hesitantly sheathed his weapon.

"May I address the Court, *Princess* Avivae?" asked Hades sarcastically. "You haven't been officially crowned. And, by right, the throne is mine."

Hades walked slowly to the first step. Avva's guards turned their staffs on him. Then Hades bowed deeply once more.

"Queen Avivae." Hades looked up, "*I crown you* on this blessed day. I recognize your rule. And with that comes the blessing of Zeus and Mount Olympus. But I do not take back what I said when I entered the chamber. Certainly, your subjects know of your relationship with your mother. I simply stated a fact. You didn't like her. Am I wrong?"

"No."

"Queen Avivae, descendant of the greater Queen Harmonia." He rose and walked back to the throne. "You spoke rightly when you said that you'll make mistakes. You will. You don't know me, and you don't know half the people who honor you today. Now, with the death of Delia, your ignorance is your weakness. Olympus wishes to take advantage of that. But I can help you." He faced the crowd. "I can help all of you. After all, I am the founder of this Amazon palace."

"We will not give gods libations," cried a voice in the crowd.

"I was the god who asked you not to, Milda," Hades said dismissively without turning to her.

"We ask no help from you, Lord Hades," Avva said.

"Take a look at my men, Avivae. I have three thousand mercenaries above the ground and many more below. These soldiers are better trained than any regiment in Atala." Sol's soldiers grumbled. "And now, with the deaths of your mother and father, war is afoot. I can help you. I was once aligned with your people. I suggest you consider my offer."

"Help her like you help my brother?" snapped Solinair, gnashing his teeth.

Hades raised a finger, but he seemed to change his mind about addressing him. "But you must first abide by Zeus's laws. The law is simple. *Any Outworlder who steps foot on Gaia will come to me.* Now, lovely queen, will your subjects abide by the law of Olympus?"

"Yes." Avva thought for a moment in silence. "Of course. My violation is my business, I do not ask my people—"

"You'll learn soon enough, callow nymph, that your mistake is theirs."

"I see … but perhaps, then, you can explain to my sisters something I have been wondering—how do I follow this edict? How does my people? The borders are unclear along the Strait."

"They are not."

"Then can you explain—where is the boundary?"

"The borders of Napea and the Hinterlands are evident," he replied with a grin.

"No, I think, I have to disagree. What if one of my subjects steps foot on the water's edge? What part of the Strait belongs to which side? The tide changes, Lord Hades."

Hades furrowed his brow. "When the ground is dry, you'll know."

"How?"

Hades shook his head.

"If the water rushes in, it shrinks Gaia and becomes part of the Outworld," Avva persisted. "But if the tide recedes, Gaia enlarges."

"I don't understand your point."

"Seems to me that if you have a law based on boundaries, then the boundary has to be clear. Allow me to demonstrate: every one of my subjects knows that I landed on Gaia. But what they don't know is that I landed a second time a couple of days ago." There were gasps. Hades lost his smile. Avva caught Sol smiling. "Or did I? When I arrived again, I landed a few feet from the waves. I walked parallel to the water. And I considered how unsure I was about whether I was violating your law yet again or not, Lord Hades."

There was laughter from the multitudes and applause as if Avva had just participated in a great contest—only she knew full well Hades wasn't participating.

"Wood nymph." Hades said with a smile, "have your people follow my edict. You may play rebellion, but don't have your people tempt fate, or you will find that, wet or dry, Olympus will decide the boundary for you. Or we might wipe away the borders altogether, flood the palace, and starve your people. Do I make myself clear?"

She nodded.

"Splendid." He turned and loudly addressed the crowd. "I come, not only to congratulate Queen Avivae, but to warn you. Not one of you nymphs may pass the boundary. Your queen's fate is sealed and she may envisage any fantasy she likes, but you all will honor Nefertiti's pact. If you violate it, your immortality will be forfeited." He reached into his pocket and quickly bowed again to Avva. "I bequeath unto you a gift for your new crown." He threw her a fruit and she caught it. It was a pomegranate. "Consider the myrle berries my offer of allegiance. Your life may now be mortal, Avivae, but you are still the Amazon Ambrosia queen. I sincerely hope we can work together in strength as we have in the past. Persephone and I extend this olive branch. We are family. Either way, I will be watching."

He clapped once loudly and nodded to his men.

Sol glared at him with hatred as he passed by.

"Oh, be careful with this one," Hades said with a chuckle, pointing at Sol. "The point of his crescent stabs you. He will lead to your fall."

Everyone remained silent until the double doors shut behind the black-armored soldiers.

8

THE GARDENS

Hanna told Avva that Sol had messaged her with a request for a private audience. She couldn't stop stupidly giggling over that. Then Avva arranged for Hanna to message him back suggesting that the queen of Azure Blue and king of Crescent Blue should meet one another in the courtyard garden. It had been a couple of days since the coronation. In truth, Avva had been dying to see him, particularly after his brazen confrontation with the god of the Underworld, but she'd been so busy orienting herself to her myriad of responsibilities as queen.

It was evening now and everything was lit by torchlight. Avva walked the palace garden, passing a fruit grove and then a dense thicket full of the smell of lovely jasmine. She made her way further down a cobblestone walkway, hearing the waterfalls by the vines at the edge of the garden and the trickling stream running by her sandals. Then she meandered over a small arched stone bridge and through a tunnel of purple and green oaks. That's when she saw him. He sat under a torch lamp on a large oak chair, with his head down, fidgeting with his fingers. He was alone.

He wore a simple brown tunic and pants, almost peasant clothes really, but with a longsword on his belt. Avva wasn't dressed like royalty either, preferring a beige tunic draping over simple pants and sandals. But Sol's long dark hair was kempt, slicked back again and gathered in a ponytail. And, though he was broad-shouldered and very strong, his features, despite scattered facial hair, seemed boyish. And cute. Very cute.

Avva's friend Eva surprised her, emerging by a nearby walkway that headed out of the gardens and toward the fields south of the palace. After seeing Sol on the chair, she nodded and covered a playful giggle with her hand—stupid Eva.

Sol turned, hearing Eva's laughter. Then he quickly stood up at the sight of Avva. He bowed deeply, gesturing broadly with an arm.

"Queen Avivae Ambrosia."

"Oh, Sol. Stop."

"I am honored to be in your company, madam. And happy to congratulate you."

"Just stop," she said with a laugh. "Stop talking so formally." As he stood upright, she hugged him. When they let go, he had a joyous grin. But then he cocked his head.

"What's the matter?" he asked.

"What do you mean?"

"You look worried."

"It's hard, that's all."

"Ruling a kingdom is very hard, Blue."

"You remembered my nickname. Thank you."

"Only now, you're really *blue*. Why? We have this night together?"

"Oh, are you busy too?" she asked.

He looked about the garden uneasily and nodded. "Aye, but that's business. Like I said, we have tonight. And I've missed you, Avva."

"Oh, Sol." And she touched his shoulder. "That's sweet."

She was surprised when he took her in his embrace again. Then, gently, so gently for such a strong man, he led her by her hand to sit with him on the wide chair. The chair was broad enough for two.

She sat quietly, regretting not being in his arms again but enjoying being near him just the same. They looked out at the nearby trees under—with some irony, she thought—the white light of a crescent moon. He gazed out wistfully.

"What do you think of our lands?" she asked.

"Back home they would only be in my dreams."

She smiled.

"I must go soon," he said.

"What? Why?" she asked, jumping, as if startled. "I mean … of course. Of course. Sure."

"Henri's very sore that I haven't returned. Our lands are in grave danger."

"Henri?"

"My chief adviser. Aye, I fear for my people, Blue. We're surrounded. It was with great effort and some concern that I came here to honor your coronation."

"I'm so happy you did."

"I am too."

They sat silently again. It became uncomfortably quiet, apart from the sound of the running streams. She looked at him and he just smiled.

"Would you like me to show you our garden?" she asked.

"Yes."

They walked hand in hand around the great gardens. They spanned a vast distance. Trails lit by torch lamps circled around blue and purple trees. A few more nymphs passed wearing far simpler clothes than at the coronation—tunics or even pants. Some were caretakers, others close friends of Avva's. Many of them were giggling behind their backs.

"I haven't forgotten our last meeting," Sol said thoughtfully, now playing with her fingers in his hand. "I've spent many evenings trying to reimagine how you look, but I couldn't place it. Funny, I couldn't believe that I couldn't remember your face. Too beautiful, I thought." She laughed and he ran a finger along her hair. "And I haven't forgotten your laughter. Before passing over the Styx, it would be my dream to hear your laughter upon my last breath."

"Thoughtful … but not very romantic."

He laughed.

"Perhaps I can send you my portrait so you don't forget my face. We have artists around the palace. But surely, great king, there are many other women you'd like to commission a painting of?"

"No." He gently turned her toward him. "No one." He looked into her eyes and ran the back of his hand along her cheek. She got lost again for a moment.

He reached down and kissed her lips. The touch of their lips seemed longer than before. Then he squeezed her in those giant arms. She felt him close as he drew his tongue along her lips, but she didn't part hers. The kiss itself didn't matter. Standing in his arms was dreamy.

They walked the pathways paralleling the bush maze. And then stopped a few more times to kiss some more.

"May I speak with you as a king?"

"Sure." But she didn't like how formal that sounded.

An older nymph with wrinkled skin, in a long gray peplos with a high collar, passed by and curtsied to Avva. Then she smiled widely at Sol. Apparently, even the elders were amused at the monarchs strolling together.

"The way you dealt with Hades was impressive. And how you spoke to your people was magnificent. I want you to know that. I'm not very good at talking with people. I am very good with my sword. I raise a sword and shout and men follow." She laughed. "It's true. But you, you, Blue, have your mother's presence. You speak like her. You hold her focus and grace. I think you will make a great queen."

"Thank you. You don't make a bad king yourself."

"Ah, but I told you once before. I am nobody."

But *nobody* continued to hold her hand.

"How do you know so much about my mother?" she asked.

"Hmm?"

"You said you weren't at the games. You barely knew my mother."

"I met her a couple of moons ago."

"Yes. Over the bridge. So I heard."

"You did?" He turned and she just about died when he peered into her eyes again, under another flickering lamplight.

Stop acting like a baby, Avivae! You're a queen.

But he is cute. His eyes are so caring. And his smile … Have I been away from men so long?

"I spoke with her. It was a gift to speak with my mother." She cringed when he said the words "*my* mother." And he seemed to back off. "I … I don't remember my mother. I like the honor of thinking yours was my own. I know she loved you."

"She didn't love me. She was a witch. I told you. She didn't care about anyone. And you know what, Sol? That time you asked me whether I was just giving her a bad name, I wasn't. You know, when you asked me if she was really a witch? She was. She was a real witch. A real one."

"She was wise and kind to me."

"What do you mean? I heard she nearly killed you."

"Many have almost done that. And many of them are now my closest friends."

"She's a witch."

"Avva, you raised a sword to me when we first met, as I remember."

She giggled. Not because that was particularly funny, but because she felt wonderful. She couldn't remember a time she was ever this happy. But then she realized how puerile her laughter probably sounded.

She grabbed his hand and ran with him, leading him deeper into the forest, away from any trail.

"Where are you taking me?"

She didn't answer.

She maneuvered around the brush using the walls of a crystal tower to guide her. The Crystal Palace shone white under the moonlight. Beside one of the walls she spotted a worn stone cottage with a thatched roof.

"This," she said, gesturing, a little winded. "This is our zoo, Sol. Here there are all sorts of animals from Napea. Creatures you've never seen in your life. I really want to show you. You want to? I want to show you everything about me … I mean, everything about Azure. Do you want to see?"

"Yes. I'd like to very much, Blue."

She chuckled nervously.

Stop acting like an infant, Avva! You were just coronated queen, by the gods! Mother would take your crown back.

But he's so handsome. And so regal. So strong. I can't wait to tell you about him, Hanna. Yet humble. I've never met anyone like him. Nobody indeed. The most significant nobody I've ever met. Because nobody can compare to him.

They stopped by the door. She could smell the animals. That wasn't pleasant. Perhaps it was stupid to show him this. But he seemed curious and he didn't seem to mind. There was the sound of fluttering. Probably the birds. And then there was a low growl.

She tugged at his hand, but he stopped her. He turned her into his arms again before the door.

No one was around. They were alone. It was dark with only the stars and moonlight over this cottage by the palace grounds. Only the sounds of chirping and the animals within her zoo could be heard. He gazed deeply into her eyes and ran his hand along her cheek. Then he touched her lips and her ears with his lips. It was as if his kisses were examining her face. Then he leaned down and kissed her lips harder, this time with more passion than ever before.

"Oh, Sol," she said in a whisper. "Stop."

"I'm sorry," he said, pulling back, furrowing his brow.

"No, I meant, I wish you wouldn't," she said, shaking her head, "you wouldn't stop." Then she closed her eyes and kissed him again. "I mean, I wish you wouldn't stop kissing … please don't stop kissing me."

"Who counsels you?"

"Huh?" she furrowed her brow, backing up. "What?"

"I'm sorry. I'm not only bad with speeches, I'm bad with manners. But I have to know. I'm worried about you. Who counsels you, Avva? I have Henri and many others from Castle Cove who help me with my affairs. But what of you? Who helps you manage your kingdom?"

"No one."

He leaned back on the stone wall, folding his arms, and shook his head.

"It's a hard world," he said. "Very hard. As you're queen, and my closest ally—by distance and, I hope, by heart—you need to understand politics. You're smart and strong, but you need help in your affairs. Who counsels you? I'd like to know your plans. Are you, for instance, my ally or would you prefer to fight?"

She burst into laughter.

"Ah, Avva, your laughter is ambrosia from the gods."

"I'd never fight you, Sol. Anyway, there've been new Amazon queens before. I'll weather this change."

"Not with the land as it is now." His smile faded and he grew serious in a flash. He was like that. She marveled at how he could change his countenance so quickly. "What I mean is, as my closest ally, I would like to be sure things are in order in your Court. I'd like to ensure your safety. *Our* safety."

"We have a group of elders. They are known as Imada. They inform me of the happenings surrounding my kingdom."

"Well, you were right when you spoke of your mother's rule. She protected your lands. She was a brilliant leader. Our father once told me that she was the sharpest leader in all of Atala, besting even any ruler from Assyria or Egypt. But there are many dangers. I know my brothers will test you. You say there were coronations before, but an Amazon queen was never in a position to fight off the continent. War is brewing. And, not sure if you noticed it or not, Avva, but none of my brothers showed up to your coronation."

She felt her face flush. And for the first time, it wasn't embarrassment or a childish crush. She was angry.

"Perhaps, Sol, I can show you my zoo now. I'd much rather do that than talk about—"

"Please Avva," he said dismissively. "I don't know when I can talk about this with you again."

"We can arrange other times."

"Avva," he said with a smile, "I'm serious. Even Queen Delia didn't have to face the threats you do. My father, our father, managed to unify Atala. But his death has broken that unification. And, in some ways, things are worse than ever. In this, Hades is right. He offered his services too. When your mother spoke to me, she spoke of this. She asked that I protect you."

"Protect me? I don't need—"

"Yes. You. I mean it. I don't mean this in arrogance."

"You're not arrogant, Nobody. But I don't need protection."

"Then you know the Tiger King is planning on assaulting my lands in the North, from Adelain?"

He waited for her answer and she just shrugged.

"He will align with my brother Balen in the Moon Kingdom."

Again, he waited like some irritating philosopher.

"Then will come Ansel's army from Castle Cove itself. They will all converge upon Crescent Blue. And then they will threaten Azure Blue."

He waited. She turned from him, beginning to not like this serious version of Sol.

"They plan, with the help of Hades, to trap me in three fronts, Avva. And when they do, they will threaten you."

"No barbarian has ever attacked our lands."

"Aye," he said with a sigh, and he finally stopped challenging her. He looked out toward the sea. It wasn't visible through the trees, but Avva knew that, of all men, this man would know precisely where it was behind the blue leaves and thickets. "No one ever has, Blue. But there's never been a unification of the Hinterlands until Darius either. And now your lands are the only lands left in the north of Atala to conquer. Perhaps an ancient fear of Amazons might keep my brothers away. But if they take my small castle, they might eventually move on to yours."

"Why are you telling me this?"

He turned and she stared into those dark eyes, searching him. For the first time, she wasn't looking at his eyes with desire. She was searching for deception and deceit.

"I am known as the Crescent king. The crescent of land bordering the Strait is all I have. But, Avva, it is a buffer from your enemies."

"So what do you want from me? Why talk about this on our evening together? You even said it was our time away. Why do this now, Sol?"

"I seek a treaty. Our two kingdoms need to unite."

"I have no interest in discussing treaties right now. Anyway, I can't help you. There's no way I'm going to have my sisters land in Crescent—"

"I would never ask for any of your nymphs to land." He sighed. "Avva, I don't want to talk about this either, but I'm desperate. I only ask you to consider a treaty. But even if you don't, let me share something with you, in grave secret, something you mustn't tell anyone. Let this secret show my trust in you. In order for my people to live in peace, I'm going to strike first. I plan to attack Torinth. I would like to sign a treaty with you and your people before I invade to help protect your shores."

And now he was the one to search her eyes.

She put a finger on her chin in thought. "I think I'd rather visit the animals instead." She burst into laughter and darted inside the building through the wooden door. He grabbed for her hand, but her fingers slipped out of his grasp.

She ran to her favorite cage. A very large bright-purple tiger with black stripes was lying on leaves under torchlight. All the cages were lit every night by the zoo caretaker. She pointed at the animal among a thicket of blue leaves.

"A Zaffre tiger, Sol. What do you think of him?"

He stood beside her. "Wondrous. Mighty. Incredible, like your lands. Amazing like … you."

She turned and he forced a smile.

"Just not now, Sol. Please. Talk of something else."

He nodded and just looked at the tiger. But she could tell his mind was not on the animal. He still looked about, pained and restless, moving his eyes all over the cage.

She reached up and kissed his beard. He turned his head, and she touched her lips to his again. Then, as he reached to embrace her, she dodged out of his grasp, giggling, and ran to the next cage.

"What … what about this one? Do you know what this is, Sol?" She pointed at a bird. It was a black bird with multicolored wings, an azure chest, and bright blue eyes.

"What?"

"This is a phoenix. It is the only one in existence. Do you know what's incredible about it?"

Sol shook his head.

"It lives forever. I've never seen it, but apparently, it can renew itself eternally. What always amazes me, ever since Engel taught me this, is the bird's discipline. He could escape as he pleases with such power. But he doesn't. He just stands in his cage. He's been doing that all my life. Of course, mother lived for nearly a century. But I'm young, like in human years. Can you imagine living forever? It's said, Sol, that this was Harmonia's bird, but I find that hard to believe."

Sol didn't seem to care. He just looked at her and ran his fingers along the hair by her neck.

"He's your standard," Sol said with a serious nod. "An honor to see it. A real honor. I don't want you to ever lose this, Azure queen."

Veering my attention right back to business, are you? Clever king. Well … No!

Avva pouted and hit the metal bars on the cage. "Oh, Sol, can't you have fun for an instant?"

He nodded sternly. And that made her laugh.

"I tell you what," she said. "If I promise to sign this treaty of yours, will you promise to enjoy my zoo?"

He laughed. The phoenix fluttered his wings and the tiger stirred. "I've never met anyone such as you, Avva. Back where I'm from, in my home in Kitheria, we would pronounce your name Anna. Queen Anne."

"Anna? I like that. Why don't you call me Anna?"

The phoenix walked close to the wooden bars, and Sol reached through and petted him.

"Magnificent," he said, running his hand over the fowl's red-feathered head.

"Will you win?" she asked.

"Hmm?"

"Will you win, Solinair? If I sign this treaty, I want to sign with the side that will win."

"I will win," Sol said, nodding with a smile. "I always win. War is one thing I am very good at." She believed him. He seemed so focused and determined. "But..." He turned back and petted the bird with a sigh. "Know this. Even if you choose not to align with us, Anna, I will tell you one more secret. I shall protect you. Either way. I love your lands that much ... just as ... I love you."

"Well, if you win. Somehow, I know you'll win. I'm on your side, Crescent King."

"You must deliberate carefully," he said. He looked stern again. "You must do what is right for your people. Speak with your Imada. Find counsel before you make a decision. You can't do it alone."

"I think, King Nobody, that I just heard you not only say that you love our lands but that you love someone else. A queen, if I am right? The Azure queen. Didn't you just say that?"

He didn't respond. Rather he held her tightly and kissed her lips again.

He grabbed her. She felt his hand with as much strength as two men grab her. Such strength. Then his other hand probed under her leather tunic and up to her chest. She had no support for her breasts. Sol found one of her soft mounds while kissing her harder, with more passion than before. No man had ever touched her there before, and it frightened her a little. Perhaps she was moving too fast? But after the week's whirlwind of events, what couldn't be happening too fast?

"Oh, Sol," she whispered in his ear between kisses. "I … I had my first kiss here."

"Is that why you showed me?" he whispered back.

She nodded. His hands moved around and massaged her more.

"It was my first … Nothing like this. My first and only kiss."

He quickly pulled away, moving his hands out of her tunic. Then he turned from her and grabbed the bars.

"What's wrong?" she asked.

"You're so delicate," he said, shaking his head. "By the gods, so beautiful, but so delicate."

"Hey, I'm not delicate!" she said with a chuckle, hitting his shoulder. "What's that supposed to mean?"

"You don't understand." He turned back with that serious look she didn't like. "Let me be straight with you, Avva. I thought I'd meet with you as a king tonight. I … I thought I could sway you for my political interests. For my people, militarily."

"So that's it! That's why you wanted to meet?" And her face blushed in anger again.

"Wait," he said, raising a hand. "No. Wait. Listen to me."

"I think I should go."

"Anne."

"My name is Avivae."

"Avivae. The loveliest name. I meant everything I said. Every-thing about love too." He lifted her chin. "And *you*. Yes, love for you. First I met you because of war. Because my lands and people are threatened. Second, I met you for the same reason I sailed alone across the Strait. Because I've longed to see you. I've longed for it for so long. I do love you, Avivae."

"That sounds a little better." She looked up. "Go on."

"I told you the dangers I face. But I need to, well, treat you carefully … I mean you're a virgin, right?"

"Right. I really think I should go now."

"Well, aren't you? Isn't that what you just said?"

"So what!" she hissed.

Sol reached for her hand and she batted it away.

"Oh, Anna, it's not just that. You're a virgin as a ruler. That's what I meant by delicate." He laughed and stepped back. "You're not delicate in will. You'd probably be my worst enemy."

"I would!"

"But you're so young in power. That's what worries me. But it's …" He cupped her chin and then ran his fingers along her cheek again. He cradled her head in his hand. "It's wonderful. You need help. Your mother told me as much."

"She would." Anna said and she turned her back on him. "You even sound like her when you speak of war."

"Anne, I want to protect you. I want to help you and your people. Will you let me? A treaty will protect you." He took her arm and tried to turn her toward him, but she was acting stupid and mad. But it was a game. And she smiled as he kept trying to turn her. "And for you to protect me, Anne. All right? I need your protection too."

"I don't know, Sol," she said, finally gazing sternly into his eyes. "I'll speak to Imada. I can't imagine ever fighting you. But I'm not sure I can disregard your brothers and take a side either."

"I understand. I spoke of this for you to consider it. I'm not asking for your decision now. I told you to speak with your counsel."

"But did I hear you say you loved me?" she asked, tilting her head back with a whimsical smile.

"Yes."

"I think I care about you too, Sol." And she grabbed his hand from behind her and leaned against him again.

He gently put his arm around her. "For some reason, we were meant for each other. I do love you, Blue. Just as I love your lands. I've never loved anything more. Thank you for this wondrous evening tour of the garden and your zoo."

"Said formally like a true king." She turned to lift her lips to his again. "But you're not going anywhere, King Nobody. I need nobody's protection tonight. After all these ceremonies, I truly want nobody. Not a king who talks of treaties or battle. Not someone to talk of trouble. Nothing. Will nobody protect me tonight?"

"If you wish it. Aye. You shall have him for the rest of my life."

"And who knows. Teach me some more. Perhaps then I will protect you, Sol."

9

HENRI

Avva left her royal chambers and ran down a cobblestone merchant street, searching all around the palace for Solinair. It was a clear day and they had planned on going riding together around the castle grounds in the evening. But Avva had needed to excuse herself from his company after being forced to preside over the trial of a thief in the throne room. Now she feared Sol had left early to return home. But he wouldn't do that. Would he? And yet, every night for the past few days all he had spoken of was how terrible things were back in Crescent Blue.

She passed a cottage with a thatched roof and smelled cooked meat. She couldn't see through the wooden doors, but she could smell the alluring pepper- and ginger-roasted pheasant. She got hungrier passing another cottage full of baked bread and cakes. Then she wound down a narrow alleyway and another street. When the green sun finally fell under a stone wall, she gave up looking and headed back to her royal chambers for supper.

The main dining room of the palace was a wooden-walled room with a matching oak dining table. The table was grand, capable of seating maybe thirty people. There were small windows along the wall. Windows of glass—something rare and not seen outside of her kingdom; she laughed every time Sol ran his fingers along one in wonder. The wooden chairs were novel too. The tradition of the time outside Azure was to eat lying on one's side. But what drew her eyes the most and made her give a huge sigh of relief was seeing two men seated at the far side of the table. They wore simple tunics with long, disheveled hair down to their shoulders and beards fashioned in a similar manner, tied near the chin. But one man's head and beard were gray. As they ate, they didn't talk, but Avva found their mannerisms strikingly similar. The young man was her boyfriend, Sol. The old man she did not know.

Sol seemed to awaken from a deep meditation when hearing her enter. He became the animated Sol she had grown to love over the past week.

"Anna! Come here! Have supper with us."

"I thought you left."

He shook his head, jumped up, and ran to her. Then he put an arm around her and led her to the other end of the room. "I'm sorry. I had to greet an old friend by the beaches."

Henri nodded but he didn't get up.

"Henri!" cried Sol. "Henri, this is Anna!"

"Of course she is." And he gestured to take her hand with a smile.

"Welcome, noble sir," she said. She gave him her hand, and he turned it, opening his eyes wider at the deeper blue of her palm. He examined her hand and handed it back as if it were a specimen.

"My queen," Henri said with a nod. He had a glint in his eye. But it wasn't just his eyes, it was his squint. He seemed so contemplative. "I'm an old man, but I never had a chance to step foot on Azure Blue, though I saw your lands across the Strait all my life. You can't imagine the honor it was for me to finally land here. Though late to your coronation, I congratulate you." And he bowed before her.

"I haven't seen you with the other men."

"I just came today."

"While you were away working, Blue," Sol said, "I welcomed my chief advisor. He came alone."

"Across the water alone?" she asked. "But Poseidon makes it dangerous."

"Sol did it to see you," Henri said. "Remember?"

"Yes. But you're—"

"Old?"

"Well …"

"He is old, Anne. But wise and strong. I told you."

"Three weeks, Sol," he said, leaning back in his chair and tearing off a piece of bread. "Three weeks in that rancid rat-infested fortress with Hades. My bones ache. I'm tired. Next time send a messenger. Or send Milo."

"Of course … of course," Sol said. "Sit, Anna. Why … I mean, it's your home, but please join us in this amazing feast your people gave us. I believe it's fish. Eggs. Cheese. Lovely berry wine. Whatever it all is, it's wonderful. Incredible."

"The fish is Yocombre," Avva said, sitting beside them. "It's a blue-green fish from the Stratos. Only found in Azure. Look at the shiny blue gills. Seems my people wanted you to try our local food."

"Umm, it's delicious," said Sol, picking it up and biting into it. "Join us. Please, love."

Henri ran his fingers through his thin gray hair. He stroked his beard. She noticed him stroking the beard more aggressively after he heard the word "love." Then he ate quietly, seeming to ignore them.

Sol was staring at Henri as he ate. Then, as Henri looked up, she realized that she was staring at him too.

"So how'd it go?" asked Sol. "Come on. Tell me." Then he turned to Avva and winked. "I sent him on a quest to speak with my brother Ansel."

"He almost took my life," Henri said, nodding warily.

Solinair laughed heartily and hit the table. "Of course he did! Aye, I would have. You think we should have left out the ending?"

"The ending was a bit much, Sol."

"Did they laugh?"

"What's so funny?" Avva asked.

Sol smiled more widely and gestured for a crystal decanter to pour her some red wine, but Avva shook her head.

"I was spared by Hades," Henri said with a nod to Avva. "Seems that although the fiend provides counsel, he let me live. The Dark Lord told Ansel that my death would be too soon after Darius's. Sol and I figured that, but I worried Ansel was too stupid not to send me to the ferryman. Sol, Hades was right. The snake is always right, loathsome creature that he is."

"Ah, hmm." Sol pulled off more fish with his teeth. "Aye, well that's why I knew my brother wouldn't kill you."

"A dangerous gamble."

"What are you two talking about?" Avva asked. She picked up some olives from a tray and threw them into her mouth.

Henri looked at his king, unsure.

"It's all right, Henri. You can trust her. There are no secrets between us."

Henri shook his head and sighed deeply. "I visited King Ansel, my queen. Sol's brother. The Sun King."

"He has no right to that title," Sol said.

"Everyone in Atala still calls him that, Sol, no matter what you think."

"Aye."

Henri smiled and rubbed his long gray-white beard. Then he dipped some bread in eggs. He spoke, with his mouth full, to Avva. "Your Majesty, your foolish friend here sent me on a mission to die in Ansel's kingdom."

"I did not. And you did not. You're alive and well."

"Yes, you did. The quest to deliver a letter was a fool's journey, and I will never do it again, or it will be the death of me, son—"

"It was a message of peace," interrupted Solinair, raising a finger. But then he laughed again.

Henri shook his head, swallowing more food.

"So, what did he say?" asked Sol.

"What do you think he said?"

"Ah, but we tried."

Henri turned to the queen again. "Allow me to explain, Queen Anne. We've spent the last season preparing for invasion." Then he turned to Sol again. "You did tell her that too, I assume?"

Sol nodded.

Henri shook his head. "With Solinair's just rule, it's not taken long to earn the people's hearts. Along with the small piece of our crescent beaches, we've gathered an army from your father. And with Sol's heart—not all kindness, mind you, but tenacity— our army doubled. Then tripled. Small it is, but full of the best soldiers of all the armies in the four kingdoms. We've trained for many moons in preparation since the death of your father." He furrowed his brow and reached out a hand. "You have my condolences for that, of course, Anne."

Avva nodded.

"An army to take the rest of…" Henri nodded his head in a bow to her. "Of your illustrious father's lands. But your idiotic lover here wanted to send an olive branch. He sent me to bring a letter to King Ansel. King Ansel, being the oldest brother, holds the Sun Kingdom at Castle Cove of Azerban—once Darius's kingdom and once Sol's and my home. I went alone to show goodwill. The letter made one final offer for peace. It simply asked that Darius's lands would be honored and that Torinth would forthwith retreat to Adelain alone and give back the lands his butchers had stolen from us. We didn't bother speaking to Torinth—"

"He's mad, Blue. Completely mad."

"Yes, Torinth is mad," Henri said with a nod. "He's always been. So I rode directly to Ansel." He put down his piece of bread and said to Sol, "You told her everything?"

Sol nodded.

"*Everything?*"

Sol nodded again.

Henri reached into a pocket in his tunic and took out a rolled parchment and placed it on the table before Avva. Then he folded his arms, leaned back in his chair, and gestured for her to read it.

Ansel, dear brother, the people grow weary of battle. Our great father, King Darius, showed respect to me when he gave me land upon his death. But now there are squabbles over the borders and dishonor. All I've ever wanted was peace. Peace for my people, peace in my life, peace with my family.

I ask for help. King Torinth continues to send bandits along the northern borders. This cannot continue. If you and dear Ballen are willing to move Torinth to relinquish his northern excursions, I will be forever in your debt. We must honor the borders agreed upon since the death of our illustrious father.

If you do not agree, be advised that I will have to take measures to force peace. I shall devote all my forces, at an unknown hour, to push back Torinth. Then I will move on to your kingdom and Ballen's. Your fate, unlike that of Torinth, who I believe is simply not of right mind, will be to be hanged from a tree surrounded by your starving subjects.

Your dearest brother,
Solinair Solinaray, The Crescent King

"Why you risked my life to offer peace but then had to threaten to hang him is beyond me," Henri said, shaking his head.

"To show strength," Sol said with a laugh. "You advised me and my father to do this many times."

"Yeah, well. Hmm. Seemed like foolhardy conceit. Go ahead and tell her the rest yourself." He picked up his fork and dug into more eggs, shaking his head.

"We've already attacked the harbor north of the Strait," Sol told Avva. "War is declared. I really sent Henri as a decoy to give my brother Torinth a false sense of security and time.

That was the other reason for the olive branch. And now I've cut off Adelain's supplies. Adelain, as I'm sure you know being so close to your borders, Blue, is a harbor town. Torinth has ships but they're of little use to him now that I burned his docks. Now his only supplies of food and rations are through Crescent Blue. The closest harbor town left in Atala is Castle Cove itself, which is far too far away to be of any use to Torinth now."

"Of course, your boyfriend lives in a dream world," Henri added. "We had a day to ward off the attack, on the off chance that Ansel actually capitulated. He still wanted to offer his enemies a chance of peace before conquering them. Very noble. You see, he loves fantasy, which is why he's foolishly in love with you."

"Henri!" Solinair yelled and hit the table.

Henri shrugged and grabbed another egg.

"You don't like me, Henri?" asked Avva, pretending to be hurt. Henri turned and gazed into her eyes sternly.

"May I speak freely, Azure Queen?" Henri asked.

"You always do," snapped Sol.

"My queen," continued Henri, bowing his head, "aside from having striking beauty, you're brave, brash, and foolish, even childish. And I'm not referring to age. You are exactly like your father. You're more like King Darius than any of his sons. More like your father than, I would bet, your mother. That's probably why Sol is so smitten with you. But I'm afraid, Queen Avivae, you don't serve my master well."

"Why?"

"You know the edict. Your love for each other will hurt one another. And just like Hades said, it will eventually kill you, Anna."

"Stop it, Henri!" shouted Sol. "By the gods, is that a prophecy!"

"You said I could speak freely," Henri said, shrugging.

"Not to threaten her life!"

But Avva was not upset. She sat in thought. "I see. Then,

dear Henri, what would you say if I told you we are in love? And there's nothing anyone can do about it."

"Then I would say you're a bigger fool than my master, Your Majesty." And he even bowed after saying that.

"Enough, Henri!"

"Does he hold prophecy, too, Sol?" Avva asked, turning to him.

"Aye, aye. Anna, he's learned magic from Magi in the East. An old fool without manners, but the best counsel any king could have. He was our father's advisor. But he's not good with women. And he doesn't know when to shut his mouth."

"The king's quite right, madam. I've gotten into trouble countless times for not knowing my place with royalty or how to speak to women." He rose. "Please accept my apology if I offended. And now, I ask a king and queen if I may retire. It's a long journey and I am very tired. Can I have a room to rest my weary old bones, my queen?"

"Only if you answer one more question."

Henri smiled and bowed again. "At your service, my lady."

"Why did you and Hades prophesy that Sol would kill me?"

"Because he loves you. But this is not prophecy. True love kills all people—a part of you, anyway. But he did not say he will kill you. He meant his love will be your downfall. Though he is accustomed to war, I don't think my son would ever lay a hand on you. But wondrous Amazon nymph, you've chosen to live among men. You defied the gods' decree. You are now mortal. I can't say much further. I honestly don't know, but I do see the beginning threads of fate. Don't you? Are you the same girl that was imprisoned in a tower a few moons ago?"

She shook her head.

"His *love* will hurt you, Queen Anne. He would never."

The old man gave them one last great bow and walked out of the dining room.

"I'm sorry, Anna," said Solinair, biting off a piece of fish. "He can be so damn depressing. And irritating."

"I like him," she said with a smile.

"Aye, aye, he's a good man." And Sol smiled at that. "A good man. But so cruel. So unfeeling, you know."

"How long have you known him?"

"Longer than your father. He took me in first, in Shadow Forest—even before the king—when I was a boy. I suppose he was my first true father."

"He doesn't fear you?"

"He fears nothing," Solinair said with a laugh. "He's family … I'm sorry if he frightened you."

"He didn't frighten me. I heard him call you his son?"

"He raised me, Blue. Foreseeing death. I hate such talk. What good is soothsaying? I would rather not know. And he has no business speaking of your future."

Avva got up. Then she forgot all about the wizard. Instead she pointed outside. "I thought we could take monokera for a stroll in the palace fields tonight again. There's enough torchlight. That is, if you're not leaving? I was so worried you were already gone."

Sol rose and took her in his arms. "I'm not leaving yet. But I will soon, Anne. Two more nights. Henri said we have that long. Then I must go to the front to face Torinth. But you, my dear, I didn't see you touch any food."

"I'm not hungry. How dreadful. The front? Well, stay as long as you'd like." And then she stood on her tiptoes kissing his cheek. "When will you start this fight?"

"Armies are forming along the border. Torinth is a man who never could control his rage. Imagine how he felt when he woke up to his precious docks in Adelain having been burned. He is the only one among us who believed in building a navy to fend off the outsiders. Now I destroyed his dream."

"How'd you do it?"

"In secret. I sent spies in the middle of the night and torched the docks."

"Sneaky."

"Aye."

"How do you know your brothers won't strike first?"

"Because they lack the means. Torinth is mad, but not stupid. He will wait for Ansel to meet him with his forces from the South."

"Then why are you waiting?"

Sol nodded, losing his smile. "We've amassed a great army, but we are still vastly outnumbered. We have to be precise with our strike. Incredibly precise. We rely on General Milo's genius and Henri's guile. We have to be patient."

"You might have a chance." She looked out the window. It was dark. Her blue lands were gray. "Do you require my help?"

"Have you made your decision?" He placed his arms around her again. Then he ran his hand along her hair and kissed her head.

She nodded.

"Absolutely not."

"Why?" she said, jumping out of his embrace. "I thought my support was part of your treaty?"

"The treaty was supposed to be for my people to protect *you*. Don't misunderstand my intentions this past week. I will never allow your people's purity and immortality to be sullied by man's wars. With the harbor burned, I feared Torinth would consider striking Azure in revenge. Now he will not do this if we are bound by treaty. That would promise battle with me before Ansel's and Ballen's forces have arrived. I think he will wait."

She shook her head and looked down. "You've planned everything."

"With the help of that old man you just met. But we're still very likely to fail. If I die, Anne," he said gently, lifting her chin and looking sternly into her eyes, "let me die alone. I don't want one Napean nymph to fall in Crescent Blue."

She shook her head again. Then she took a deep breath, leaning her head back into his chest.

"Promise me." He kissed her head and held her again. "No matter what the price, don't send your people into battle."

"Don't ask me to do that."

"I ask you to stay back. By the will of the gods, we will win, but stay back. If we don't win, make peace with my brothers. My elder brother is my greatest enemy, but he is the strongest. If you placate Ansel, you can stay out of war."

"But you said fighting them all is inevitable anyway?"

"For me, yes. For you, if you use your mother's strategy, maybe not. There's still fear in men's hearts of Amazon. Though eons have passed, my people haven't forgotten Harmonia. No one dares fight you. Use diplomacy, like your mother, if my land falls."

"I don't want to talk about this anymore," she said, shaking her head. "I won't make deals with anyone while watching you die."

"Just take care of yourself." He drew her into an embrace and nodded. "You should eat supper, my love."

"I love you," she said, leaning her head against his chest again. "I love you, Sol."

"Aye. I love you, Anna."

"I don't want you to go."

10

____

IMADA

ANNA DESCENDED THE DUSTY STEPS INTO THE PRIVATE BASEMENT in her palace. She was solemn. She had permitted herself to cry alone in her bedchamber for many sleepless nights, but never publicly. Sol had been gone for some time now, but she seemed to miss him more every day.

Being down in the depths, lit by a few torches on a stone wall, reminded her of a crypt. It smelled of death with a stale and dusty odor. She sneezed a few times. She had been told by her mother that this chamber was secretive and perfect for planning the Amazon hidden agenda. She had never been told exactly what that agenda was.

Indeed, as Avva entered a hallway through an open wooden door, torchlight flickered over five elders, wearing formal black robes, who looked more like dead specters or evil sirens than the counsel of Azure. The room was windowless with a long wooden table. Their robes were plain but regal. Each robe ran from a tall collar with many gemmed golden necklaces over wrinkled skin.

All the witches flashed fake smiles before Avva.

Take a deep breath. You can do this.

Milda, the eldest, sat at the center of the table. Her curly white hair was as ugly as her smirk. She gestured with an arm for Avva to sit across the table. Then all the hags stared at her.

"Imada welcomes you once more," Milda said with another stupid fake grin. "We recognized you after the coronation. Now we extend the same greeting moving forward."

"Thanks."

They had met not long after Sol had left. That meeting had been quick, more ceremonial. Now they had asked to meet regarding a pressing matter. But having already spoken with Henri and Sol, she didn't expect much of a surprise.

"There's a great deal to deliberate on, Queen Avivae," said another elder woman. Avva didn't hate this one as much as Milda, because she didn't seem as phony. But instead of smiling, she sort of scowled as she pushed some rolled parchments across the table. Avva grabbed them. "Did you bring your royal seal, dear?"

Avva nodded.

"Queen Avivae," said Milda, "our position in Atala is more dangerous than it ever was when your mother was alive. I can't remember a time more perilous. And I've lived to see every Amazon queen since Queen Harmonia. Not even when I advised the great Queen Nephratee, or her mother, revered Harmony, have the times been so dangerous to the survival of our people."

"You knew Harmonia?"

The witches laughed—no, more like cackled—at her question, and Avva tightened her fist under the table.

"I was Queen Harmonia's trusted advisor, dear. She was the greatest leader that ever lived." Milda turned to the empty stone wall and sighed. "The greatest, child. She should never have left us. But that was long ago. Back then, centuries ago, our shores were threatened too, but Harmonia was so shrewd, so feared, that no man ever dared touch upon Napean shores. There was no need for any edict. All feared her. Now things are different."

"Perhaps I should rule like her."

"Yes." Milda nodded, looking right into Avva's eyes. "Yes. Yes. Perhaps you should. I would like that. And I can help you."

Milda paused and looked at the wall again, and Avva noticed that no one else dared say a word. Milda was their absolute leader. When she looked back at Avva, her dark eyes narrowed. Avva felt a little sick.

"When you stepped foot on Crescent Blue, child, you broke the treaty made between the great Queen Nefertiti and the god Hades. It had consequences not just for you, you brought harm to your people and an affront to the balance of power in Atala. You must think like a queen now, Avivae. Everything you do affects your people. Lord Hades himself told you that. So did your mother every day of her life. Your personal life is not important. What affects your subjects is preeminent. Do you understand?"

This was exactly the sort of thing her mother would say. And it made her hate Milda even more.

"Your mother, Queen Delia, knew these things. She knew how important it was to consider the consequences of her actions for our people. You—forgive me queen—do not."

"She's young yet, Milda," said one of the crones.

"Yes, yes," Milda said, raising a hand, "but there isn't time." Milda took a deep breath and said, "You know we are threatened, Avivae, by the violence across the Strait?"

"Yes."

"Well, we are Imada, child. I will tell you more. Of course, everything within this room is secret."

Avva nodded.

"Our agents inform us that Hellena is stronger under Zeus's will. Within one generation, the Greeks will be the most powerful force in Gaia. Not Atala. Not even Amazon. The Greeks have technology, they have heart, they hold discipline and, most worrisome, they are building ships. But, like our closest neighbors, they are broken up into many kingdoms. That is their weakness.

"One day it is feared that, unlike Adelain's harbor, now in ashes, the Greeks will bring ships to overrun our shores. Not the

Assyrians. Not the Egyptians. And certainly not the barbarians across the Strait."

"I've heard of the Greeks' power."

"From who, child?" asked a crony with smugness.

"Engel told me. Engel said the Greeks are very resourceful."

"Engel, I see." Milda leaned forward. "Allow me to give you my first piece of advice as queen. Never listen to a Mandrigel. Ever. They are weak. They are born slaves."

Such words were heresy for a normal Amazon. Nefertiti had taught her people the importance of freedom for all and, legend said, she had been willing to die for the Mandrigels' freedom. In fact, Engel had been revered around the kingdom since Nefertiti's reign. Apparently the Imada thought differently. But Avva loved Engel more than anyone in the palace. And, in that moment, the clever witch Milda blinked, seemingly flustered, possibly remembering this too.

"Perhaps I can listen to your advice if you stop referring to me as a child," Avva said.

"Hand our new *queen* the charts."

One of the oldest ladies beside Milda picked up some rolled papyrus on the table, rose from her chair, pulled them out of a golden ring, and laid them down, with a shaky hand, over the ones already piled next to Avva. Unlike the others, which showed writing, these appeared to be geographic maps.

"Take a look," Milda said. "We shall wait."

They were ancient maps, many appearing worn and ready to crumble in her hands. She was dazzled by their detail. It spanned from Shadow Forest across the Crystal Kingdom and into Kitheria, and even beyond the continent of Atala to the Strait of Aethiopia. But not only was there a map of Atala, there were maps of Egypt. And distant lands named Sparta, Corinth, and Argos. Further details—far south, beyond even the Nile, showed territories only dreamt of, deep in a vast land known as Aethiopia. And there was even a map of a larger land far to the west of a great sea. This map was round and showed her home as just a tiny dot in a huge spherical plane. And upon this circular map was water that looped far below Aethiopia and back around to what Avva had been taught was called the Indus. There, among the Indus, were more cities. And further snowy lands she didn't even know existed in the far North.

When she looked back at Milda, the nasty old hag smirked. Milda nodded and gestured to the other nymphs in the room.

"We are Imada. There are many more of us living in secret in your palace, Your Majesty. We have knowledge that goes far beyond man's. It is this knowledge that has kept our people safe and prosperous for half a millennium."

"How did you get all this information?"

"Monokera," Milda said with a shrug. "The gods. Much surveillance was ordered by Harmonia during the Amazon wars. Harmonia had eyes far beyond the Atalan continent. Indeed, her dream was to conquer Argos, said to be the home of the gods in Hellena. And beyond that, when speaking to me in secret, she intended to rule the entire world. But Argos was her first step toward that dream. Argos, at the time, was the most powerful settlement of the Greeks. Even then she had the foresight to know that any people favored by Zeus would be the most power-ful. Those Greek men would have to be conquered and subju-gated. Had not Zeus himself stopped her, Harmonia would have continued her conquest to the far edges of the world.

"Now, we benefit from the knowledge of geography from the sky. In addition to aerial surveillance, some of our most ancient information comes from Lord Hades himself. But now, instead of planning a conquest, your mother, Delia, ordered us to watch man merely to ensure our safety. Do you understand all of this, Queen Ambrosia?"

Avva nodded.

"Good." Milda acted as if their conversation was over. She picked up a single rolled parchment on the table before her, spread it out, and looked it over. "Now for some unpleasantness. There is word of a fierce young barbarian across the Strait. A mighty warrior. He goes by the name of Solinair Solinaray." She looked up and glared at Avva for a moment as if waiting for her words to sink in. "This name was bequeathed to him by your father, Darius Solinaray. He is a bastard born from Harkist in the disorderly barbaric lands of Kitheria. This bastard is causing quite a stir in the Hinterlands. Mainly, I believe, because of the help of King Darius's counselor Henri Untair. Do you know this man?" Milda steepled her fingers and stared at Avva with that infernal fake smirk again.

"I ..."

"May I remind you, we are Imada. We know news from all the far reaches of Gaia. And be assured, young queen, we know the events within our own halls."

"Then why are you asking me?"

One of the other ladies cackled at that.

"At this moment, there is a regiment forming over the northern borders of Crescent Blue, not far from the Crescent boy's fortress," Milda continued. "And currently making their way through Shadow Forest, there is another army, including Eruboi mercenaries from Lord Hades, marching to close in from the south. Among them, we believe, are even some of King Ballen's, the child king's, soldiers. They have been gathering in strength for the past moon. And there is word, though the cowards wait along their borders, that even soldiers of Caravia are amassing near Crystal Lake. Like vultures, everyone outside of the continent hopes for enough damage in Atala to move on to the Sun Kingdom itself and threaten King Ansel. Basically, Avivae, the men are doing what they do best. Killing themselves. Their stupid squabbles weaken Darius's great empire, fragment it, and allow outsiders from the east and south to encroach upon Napea. This must be stopped. Or quickly put to an end."

"I understand."

"No, forgive me, you don't. So I'll ask you one more time. And I warn you, the group before you can help you. We can work with you, but we must work in trust. Don't lie to me. Do you know this boy king?"

"All of you saw him at my coronation defending me. Who is

the one lying? Why ask me what you already know? And he is no boy."

"Word is," Milda said with a nod, "that you've become quite fond of this Crescent boy. Having sex with men is permitted, of course, as a necessity for procreation, during our festivals. Of course, it is preferred then. But lately we can—"

"What business of that is yours!" she snapped, feeling her face redden.

"The business of an Azure queen is Imada's greatest concern, child. Including base tendencies. Queen Harmonia once said that aversion to things such as blood, sex, and shit weakens Amazon and brings us down to the likes of man. We have to deal with everything in our natural world. Everything. Hades knew this too. Only Greeks and Zeus teach you to avoid your natural self. Through order and acceptance of our base instincts, we can become a greater force."

"You disgust me," Avva cried.

"No, you disgust us," Milda said calmly. "Solinair is your brother. Not by blood, but still Delia and Darius's adopted son. You are an Ambrosia and can carry on any foolish way you wish, of course. I said your personal tastes don't concern us. But part of your power depends on your public image. Involving yourself with your *brother* taints your rule."

"Is that a threat, Milda?"

"Calm down, child," said one of the other elders. "Please. Calm yourself."

"Stop calling me a child!" Avva hit the table. "And don't ask what goes on in my private life."

"Then I'll move back to politics," replied Milda, unperturbed. "Imada's made a decision. Be like our revered queen, your mother, Queen Delia, who never let her personal interests affect her decisions. Delia was good at that. That's what kept the peace. Do I have your attention?"

"Not for long."

"We advise you to back Sol's brothers. Allow them to quickly defeat this Crescent boy. If you do not, we predict Sol will cause more damage to a very delicate Atala. He will hurt Azure Blue."

Avva was ready to jump up and leave. But then another, one who had been silent, spoke. She was so frail and pale that it seemed to be a chore just to turn her head. And her head shook as she spoke.

"Dear Queen Avivae, please listen to Milda. She can be … a little brash. But listen. We've watched your lover. He is a powerful warrior and could defeat any of his brothers in single combat, but he doesn't hold a chance against them in this war. They will conquer his land. When they do, we can work for peace among the other three kings. Let him lose."

"Torinth is mad," objected Avva. "Surely you ladies know that? You can only imagine the sort of damage Torinth will cause upon our shores. You wish me to align with him?"

They nodded.

"And Sol said Ballen is younger than ten. His advisors rule him."

They nodded again.

"Ansel is known as a butcher to his people and has caused the Sun Kingdom to fall into shambles. He seems to kill his own subjects for sport, and beggars are everywhere, living in squalor. He's damaged everything, even the legendary Castle Cove. Surely your intelligence knows all of this?"

The witches, infuriatingly, nodded again.

"Sol is the best king of them all. He's no boy. He's a better man than I've ever known. And, word is, Delia asked him to help protect our kingdom. Do you elders believe Darius to be a fool? Darius knew his sons. And according to my mother, Darius knew his adopted son was the greatest."

"So King Solinair says to you," replied Milda. "But then why did your father bequeath him a land so easily taken?"

"Because it was the only possible way for peace. Darius hoped to bring peace. He hoped his sons wouldn't fight. And he hoped that giving Sol—a bastard, as you insultingly said repeatedly—a small parcel of land would keep the peace. Doesn't that make sense?"

"Interesting theory, Avivae. But another would be that King Darius knew his adopted son would never amount to anything and that a small piece of land would appear fair but take care of his share of his inheritance."

"That's not what my mother told him."

All the women looked away. Many sighed and stared at the walls.

Then another spoke. "None of us in this chamber believes that Sol is not a good king, Avivae. We won't even refute your theory of favoritism. But all of that is unimportant in the tide of war. We are advising you for the future of Azure Blue. If you wish your kingdom to get out of this safely, you need to side with Ansel."

"Ansel is aligned with Hades."

"So was Harmonia," said Milda.

"Well, I am queen now," she snapped.

"Apparently." Then Milda turned to the nymph beside her. "She's too young. I told you this. She forced this out of Delia too early at a terrible time."

The nymph beside her nodded.

"I am young," objected Avva. "So is Sol. But we both deserve the crown."

"Think quickly and carefully, Avva," Milda snapped. "This isn't about deserving anything. This meeting is an introduction to your counsel. Imada. You have to trust us. I worked personally with Queen Harmonia to build the kingdom you've inherited. You lack experience. And I can tell you, even if you're foolish enough to side with the Crescent king, he will lose. There is no way for him to win."

"Then I'll help him fight."

All the witches' eyes bulged at that under the flickering torchlight.

"My mother once helped Darius," Avva said with a shrug. "I'll help his best son."

"What do you intend to do?" asked Milda. "Kill your new immortal subjects in battle as an introduction to your rule? If you wish rebellion, you'll get it."

"I don't know. But I know who I side with. And I ask you, our Imada, to help me. You claim this meeting was planned to see how we'll work together. Well, how I act is not all that matters. How you act is important too. I've already decided that my allegiance is with Sol. If you support me and my Ambrosia family, you will help me."

Two of the old women leaned over and whispered something into Milda's ears. Then Milda nodded and flashed one of the most ingenuine grins Avva had ever seen.

"So be it," Milda said.

"What?" asked Avva.

"We are Imada. We've predicted this vapid puerile crush. And Imada is quite aware of your obstreperousness and tenacity. You are an Ambrosia. We are Imada. We advise. It is up to you to lead. Even if it results in our destruction."

"Good," Avva said, standing up. "Help me side with Sol then."

"We can help you gather the army," Milda said. "It's been centuries and they're rusty, but we've decided it's time to rebuild and be ready anyway. Delia saw all this coming, so we are not as unprepared as our enemies imagine. You may amass our soldiers, but not one of us will support you landing outside Napea with our people. Not that I would object to disobeying the edict. Understand me, Avva, I objected to that law laid down by Nefertiti more than anyone. Only when she left as pharaoh and gave us the great Queen Dainya were we satisfied. But, you see, we must follow the edict of the gods. It is too dangerous not to."

"Then this meeting is adjourned, ladies. Thank you for trusting me with your great knowledge. Gather our weapons and armor. Ready the monokera in the tower stables and arrange a regimen under Cambria. I will need them battle ready in one week."

They laughed. "One week!"

"Aye. One week. And tonight, I already need you to survey their armies from above. I shall go into the air myself. Not to land, but to watch in the clouds."

"He plans to strike so soon?" asked Milda.

"You tell me. I thought you Imada were all-knowing." She shook her head. "I can tell you the day, if you wish. Goodnight, ladies."

They all rose as quickly as their old bones would allow before she could walk out the wooden door alone.

"When?" asked an elder.

"What day?" asked another.

"Tell us, Ambrosia."

Avva relished not telling the witches another word.

When it was clear she wouldn't say a word, they bowed.

"You have the backing and recognition of the Imada," Milda said. "And let me congratulate you once more. We are overjoyed at your new position. Bless Queen Avivae Ambrosia, Napean sovereign, ruler and queen of Azure Blue."

"Hail!" they all said.

But as they walked behind her up the musty stairs, the atmosphere hardly felt collegial. No one uttered another word.

11

THE CRESCENT KING

AVVA HAD NEVER WITNESSED BATTLE. SHE HAD BEEN TRAINED, along with all Amazon nymphs, to fight since she was a little girl, but she had never seen people fight to the death. Nor had she ever killed anyone. Rumor had it that her mother had. And, indeed, Sol had confirmed it when he told her that Delia had once sent the monokera to help her father along the shores of Castle Cove. Now, despite strong objections from her Imada, Avva flew Antilus above the clouds. She wore an ancient scarlet helm, matching leather pteruges, and the phoenix standard on her armored breastplate. She looked like the royal guards wearing the hoplite armor of her ancestors, though it was polished and clean, as Hades had said it was. She had with her a hundred soldiers in similar garb, flying with her in the clouds, the finest regiment from Azure Blue. Beside her flew Cambria and her dear red-haired friend Iris.

It was difficult to see below. The armies had lit fires, and with the flames came smoke and the terrible stench of burning bodies. Peering as best she could through the gray smoke, she saw a river flowing along Polis Canyon, east of trees surrounding the beaches of Crescent Blue. The water under the smoke had turned crimson.

"Avva," Cambria hollered through her helm. The wings of her unicorn flapped under Avva's general. Cambria pointed and exclaimed, "That's him!" She pointed at a group of soldiers wearing sky-blue armor, on horseback, riding quickly into the valley beneath them. "Like your father, he's known to use speed on horseback to shock the enemy. It seems he's cornered the Tiger King."

That's when Sol's blue hoplites crashed into a group of soldiers wearing golden yellow armor. The enemy held shields and spears in an orderly phalanx. This phalanx was an ancient "turtle" formation said to have been invented by Harmonia during the Amazon wars. The enemy soldiers held shields at all sides and led carrying spears.

In an act of sheer madness, Sol leaped off his horse onto the shields of his enemy and swung his sword violently at anything he contacted. The act was explosive. It broke the phalanx. His men followed, throwing themselves with equal violence upon the enemy. Avva had never witnessed such savagery.

She spotted Henri, wearing the same blue armor as Sol, but with his long gray hair flowing behind his blue helm and along his face. It was an odd sight. He wielded his sword, twirling it around with perhaps greater finesse than Sol.

After the horses in the phalanx had been speared, many men of the Crescent army fought on foot, hand-to-hand. One was missing a limb, but even he fought on. Others wrestled by the red river, jabbing each other with knives or even fists. Avva found it hard to discern which side some were on, so drenched in blood were their breastplates and pteruges. All the while, fire spread along oak trees by the sides of the canyon.

"Look," Iris hollered. She was beside them on a black unicorn. She pointed in another direction. "Oh, look, Avva. Look over there along the trees. The Sun King's army marches to trap him."

It was King Ansel's men—marching through the forest into the valley—and, with them, many mercenary Eruboi in black armor.

She spotted Sol again through the gray smoke. He wielded his sword swiftly, almost elegantly like a dancer, charging his enemy. She watched him crack open his foe's helmet, spin around, and then, with perfect aim, decapitate his foe. Then Avva jumped as a man leaped on Sol from behind. But with great strength, her lover threw him off too. Then Henri twirled his sword just as elegantly as Sol, cutting down a soldier charging at Sol.

Solinair's and Henri's skills were unmatched. Indeed, just as he had told her, Sol was very good in battle. Their movements made fighting look easy. And they expertly wielded multiple weapons: bows, daggers, axes, Sol's long sword, javelins, and even bare hands. And they never missed. Nor did they flinch. But no matter how skillfully they fought, Avva saw a force four times larger marching toward them.

"Say the word," Cambria said, watching the incoming reinforcements and nodding sternly.

Anna felt a lump in her throat. And she perspired under her heavy armor. Part of her wanted to obey the Imada and fly back to her castle. Antilus helped. Her unicorn turned her head away from battle, urging Anna to flee. But then she watched the man she loved. He was fighting back three men. And then Henri hacked away another. Just when she thought he was finished, he fought some more.

How strange. How could a warrior so brave and mighty lose? But with the enemy arriving with fresh troops, how could he win?

Cambria raised her hand at the others, staring wide-eyed at Avva. A raised hand was the signal for the archers to ready their weapons. Avva grabbed her bow from her back then reached for her arrows with her shaky left hand.

But then came the sound of the war salpinx from below. Cambria turned. Avva spotted Sol turning at the sound too.

"Now, Your Majesty," Cambria cried. "Now or never. They've arrived. They will run him down."

Avva shook her head. Cambria nodded, seeming to understand. Her general probably thought she had chosen to retreat.

She hadn't. But like Sol had told her, battle had to be timed perfectly.

Then she witnessed the unexpected. Sol, now battered and weary, so worn that he tossed his helmet to the side, got back on his horse. His armor and hair were streaked with dripping blood. He reached into a bag on his horse and removed a horn. Then he blew a horn of his own.

"He's gathering his men," Cambria shouted. "It's hopeless, but he's making a last stand, Avva. We either help now or it's too late."

Solinair sat on his horse with Henri by his side and another huge broad-shouldered man. These three soldiers waited for their battered army behind them, who were still fighting, to form a line. Sol shouted something at his men. But Avva was too far away to hear his words.

Avva looked down at her bow. It was shaking. No, her whole hand was shaking. She felt sick. She coughed from the smoke. The stench was pungent, smelling of iron and excrement, turning her stomach. Her heart felt like it was going to break. She blinked, fighting sweat from her eyes. Cambria shouted something, but Avva didn't look anymore.

He was going to lose. If she didn't help him, he was going to lose. And yet Sol and Hanna had told her that her mother had trusted him. And Avva loved him.

She directed Antilus to fall from the sky.

"*My queen!*" shouted Cambria from behind. Cambria shouted, "*The queen's descending! Avivae's falling! Fire now and accompany her! Fire and defend Queen Avivae!*"

Avva felt her stomach rise over her head as she was surrounded by the hiss of wind and then the streak of arrows as the ground rushed fast, closer and closer. But the arrows did not come from below, for she hadn't been spotted yet. They rained down from her army behind her.

Then she saw the man she loved. King Sol was riding hard on horseback, then charging, a final suicide. He cocked his head as he rode and seemed to recognize her. Yes. He saw her. Their eyes met. At first there was surprise and then a strange expression. Fear? But she did not believe this man could be afraid. He hadn't appeared afraid during the entire battle … unless it was fear for her?

Avva swooped close to the ground and aimed her arrows at incoming soldiers. She shot arrow after arrow. She had been trained in the games to balance herself and fire. As an Amazon, she had been trained since she could walk. She was an expert markswoman. So was the army that followed her. She saw her enemy fall from horseback or on foot as her arrows struck her first kills.

A thunderous chorus of cheers, hurting her ears, rushed under her—from the blue hoplites—as she strafed over the battlefield.

Now it was Sol's turn. With the backing of the Amazon, his horses crashed into the fresh rows of soldiers. The blue Crescent flag was raised. It flew into the standing crowd of gold foot soldiers and the yellow-and-black flags of the Tiger King.

The rush of screams and the sight of men becoming things other than men was terrible. She watched as her arrows mercilessly penetrated chests, necks, and even eyes.

Then, in a matter of seconds, she found herself only a few feet from the ground. As she pulled Antilus up by the neck, she heard arrows whoosh beside her ears, but she hardly had time to think of it. Then some of the foot soldiers in yellow began throwing javelins at her from the river.

Antilus's hooves skimmed over the water so closely that waves formed under her. One spear rushed right by Antilus's leg, and Avva was almost thrown when the unicorn turned to evade the blade. Her unicorn had not forgotten how to fight either. As Antilus straightened, grazing the rushing red water with her hooves, she saw the unthinkable: above her, a nymph plummeted from the sky. The Amazon fell hundreds of feet and slammed into the ground.

Avva pulled Antilus's mane up and clutched her tightly as the unicorn rose and then turned so sharply that she thought she would be thrown off. She felt her beloved unicorn resisting as they circled back to a pack of yellow knights. Then, when close enough to the water's edge, she leaped from Antilus.

Above there was shouting and from the corner of her helm she saw some monokera still soaring like birds in a tumult above her. But no one dared land with her.

Avva slid along the ground and leaped over dead bodies. She ran to the fallen nymph. She pulled off the helm only to find, to her horror, a lifeless red-haired Amazon. One of the only red-haired nymphs in the kingdom. Her childhood friend Iris.

"Iris!" Avva, in tears, lifted her head. "Oh, Iris. No!"

Iris was dead.

Avva turned to her right and saw Sol's army, close by, charging on their horses alongside the river, running over knights, spearing or hacking at their enemy. It was enough to distract the yellow soldiers from attacking her. Across the river more soldiers were sword fighting. A few were even wrestling along the river.

"She's grounded!" One soldier in yellow shouted. "Kill her! Kill the Amazon!"

Then came a yellow knight. The soldier's armor was bloody orange from battle. His helm was off, and his long hair covered a muddy red face where only the whites of her enemy's eyes seemed to shine before her. He raised his sword above his head ready to smite her. Something in Avva's training caused her to pull out her royal Mandrigel blade, a sword not used in centuries, glowing azure like her home. The enchanted blade cut right through her opponent's sword, splintering it into pieces and piercing through the armor and into the soldier's gullet. The man fell on top of her, so heavy. She smelled his putrid breath and the smell of his blood. But then those white eyes closed and his breathing ceased.

She yanked her sword out and rolled him off her. More arrows landed beside her. Unicorns swooped down, nearly touching the ground, their riders firing arrows at any other soldier daring to approach their queen.

She crawled back to Iris.

"Oh Iris, can you forgive me? Iris. Dear Iris."

A whole group of yellow knights were trying to get to her from three sides, but many were falling to the ground, struck by the arrows raining from her guards.

Then came the sound of hooves.

"Get back on your horse, brave queen!" cried a horseman. She recognized his voice. Sol. The king leaped from his horse and grabbed her, pulling her up. "We're not finished yet, Anne!"

His face and long hair were so worn, muddy, and stained with blood. And Avva saw a gash along his leg and even a piece of an arrow penetrating his blue breastplate. Henri and another group of horsemen turned their horses and shielded Avva from the surrounding chaos.

"You promised me you'd win," Avva said.

"Mount your horse, Anna!" cried Henri. "Rise in the clouds and get out of here!"

"You promised," Avva repeated, looking at Sol.

Sol was about to answer, but then he fell into a sword fight with a soldier trying to break through the protective wall he had formed around her.

"Aye, with your help, madwoman," he said, hacking. "I'll win. Now rise back to the clouds, like Henri said, where you belong."

"No. Help me take my friend back," Avva said, shaking her head. "I'll go only with her. Any nymph that falls must be brought back home."

"My lord!" cried Henri, swinging his sword at another. "No bodies. We can't."

Sol shook his head, but Avva wouldn't budge.

"Stubborn Amazon," Sol snapped. Then he turned to another soldier. "Bring the fallen nymph with us. We shall return them to Azure in honor of what her people have done for us. Any nymph that falls, gather her and honor her. They've saved us."

"My lord!" objected another. "We aren't even taking our own."

"Do as I say!"

Then Sol lifted Avva back onto Antilus.

"I love you," she said.

"Aye. Aye, mad Amazon. What man wouldn't love you, eh?"

Sol hit Antilus's butt hard, sending her running, flapping her powerful wings and soaring back into the clouds.

In the clouds, through the smoke, she watched him continue to fight. Far from a Crescent, he fought to the death like Darius, the Sun King, with full courage and glory, while his cowardly brother was spotted far off in the hills fleeing back toward Shadow Forest.

Watching Sol and his men persevere, she knew, as her mother had known, that this man was the true and future king. And with her help, with a continued volley of arrows from above, he managed to do the impossible. He kept one brother at bay in the north while forcing the others to retreat south along the shore and back into the forest. Imada had predicted that the boy king wouldn't win. They had been right. But they never anticipated their queen would provide aid with her own sweat and blood.

The battle continued throughout the rest of the night. There were continuous screams of agony, the smell of fire and death, and constant smoke. Her people continued to watch from above, flying home out of exhaustion, but returning to continue their aerial surveillance and aid.

12

THE OUTSIDERS

As the red hue of dawn fell upon the horizon and Avva fought with her eyes to not let them drift asleep atop Antilus, the unthinkable happened. She spotted smoke, not just below, but far across the sea toward the rising sun. A brown hue, not azure, coming from home with clouds rising high above the ocean.

"We must return, Avva!" cried Cambria, flying up beside her. "The smoke's from Napea! We must defend Azure."

"Back!" Avva shouted. She turned to the others, signaling. "Back home! We must go back to defend!"

Avva allowed one more glimpse below. No longer was the battle fought along the Polis and within the river canyon. Now the battle had extended along the beaches. Sol was winning, but none of that mattered now. She couldn't help him. She had to help herself.

Avva swooped back, close to the waves, over the sea. The sky turned smoky hazel, then red, then ashen. She spotted her beaches in the distance with man's ships along the shore, silhouetting the coastal forests, now aflame. Her kingdom was being invaded, the first invasion since the founding of Azure Blue. And all because of her. Because of a fool's love. A fool's crush. This was the greatest shame in her life, far worse than her mother's slap. Imada, even that witch Milda, had been right. Avva was the worst nymph queen there ever was.

As the smoke thickened, she began to fight off a volley of arrows from the beaches. Invaders in gold hoplite armor were lined up in rows preparing to march through the burning forest to her palace. Their entire navy had been mobilized to wreak vengeful havoc on Napea.

Antilus dropped, expertly dodging an incoming arrow that nearly passed through Avva's helm.

She rushed over the burning trees by the coast. Then she spotted the Crystal Palace on the horizon. It was oddly tranquil under clear skies away from the burning coast. She dodged another arrow close to her shoulder. Two of her companions on monokera fell beside her, this time not on Hinterland soil, but in her own kingdom.

Along the purple fields, Avva saw soldiers rushing toward the palace. Ansel had ordered hundreds of foot soldiers. Here they weren't marching; they were charging forward. Some were hurling flames at the crystal palace. The drawbridge was up for the first time—perhaps the first time ever—over the dry moat. And arrows were falling like rain from the castle towers, shot by nymph archers. As before, their aim was sound, but there were so many foreign fighters rushing to the walls. Then she saw azure soldiers, her sisters, in red hoplite armor, flying down from the stable tower into the fields to face them alone. Far outnumbered, they bravely rushed down with bow and arrow, but many more fell from the sky than before, plummeting to their deaths by staff, by arrow, or simply unbalanced by the high elevation.

Then her people along the crystal towers saw her. She was surprised that, in all her failure and shame, the nymphs cheered her as she flew over the crystal walls. Somehow their cheers felt like another slap in the face.

She landed with Cambria on a cobblestone road near the town center. Hundreds of nymphs were running to secure the ramparts and palace battlements. Battle had come so fast that most were not wearing armor. Never in Avva's life would she have imagined that the wooden ramparts and towers built by the legendary Queen Harmonia centuries ago, to fight off invaders, would actually be tested by an enemy outside their walls. According to legend, they had never been tested before.

"Go to the walls," Avva barked to Cambria, leaping off Antilus. "Don't let them breach. Fly the archers by monokera to attack from above and keep them at bay."

"Yes, Your Majesty," Cambria said with a bow. Avva noticed Cambria's eyes. She was exhausted. They had been in battle across the Strait for so long; now this. "I suggest, queen, you return to the throne room. You'll be safe there."

Yes, even though lovely, surrounded by the gardens of the palace, Harmonia had built the throne room in the center of the city for defense. Everything in the Crystal Palace had been built by the founder of Amazon for war.

"I shall prove to the beasts who rules Azure," Avva answered, narrowing her eyes. But she spoke more to herself than Cambria.

"What are you planning?" Cambria asked.

She didn't answer.

Then Hanna, almost unrecognizable in scarlet armor, surprised her by running into her arms.

"Oh, Avva. You're all right. Thank the gods, you're okay!"

Avva was so tired. She breathed better in the thinner air, but she felt the sting from an arrow she had pulled out of her upper leg, under her pteruges, earlier in the night. In Hanna's sweet arms, for just a moment, she wanted to go to her bedchamber and sleep.

"Stay by the wall and don't let them enter," she said to Hanna. "Fight and protect the palace."

"Yes, Blue. But what of you? Are you going to take sanctuary in the throne room?"

Avva didn't reply.

Avva ran as fast as she could through the streets and into the main chambers of the palace. People were in such haste that they didn't bow or even notice her. She limped her way past the spiral stairs in her favorite part of the halls. Her two guards stood, as they always did, completely still, guarding the stairs up to her bedchamber. But for the first time, they didn't stand in stoic contentment. They stared ahead, wide-eyed. She couldn't resist following their gaze through her favorite three-story window. She wished she hadn't. This was the view, which she had longed for every day of her childhood, of her father's lands. Now flames engulfed everything off the shore.

That pushed her to run harder, ignoring her pain, through more halls until finally reaching the main throne room. Falena stood holding her staff with a shaky hand by the doors. She nodded as Avva ran through an open door into the empty throne room. Then Avva ran down the aisle to the bottom step leading to her throne. There she opened a wooden chest and grabbed what she had come for. A small golden rod. The Scepter of Azure.

She had considered bringing the weapon into battle but had decided against it. If she were to die, she did not want it to be lost.

Despite exhaustion, she limped back and cried for Antilus near the walls. She whistled frantically. Antilus was so wary that the unicorn had to be led over by an Amazon. Avva mounted her.

"It's okay, girl," Avva said softly to Antilus's ear, petting her mane. "One more charge and it'll all be over. I promise. But I need you now. Azure Blue needs you more than ever. You can run, not fly. We'll charge like Sol. Ride to them, girl! They dare threaten us? Our home? Harmonia's palace? Ride and I'll stop them! Ride!"

Antilus nodded her head violently and squealed. Then Avva ordered her into a gallop toward the main gate.

"Open the gates!" Avva cried. "Open them!" She shook her golden scepter in her right hand and enlarged it into a staff.

"Avva?" It sounded like Hanna's bewildered voice. She was standing by the wall with other soldiers, using a bow.

"Stay back, my queen!" one warned.

"It's unsafe!" cried another.

A hundred nymphs standing their ground along the ramparts looked down at her as she and Antilus rushed below them.

"Open the gates! Stay back and open them! Upon my order. Open the gates now!"

The drawbridge fell and she looked upon a terrible sight. Golden-clad hoplite men, splashed with red, were now sword fighting Amazon soldiers in scarlet. Other lines of soldiers were charging at a few Amazon nymphs bravely standing their ground before the palace. Only a handful were trying to keep back a hundred. Meanwhile, many of the enemy's captains seemed to be trying to gather their men into a phalanx.

Antilus's hooves ran over the bridge, clapping against the old wooden platform and, once more, a hundred arrows shot down from monokera in the sky above to protect their queen. An arrow whizzed by her right ear. A few more inches and it would have meant her end.

When she rode off the long bridge onto the fields, she and her unicorn stood alone in the midst of a hundred enemy soldiers. Then she lifted her mighty staff in the air. A few of her Amazon fell to the ground, guessing her intention. Tragically, many more nymphs on the fields just stared dumbfounded.

Avva shouted the ancient words:

"Eneich Aneu Loriaan! Eneich Aneu Loriaan! Eneich Aneu Loriaan!"

The ground shook and ice rushed from her staff, turning everything she faced into ice. Even flames along the fields instantly thawed. Then the cold advanced in a circular pattern, affecting hundreds of soldiers on the battlefield. Some soldiers turned to run, but most could not evade the icy storm. Some fell to the ground, shattering into pieces. Others froze, motionless.

Avva's heart had been cold to any consequences of her plan —until now. Now that she had committed the act, using the enchanted scepter, she was disgusted by the terror she had wrought. It was bad enough to cut an enemy down with a sword or arrow, but to freeze their bodies to death was morbid and unnatural.

Those that lived ran. In panic, hundreds who had stood

ready to march and charge the castle ran from her, some fearing her very gaze as if she were Medusa. They ran toward the burning trees along the beaches. And then a thousand nymphs cheered, behind her, from the walls of her palace.

Avva rose in the air on Antilus. Hovering higher. She watched them until they fled all the way back to the scorched and blackened trees of her beaches. Then she saw ships. She squinted and saw the blue standard of the Crescent king. Sol was using his navy, likely his entire navy, to fight and provide aid. But he was too late. She had already sent Ansel's and Torinth's armies fleeing.

When the enemy returned to their ships, some of them were attacked in the waters by Sol. But many more escaped northeast. Avva guessed they were heading past Mount Ambitus to escape the continent and return, around the forests, to Azerban.

Avva landed and jumped off her unicorn. Antilus seemed too tired to even turn her head. Avva cradled her head in her arms. Then she looked around her fields, much of the beautiful lavender charred. As her subjects continued shouting and cheering for their queen, Avva leaned on her unicorn and wept.

HOPE AND DISGRACE

AVVA WANDERED HER BLOODY AND SCORCHED FIELDS AS SOLDIERS in light-blue painted armor stacked dead bodies on the ground. She covered her mouth with a white linen cloth, but it couldn't completely shield her from the stench. Her blue world had become black. And as the sun set, it lacked its usual lovely indigo, glowing an ugly smoky umber.

Many soldiers still stood motionless like statues, petrified by the violence of her golden staff. That was the worst. But they were no longer iced. Their open eyes were glassy with water dripping down their beards, helms, and breastplates. Now wet, with a mist forming around them, but still stuck in frozen rigor mortis. Unfortunately, the ice didn't stop the smell of their rancid sweat, blood, and flesh. It was the smell Avva now associated with war, much like the battlefield in Polis, but this time, bizarrely, in her home.

She passed Amazons lying on the ground with the same scarlet armor she still wore. Women with pointier ears than humans and faintly blue skin—a bit bluer upon their death. She recognized all of them. A handful had been frozen by the terrible gilded weapon she still carried, now shrunken in her belt. She stopped by some, crouched over their bodies, placed coins on their eyes, and prayed for a swift journey to Elysium. She had become so accustomed to her own crying that the sound of her whimpers under her cloth occasionally startled her as if coming from someone else. Over one of the dead—Gavria was her name—Avva's whimpers were disturbed by the sound of snapping sticks and leaves.

A huge dark-skinned man approached.

Avva had seen this man fight with King Sol and Henri. He was as skilled as they were with the sword, and now he looked as weary as she felt. Dry blood stained his face. He had a gash on his right arm between his blue leather elbow pad. Sol was taller and larger than Avva, but this man looked like two of Sol.

"Your Majesty," he said kneeling on the ground. He removed his blue helm from a bald head. "King Solinair Solinaray has arrived as a guest on your shores and requests audience."

"Where is your king?"

"He surveys the fields like you, my queen." The man attempted a smile with chapped lips.

Avva spotted Sol for the first time, wearing worn armor and, indeed, doing the same thing she had been doing—crouching down and placing coins on the fallen.

"My name is Milaius. Milo." And he dipped his head again. "I am the chief general of the Crescent army."

"Your army is no Crescent army."

"Aye. After your help, no. No, we aren't. Sol and I, and every man from our kingdom, wish you our deepest gratitude. What happened in Azure is dreadful, but what you did on our shores, Queen Avivae, saved us all. None of us will ever forget you."

"You're welcome." She watched Sol kneel before another fallen body.

That's when she realized something almost as terrible as the invasion. Sol was honoring the dead of his enemy. These were not his men. His soldiers had not yet arrived on the shore to fight. These were Ansel's and Torinth's yellow-armored men. This war was so despicable that Sol's enemies were his friends.

"I take my leave, Queen Avivae," Milo said. "It is an honor to meet you."

She absentmindedly nodded.

Milo crossed paths with Sol and said something inaudible, gesturing to her, and walked south toward the beaches and the charred forest.

When Sol was close enough, his features seemed so misplaced, completely at odds with his demeanor. Naturally he was young, but no one she had ever known looked so young but so worn. Behind blood and dirt was still a boyish face, but with an expression of knowing and sadness that seemed ... old.

Antilus was near. Before Sol caught up with her, Avva mounted her unicorn. It was a strange act, but she realized it was to stop him from embracing her. She felt an odd mix of adoration and hatred for him now. Then she gazed down at him, covered her mouth with her white cloth again, and nodded in the same stern fashion as his general.

He waved a piece of a golden flag before her. It was a part of the yellow sun on a white flag. Ansel's standard. Similar to Torinth's, but Torinth's was striped black representing a tiger. Sol sighed. "This is a piece of the flag he intended to hoist over your castle, Blue. The fiend intended to overrun you—while, of course, leaving his army like a coward and returning personally to Azerban. I gathered all my ships to rescue you, but what a fool I was forgetting once more that you don't ever need aid."

"I stopped him."

"Aye," he said, nodding. "Aye, you did." He looked around the field, and she saw him grip his fists and clench his teeth tightly. "I asked you not to get involved. I wish you hadn't, but now ... I am forever in your debt."

"Will you be putting your flag up instead, Sun King?" He turned and looked at her queerly as if he hadn't heard the words. She was very earnest. "I hope you don't intend to put *your* flag on my palace towers instead."

He looked around and took out a white cloth to cover his mouth from the stench. It seemed so white in his dirty hands.

"Your men landed on my shore without permission," Avva explained. "My ancestor's edict, Harmonia's, forbids that. Even you, King Sol, are not allowed without permission. No man is allowed. If you intend to invade, I will ready my army at once."

"I came to help," he said, furrowing his brow and shaking his head.

"Very well," she replied with a nod. "Then I shall give you my terms. Those bodies of men you gather are to be taken out of Napea. Cleanse our hallowed ground, which you have defiled with man's filth. Take every body and sail with it back to your kingdom. Do not burn them here. Clean Napea. We want no part of this."

"Why?"

"I am disgraced and humiliated by this invasion. I want to wipe all I can of it from my memory. You are also expected to restore the trees your brother burned."

He laughed, but she frowned. He quickly turned serious. "Very well, of course, my lady." He bowed graciously. "Your wish is granted."

"I'm not done."

He bowed. "You have further terms for your ally?"

She nodded.

"What is it, Azure Queen?"

"I'm pregnant." She readjusted on Antilus and sat taller. It was said as if it were an amendment to a treaty. Then more tears formed in her eyes. She turned, blinked to try to get rid of them, and readjusted again on her unicorn.

"Excuse me, Anna?"

"I am pregnant."

"By whom?" he asked with his eyes now wide.

"Don't be stupid, Sol."

Then, in fact, his mouth opened stupidly. "I am … overjoyed to hear the news, my queen." He paused pensively. She said nothing. She just sat tall on Antilus.

One of his advisors rushed toward him, but he quickly signaled the rider to leave.

"It seems I picked the right side."

"Indeed. Maybe that's why I helped. Not only because you are the rightful king. But I am Amazon. Of course, I will raise my daughter myself and need no assistance from her father." Then she finally looked down and forced a smile. "Though I shall tell her one day of her father's bravery. And how we worked together. King Solinair Solinaray, the true Sun King, and Queen Avivae Ambrosia, the true Sun Queen."

"Perhaps I can tell her the tale myself one day, Anne."

"I'd like that."

Sol touched her leg. It was bandaged now. He ran his hand gently over the bandages.

"You're hurt," he said. Avva felt a lump in her throat. "I am … sorry. I hurt you."

"Sol …" she started, but then failed in her words. The tears fell now and she couldn't stop them. "Look around at what I've done. I am a monster. A disgrace to my people." She turned toward Mount Ambitus. She saw a group of monokera flying overhead, likely upon orders of her Imada, watching and defending and not trusting this man-king. They were so high up, they looked like insects in the distance. But they watched. And for a second she shuddered to think that Imada, too, knew of their unborn child.

"May I speak with you now as a friend, Sol, not as a queen?"

"Always, Anna."

She dropped her hand. He took it and played with her fingers.

"I'm ashamed. Disgraced. My mother would think less than she already did of me. She once slapped me in front of the whole Court. If Harmonia were still alive, she'd slap me now."

"We were forced into this. You had to pick a side."

"I could have chosen diplomacy."

"Look at what my brother did here. He landed on your shore to torch your palace and your island." He gnashed his teeth. "I hate him more than ever for not appreciating the beauty of your lands and your people. Even without our love, Anna, I think you would have had to defend this. And even without our love, if Ansel had done this to Azure Blue, I would have despised him and sided with you. But now, with our love and with our daughter—"

"I failed my people. Delia never had a battle on our shores; neither did Dainya, Nefertiti, nor certainly Harmonia. I am the only nymph queen who has disgraced the Amazon. And, my love, it is because of you. Perhaps Hades was right."

Sol gave no reply to that. And, for a moment, there was a strange, unsettling stillness in the air. Among a hundred slain bodies still lying on the purple and black fields, there was only the sound of Sol's breathing. And the warmth of the hand he had not removed from hers. And even now, as she hated him, hearing his breathing and feeling the touch of his hand, she loved him.

"Avva, let me … let me try to speak to you with words that can win your heart. I have already lost my dear little brother, Ballen, due to my failings. Please, don't let me lose you. Love has done things to both of our kingdoms. Love has driven me to pull all my resources to rescue your people at the cost of mine. I've left my kingdom unguarded. For you, your land, which I treasure more than my own. Truly, as I said, even without you, I would treasure it. But also for our love. It's what binds us. I … I do not think that you and I together is bad. I don't think that you and I are wrong."

She said nothing.

"I killed my poor brother Ballen. I could not convince my little brother to join me. It was savage, but Henri knew it was the right thing to do. Just as it was right to fight Torinth and Ansel. My younger brother is dead by my hands." His voice broke and it tore at Anna's heart. "For sand, Anna. For a desert of sand." He violently shook his head. "I did not start this war. Don't let it consume you. Don't let it take you … It seems, I'm sorry … I don't know what else to say. I can't speak the right words."

"You're a king. You need words more than your sword."

Her mother, Delia, would have said that. And she regretted

uttering it. Then she felt tears form again. But she wouldn't cry. No, she couldn't do that anymore. But it was her fault. The rancid stench. It was not only Sol's men or the enemies. It was Amazon bodies. Her harsh words were not only to him; they were meant for herself.

"Aye. I will try to be a good king, dearest Anna."

"Why should I trust you?" And she finally pulled her fingers back from him.

"You have my heart. Do with that what you will. Your love has poisoned me. I think mine has poisoned you. But is that such a bad thing? We can't be concerned with what people think. You've saved my kingdom. I shall protect yours. And this daughter that's coming. I'd like to protect her too."

"Your words are not so bad, Sol," she said with a smile.

He took her hand again, squeezing it with a sudden fierceness. "Don't abandon me like your mother did, Anna. Don't do that. Darius was never happy. I can tell you, it was the one thing he hated about your mother. It made him miserable. Hiding won't stop man from touching your shores. You knew this when you broke the edict and met me that first time."

She merely nodded.

"Enough of this. You've done well, Blue. And you've made no mistake falling in love with me. Not only are we united in love, but our lands are united by me now."

"You're so conceited," she said with a laugh.

He took a deep breath and closed his eyes. "Ah, your laughter is an elixir of the gods."

Anna covered her mouth again with her white cloth. Then she looked down at his grimy hand holding hers. She could feel his cuts. Even his hands were raw from holding his sword during the terrible battle.

They peered together at his distant kingdom across the Strait, and she permitted herself a little happiness again just being beside him.

"You know, a king has to have a queen, dearest," he remarked.

"I hope that wasn't a proposal, Sol. Such a thing needs to be done with chivalry. Especially when you're proposing to the queen of Azure. Do not dictate facts to me. Anyway, I told you that Cassandra and I can take care of ourselves."

"*Cassandra?*" He whirled back and looked at her. "You've already named her?"

"Aye, my king. Do you object?"

"Cassandra is a wonderful name." He nodded. "Fitting for a beautiful girl."

"She could be an ugly duckling. But I am sure she'll be strong like her father."

"She won't be ugly. Not from such a beautiful woman as yourself."

"Stop flattering me." She felt herself blush. "She will be strong from a man with such courage and honor. And, yes, beautiful from such a handsome father." She sighed. "Will the Sun King be needing lodging in Azure Blue for the evening?"

"No. I'm sorry, Blue. I must return to defend Shadow Forest. Ansel's on the run and Torinth has been captured, but the land is hardly safe."

"When will you return to me, Sol?"

"As soon as I can." He took her hand once more and kissed the back of it. "As fast as I'm able. I promise you that."

"I love you," she said.

14

THE HANDFASTING

It did not take long to clear the kingdom of the dead. King Solinair fulfilled his promise. What's more, after a moon passed, he brought carpenters to rebuild the furniture and walls that had been burned down by stray fiery arrows. They did what they could, but the ancient palace had been constructed by Mandrigel and neither humans or nymphs knew how to replace some crystal sections. Then Sol ordered that the reflecting emerald walls be washed. He even replanted trees. But he could not heal the beaches. The greatest tragedy was the ancient azure oaks and ferns, which had grown for a millennium near the shore, now lay charred and leafless along the purple sand. It would be a long time before the coastal forest could guard Avivae's kingdom again. But he helped repair everything as if it were his own. And soon it would be his own. And that thought was what kept Avva's step light despite the dawn of war.

One very pleasant breezy afternoon, Avva walked with Engel, holding the dwarf's stubby hand. They sauntered along many of the paths that Avva had walked with Sol when he visited the palace gardens. It was one area that remained completely untouched and tranquil after the invaders' terrible incursion.

"So, what do you think, Engel?"

"Hmm? About what, Blue?"

"About him? About marriage?"

"Not the king again?"

Avva laughed as he jerked his hand from hers and shook his head.

"Just wondering," she said with a shrug. "I've been thinking, I never really asked what you thought of him. I mean, I talk about him, but I never asked you. In a way, out of all my subjects, you hold my mother's spirit—the tiniest good part, of course. I feel like your opinion would be hers. Your thoughts are like hers."

"Then you wouldn't want to hear them, would you?"

She tried not to laugh, but she did. Then she grabbed his stubby fingers.

They walked over to the great blue-green maze. It was full of turquoise and blue trees and white jasmine bushes with that lovely scent. Avva had walked it so many times that there was no way she could ever get lost. But she enjoyed wandering through it anyway. Thank the gods, it had not been damaged by the invaders.

As Avva ventured through the entrance, she remembered Engel frantically searching for her and Hanna when they used to hide from him. She had been a very naughty little girl.

"So? Whatcha think?"

"Hmm? Humph. He's human."

"Yeah? So? A nymph must find a man eventually—particularly a queen, if she is to have an heir. Even Mother knew that."

"Yes, but you can't marry him."

"Why?" She turned and pouted. "What do you mean?"

"You're not allowed to marry. And he's your brother."

"Oh stop," she said with a laugh, resuming her walk. "Come on. He's adopted. And we never met till now."

"No," Engel said, but he resisted commenting further. He was too wise to argue.

So they kept walking. There was no way to see outside the garden, the bushes climbed so high, but they both knew the way.

"What's your intention, Blue?" Engel finally asked.

"I'm going to marry him, of course."

"Then why ask me?" He snorted.

"You're so funny when you're mad." Avva squeezed the little dwarf's blue hand harder and continued walking. "Tell me what you're thinking."

"No."

"Go ahead. Tell me. Times change and so do the rules, eh? I think it was the biggest fault of my mother not to see this. And her mother too. My grandmother, based on the little I've been told, may not have been as cruel, but she was very boring."

"Your grandmother followed the rules. Dainya was a good queen. And yes, less unruly than you."

"Than my mother?"

"Delia was as naughty as you."

"Humph. I don't believe it."

"She was old when she had you, Avva. When she was young, she was very much more like you than you'd want to think. And in some ways, Dainya had more trouble raising Delia than your mother did with you."

"Did Dainya send her away to the prison tower?"

"No."

"See, mine's worse."

Engel didn't fall into the trap. He kept his mouth shut as they turned a few more corners.

"No one ever wanted to change, Engel. That's the problem. No one ever wanted to do anything since Nefertiti dared to defy tradition. But your Nefertiti was something, wasn't she? And you liked her the best, didn't you? Even more than me."

"I loved her." Engel pulled his hand away, and stopped, by a bush wall, folding his arms. "But I love you, Avva. I always will. Your family was given to me by Nephrea, and I swore to care for you. I have loved each and every one of you."

"You have," Avva said, leaning down and touching his broad nose with a single finger and a smile. "And I adore you. But you didn't answer me. Did you like her more than me?"

"Oh, stop acting a child," Engel said, resuming his walk. "You're queen now."

They grew silent once more. Engel turned left at a fork in the road, but Avva didn't join him. That was the way out. She turned the other way. Then she laughed inside hearing her favorite man hobble over leaves behind her.

"Well, Engel? You did, didn't you?"

"Nephrea cared only for others. When you do that, when you sacrifice and live for others, then I'll consider you as mighty as her."

Avva reached behind her and waited for him to take her hand. Then the two of them made a few more turns along the maze.

"Well, my mother was a witch. She never said she loved me. Not like you. Really, you've been the only one for me."

"Your mother did not cause humans to invade our shores."

She stopped cold. It was the wrong thing for him to say and it hurt. She just stared at a withering dark cherry and mauve bush.

"Blue. Blue." He touched her back. "Blue. I'm sorry. Blue …" Those words sucked the joy out of her. "Avva, I'm sorry."

"Imada thinks the same," Avva said with a nod. Her voice sounded so serious it reminded her of her mother. "Milda blames me for the damage to the palace. Imada threatens the crown, but I don't have to be reminded of it by you."

"I know. I take it back. I didn't mean—"

"I may still be young, but I'm not stupid. I live with my mistakes every day. All those people, my people, who lost their lives, I know the wrong I've done. But was it so wrong? Sol thinks we didn't have a choice. And I had to help him. I—"

"I know, Blue. You don't have to explain. I'm sorry. It's just … you hate your mother so much, I wanted to defend her. Forget I said anything."

He touched her fingers. She hesitated, but then held his hand again.

"Times are changing," Engel said. "You're right. Perhaps

that's why I'm uneasy. Don't blame yourself for the attack. It's the way of this hard world. You did what you had to do, and the people who really count in the kingdom know that."

They walked together, now more slowly. She turned aimlessly and he accompanied her.

"And as far as Imada," Engel continued, "I can't remember a queen ever getting along with Milda. Nephrea and Delia hated Milda. Nephrea once told me her mother, Harmonia herself, hated her too."

Avva still didn't say anything. She almost wanted to just head back to the palace.

"And as far as King Solinair," said Engel, "your mother doesn't object. She told me before she died. I think you still don't understand her. You never did. You won't accept why she imprisoned you. It was a message to the gods, not meant for you. You won't accept that she did it out of love for you. She did it to protect you."

"I will never forgive her," Avva snapped. Then she shook her head. "I will never forgive her for striking me in the face at my father's funeral. And there is a list of other things. Many more. No, Engel, I won't ever forgive her." But then she turned and smiled down at him. "But I have you." She pulled a red flower growing from a vine along the blue bushes behind him, and she felt a grin on her face again. She handed it to him. "We're going to get married in front of the palace on the grassy fields. What do you think of that? By then, all the black and white ash will be gone. It will be spring and it will be lovely. He's agreed to marry in Azure, due to Nefertiti's edict, so that all our sisters can bear witness to our love."

Engel merely nodded.

"Oh Engel, I'd really like it if you went with me down the aisle. You've been my real caretaker. More than Delia or Darius ever was. Will you hold the torch and support our union? Will you come down the aisle with me?"

"Yes, Blue. Of course I will."

"Oh, it's not right, Alexia!" Avva grabbed the brush from her friend and ran it through all the kinks in her long black hair. "Why do I have curls! Why not straight? Think of Hanna— straight as an arrow. She takes a minute, then her hair's ready. My hair. Sard the whole thing! And what's the point when we're covering me in a veil?"

"Stop moving, Avva," Alexia said, grabbing back the brush. "Let me work!"

Hanna walked into the beauty room. "They're seated, Avva." And that was far worse.

"Late to my own wedding? Dreadful! Humph!"

Avva jumped up. Alexia, who was a short girl, just kept working, reaching up and following the queen's head as she moved all over the room.

Avva walked over to a large mirror and gazed at herself in her long white dress. Alexia accompanied her, all the while combing her hair.

"Avva, that's the same dress you wore when your father died!" exclaimed Hanna.

"So? Only *you* know that."

"The whole kingdom knows. Don't you remember the scene you caused?"

"But I'll be under a veil. Where is that hideous red thing, anyway?"

"Change the dress," insisted Hanna. Alexia finally put down the brush on the wooden dresser. Her hair was still wavy, but did it matter? It would be hidden under an ugly veil.

"This is my finest white dress," Avva answered. "My *only* white dress, for that matter."

"We have a thousand dresses," said Hanna.

"But they don't fit right."

"If I had recognized that you wore that at your father's funeral, I wouldn't have brought it over to you."

"It wasn't a funeral. It was a meeting with my beloved mother." Avva turned from the mirror to her friends and smiled at their expressions. Then she stuck her tongue out at them.

"You should change it, Your Majesty," Alexia said, nodding. "Just don't wear white then."

"Change it," Hanna repeated. "Besides, you're showing too much in it."

That did it. Avva pulled her dress right off and gave out a scream.

"Avva, hurry!" said Hanna. "Here's the veil." She shoved another dress into her hands: a huge scarlet wool cover that reminded her of her battle armor.

"Get me the blue peplos, Alexia. It's in my bedchamber. The one I wore at the coronation. It was all baggy at the ceremony. It'll fit. You know, the azure blue one."

"Blue, queen?" asked Alexia. "And that peplos is so heavy for the aisle."

"You just said I could wear any color."

"Okay, Your Majesty," Alexia said with a nod. "Blue for Blue. We'll change to a blue peplos."

"Hurry," Hanna said. "Hurry. They're waiting. Get the blue one on, guys."

"You haven't been outside, Avva," Hanna said with a nod. "Solinair has a whole legion outside on the fields, at attention, waiting for you."

Avva screamed.

"What's going on in here?" exclaimed Engel, hobbling in. "Aren't you girls ready yet?"

When he saw the queen in her undergarments, he turned and covered his eyes. Engel was dressed formally in a pressed dark blue chiton. His hair was slicked back. He looked very formal and cute.

"I'm trying to fix my hair," said Avva.

"Who cares about your hair?" Engel said frantically. "It'll be under a veil. You have to leave now."

Alexia returned to the room with the long blue dress.

"Blue for a wedding?" asked Engel in shock.

"Well, I can't wear the white one," Avva said. "I wore that at my father's funeral. Remember? Or do only they remember?"

"So?" asked Engel, rubbing his eyes and shaking his head. Then he snorted. "Just wear the white one."

"I can't. I'm showing. Ask Hanna."

Engel hit his forehead with his palm.

"Hanna," Avva said, adjusting her blue sleeves, "Can you tie the Hercules knot? And don't squeeze Cassandra too hard."

"Okay, Avva."

As Hanna tied the elaborate knot, Alexia put on the thin scarlet veil that draped down her body. It was red to ward off evil spirits, per tradition. Then Alexia handed her a bouquet of flowers.

Avva slowly made her way through the palace halls and out into the fields holding a bouquet of roses, lilies, irises, and violets. Engel held her hand with one arm while holding a dimly lit torch in the other.

She had learned as a little girl what the wedding bouquet represented. The lily was Hera, the goddess of marriage; lilies were said to be Persephone's favorite. The iris symbolized the rainbow, a fabled messenger of the gods. Violets represented Io, a mythological oceanic nymph. This bouquet was the extent of her people's worship of Olympus, celebrated in weddings in honor of Persephone. Legend said they were flowers gathered by the venerable Persephone before her fall. Sol's people followed the traditions of Olympus. They married among statues of Olympian gods and provided libations and offerings to Mount Olympus. But those things would not be permitted in Napea. Amazon gave reverence only to Persephone, it was said, by ancient decree by Nefertiti.

Outside it was a gorgeous day. Midday. The green shone brightly, the flowers were blooming along the emerald palace walls again, and the fields had resumed their lovely lavender shade. Hundreds of people sat in rows of wooden chairs, many of them brought out from the throne room. The seats were full of her nymph subjects, and hundreds more stood to the side.

She could see the distant Strait and a number of large ships. Many moons ago, seeing the Strait from the fields would have been impossible through the coastal forest—before the trees were burned to the ground.

When she walked outside, there was a lot of chatter. But as she and Engel appeared in the aisle, all grew quiet. At the end of a long aisle of chairs was a small bonfire.

By the central fire stood Sol, with his long hair slicked back, wearing a pristine beige linen tunic, leather pteruges, and sandals. Even now, he held his longsword on a belt by his side, and the polished gold scabbard shimmered under the green sun. His chief advisor, Henri, stood beside him. Henri was formal, too, similarly dressed with his long gray beard and gray hair combed back. Avva laughed to herself looking at Henri's hair, remembering how she had complained about kinks and curls. She would have died if she had this old man's head.

As she walked down the aisle, Hanna, Eva, and Alexia, in their matching blue dresses, carried the long red veil from behind.

Standing beside Sol, Avva caught a glimpse of an ancient Azure woman sitting by the fire. This was her sweet nana, Maina, who she had loved since she was a little girl. As much as Engel was her father, Maina was her mother. And the old woman's nod brought tears to Avva's eyes.

Henri began the ceremony with some ancient words from a rolled parchment. Then he spoke of the importance of love conquering evil and other such stuff. Avva paid no attention. She faced Sol and got lost in his eyes. Her heart quickened as it always did as he touched her hand. She missed him, for not only had they not seen each other out of tradition, they hadn't been together for many moons because of war.

Henri took the king's wrist and tied it to Avva's gently with a white cloth. Then thin gold crowns were laid on their heads by Maina and her two other elder friends. Cheers rang throughout the valley. Red flowers were dropped over the crowd from monokera above.

Avva sighed with relief. Then the king turned to the queen and gently kissed her lips before the thousands. Then he kissed her some more.

15

THE HUMDRUM COURT OF
PRINCESS CASSANDRA

Time passed quickly. When Avva's beautiful baby girl was born, Cassandra was doted on by the whole kingdom. Everyone wanted to hold and play with her. By the age of five, the poor unfortunate had five parents: Avva's best friend, Hanna, who spoiled her rotten with toys and games; Engel, who took the role once more as the Ambrosia child's guardian; her father the king, who, indeed, had set the Azures as his home and seemed to organize his war campaigns around visiting her; her Uncle Henri, who loved showing the little princess tricks and sorcery and giving her simple trinkets from the Hinterlands; and, of course, the queen. Perhaps all this attention was what made the girl so unruly.

By the age of seven, she became best friends with a nymph with long golden hair named Lalaina, Cambria's daughter. As the years passed, one could see Cassandra and Lalaina running through the Court kitchen with Engel chasing close behind.

One particularly improper day, Cassandra stole a stick from Uncle Henri's pocket. It was a small light stick the Magi was fond of showing her tricks with. Casey rubbed the stick over Lalaina's lovely golden hair. Lalaina clapped excitedly as a bright purple-blue flame engulfed her head.

That had been two moons ago.

More recently, on Lalaina's birthday, a temperate winter day, when Engel had taken the girls to a natural spring near the palace, Engel got called away. When the girls were alone, Cassandra tugged Lalaina with a rope near the deep end of the pool. Lalaina fell in. This seemed harmless, only Lalaina couldn't swim.

"What's the matter with you!" screamed Avva, staring down from her throne.

"Sorry, Mama."

"Sorry? You nearly killed Lalaina. And it was her birthday!"

Cassandra was forced to kneel before the empty throne. It was dark, and torchlight lit the hall during the early evening.

"I'm sorry, Mama. I didn't know she couldn't swim. Well … I think she can swim, she just isn't very good at it. Can we go back next week?"

Avva clenched her hands tightly and she felt her eyes bulge.

"She didn't mean any harm, Blue," said Engel, standing beside her daughter. "She just didn't know."

"You're not off the hook either. I thought you were watching her."

Engel sat down at the foot of the steps leading to the throne and folded his arms. Avva came down from her throne and started pacing the rows of chairs.

"How am I to make amends to Cambria? Hmm? By the gods. Her daughter almost drowned. On her birthday! Hmm? … I tell you what, Casey. I'll summon her. How's that? You tell her." Avva ran back up the steps to the throne and shouted, "Cambria! Cambria!"

Casey started crying. Engel embraced her.

"Get away from her, Engel," Avva yelled. "You spoil her rotten. Everyone does. Let her cry."

"I'll give her my unicorn!" Casey said. "Okay, Momma? I'll give her mine! I didn't mean it. She can have mine."

Avva thought for a moment. Then she nodded. "A fine idea, princess," Avva said, opening her eyes wide and nodding. "Sure.

Yes. A princess's unicorn for her friend's horse. Your unicorn, Naya. Your birthday gift for hers … very well. Give her your royal unicorn and apologize."

Engel held Cassandra as she cried and cried in his arms.

"By the gods," Avva snapped, rolling her eyes and shaking her head. "Let her go, Engel."

But the princess wasn't pleased. Avva figured Cassandra had suggested the sacrifice simply to calm her anger. She didn't seem ready to actually part with it. The girl jumped up. Then when Cambria, wearing her scarlet armor, walked into the throne room, she darted down the aisle toward the exit.

"Casey!"

"Just let her go, Blue," Engel said.

"She's a walking disaster. I spend more time apologizing than running the kingdom. And you, Engel. You're supposed to be watching her. We can't leave her alone for a moment. I mean, she nearly drowned. I never—"

A metallic crash vibrated outside the throne room and made them both jump. Cambria rushed back outside. Then she heard Casey's voice wailing outside the double wooden doors. Avva ran down the aisle with Engel chasing close behind.

In the hallway outside the throne room, Cassandra lay on the stone floor amid a pile of ceramic pottery pieces. An ancient vase the size of a person was now strewn across the floor. It was a pair of matching vases, with a painted mural depicting the ancient Napean wars with the Mandrigel, that stood beside the great wooden doors. Avva had been told as a child that it dated back centuries, to Harmonia herself. Apparently, the girl had knocked it over running.

"*Casey!*"

Avva lifted the child by the elbow from the pieces of the vase. Casey cried more.

"I didn't see it, mother. I was running—"

"*Casey!*"

Avva dragged the girl by the arm back into the throne room. A few subjects stared from down the hall. Then she pushed

Cassandra onto the floor by the aisle and slammed the doors shut behind her.

"My queen," Cambria said, in her shiny hoplite armor, nodding. She was still by the doors. "You called for me. Is everything all right?"

But Avva was too busy shouting. She wasn't even sure what she was saying. And Engel kept tugging at Avva's arm, begging for Avva not to strike her.

"*You half Hinterland dog!*" Avva said to Engel, raising her hand over the girl. "*Deisa! A mangy deisa, you are.* It must be your father. And, Cambria, she nearly drowned Lalaina! You wouldn't mind a good punishment, would you?" Engel held Casey again. "There you go! There you go again. Go comfort her like everyone else. That's why she's spoiled. Stop crying and act a princess. Or, so help me, I'll…"

"Yes, Momma," Cassandra said, wiping her tears with the sleeve of her tunic and looking up at her.

"What's the matter with you!"

Cassandra just turned her head and leaned into Engel's shoulder.

"Tell Auntie Cambria what you've decided. Hmm? Tell her. Your wonderful idea on how to make amends to Lalaina. Go ahead."

Cassandra said nothing. She stubbornly shook her head, still burying it in Engel's embrace. After a long pause…

"Tell her! Tell her now about your unicorn. Now, before Engel doesn't stop me from swatting you like the pest you are."

"I want to—"

"Speak louder. Talk loudly and address our general like the princess."

"Lady Cambria," Cassandra said, raising her wet, bloodshot eyes. Her formal words and demeanor, even now, in this turmoil, looked cute—a cursed cuteness that had won over everyone in the Court. And right now, it seemed to be winning over her royal guard. Cambria was smiling. "I'd like very much to give Lalaina my unicorn for her birthday, Lady Cambria. I … I'm so sorry for what happened. I think it would be a lovely gift. I want—"

Cambria smiled. "No, dear. Not your monokera. Naya is a royal breed."

"We owe your family a great deal," Avva said.

"Thy will be done, Queen," Cambria said with a bow. "But your daughter did nothing on purpose. Lalaina merely fears the water. And Casey got her out safely. I know they love each other dearly and are very close friends."

"Nevertheless, she must take responsibility for her actions. She's spoiled. She needs to be taught a lesson. Besides, she has a heart. I know she feels awful. There's a part of her that would enjoy your daughter's happiness."

"I'll accept the gracious gift if Lalaina wills it, my queen," Cambria said, bowing again.

Cassandra looked at Cambria with her teary eyes and then spun back and stared at her mother. She lost all formality and scowled.

"*No! No!*"

She leaped out of Engel's embrace and darted out of the room again.

"Casey!"

Engel hobbled after her.

"Let her go, Engel!" Avva cried, putting her head in her hand. "You said it yourself. Let her go. I'll punish her later." Then she turned back to her chief guard. "I'm so sorry for what happened, Cambria. I'll talk to her. And Lalaina shall have Naya as our gift."

Cambria bowed deeply. Then she left the room, closing the double doors.

Avva wandered slowly back down the aisle and up the steps of her throne. Then she put her head in both her hands. She felt so heavy.

Rain splashed against the side windows and the crystal dome above. A white full moon passed through dark gray clouds. Sheets of water washed along the side of the glass. And then she looked at the vines and flowers running along the aisles of her throne room, lit by torchlight. The brightly lit chamber with the many vases was tranquil compared with the dark stormy night. Even with the bad weather, her throne was beautiful. How could she feel so miserable in the midst of such loveliness?

Engel returned to the throne and did what he always did. He hobbled over to the bottom step and sat down at her feet. She wondered if he had been doing that for centuries.

"Would you permit me to speak, Blue," Engel said, leaning his head back.

"Of course, you were right," Avva interjected. "You're always right. I love Casey more than myself, but she's more difficult than running the kingdom, I tell you. I can't keep chasing her. Perhaps it'd be better if I let her be bad."

"I'm here to help."

"Yes."

"Be patient. Your daughter means well, but she has your stubbornness. You were a handful too. Why do you think your mother was so hard on you? But Queen Delia loved you more than herself."

"Humph. She had an odd way of showing it."

"She sacrificed herself for you."

"You've said that many times. I don't care. I hate her, Engel. I really don't care what she did, and I wish you'd stop talking about it."

"The campaigns of the Crescent king rage outside Shadow Forest," Engel said, changing the subject. "Now they encroach on Azerban. It should be soon that your husband fights Ansel one last time and takes Castle Cove. But there's word from the elders that they have seen a royal caravan traveling to Crescent Blue. If it's Sol, and it probably is, he should be here in only a few days."

"I've heard the same from that infernal witch, Milda."

"He'll be here, Blue. That's all. It will be easier."

"Oh, Engel, it's not just that. You stopped me from hitting Casey, but what of Lalaina? She burned her hair! And imagine if the poor child had drowned. Would you have stopped me from punishing her then? And would Cambria?"

"Yes. Because it would have been a mistake. I would have forgiven Casey and so would Cambria."

Avva shook her head. Then she took yet another deep breath. She was growing tired of taking deep breaths.

"Perhaps you should consider sending her to the Hinterlands with her father."

"I can't do that. For one thing, it isn't allowed. For another, Sol would probably laugh all this off."

"Yes. Perhaps you should too, Blue."

She looked out through the walled windows again. It was pouring now. She liked the sound of rain splashing against the glass dome and crystal walls. There was something about being inside, away from the cold rain, that was always pleasant.

Her favorite thing when it stormed so much was to watch the rain through the grand three-story window by the double-spiral staircase. Perhaps she would do that. Perhaps, if she could make up with her daughter, she'd do that with Casey tonight.

"What are you thinking about now, Avva?"

"Hmm? Oh nothing, Engel. Just waiting for the next vase to fall."

HENRI RODE on horseback through the forest of the Stratos as Cassandra clung to his waist. He had promised her they would go to the Mount days ago. Now he just enjoyed his "niece's" breath against his neck and her cute voice as they rode across Napea. But she did not speak like she usually did. Usually, she was a chatterbox.

"Princess, what's the matter?"

"Nothing."

"It's something. You're not talking."

"Well, Mother gave my unicorn away," Casey said with

broken words. "My beloved unicorn, Naya. And I haven't been able to play with my best friend for weeks."

"I'm sure she had good reason for it."

"Hey, look!" She pointed at a small bright multicolored squirrel. Its wings spread like a multicolored peacock. But, upon seeing the travelers, it quickly folded them and hid in the bushes.

"Incredible. We don't have animals like that in the Hinterlands."

"And look over there, Uncle! Another flying squirrel!"

"Doesn't your mother let you travel to the Mount? You act like you've never seen this before."

"Well, yes. I've ridden a few times with Engel. But only every moon or so … look, there's a winged lapis deer, uncle!"

"How old are you now, Casey?"

"Ten. You know that. You sent me a necklace for my birthday many moons ago. Don't you remember?"

She leaned forward and he laughed at the sight of her jovial face. She was such a cute girl. Her expression was childlike, but wise. Too wise. She was sneaky too, too smart for her own good. But she had Sol's energy and Anna's rebelliousness and loveliness. He adored her.

"You know I'm old, Casey. Perhaps forgetful."

"Not that old. You're not as old as those elder hags. Imada are old hags, you know, Uncle."

"Casey. Really."

She giggled. "When's Papa coming home?"

"Soon."

"It's been so long."

"He'll be here. And he'll expect a full report of our quest when we return. You must jot down in your mind all the creatures you show me and then write about them later."

"All right. Hey look, there's the winged deer between the trees."

"Don't be too loud. You'll frighten her away."

The horse followed a trail deeper into the woods, under a canopy of blue-green oak trees. The trees towered over them now, and Henri could hear a stream rushing by. They galloped across a brook, and he marveled at the blue glow of the waters. Then, between the trees, he saw the endless wall of Mount Ambitus, so high that the peak touched the clouds. It was a clear day with a green sky, but he could barely make out the sky above the Mount.

They reached an ascent along the trails. Henri could just make out the Crystal Palace, reflecting the surrounding azure-turquoise forests so blue it looked like a sapphire. He showed Cassandra.

Then they approached a tributary of the great Stratos River and Henri stopped his horse by the edge of the water.

"We should dismount."

They walked with his horse along a dirt trail paralleling the water.

Further on, there was a sound in a thicket, and he caught the girl's eyes bulging. She pointed with a shaking finger.

"Zaffre," she said in a whisper. "In the bushes, Uncle. Do you see it?"

"Aye," he said. He moved toward it, but the girl grabbed his arm. "It's all right, princess. Shh … quiet."

He walked slowly toward the shrub. Casey stood far back. Inside a bright red bush was a wild cat with a bright purple hide and black stripes. Its eyes were a deep onyx.

"Would you like to keep him, Casey?"

"Oh yes … but—"

"Shh. Stay quiet then."

Henri walked toward the cat. It stood frozen, staring at the old man through the leaves.

"Be careful, Uncle. He'll bite you."

Henri approached the cat. The tiger shifted. Henri slowly took something out of his pocket. The cat stared at it. Then he quietly started talking to the animal in the feline tongue of the ancients. He sat down, calmed his breathing, and turned with his eyes half closed while signaling repeatedly for the princess to stay back.

The wait took a long time, and he could feel Cassandra growing impatient. But every time the girl started to stir, Henri motioned for her to be still. For a while, the cat became as still as he was and only the sound of the trickling water could be heard.

The cat walked slowly out of the leaves toward him. Henri fed the animal some dry meat from his palm. Then Henri took out a rope from his knapsack and slowly circled it around the animal's neck. He walked the animal back to the girl with a leash. And it was done.

"Now you be careful, princess. This is not like the domestic cats of the castle. This is a wild cat. He can appear calm and peaceful, then the next moment bite off your finger. Do you understand?"

She nodded and smiled excitedly. She stood transfixed staring at the beast.

"Well, come on." He took her hand and gave her the rope. "Try to pet him." She reached out but then quickly pulled her fingers back. Henri took the girl's small hand and softly petted the fur with her. She giggled.

"Now you lost a unicorn, but look what you found. A Zaffre tiger. How's that? Feel better? Tigers are very lucky, Cassandra. Try to spread the luck between you and your mom when we return, will you?"

She wasn't listening. She was too enraptured by the beast.

"But what if Mom doesn't let me keep him, Uncle?"

He laughed. "Don't worry, your father and I will talk to her."

"A wild cat in the palace!" shouted Avva. "Have you lost your mind, Henri!"

Engel couldn't stop laughing at the bottom of the steps. Henri stood holding a brown leather hat in his hands after having bowed to her. As usual, Cassandra ran the moment her mother started screaming.

"*Look at what I brought in, Mom?*" Avva continued rolling her eyes. "What does she mean '*look what I brought in*'? Are you both mad? That animal is as big as she is! He'll eat her."

"He's a luck tiger, Blue," Henri said. "A Zaffre Tiger. All tigers are lucky. Why, I gave Torinth a Bengal Tiger from the Indus when he was a boy ... and she had just told me how you took away her unicorn."

"Torinth is an imprisoned lunatic in Adelain!"

Just then, as if on cue, there was a roar from the tiger. Avva put her head in her hand.

"What's the matter, Anna?" asked Henri.

"What do you mean!" she snapped. But then she looked at the old man's kind gaze and felt ashamed of yelling at him. "I ... I have a headache."

"I can try to mend it. Or perhaps Engel can."

"I'd very much like to dine with you this evening. That is, if the animal you brought doesn't eat my daughter. Perhaps that's your intention? Is that what you meant by saying you knew how take care of my troubles?"

"No, Anna, I have a far greater surprise in store for you. Something that might just cure that headache of yours."

"Hmm? What?"

Then, as if on cue, the two wooden doors of the throne room were thrown open. With it was the sound of her daughter's laughter. A large soldier rushed in wearing polished blue hoplite armor. Casey was carried as if she were baggage, laughing and jerking hysterically in the soldier's arms as he bounded down the aisle. He was so large that it was as if he were carrying a baby. This "soldier" was her husband, Sol, of course.

Engel rose from the bottom step and fell to the ground bowing before the king. Avva sat on her throne staring down at him.

"I seem to have found a brigand in your palace stealing cakes from the kitchen, illustrious Amazon queen," Sol said with a broad gesture of his free hand. He bowed, still holding Casey in the other arm. "What would you have me do with this ruffian?"

"Stop it, Daddy," she said, laughing. "Let me down. Let me down."

"To the dungeon with you!"

Anna permitted a faint smile. Then she heard the roar of a tiger. That made her lose her smile.

"Ah, that too, Queen Anne. That was her accomplice."

"I thought my surprise was a killer cat, Henri?"

Avva hadn't seen Sol in so long. Usually his beard was trimmed thin. Now it was shaggy and there were wrinkles under his eyes. Still young but, from constant campaigns, her husband looked like a man of middle age, not the young Crescent king of North Atala. And although he was jovial, he seemed so worn.

"Well, woman? What should I do with the scoundrel? Hmm?"

"I am the queen," she corrected. "Not a *woman*."

"Engel," Sol said with a nod, looking down at Engel, who was still bowing. "Get up, friend. You never need bow to me." Then Sol whispered something in Cassandra's ear and the girl nodded. He put her down and walked to the lowest step, bowing with a broad gesture of his arm.

"I beg your pardon, Amazon queen. How rude of me. Do I have permission to step foot on your lovely Napean shores? Beautiful they are, 'tis true, but not nearly as lovely as the sight of their ruling queen before me."

"Aye," Avva said with a big smile. "You may enter."

Sol bounded up the stairs. A single tear fell down her cheek as he embraced her tightly.

"Oh, Sol, six moons," she said in his ear, shaking her head. "Six moons. It was terrible."

"I came as quickly as I could," he said quietly. A growl echoed through the walls and Avva finally laughed in his arms.

16

EMBRACE

The light shone through the white curtains, causing a dim aqua glow on the white sheets of their bed. It was morning. When? She didn't care. She was enjoying the sound of Sol's breathing as he slept. Her poor husband was exhausted. It seemed he hadn't slept since the last time he was in her kingdom.

He faced her, naked, on top of the covers. She watched his mouth, under his thick beard, slightly open and close in the rhythm of his sleep. She wasn't sure for how long, but she liked just watching and listening. She could watch him sleep forever. Her eyes wandered over the thick ropes of his muscles. She traced the triceps and biceps and then squinted at a healing gash along his chest. Despite his objections, she had tended to it last night. It had been deep but was now closed. The bruising followed the wound from the chest all along his side, and he had winced, at times, during the night as he turned. He claimed the cut was old and all was well, but Avva knew better. She had learned the basics of wound care from her military training as a young girl. This was a fresh wound and, despite his objections, she had sewn it. Looking at all his other scars—many now large disfigured gashes, where he hadn't had his wife around to tend them—she dreaded knowing how many battles he had fought since she last had seen him. Then she saw traces of scars along his shoulders. If she turned him, she would see a trail of them all over his back. But she had seen those since they had first met. He had never told her how his back became disfigured. There were some mysteries, perhaps, she'd never know.

Sol opened his dark eyes and gazed at her in the dim light. He smiled.

"I know no other pleasure than waking up to your gaze, Anne." He listlessly ran his large chapped hand along her side. She closed her eyes. His fingers glided along the curves of her breast. She turned, exposing herself more. She was naked over the covers too.

"Oh, Sol. Don't leave me alone anymore."

"I wish." He kissed her on the lips. "I wish it." Then he danced with her tongue inside her mouth. "If only I could stay. Ansel's finally on the run. But our troubles don't stop there. After all, it wasn't my brother who broke our father's kingdom. It was the animal Morteus that murdered your father."

"King Morteus?"

"Aye. He's nearly as old as Henri now. Just as wise but, as Henri is good, Morteus is evil. And despite our achievements, he views me and my brothers—and you, Anna—as children."

"Oh, Sol," she said, hitting his shoulder, "when will this end? It's been years."

She turned from him. He put an arm around her. At first she batted it away, but it was only playful. He ran his hand along the curves of her breast from behind again. She took his other hand in hers and kissed the back of it. Then he clutched her tightly.

"I want it to end, but every time I charge Castle Cove, Ansel fends us off. Darius created many fortifications."

"Why not just burn it?"

"Burn Castle Cove!" he exclaimed, nearly jumping off the bed. She turned and faced him, nodding. "Anna, are you crazy? Castle Cove is the symbol of your father. No one would ever desecrate that castle. Not from within Atala, anyway. That would be like desecrating King Darius himself."

"So Ansel sits imprisoned, like Torinth, in his own castle."

"Aye. Exactly."

"I need you here," she said with a long sigh. She ran her hand along his long curly hair. "I like touching your hair. I'm losing mine over Casey."

He laughed. Then he kissed her head. "I see a lot of hair. A lot of very beautiful hair."

"It's not funny. Casey's driving me crazy. Can't you … hurry this war thing up?"

Then they heard a tiger roar. And that made Sol laugh again.

"That's not funny either," Anna said, hitting Sol's arm. "Your friend brought a wild tiger into my palace."

"Torinth had one when he was a kid."

"Torinth's crazy!"

Sol laughed even more and embraced her tightly.

"Stop it. I'm very serious."

"But you're funny. Oh, Blue, I'll fight as fast as I can. My stop here is a break before our move into Azerban. These fights are the last. When I finally win Castle Cove, Atala is ours. The dream is ours. And then you can genuinely call me the Sun King."

She nodded, but sighed. He put an arm around her once more, but she pushed him off. "Then there will be Morteus. And then Philipp of Kitheria. And Lanius. And then the foreigners. No, Sol, I don't see this war ever ending. And next, when you have all of the continent, you'll be sailing across the Strait of Aethiopia. Or heading to Hellena."

"Aye, the Greeks are building a navy."

Avva hit his arm hard this time. "It's not funny, Sol."

"You married a warrior. What did you expect?"

"Peace. Real peace. Even when there was a truce, you still fought. You need to spend time with me and your daughter and end this war."

He reached for her. Yet again she turned and knocked his hand off.

"Isn't a little time better than none?"

Yes. Even a little. A little time to smell his breath, feel his arms and the warmth of his skin. It was an eternal happiness for her. And the odd mix of his thick musculature surrounding the most delicate heart of any man she had ever known. Yes, he was better than an eternity with any other. But …

He put an arm around her and she finally let him.

"Of course it is," she said in a whisper. "But it hurts so much when you're gone."

"I love you, Anne."

"Show me," she whispered. "Make love to me. Make love to me again. Do it forever."

She felt the dry, chapped skin of his worn hand run along her body. The cracked skin glided down her back and hips, making her giggle. Then it ran down her back to the curve of her butt. He held her, holding her so tightly, as if not wanting to ever let her go.

"I love you, Anne. If I could spend an eternity on this bed, believe me, I would."

"I know. Do what you do, fight, then come back to me. Win. But come home soon. Then don't ever leave me again. You don't know what it's like to think that every time you go, I may never see you again. That's the hardest."

He merely squeezed her tighter. "I love you."

"It's not enough. I want to be with you always." She grabbed his arm and wrapped it around her neck as if holding him so he couldn't leave. "I love you more, my Sun King."

17

AZERBAN

Sol's army gathered at midday along orderly lines by the fields of Azerban. He met them on horseback alongside Henri and his chief general, Milo. Azerban consisted of a vast grassland bordered by the dark Shadow Forest in the north, ugly marshes in the far south, and the sandy beaches and cliffs of the sea in the west. It was the first open land one encountered when entering the southern part of Darius's empire. The vast fields were ideal for tilling. Therefore, at one time, it had been the richest land in all of Atala—before Sol's brother Ansel spoiled it. Now the dead fields were the perfect arena for battle.

Sol removed a glass scope from his coat and looked toward the castle on the hill in the distance, once his home. High among thick green moss, trees, and waterfalls lay the beautiful palace. Ansel could enslave and break the surrounding lands but not even he could destroy Castle Cove. This beautiful landmark had been Darius's answer to his vision of Azure.

Over forty regiments of foot soldiers stood in single file behind Sol. Directly in front of them was his seasoned cavalry of fifteen hundred men. With the help of Henri's swordplay arts from the Far East and Milo's expertise with the cavalry, this army was the finest military power on the continent, perhaps the world. But the Crescent king faced a force far larger. Starving and forced to fight, Ansel's soldiers left the protective stone castle walls. Now a motley crew of gold-armored men, hardly standing in order, but with a force twice the size as Sol's, gathered on the opposite side of the field.

Ansel's cavalry rode with him. Darius had taught his sons the worth of a strong cavalry. Then Sol spotted more of his enemy. First the striped black-on-yellow flag, with Torinth's remaining loyal fighters in gold armor much like that worn by Ansel's soldiers, but black helmed, fighting for their imprisoned king. And then some black-armored Eruboi from Hades. And even the ancient hoplites of Caravia, shining in their bright emerald green. Truly, though Sol fought for what he considered his rightful home, he fought the entire continent today.

Worse, he spotted flags from villains outside of Atala. Many were from the city nations of Hellena. They had been told that Ansel was the rightful heir to the kingdom and, though there was some truth to it, it was likely that the foreigners did not understand the extent of Ansel's tyranny.

Then Sol spotted the strangest thing. He pointed and showed Henri. A row of elephants from the furthest lands. It was the first time he had ever laid eyes on such creatures. He had learned of them in drawings. Soldiers on saddles rode these giant creatures. They formed along an eastern flank near a river.

"Now would be a good time, sire," said Milo. "Unless you'd prefer to fight the Egyptians and Assyrians too. I believe they're the only ones in the world not here yet."

"Are you ready, Sol?" Henri said. Henri's beard was now completely white, running down to his battered bright blue chest armor. "I, for one, could do for some ale."

"Here," Milo said, offering a leather pouch. Henri grabbed it and drank heartily.

"Is it even possible, Henri?" asked Sol, shaking his head. "Ready for what? For the water to turn red once more?"

"If need be," Henri said and shrugged. "Whatever happens, I die with you, son. That is my choice. For whatever comes of today, you are the rightful king of Atala. Don't forget, though outnumbered, you have the most loyal warriors, better trained, and better fed. And a far greater advisor."

Sol nodded and tried to smile, but he couldn't. He looked behind him and saw the look of terror on the faces of his troops, who were standing at attention. He fumbled with his scope again, watching the enemy slowly march closer, holding their flags.

It was then that he saw someone that nearly made him drop the scope and fall from his horse. Morteus. The villain was here. Sol spotted the fiend on horseback, in bright green armor, with his Caravian soldiers. The Mangus line of the Crystal Kingdom, said to be descendants of Caravians, also wore emerald armor. But Sol would never have thought that the man who killed his father would stand and fight with his brother. Morteus was short, more fat than strong, and beardless, with thin gray hair.

Sol's eyes narrowed.

"Do you see who rides with them, Henri! That sarding turd, Morteus! Do you see him? My brother fights with Morteus!"

"Aye, Sol," replied Henri with a sigh. The old man didn't seem surprised. "Ansel's heart is blackened by the Dark Lord. Hades' mercenaries ride with him too. But that is why your father gave you power. As I said, you are the true Sun King."

"I've despised my brother for destroying our lands!" Sol shook his head violently. "But this, this I will never forgive! To fight with Morteus? Our father's torturer and murderer!"

"Calm yourself. Be true to the battle. Ansel's desperate. Thank him for wiping away your doubt over fighting him."

"But, Morteus!" Sol spat on the ground and then stared at Henri. "Surely my eyes lie!"

"I've known Ansel since he was a babe, Sol. He's a fool. And now you see why Darius gave you, a bastard in all other eyes, the keys to his kingdom."

"He gave me a crescent."

"He gave you Anna."

Sol finally calmed down over that. Henri nodded and turned to the incoming forces. "He gave you his greatest treasure."

Sol lowered the scope and angrily stuffed it in his tunic. "Well, now's no time for sentimentalities, old man."

"It appears it's time to fight, my lord," said Milo. "You both might notice there are soldiers marching toward us. Perhaps we should do something."

"They seem to be," said Sol, wiping his face as if trying to wipe the sight of Morteus from his mind. "Aye, we're better prepared. Our army is strong. But we're outnumbered two to one."

Sol uncomfortably watched the lines of soldiers, carrying their spears up high, bearing shields, and wearing golden armor, slowly march forward. But then they were signaled to stop. And with Sol's naked eye he saw two single riders, all in black—Eruboi—break through the line. They rode fast toward Sol.

Milo turned his horse, ready to greet them. Sol raised a hand and shook his head.

"My lord," Henri said, "Let Milo speak to him."

"There will be no discussion with my brother, Henri."

"That's not your brother. Look again."

Sol looked through the scope. One man in black armor rode carrying Ansel's yellow sun flag. The other was a tall man with a hood over his head, much taller than the first rider. He had on a black cloak with pitch-black armor underneath.

"How did you see him? I thought your eyes were old?"

"I felt him. Have Milo speak with—"

"No, I will." Sol reached down and grabbed his horse's reins. "You, stay back."

"My lord!" objected Milo.

Sol launched forward and it was too late to stop him.

Sol rode fast. As he drew closer, he witnessed the thousands now halting at attention waiting for battle. Hades stopped fifty yards before Sol and dismounted. When Sol was close enough, he drew his sword and leaped off his horse.

"Here to fight me, god?" Sol shouted, brandishing his sword. Hades smiled under his dark hood. His Eruboi companion held his black flag and did not dismount. "Why is a god of Olympus here?"

"Put the blade down, Solinaray."

Sol didn't. He kept it raised as Hades walked right up to him, but Hades didn't bother unsheathing his sword. Nor did Hades remove his hood.

"My family watches you and Queen Avivae with interest," Hades said. "How can I miss this? This battle decides the fate of the continent. You might, indeed, take your father's empire back. But if you do, Sol, I'm afraid my family is not fond of you. They don't like you. Particularly, they're not fond of your wife. You know her sins. It's all I can do to stop Zeus's lightning from striking her down."

"What sins?"

Hades afforded another sly grin. "Touching down on Crescent Blue. Battling men." He opened his eyes wider. "Freezing them. And then marrying one. Even Queen Harmonia didn't marry. No nymph has ever been permitted formal marriage. Must I continue? Your wife has broken every edict. We're not pleased."

"Haven't you diseased my brother's mind enough!" Sol swung his blade close to him. Hades did not flinch. "Ansel fights with Morteus? For that I shall behead him and give him no honorable burial. And I believe it's your doing. Where is the coward?"

"Ansel doesn't bother to talk to you," Hades said dismissively. "I'm not here to dictate terms. I'm here to discuss what happens after."

There was a pause. Sol was still pointing the sword toward his head.

"*If you win*," Hades said, looking behind Sol. He turned and looked at Ansel's army behind him. "*If you win*, Solinair Solinaray, I offer you one last chance to make amends with my family. Abandon Avivae. If you abandon her, politically and, need I say, by flesh, I promise you favor from my family on Mount Olympus."

"And if I lose?"

"Delia knew you wouldn't. So did Darius. Do you doubt yourself?"

"Then why have you been aiding Ansel?"

"Are you good with your sword, but not with your head? If bees don't come out of their hive and you need a sting, what do you do? You stir the nest. Hit it with a stick. Do you think I wished for you to remain a Crescent forever? You are the greatest warrior of our time. Do what you were born to do. Kill. Then take your rightful seat on your throne as emperor."

"Anna will never agree to your terms."

"Why are the greatest conquerors in the world the worst men at home?" He leaned his head in his hand and shook it. "I didn't suggest you ask her. Treat Anna like the sarding woman she is. Abandon her. That's enough." Then he wagged his finger. "If you don't, you won't like what comes next. Return the laws to the way they were before Queen Avivae. Return to the time of Delia and abandon Avivae. Be warned that these wishes come from Lord Zeus himself and you risk his wrath if you don't."

"Why Zeus? It was your edict that she broke."

"My edict was an agreement made with Nefertiti by my brother. Like you, I loved the nymphs. I didn't make that edict, Zeus did."

"But you do wish to stir the nest, as you say?"

"Of course, you're not such a dullard. Do as you will, but when this battle is over, and *if* you have your victory over Atala, consider Zeus's wishes carefully. Be warned or things will not bode well for you."

Sol sheathed his sword, turned from the god, and mounted his horse. "No."

"Good luck, then."

"Back to the depths with you," Sol replied, gnashing his teeth. "Only you could be such a snake as to aid my enemies and then root for their destruction."

"I fight for the long haul, Sol."

Sol did not return to his general and advisor. As he returned to the line, he grabbed a blue Crescent flag from one of the foot soldiers. Then he fell into a gallop before his men, pointing at the enemy across the field. Men's feet thundered and cries bellowed from their chests. He saw their faces fly past and caught some of their expressions. With the return of their king, many now lost their look of fear in support of him.

"Are you afraid?" he shouted.

"No!"

"Do your legs quake?"

"No!" they shouted, banging their shields and stomping.

"Are your hands unsure?"

"No!"

"Watch villains gather from every corner of the world! They send everything. Why? because *they fear you!*"

He turned about and rode along the line for another charge. They cheered him on.

Sol saw the faces of children among his ranks. They were so young. They were surely afraid. And elders with long white hair, like Henri, veterans who had once fought alongside his father. They all held their long shields and spears aloft ready to advance. He knew all of them by name. They hit their shields and stomped on the ground and shouted as he flew past them.

He stopped at the center of the front line.

"Today is our glory! Those that return to their wives shall sing songs. Those that do not shall be in them. There is no fear. For this day, you all shall be remembered. This day you fought with a boy king, a Crescent, who was given a small seed. Watch it take root.

"I am not my glorious father. No. But look across. Look at the tyrant who claims to be his son, so desperate he fights alongside the man who killed Darius. The man who killed our king and emperor!"

He fell into a gallop again, rushing along the line as the crowds thundered. He could see no one now, but he felt the wind along his face and the thunder of his hooves. And yet the line continued on and on, so many shields and spears held aloft for him.

"For Darius!" he shouted, raising his flag high above his head at full gallop. "For the lands stolen, I return them to you. We will triumph. Not because of numbers." He slowed his horse once more. He waited for them to stop pounding their swords and shields. And then there came a strange silence. Behind him, he caught the enemy watching him too. "But because, unlike them, we embrace fear. For in the face of death we are free! Fight to live free before all who threaten to enslave you!"

Their shouts rang across the valley. Sol quickly pulled out his scope once more to look upon the enemy. He saw what his speech had been intended to do. It was meant not only as a rallying cry for his men but to instill fear in his enemy. They must have thought he was mad to charge the line, yet it answered the cowardice of their generals who still stood far back, in false security, by the castle walls.

Solinair rode back to the front, handed the flag to a soldier, and joined his general and counselor.

"Now we go," he said to Milo with a nod.

"Apparently," replied Henri with a smirk.

"They love you, sire," Milo said with a broad toothless grin.

"Only if we win. Is the line ready, general?"

"Aye. They're ready, Sol."

"Then let's move. Now!"

"Ya!" Sol reared his stallion up on his back legs and then charged.

He had waited painfully for so many years for this fight and now he would be the one to make the first move. He did not wait for the salpinx. Nor did he wait for his men's shouts. Many were still cheering his speech, but he heard nothing. He charged alone into the valley with his royal guard moving fast on his tail. Finally, he would take back his home.

And so Sol was first to meet a volley of arrows. They moved fast, one arrow strafing his helm. Then, to his right, the first man fell: Toric of Azerban. A brave boy, too young to die, that Sol had known in Darius's Court. The brave man had been struck with an arrow through his helm. Then more arrows fell like rain as they approached the lines of golden hoplites. The golden rows lifted their shields and formed the dreaded phalanx. The enemy signaled for them to move forward. It would be the bloodbath Sol dreaded. A thousand horses in Sol's cavalry stampeded straight into their spears and shields.

But as they nearly touched the enemy's shields, the king signaled to change direction. Many of the enemy laughed and jeered as they turned.

"They think we're cowards, Henri," Sol shouted.

"No one in this battle is a coward, my lord."

Sol looked back and saw his general, Milo, signaling to march forward with his foot soldiers in a phalanx of their own, now ignoring Sol's cavalry. Their forces gathered in turtle formation, shields out, long spears jutting toward the enemy. Like a horrible machine, they would collide with one another.

More soldiers on horseback fell by Sol's side. One was shot in the back. Then his cavalry entered an opening on the right flank and climbed a woodsy hilltop.

It was a sharp hill with large trees scattered about, shading them. The horses had to climb hard. This slowed them, but they were farther from the enemy with fewer arrows and, predictably, the enemy did not give chase, thinking Sol had fled. For a fleeting moment, Sol enjoyed the view of a waterfall cascading through a circle of oak trees. How beautiful in the midst of battle.

This illusion of serenity broke as Sol's cavalry approached the castle wall. Soldiers armed with bows aimed at them from the ramparts and more arrows fell. Sol had expected this. With surgical precision, he had planned to slip through the most sparsely guarded side of the enemy's formation and then do his best to avoid these arrows from the castle, but he knew it was impossible to evade everything.

When they passed the castle wall, one of his men cried out "Morteus!" Here there were two paths: the grassy knoll above and a woodsy path down a hill that led back to the battlefield. For a flash, Sol remembered when the grassy hill above had been a place of recreation and rest for him and his friends in the castle. Now a knoll was being used as a ramp for emerald soldiers to ride down and attack him. These forces held the green flags of the Crystal Kingdom, Morteus's cavalry. It was a small group, but enough to slow his advance.

Sol turned his cavalry toward them and up to the hill to face Morteus.

"It's a trap, Sol!" Henri warned, riding beside him. "Turn back! Morteus is trying to lure you. You'll lose the high ground we gained. You'll lose everything."

"Ah!" cried Sol, slamming his leather pteruges with the hilt of his sword. He stopped and turned his horse in a circle. "Ah, but we could ride through the grass right up his ass, Henri!" He gazed at the hill the enemy was riding down. "For Onos and Darius, Henri! We could avenge their deaths now!"

"And lose Castle Cove?" Henri said, shaking his head. "While Morteus runs? No, Sol. Stay the course. And what of Milo? You wish them to die with no support?"

"Ah! … ah," Sol cried, riding his horse in a circle again. "Ah!"

Finally, he nodded to his advisor, grabbed the reins, and did one of the hardest maneuvers he had ever done. The green soldiers charged down, hitting only the tail of his cavalry. They met other enemy soldiers on horseback already giving chase, and Sol charged down the forest path.

Sol could see the grass fields again. Blue and gold phalanxes were in disorder, fighting desperately to breach either side now. Shields and spears hacked. Their resolve tested. And Milo had most of the enemy's cavalry charging down on him without Sol's support. But Milo's army and Sol's army, Darius's finest, were better trained and would not break.

When close enough, Sol raised his sword and cried out something inhuman. He stormed his thousand into the flank of the enemy. Sol heard cheers from his men.

Sol did not slow his horse. Neither did the thousand. And an already broken gold phalanx splintered into pieces, despite the shouting of the enemy's leaders, as Sol violently rammed into the enemy's shields. Sol's right leg hit a shield and he wondered if his ankle had snapped. He ignored the pain and, far worse, watched many of his men get cut down by the mad charge. But for every Crescent soldier killed, it seemed four to five of Ansel's golden-armored men fell.

Then Sol met his first joust. Sol hacked at a giant soldier on horseback who was now without his helm, blood dripping along his long, stringy hair and beard. Two other men tried to spear him. Then more of his horsemen exploded into the line.

Although surrounded by foot soldiers, Sol knew his plan was working. The foe was now fighting without order, while General Milo's army had maintained order.

Sol struck his sword, a Mandrigelian blade, through an enemy's blade running it into his chestplate. Right beside him, old Henri stabbed a sword into the neck of another. But the stampede had made quarters too close. A few soldiers were crushed to death between the horses. Shouts, heavy breathing, and shrieks from the horses surrounded him.

After more died, a group of blue knights cheered over an opening. The bottleneck released. Sol broke free after dismembering a soldier's arm.

Somehow Milo met up with Sol here. His bloody gloved hand clasped Sol's. With Henri and Milo together again, he knew victory was nigh. The three had shattered the enemy's phalanx and were now mowing into the castle itself.

Sol was surprised at the lack of resistance. By the castle wall, Milo removed his helm, his long hair wet, and with a big tooth-less smile embraced his king again. He pointed back at the now-splintered phalanx of the enemy's army. Many gold and green knights were now fleeing to the woods.

But victory was short lived. The ground shook. There was a

terrible crash of chariots and screams. Gray-painted silver hoplites atop elephants stampeded down into the field. It was a senseless charge by Lanius the Fox. Some were still fighting when the mastodons rode over them. This violence saw no friend or foe, such were the bloody alliances Ansel had made. But as their elephants cleared a path, Lanius and his army ran into the forests to escape and abandon Ansel.

"Sarding rats!" cried Milo. "What's the meaning of this?"

"No meaning," said Henri solemnly. "War." Then he turned to Sol and warned him again, "War. Again, don't give them chase. Let the cowards run."

"Your advice is a hard medicine to swallow, Father!" Sol said, grinding his teeth.

"Leave it, Sol."

"Revenge later, eh?" Sol nodded, gripping his fist tightly. "More traps? Aye, Lanius will be punished, Henri. I swear it!"

It was this stampede that finally succeeded in breaking the Crescent army's phalanx. No army could be well-trained enough to hold back beasts running through their ranks. And for the first time since King Darius's campaigns, many of Solinair's soldiers retreated. But Sol turned back to the castle and watched others fight through an opening into the castle wall. Then his eyes fell on the kings he despised, standing beside their tents inside the inner courtyard, running about and planning—likely—their escape. Sol raised his sword and rode forward through the castle's inner courtyard.

Morteus, fearing for his life, jumped on his chariot and motioned to his driver. The charioteer pulled the reins. Sol was within only a hundred yards of his prize. Morteus did not meet his gaze. His charioteer drove madly over any object, or even body, in their wake.

Sol would have given chase this time, but now he was fighting sword-to-sword, blow to blow, with thin protection inside the castle.

He spotted his brother beside a tent. It seemed Ansel was about to jump in a chariot and run like Morteus.

"Ansel!" shouted Solinair as he fought. "Brother, I have a score to settle! Something about a squabble over my wife's property!"

"Bastard!" Ansel cried back. "Come, let us finally embrace again in *my* father's castle!"

The two kings ignored the chaos between them. Sol ran to his brother with his bloody sword drawn. Yet his right foot dragged. Indeed, it must have broken.

Ansel removed his Mandrigelian blade, shining red, waving it menacingly about his body with speed and finesse. Ansel and Torinth were expert swordsmen. Sol charged against Ansel's shield; then Ansel shattered Sol's shield with the enchanted blade, breaking it in half. Ansel swung at Solinair's head and cracked his helmet. That hit was followed by an arrow from the castle walls that landed on Sol's right leg. Sol fell to the ground, now completely lame on his right side. Ansel swung madly with his sword as Sol lifted his own sword for simple protection. He may have finished Sol, if it wasn't for a huge blue-armored soldier who rammed Ansel. But Ansel thrust his sword deep into the back of the hefty Crescent knight, killing him instantly.

Sol got up on his knees and lunged at Ansel with a knife.

"Like old days, huh, boy?" said Ansel, looking down at him. "Playing with toys under me?"

"But Father's dead and you disgrace him. You fight with Caravians and Morteus. Aye, for that I will kill you."

"*My father*, King Darius, you bastard. Never yours!" corrected Ansel, out of breath. "And you fail to see that you're the one on the ground."

Ansel uttered a scream and, with both hands, thrust his sword at Sol, but Solinair turned the move to his advantage and tripped him. He then whirled around and positioned his knife upon Ansel's throat.

"Swear allegiance to me!" Sol shouted with Ansel caught in a choke hold. The knife glided along his throat. "Even now, I offer you mercy if you take me as your king."

Ansel spat in his face.

"Swear, or I'll kill you, brother! I will!"

"You're not my brother. You never were. You're a bastard, barbarian!" Ansel laughed and spat at him again. Sol promptly dug his knife into Ansel's throat. Ansel still laughed, but he opened his eyes wide. He kept laughing as blood formed along his mouth until he became lifeless in Sol's hands.

Solinair dropped the knife, exhausted. Then he lifted his painful right leg with both hands from under his dead brother's weight.

"My king!" the red-headed Kaios said, sliding beside him. "We must mount. We're in enemy lines. We'll be overrun!"

Sol turned and saw the golden- and green-armored soldiers fighting their way through his men toward him. His men had done their best to protect him as he fought Ansel.

"Who do they fight? Their king is dead. And the others are cowards."

"My lord, praise the day!" Kaios looked down and noticed Ansel. "Perhaps they don't know. But we must go."

Kaios had to help Sol mount his horse. Once on, they rode swiftly back to regroup with their cavalry.

The soldiers fought in the inner courtyards until nightfall. Indeed, many didn't know that their kings had abandoned them.

When the enemy had retreated into the inner buildings of the castle, Henri finally met up with Sol, under torchlight, by the walls. They witnessed lines of soldiers kneeling with their wrists tied behind their backs, surrendering at sword point.

Using a wooden cane, Sol limped to Henri.

"Our home has been returned to us," Henri said with a smile, laying his hands on his shoulders. "Your father would be proud of you. He once told me that he knew you would be his successor."

"With your help, we did it. But Darius was not my father, sir."

"Oh … but of course, sire," Henri said, raising his brow. Then he nodded. "My apologies. Your father was a king from Harkist."

"No, old man," Sol said, shaking his head and patting his back. "My father's right here."

HER DAUGHTER

Avva and Cassandra flew together on Antilus above their kingdom. Casey had never traveled this far in Azure by air. The girl was so excited by the view of Napea below that Avva had to stop her from leaping off Antilus. They headed beyond the thatched roofs of the grassland homes, beyond the great forest, up to the north hills. Avva knew the way. She had traveled it so many times before. Then they headed west to Mount Ambitus.

The lands below the Mount were the most beautiful. They followed a bright blue stream along the hills, then flew upward beside a waterfall, and then up higher among purple and green bushes hugging the crests of the hilltops.

They landed on a purple soil plateau. It was Avva's favorite spot, affording a beautiful vista of her kingdom. Avva helped her daughter off the unicorn.

"Thanks, Mom."

Standing up, Avva reflected on how Cassandra was growing. She was becoming a beautiful nymph and, for a moment, as she gazed along the valley, her daughter looked like a lady.

"What do you think of the view, Casey?"

"You can see the palace. But it's so small." She ran her palm along Antilus's hide. "Good girl, Antilus." The horse neighed.

"Casey, I first came to this spot before your grandmother passed."

"Did she take you here?"

"No, Casey. My mother never took me anywhere."

"Look at the glowing waterfall, Mom. The water running all the way down that tall hill. It's so pretty. Henri's taken me up the Mount by the river and I saw it in the distance, but never this close."

"That's called Kal-edor. And it runs down the glowing streams of Inste to the Stratos."

"And above it is Nefer's peak. And then the sheer wall. And above that is Mount Olympus," Cassandra said with a nod. "I know, Mother, Engel told me many times of these places."

"Mount Olympus and the gods," Avva said, nodding and looking up in awe. "No nymph or man has ever climbed it, except the great Nefertiti. Legend says she was forced to return from the top of the Mount to escape."

"Why?" Cassandra asked.

They both stared at the clear green sky; the top of the Mount was shrouded in clouds.

"She had no other way to go," Avva said with a shrug. "So the story goes. I don't know."

"Can we go up there?"

"It's too dangerous," Avva said with a chuckle. "The gods create storms higher up to keep monokera, even birds, from the top. And poor Antilus is far too old."

"Well, maybe if you finally get me a unicorn, Lalaina can take Naya and we can fly up to the top and—"

"That's precisely why you still don't have one."

"Humph," Casey said, pouting. "I'm old enough for a monokera. It's been over a year since the pond."

"Since you nearly drowned your best friend? Look there, Casey." Avva quickly pointed to a flock of birds circling under them. They were small bright green birds. She was trying to change the subject. She really didn't want to fight.

"I hate birds," Cassandra said, seeming to still sulk.

"I see." Avva laughed. "Just pointing out how beautiful they are."

Cassandra picked up a large rock. It was an unusual multicolored rock, purple with green and red stripes, very beautiful.

"Look," she said.

Avva picked it up from her daughter's hand. "That's very rare, dear. Pretty enough to be from Olympus itself."

Cassandra grabbed it from her mother and tossed it down the hill. "We sure are high up."

"Casey, I thought you'd keep that rock."

"It's just a rock, Momma."

Cassandra walked along the ledge.

"Be careful, dear."

Avva gazed across the Strait toward Gaia. It was a clear day, and even from this distance, she could make out the shore. For a moment, that made her worry. She was tired. So many sleepless nights over so many moons worrying over a war that seemed to never end. Even now, after the castle had been taken, strife continued. But far worse, Sol wasn't here. She so missed him.

"Will Dad be back soon?" asked her daughter, reading her mind.

"I hope so." Avva took a deep breath.

"He promised me a new unicorn."

"Did he?" she asked, stepping back, amused.

"Yeah. *He* did. Remember? He said that I had grown older and when he returned, I deserved one. Now it seems all my friends have one. Except me."

"We'll see." Cassandra scowled at the ground, and Avva couldn't help but laugh. "Now that your father has been crowned the Sun King, he's at Castle Cove and there's so much to do."

"But he won. Why isn't he home?"

"You have Uncle Henri. He's visiting soon. You know, my mother never let me see my dad, ever. And when your father returns ... perhaps, aye, perhaps then we shall get you a new unicorn."

"Really!"

"Yes, princess." And Avva pressed her daughter's nose. "The moment you do something noble." Casey scowled again. "You're a princess. Act with kindness, help others, act princely. The Ambrosia family holds many privileges, but you must show the people that you deserve them. A good queen sacrifices for her people. You must sacrifice and do something special for others, or at least someone else. Perhaps do something noble for your best friend, Lalaina?"

Avva was going to carry on, but she realized she was speaking like her mother. And, indeed, Cassandra was completely ignoring her anyway. Casey was focusing on a multicolored grasshopper.

"Look, Mom."

"Just don't throw it over the cliff, please."

Casey looked up at her mother with a sly look.

"Were you even listening to me?"

"Yes."

"Let me show you why we came here. This is very important."

Cassandra nodded. She put down the grasshopper on a rock. Avva gestured to the valley.

"Look down at Azure and the Isle of Napea. Far down, you see our Crystal Palace. And there, you see our harbor with Dad's ships. And there you see the forest along the shore. And further you see the hills to the far north. All the land on our island of Napea is ours. We Ambrosia care for these lands and our people. You will one day rule. I will leave, and you will be queen. Everything will be yours. That's why you must act noble. Because, in our lives, we have been given great things, but we must give back to our Amazon in order to keep them. If you live selfishly, the kingdom will fall. Do you understand?"

Cassandra shook her head.

"Oh, Casey."

But Avva didn't blame her. This was precisely the drivel her mother used to tell her all the time.

"I understand," Casey said, laughing. "I'm only joking. Thanks so much for bringing me up here, Mom."

"You're welcome."

Cassandra played with the grasshopper again. Avva knelt and kissed her daughter's cheek. Then she sighed and looked out toward the Strait and the Hinterlands again. "I love you, Casey."

19

MOUNT AMBITUS

Lalaina sat on her knees in the den, leaning against a windowpane, looking at shops across the street near the palace walls. There was the sound of a metallurgist banging metal and the delicious bakery smell from tents across the street. She watched nymphs, already up in the early morning, shopping or eating. That made her wonder what her crazy friend was up to. The princess always had something naughty planned. A couple of days ago, they had ridden to the beach with the silly excuse of playing by the waves. Cassandra led them to the West Harbor near Ambitus. There they had watched the Hinterland soldiers manning the ships by the docks. All to look at boys. Lalaina hoped they'd do something like that today.

Her den was adjacent to the kitchen, and she could smell her mother's oatmeal being prepared by the stove—the smell of oats, a very nice familiar breakfast smell for nymphs.

"Too bad I have to be in the castle, dear," Cambria said. "Is Debra coming to give you lessons this afternoon or tomorrow? I can't remember."

"Tomorrow, Mom," Lalaina said, still staring outside. "No lessons today."

"Then it's really too bad. I wish I could spend the day with you. Maybe you and the princess can play by the beach like last week."

Lalaina laughed. Her mother turned and smiled, sprinkling cinnamon from a metal jar over the white stew. Then she transferred the smoking pot to a dish. As she walked over to pour it into a wooden bowl by the table, there was a knock.

Casey! It must be her!

"Can you get that?"

"Sure, Mom."

Lalaina ran to the entryway. She opened the wooden door and jumped back at the sight of a large unicorn at the door. It was her brown unicorn, Naya. She had gone missing yesterday. Then Lalaina jumped back again as the princess popped her head in.

"Hi."

"Casey," Lalaina shrieked.

"Shh, quiet." Cassandra put a finger to her lips. She looked around then signaled for her to follow her outside.

They walked Naya to the side of the cobblestone street, away from her house.

"What are you doing here?" Lalaina asked.

"Leaving," she said with a mischievous smile.

"Where?"

"Away." Cassandra pointed to the mountain.

"Where?" Lalaina said loudly.

Cassandra shushed her and pointed to the Mount.

"Where, Casey?"

"Flying over Mount Ambitus. Want to come?"

"Are you crazy?" Lalaina asked, opening her eyes wide.

Cassandra nodded and then shushed her once again, struggling to suppress a laugh. "I thought we could go today. Last time I went with Mom was many moons ago, and I've been dying to go back since. Now it's warm and perfect. We'll walk most of the way, that way the monokera will have enough energy to fly over the mountain."

"Over Mount Ambitus! Are you crazy?"

"Stop asking. You know I am. The weather's perfect. You could follow me with Naya."

Lalaina looked at Naya and then looked around. "Where's Inghorn?"

"She's coming—slowly. Engel's got her." Cassandra laughed. "You should see him trying to fly her." Lalaina laughed too. "It's hilarious. I couldn't get her past the stables myself without Mom hearing it. I brought Naya instead."

"You had Naya yesterday?"

"Um-hmm."

"So that's where she was. You've been planning this since yesterday?"

"Yep," Cassandra said with a big grin. Lalaina laughed. She couldn't help herself. "No, I've been planning it for far longer."

"Is Engel coming with us?"

"Are you kidding? Of course not. But I need him to bring my unicorn and keep Mom off our trail. He's riding with Sandra."

"Sandra," Lalaina said with a nod. "Good. Well, I'll have to tell Mom I'll be away."

"No, there's no time. I told Engel to meet us. He'll be here any moment. We'll follow him, then ditch him. Then we'll check out the Mount alone. We don't have to go all the way, but we can climb till sundown. I've told Engel we're going to gather berries."

Lalaina looked back at the house. "But what do I tell Mom?"

"Tell her your crazy princess dragged you on a *quest*," she said with a big grin. "Or … Oh I don't know, Cambria will understand. She never punishes you like Mom."

"But why, Casey?"

"Why not?"

Lalaina saw a unicorn far away, dipping up and down in the air, looking like it was about to plummet or crash into a tower. It made its way clumsily down to the street below. Cassandra pointed and laughed. Engel was in front steering while Sandra clutched his chest from behind. But then the princess lost her smile.

"Damn!" snapped Cassandra. "You dummy, Sandra! I told you to bring Aris. That's one too few monokera."

"Sandra's too sweet to be involved in your scheming," Lalaina said.

Cassandra furrowed her brow and then nodded.

Inghorn skipped along the stone road to a halt. A few nymphs whirled around and stared at the spectacle, likely thinking how peculiar it was for a dwarf to be riding a unicorn.

"I much prefer to walk, girls," Engel said in a huff.

"We'll have plenty of time to walk later," Cassandra said.

Lalaina tugged at Cassandra. She signaled back to the house. "I have to tell her."

"Oh fine," Cassandra said. "Go tell your mom and then come along."

Lalaina ran inside the house. She felt the normal excitement and terror she had always felt with her childhood friend. Sometimes she loathed it, other times she adored it. This morning it was just the fun she had been looking for.

When she returned to them, Engel was shaking a finger at the princess, disciplining her as always. Sandra was staring at the princess with her eyes bulging.

"The Blue River?" Sandra asked Cassandra quietly.

Cassandra nodded with a big grin.

"Why so far, Casey?" Engel asked, shaking his head. "There's myrle berries closer to the palace. Or even the garden. Why the long trek?"

"This is our special spot," replied the princess. "Don't be boring, Engel. There's a whole field of the best berries in all of Napea there. You said Mom was okay with it. And it's closer to the mythic fields of Harmonia. The last time we picked pomegranates there, the seeds were so good. And you know it'll be Mom's birthday soon." Engel folded his arms and snorted. That made Lalaina laugh. "And your birthday too, Engel."

Engel shook his head again.

Lalaina went over and petted Cassandra's unicorn. Inghorn neighed. She was a beautiful monokera, almost as elegant as the queen's white unicorn, Antilus. This steed was pearly white like Antilus. She was strong and fast like Antilus too. Sandra led Inghorn to a tree with Naya.

"Well?" Cassandra asked, tapping on Lalaina's shoulder. "What'd your mom say?"

"She's fine with it," Lalaina said with a shrug.

"Of course she is. By the gods, if only my mother were like yours." Engel caught the words and squinted suspiciously.

CASSANDRA RODE with Sandra on Inghorn. Lalaina took Engel on Naya. She was leading them—where? She had no idea. But the light occasionally shimmered, calling for her.

Over the past few moons, since news of Father's victory, the Mount had sung to her every morning. No one else heard the lovely music. Whenever she looked at the Mount, even when dark and rainy, she caught a glimpse of a shiny gold light. Part of her thought she was crazy. But whatever or whoever it was welcomed her. And now was her chance to see it. But the light was far from the base of the mountain, and she would have to fly to it.

Her only plan with Engel was to travel to the shiny Blue River. The Stratos. In actuality, no one really knew the location of the Myrle Berries of Harmony—the field where it was said Harmonia had tasted the forbidden pomegranates that began the war with the Mandrigel and created her Amazon kingdom.

They walked some of the way by foot, so as not to exhaust the unicorns, though Casey told Engel it was to enjoy the trails. They traveled throughout the morning into the afternoon, passing through blue fields and scattered thatched-roof cottages, soon abandoning all sight of her nymph settlements and entering lovely empty blue grasslands. It was a beautiful day under a bright green sun. The temperature was temperate, but not too hot. Pleasant.

At one point, when they passed a heavily wooded trail back

into a vast field, Lalaina walked up to Cassandra and whispered in her ear, "How much longer? And how are we getting rid of him?"

"He'll go back with your unicorn soon enough," she whispered back. "Trust me."

"Naya?" Lalaina snapped quietly. "But then how will we get up the mountain with just Inghorn, Casey? Sandra forgot her mother's unicorn."

"I know." Cassandra laughed and then whispered, "Well, Engel can fly Naya back to the castle. Then Naya can fly alone back to us."

"But that will take forever, Casey. You're not thinking. How long are we to be gone? It's already midday. The sun will go down and we'll have to get back home."

Cassandra hadn't thought of that. She wasn't sure how long the excursion would take, or when they'd return. She thought she could do the whole thing in a day. She carried a knapsack of food over her shoulder, but it wasn't a lot, maybe a day's rations.

"We'll be fine," Cassandra lied reassuringly. "Relax."

They reached vast purple fields. It was quiet and far from any settlement. No longer could they see nymph cottages or farms. They were alone.

Engel seemed to be getting tired of being worried and searching around him. Now he just stared forward at the woods, far ahead, that surrounded the Stratos. But he always averted his eyes upward at the wall of a mountain towering over it. Engel had always had an aversion to looking at the Mount, but he had never told Cassandra why.

"Princess, there are some trees over here," Engel said, pointing, "They look like myrle berry trees. Surely we're at our destination?"

Cassandra looked around and leaned her chin on a finger. Then she pretended to be lost. "Hmm, well, I haven't been here in so long, Engel. I can't remember the exact location."

She reached down and ran her blue fingers through some purple weeds. She pulled some up by their roots and examined them. Henri had taught her how to track. She knew how to navigate, even determine the time of day, by looking at the sky or her surroundings. The position of the sun or the stars could help provide her location and direction. She sniffed the weeds. Then she shook her head, feigning stupidity.

"I'm not sure. I know I've been here before. But I can't remember where the Myrle Berries of Harmony are."

Engel stomped on the grass and snorted. "They're everywhere, princess. Why must we go to the exact spot? There are pomegranates in abundance on every twig, bush, and tree surrounding us."

"It's a famous place, Engel," said Lalaina. "We should find it."

"You found it. It's right here." And he stomped on the ground, snorted, and gestured again to the short trees.

"No, this isn't the right spot," Cassandra said. "The berries are better closer to a brook. I think that's where the spot was last year. Further in toward the Stratos. I just can't seem to find the place. Don't worry, Engel. We just have to get closer to the Blue River."

More time passed. The girls came closer to the mountain. And Engel looked like a nervous wreck.

And it was getting dark.

Cassandra decided it was time. She wanted to fly the rest of the way, but she had to get rid of her dearest dwarf.

"No! No! No!" she said in a huff. She jumped off her unicorn. "It just won't do! I think we took a wrong turn a while back. I think we already passed it."

She grabbed some random soil and weeds from the ground. Then she looked it over, sniffing it again. Lalaina was trying not to laugh. Sandra looked concerned, still not being in on the plan. Cassandra kept searching the area for a long time. Finally, she turned to her friends, threw her arms up, and said, "Sorry. I can't remember."

"Well, we'll just have to turn back then," said Engel, folding his arms and snorting, sitting atop Naya.

"Turn back?" yelled Cassandra. "Are you crazy! I didn't go all this way just to turn back. I want to see the myrle fields. Legend says Harmonia picked the best berries in Napea there. That's why we went to war. I remember. They were so yummy."

"She warred with my people."

"Oh, yeah. That too, Engel. Sorry. But that was a long time ago. You weren't in that fight, were you? If you were, maybe you can show me the way."

Lalaina finally couldn't suppress a laugh.

"I'm not that old, Casey."

"Well, last time we found it, the berries were so delicious. You could see why our famed queen warred over them."

She took a knapsack that had been tied to Inghorn. Then she started emptying all sorts of things, fire rocks, a knife, some dried meat. Then she angrily threw the bag on the ground. "It's not here!"

"What's not here?" asked Engel.

"My map."

"*You had a map all this time!*" Engel cried, running his hand down his face.

"Yeah. But it's gone. I can't find it. I thought I'd just remember." Cassandra sat down by a large stone and put her head in her hands. She was debating on whether to pretend to cry, but she often found it very hard to make fake tears.

"It's okay, we can just go back, Casey," said Sandra. Sweet Sandra got off Inghorn and patted Casey on the shoulder to comfort her.

"Oh, Casey! This is ridiculous!" said Engel. "We have to return now."

Cassandra looked up sadly at Engel. "Engel, can you return to the castle and get my map? Please. I remember now, I left it in my room. I know exactly where it is. It's in my desk in the third drawer. Our grove is drawn near the river. You can follow the fields. It's pretty easy to find once you look at the geography. There's even dirt trails drawn. You can—"

"Princess, I'm not traveling leagues back to the palace to get your map. We'll go home now."

Cassandra put her hands in a begging position. "Please." Then, finally, she managed a couple of tears—somehow. "Please. We've gone so far. I so wanted to pick the berries for Momma. You don't know how wonderful they are. It was going to be a present for Dad too. I hear he might be coming this week. I really want to do something for them. You can fly back on Naya. It will only take you a little while by air. Please, Engel. Then quickly return. Please?"

She kept begging. She would not take no for an answer. And she was counting on his heart, the gentlest heart in the whole kingdom.

"Fine, I'll go," he said with a snort. "I'll return soon. You just stay right here, girls, so I don't lose you."

Cassandra nodded. Then she jumped up and down and threw her arms around Engel, who was atop Naya, and kissed his cheek.

"Stop. Just stop it! I don't like flying that beast, you know."

"Oh, I know, but I love you, Engel. I love you so much! Thank you!"

Lalaina slipped off her unicorn. Then Engel said farewell. The three girls watched him bob up and down in his attempt to fly back to the castle. When he was well out of sight, Cassandra turned to the others.

"Let's go."

Casey climbed up and mounted Inghorn with Lalaina.

"But Casey," Lalaina objected, "We only have Inghorn."

"Can't be helped. We'll have to fly on Inghorn. We're light. She's a mighty horse. She can take all three of us to the mountain. I mean, really, all three of us are probably not much heavier than your mother in armor."

"Where are we going?" asked Sandra, standing under them.

"Up the mountain," Cassandra said with a smile.

"Up the mountain!" Sandra exclaimed. "Are you mad? I thought we were just going along the river? We'll get in so much trouble if we go there, Casey. We won't get back to the palace until late tonight or even tomorrow."

"Well," Cassandra said, shrugging, "you can head back to the palace alone if you want to."

Poor Sandra looked distraught over that. Lalaina angrily hit Casey hard on the shoulder and the princess frowned, but she couldn't let Sandra stop her.

"Casey," Lalaina said, "Inghorn won't be able to take us to the top. Not all three of us."

"Whatever. We'll go as high as we can. The view will be amazing. And we can just look down at the kingdom on foot, instead of unicorn-back."

"I can't go back home alone," Sandra said, shaking her head. "I don't have a unicorn, Casey."

"I know. We should have taken *three* unicorns, *Sandra*, like I asked you for, thank you very much."

Lalaina hit Casey's back again, this time very hard. "She and I should leave you here alone."

Cassandra smiled down at her innocent friend. Then she reached out her hand. "Well, come aboard."

Sandra hesitated. But then she mounted the unicorn behind Lalaina. Inghorn galloped hard and took off from the ground.

THE GIRLS FLEW HIGHER and higher. Cassandra felt Lalaina's hands shaking as she held her stomach from behind. Of course, the girls had not flown together often and they had never flown so high.

They passed above the beautiful cascading glowing blue waterfall of Kal-edor as they made their way up the mountain. Lalaina pointed to a wolf. It was a red and blue striped wolf, rare in these parts, and two to three times the size of wolves in the Hinterlands. It seemed to be following them.

The area was serene and, for Lalaina and Sandra, being this high up was probably completely new. But not for Casey. She had traveled here with her mother and she had been dying to return since.

Cassandra landed the unicorn on a ledge by another large, lovely waterfall. There was no name for this one, and Casey thought that perhaps it was because few nymphs had traveled this high.

"Inghorn needs a break, girls."

They removed their sandals and waded in a nearby shallow stream. The glowing blue water touched their blue feet. It was cold, but the cold was refreshing under the hot green sun. After stupidly splashing each other and playing in the stream, they rose back into the air.

Cassandra looked up and a rocky wall edged straight up. But the thrill of the steep climb would be worth the ascent. They followed the wall as purple-green trees raced under them.

A flash of yellow-white light appeared between clouds above, a golden bright light that was like her singing morning star. Had she found it? Or was it the sun? But the sun was always green.

They rose higher, then, all of a sudden, dropped a few yards. The girls shrieked. Inghorn shrieked too and flapped her wings harder. The air was fogging and Inghorn's breathing was labored.

"She's tiring, Casey!" Lalaina hollered through the wind. "We're getting too high."

"She can get a little higher. I see another ledge above. And light ahead. We'll rest there and have a look."

My yellow light. My yellow light. But where is it now?

Cassandra gripped Inghorn's neck tightly and gave the unicorn a kick. Lalaina was clutching her and Sandra cried out something behind her.

As they climbed only a little higher, the clouds quickly enveloped them, turning the air ashen. For a moment, in terror, Cassandra could not see the ground. Then she heard thunder. The air grew frigid. Icy rain started pelting down at her eyes. Inghorn pushed higher, toward another bright yellow opening in the clouds. Her star? But they were too high up. Inghorn flew over another cloud, bucking and then jerking side-to-side in a fight to stay airborne and, for a moment, she couldn't see up from down again. Then they fell once more, for a longer time than ever before.

"We have to turn back, Casey!" shouted Sandra.

"I know," said Cassandra. "I know."

Inghorn fought hard against the wind, her great wings flapping through the rushes of rain and sleet. A yellow opening appeared once more in the clouds, and Casey could see the crest of the mountain. The yellow light was blinding. This wasn't her star, it was the sun. Only, somehow, through the clouds, it had turned yellow.

A cloud passed over what appeared to be the summit of the mountain. And another wall of earth rose higher, above more clouds, with no foreseeable break in sight. She couldn't land anywhere. And looking down, she could no longer see the ground through the clouds.

All of a sudden, Inghorn dove. The girls screamed. Lalaina was holding on to Cassandra as tightly as she could, possibly falling. Cassandra's travel tunic must have been horrifyingly slippery from the rain. They leveled off, but the unicorn's wings stopped flapping and they plummeted again. Cassandra felt Lalaina lose her grip and clamor desperately to grab her slippery tunic again. Worse, she heard a scream from behind Lalaina.

Cassandra turned and looked behind Lalaina. She couldn't see Sandra. The terror of losing her friend nearly made Casey faint.

The horse leveled off, descended, and started beating its great wings again.

Casey searched frantically under her, but she couldn't see through the clouds. She heard Lalaina scream something, but she couldn't make out her words in the midst of the rushing wind and rain. But then, under white clouds below, she saw a body falling like a rag doll.

Inghorn regained control due to the drop in weight. But then Lalaina screamed even more as Cassandra pushed Inghorn's neck straight down toward Sandra. Lalaina screamed again and again—desperately trying to hold on—and, for a flash, Cassandra marveled that Lalaina was still clinging to her back. At a couple of points, it seemed her friend was flying airborne behind her. Even Casey's legs let go of Inghorn a few times during this descent as she clutched Inghorn's mane for dear life.

Lalaina's grip was so tight that it hurt Cassandra's stomach. Meanwhile a wall of earth was dropping before them. Some clouds dispersed during their fall, and Cassandra gasped, finally seeing the ground. They were still so high up!

She could no longer see Sandra. Had she hit the ground and died?

In the clearing in the fog, Inghorn straightened and regained control, flapping its great feather wings. This far down, the green sun shone on them again.

"Where is she!" cried Lalaina. "By the gods, where is she, Casey! Where!"

"I don't know! I don't know!"

They stared down, searching for their friend. But Cassandra had lost hope that Sandra had survived.

Finally, Lalaina laughed. Her laughter was shrill in Casey's panicked ears. Lalaina yanked Cassandra's arm and pointed. A brown bird had appeared out of nowhere, far down below, over the forests of the Stratos. And atop the back of the bird's wing lay a girl. Sandra? Of course. Cassandra realized then that the "bird" was not a bird at all—It was another unicorn. And at the helm of the unicorn was a dwarf: Engel.

Engel signaled for the girls to land on a cliff below.

Inghorn was panting, completely exhausted, as they landed. Engel leaped from the unicorn, ran up to Cassandra, and pulled her off Inghorn. Cassandra hardly resisted. She could barely move.

"*What were you doing!*" cried Engel, searching her eyes. "*What's gotten into you?* What was this all about? You're going to get yourselves killed!"

Cassandra couldn't speak. She looked down at Sandra, who

was lying on her back. She looked dead. Lalaina knelt down before Sandra, crying.

"Casey! Casey!" yelled Engel. He shook her shoulders. "What was the meaning of this? What were you doing up there?"

Casey looked at Engel. Then she kneeled over to check Sandra. Then she cried with Lalaina.

Engel stomped on the ground and this time it wasn't cute. He was furious. Cassandra had never seen him so mad.

"Lalaina!" said Engel. Apparently, he had given up on Cassandra. "What were you girls thinking going up the Mount?"

Lalaina looked up at Engel with tears flowing down her face. Then she opened her eyes wide in fear. She began to struggle with breathing. She started gasping for air. "I … I … don't know … what's wrong … Engel. I can't breathe."

Engel grabbed Casey's knapsack. He threw the contents out, then took the leather bag over to Lalaina and forced it under her mouth.

"Breathe in this," Engel said.

Lalaina nodded.

Cassandra started poking at Sandra. Was she dead? Had Engel rescued her only for her to die from the fall onto the unicorn? But she didn't look injured. No, Sandra was breathing. She was asleep. Or unconscious.

Engel walked under a tree, folded his arms, and sat down, looking away from them.

They were all startled when Sandra awoke, screaming.

"Pomegranates," said Engel to himself, shaking his head. "All for pomegranates. The best myrle berries. Hmm."

"How are you even here?" Cassandra finally asked, looking at Engel.

"Oh, you can talk now, princess. Good. You know, Casey, I may be smaller than you, but I'm not stupid. I circled around the forest then headed back to see what you girls were up to."

Cassandra ran over to Engel, tackled him with a huge hug, and started kissing him.

"What's this!" Engel yelled. "What are you doing?"

"You saved her! You saved her, Engel! Thank you! Thank you!"

"Get off me!" shouted Engel and he pushed her off. "Princess, it's too bad you three survived. It'd be better to have hit the ground than face your mother. Now Avva can kill you."

"But you saved Sandra, Engel! You saved her!"

"Yes, I did," he said and turned away from them again. "And you almost killed her."

"Oh, I could kiss you, Engel!"

Engel shook his head. "You did."

Cassandra knelt down next to Sandra again and put an arm around her friend. "Are you okay? I'm so sorry, Sandra. Can you forgive me?"

Sandra blinked her eyes, sat up straighter, and started to cry. That got all the girls crying once more. Cassandra caught Engel shaking his head in a huff and turning from them again.

"I told you ... Casey," Lalaina said. "The unicorn couldn't carry us all."

"Seems you were right," Cassandra said with a laugh.

"I should push you off the cliff, princess!" snapped Engel. "Humph. Something funny now?"

"Watch your tone, Engel, I'm still your princess."

"Well, *princess*, you have to be more of a leader if you want to use that title."

"Now you sound like my mother. But I don't care what you say. Anyway, you saved her, Engel. Nothing could make me love you less now."

She almost charged him again to hug him but saw his expression and thought better of it. All three girls gathered together and some of their tears became laughter.

"*Princess*," Engel said, more softly. "Take a look at the mountain and tell me what you see?"

"What?"

"You see that big green ball. Do you see it?"

Cassandra nodded.

"Let me teach you something because, apparently, nothing I

ever taught you before has sunk in. The sun is disappearing under Mount Ambitus. The sun's setting. Which means it's going to get dark. And that means we have a limited amount of time before it will be cold. Now, the problem that we're faced with at the moment is that we have no transportation. And we're still quite high in elevation. Do you know what happens at night on a mountaintop?"

"Engel, stop talking to me as if I'm an idiot."

"Of course, Casey, our unicorns can easily fly us back, right?" he asked sarcastically.

"Sure."

"No. Inghorn might not even be able to walk. And Naya is hurt from Sandra's fall. Her wing might have stopped Sandra, but it severely damaged her side. I know Naya can't fly back either."

Cassandra's jovial mood faded. Then she nodded, sat down on the ground, and leaned her chin on her hands.

"Simply put, you're in trouble again."

Cassandra looked up at him. He shrugged and hobbled over.

"What should we do?" she asked Engel.

"I thought I was stupid?" But he looked into her eyes and forced a smile. He shrugged. "I don't know. It's going to get very cold here soon."

Sandra approached Engel and spun him around in her arms. She kissed him.

"What's this! What's going on!"

"You saved me, Engel! Thank you. You saved me!" Sandra said with a big smile.

"You did," echoed Lalaina.

"Oh, by the gods, girls! Just be glad I wasn't stupid enough to fall for your ruse. Why did you do this? Why did you climb the Mount, anyway?"

"I wanted to play on the Mount and enjoy the view, Engel," Cassandra said. "Anyway, I have been telling you about the golden shine from the Mount for many moons. My morning star.

My star of Aphrodite. I told you. It calls me. Ever since my mother brought me here, I had to return."

"We've got to do something, Casey," said Lalaina. "We can't stay on this cliff. Engel's right. It'll be dark soon. And cold. We have to find shelter."

Cassandra nodded. "I'll look around."

She set out alone. No one stopped her. She figured they probably hoped something bad would happen to her. She searched the trails. There was one narrow path, but it had not been made by people. It was naturally steep, angling down a grassy violet knoll, covered on both sides by blue bushes. The trail headed all the way to streams far below. At first Cassandra thought they could go down this way, but it was too steep.

Then, on the other side of the cliff, she caught a sudden shimmering light. Her heart quickened. It was a yellow light. Her star? Had she found it? It was glowing in the distance and, for a moment, she heard singing. A gloriously lovely song that seemed to call her. It was voices, though nothing spoken in any tongue she recognized. And now, after seeing a yellow sun through the clouds, the light reminded her of that. This was the light she had seen for many moons. It was the light that had driven her here in the first place.

She rushed along the trail. It was narrow and a couple of times she feared she would fall from a high precipice. Then there was a flattening along the edge. By the end of the trail, and by nightfall, she found the source of the light. It was a reflective ancient metallic door, partly cracked open, no longer reflecting yellow but white from a bright full moon above.

When she arrived back to tell her friends, Lalaina and Sandra were arguing. Engel was gathering up branches in his arms and stacking them under a tree.

"She probably fell down the mountain," said Lalaina. "Or got attacked. Remember the wolf! I'm so worried."

"Don't talk like that!" said Sandra. "Don't speak like that about our princess. She can take care of herself. I know she's fine."

"She almost killed you, Sandra."

"So, I don't care. I want her back. I'm sure she'll—"

"Here I am," said Cassandra.

"Casey!"

"I found a cave."

Engel looked up, furrowing his bushy eyebrows. He still looked mad.

"It's close to here. The setting sun was shining over metal on the floor by the entrance. Now the moon shines over it. It's the 'star' I've been seeing. It's a metal door. I want to show you guys. It's simply lovely, Engel. The path's a bit windy and steep, but we can make it if we're careful. Only thing is, I'm not sure about Naya and Inghorn. They're much too big to travel the narrow paths and enter through the door."

"We can leave the monokera," said Engel. "They can fly back when they regain their strength tomorrow. Or even return by foot along the trails here. What sort of light is this? What do you mean it's been singing to you?"

"I told you. It sings in the morning. Now it's singing here. But it's not a star, it's a door. It wants me here. I can't explain. I hear it sing to me when it's brightest."

"That doesn't sound good."

"Whatever. It leads to a cave. There's shelter there."

"It's cold," Sandra said rubbing her arms outside her white tunic. "Inghorn and Naya should come with us."

"They can't, Sandra," replied Engel. "Anyway, unlike us, they can weather this night with their hide. And when they have enough strength, they'll go back."

"All right," said Cassandra. "But you said yourself, Engel, we need shelter. Follow me to the golden door."

"Of course, *princess*," Engel snorted. "Anything you say."

THERE WAS an opening by the door. It was small, but with Engel and the three girls pushing, they managed to open it wider.

Cassandra searched her pocket and found one of Henri's special fire rocks. She had three. They were small enough to fit in her hand. She gave them to Engel and Lalaina. Engel shared his with Sandra. When Casey shook her rock the way Henri had shown her, she had to shield her eyes. The glow wasn't from her rock, it was from the walls. The hallway was gilded. Perhaps that also was the source of the brilliant light reflection. Thankfully, dust coated it. Without the film of dust, it probably would have been brighter.

Engel grabbed Cassandra's arm from behind. He shook his head.

"No, this doesn't feel right, Casey." His voice echoed in the long hallway. "This is made by the gods."

"So? It's warm."

"I vaguely recall something about this chamber. It was long ago. One of your ancestors told me of it. This is Hermes' lair. And you being *called* here is surely not good. We should go elsewhere."

"The messenger god? But I have to know. I—"

He shook his head.

"Well, it's warm, Engel. We have each other. Can't we just use it for shelter for the night? We can stay close by the door."

Engel turned toward the outside and folded his arms in thought. She walked further inside, not waiting for his reply.

The hallway became very wide, but it opened into pitch blackness. Here she seemed to have entered a simple cave chamber with earthen walls. Henri's lights were bright enough to light some of the huge chamber, but there was a great deal of darkness further along. She thought her friends weren't following her, but then she heard their footsteps from behind.

"No further, Casey," Engel said. "Just use this as shelter. We shouldn't go any further inside."

Cassandra shrugged. Then she laid her knapsack on the ground and reached into the bag. The bag was the size of two fists, but she reached her entire arm inside. Engel stared in amazement. Casey took out three long blankets the size of her.

"Enchanted," he said with eyes wide.

"Henri's," Cassandra said with a nod. "We have three blankets. Someone's going to have to make do. That will be me."

"You've been around that Magi too much," remarked Engel.

Cassandra shrugged and removed a metal box from her bag. This was Henri's too. She lit the device aflame for a small fire. She placed that in the center of the sleeping blankets. Then she gripped the rocks, dousing them out.

"Just like camping in the forest, but a little darker," Lalaina said with a smile. "And with more echoes."

Then Lalaina cupped her hands around her mouth and yelled, "Echo." Her words echoed.

"Shh!" cried Engel. "Stop playing!" Lalaina frowned and Casey laughed.

"I'll keep the fire going," Casey said. "I'll stay up all night on guard. This is all my fault."

"Yes, it is," Engel remarked, annoyingly. "And yes, you will."

"Anyway, goodnight."

20

AMPHIUMA

Cassandra was Avva Ambrosia's daughter, and her father was a great Kitherian warrior. Not only did she inherit strong Amazon and warrior stock, she inherited their spirit of rebellion and curiosity. Sitting in an open cave, she couldn't help but take out a rock light and walk further along the chamber alone, exploring, as her friends slept. And, anyway, the lovely music was beckoning her.

The further she walked, the more the walls lost their dust and shone golden. That helped light her way along a dusty earthen cave.

Despite the light, she fell, tripped on a couple of steps, and landed a few steps down. Her brown tunic was long, but she wore short travel pants, now torn at her knee from the fall. She touched what she thought was a dirt ground. It wasn't. It was stone with grooves. Shining the rock light around, she also saw stone Doric columns, like the ones in the palace, holding up the earthen walls.

The cave opened to a grand entryway. Here there was enough golden light reflecting off the walls to light up a hallway the size of the throne room in the palace. On the ceiling, there were golden stalactites and gems of red, purple, and green. So glistening the jewels were that her single fire rock lit the entire room. The floor was a shiny white, with the exception of sporadic water pools in holes on the ground. But even the water reflected the bright yellow light in the hall. And the music, the tranquil music, now sounded clearer than ever.

"Incredible," she whispered to herself.

She couldn't wait to get back and tell her friends. She walked the breadth of the grand room. It was silent. Empty. Her sandals tapped and echoed along the hall. The music was there but, oddly, it seemed to come from a darker region at the end of this golden room.

At the end of the chamber was some sort of lookout. She went to the ledge, and then involuntarily lurched back. There was a dark abyss. Then, to her sides, lay dirt walkways. But to her right, the trail over the sheer cliff ended in complete darkness. There was a trail to her left, but it appeared rocky. She shone her rock in that direction and walked only a few steps. She didn't dare pass further. This trail, too, appeared damaged, and the fall could be treacherous.

She had to move carefully back. She looked down again at the empty abyss. Very faintly, she heard water rushing below.

Then she thought of the others.

Are you an idiot, Casey? If they wake up, they're going to think something happened to you again. Go back or you'll be in more trouble with Engel.

More trouble with Engel? No. It's not as if I'm not in plenty of trouble already. There's no way he won't tell mother about Sandra.

But why had she traveled so deep into the cave alone in the first place? That was foolhardy and stupid. Here the music played loudly. It seemed to be raging. Right here at this spot before the chasm. It was so alluring. Why?

She quickly headed back to the golden hall.

To her astonishment, a figure now sat in the center of the large chamber on what looked similar to her mother's throne. She almost passed him without noticing him in the shadows, he was so still.

He was black and red striped, about the height of Engel. He

was crouched downward with long, unnatural hands over his knees as he sat on the golden three-step throne. And he had hideous thin scarlet hair and bright glowing blue eyes. His lips were crimson and curled around two sharp fangs. His teeth and eyes glowed white from the fire stone in her hand.

"Who are you?" she exclaimed, jumping back. "Sorry, I didn't know anyone lived here. Your home is … beautiful."

He laughed. But the laugh sent shivers down Cassandra's neck. It was harsh, inhuman, almost sounding more like a bark.

"What call you? Hmm?" The creature's voice asked, very hoarse.

Cassandra started searching her pockets for her camping knife. It was sharp enough and she knew how to use it.

The creature made its way off the stone throne. He didn't walk, he slithered.

"Step no further!" echoed her voice as she pulled out her knife. The room became black as she nervously covered the fire rock with her left hand. She quickly opened it.

"What call you? What call you?"

The creature stopped about three yards away and crouched on its knees with a big grin. A long thin tongue licked his lips. Cassandra shrank back.

"Name? What call you?"

"Cassandra Ambrosia," Casey replied with incongruous pride. "Princess of Azure Blue."

"Found." The serpent snickered.

The creature approached a little too close. Cassandra was repulsed by his dry, leathery skin and dripping sweat. And he had a foul odor. Sweat covered his black-striped face and torso. He started to sniff her. He began licking his lips.

"Ambrosia? Ambrosia? Taste. I'd like a taste. Permit me?"

"Stay back!" Cassandra brandished her knife. The creature reeled back, feigning fear.

"Stand back!" she yelled again, her voice echoing in the chamber.

The creature came closer, ignoring her. Then, with disgust,

she noticed this creature moved like a snake because he had no legs.

Cassandra started slashing the air between them. Every time, the creature seemed afraid, but it didn't stop its slow advance. Cassandra kept walking back.

He oddly raised a hand and pointed behind her. She cocked her head back. She was standing at the ledge of that great dark precipice. Her heart pounded in her chest. She was trapped with the beast in front of her and the abyss behind.

"Back off!" Cassandra warned, slashing the air again. "I warn you."

"A lick is all. Then go, Ambrosia."

"Back away from her!" cried a voice behind him. It was Engel's voice. He and her friends were behind her. Once again, her caretaker was saving her.

"Not you …" The creature gazed at Engel. "Not you. Here for Ambrosia."

The creature whirled back to Casey. Then hurled his whole body at her.

Cassandra felt air rush her face and the sensation of the ground falling from her as the creature clamored, wet hands along her body, falling with her. It was pitch black. She was falling. It was like falling from Inghorn again, but this time it didn't take as long to hit the ground.

She expected a painful crash and instant death. Instead there was a rush inside her ears and a sudden sensation of icy cold. She was in water. She could even push against a current. But she didn't know where to go and, with only a dim violet glow above, she had difficulty seeing the surface. She pushed up, looking for a way out of the water to breathe, but then the beast grabbed her and dragged her down again.

Somehow, she found the surface. She gasped for air while coughing and spitting out water. But then the snake pulled her in again. She submerged and surfaced once more. The creature slithered by her ear, "Wait! Only taste and bite!" She grabbed him blindly, hitting and kicking him. She heard the snake's fangs chomp near her face. Casey struggled to stay afloat but thankfully she found the monster weighed as much as Engel. She flipped him in the water. But the creature wrapped his body around her again, rolling her. She gained her last bit of courage and, remembering what her uncle had taught her, managed to wrestle the beast. It squirmed and hissed under her weight near the surface. She grabbed its neck and choked him with all her strength as they continued to move with a current. She rose above the surface of the water and took a deep breath just in time, but she didn't let go of the creature's neck. Then they were submerged for a long while, until her body slammed against a rock. The beast gurgled and howled when she surfaced in darkness. She still held his neck. She squeezed it as tightly as she could. Under a strange purple light, she saw his hideous snake eyes close and his tongue come out of his mouth. When he finally stopped struggling under her hands, she let his limp body go. It sank in the water.

She pulled herself onto a sandy shore. Only a dim purple light lit the rushing water and sand. Then she heard Engel's voice desperately crying for her from above. It was so faint, but she could hear him shouting her name. She shouted back but he didn't seem to hear her.

She lay on the ground, exhausted, clutching her arms tightly around her. Only now did she realize how freezing cold the water had been. She shivered. Engel and her friends kept hollering from above. She finally spotted a golden yellow light, but it was so far up above her. She had fallen so far.

Then, still shivering and exhausted, she sat with her head in her arms, shaking on the sandy floor. She shook for a long time. Then … she cried.

SHE CRIED FOREVER. The tears kept coming. But eventually she tired of crying.

She stood up, tall like a princess feigning honor. She became determined to find her way back up to her friends. She wrung out her wet tunic. Then she brushed the mud, sand, and grime, from all the dirt collected along the stream, from her legs. She checked herself for wounds under the strange violet light. There was a gash on her right arm, likely from the monster's bite, but that was all. It was thin, clean, and only bled a little. She tore a piece of cloth off the bottom of her brown tunic and wrapped it around her arm to stop the bleeding. Then she shook from the cold again. She considered looking for wood to make a fire but quickly gave up. There was nothing to stoke a flame, only sand.

Then she did the only thing she could do. She walked into the violet light emanating from a cave.

2 1

CAVERNS

CASSANDRA CRAWLED DOWN MANY NARROW PURPLE PASSAGEWAYS for what seemed like leagues in this underground cavern. The trail always dipped downward, and some of it was nearly as small and narrow as her body. She discovered that the purple glow emanated from huge purple mushrooms that grew on the sides like bushes or lay flat, growing on the earthen ceiling. Soon the mushrooms gave way to large glowing yellow leaves. Some of the hallways seemed to be supported by white columns, though most stone structures were cracked and in pieces.

She slept and walked repeatedly with the desire to simply find her way up and out. But the caves seemed to mock her efforts, forcing her to descend further and further down.

In time, the caves changed into larger chambers. They contained orchards of strange draping green-leafed trees with yellow fruit with red stripes. She was hungry, but she feared tasting it. Hunger got the best of her, and she bit into one. It was delicious. It reminded her of the peaches in the palace garden. It was sweet like a peach, but hard like an apple.

The large cavern gave way to another room. Then another.

Finally, she gained some hope as the trail led upward and even over some stone steps. This opened into a vista her eyes could not believe. A vast valley that seemed to have no walls or ceiling with bright yellow light emanating from above. At first, she thought she was outside the Underworld. Perhaps this was the yellow sun of her father's lands? But as she squinted, she did not see a blue sky, only an earthen brown enclosure far above.

Straining her eyes she could see for over a league in the distance, and she looked out over the valley below. Another orchard of the strange fruits was directly below, and a lovely river flowed, with many streams as tributaries running in both directions. There was another large opening at the far side of the valley, so far away that it looked blurred. Out there she thought she spotted people and settlements.

The yellow "sun" was dim. She had seen the lights dim and brighten, as if mimicking day and night, in the caverns and she guessed it was the same here. If this was true, as it had been bright for a long time, she guessed it was dawn or twilight.

She jumped at the sound of a bird chirping. On a cliff beside her was a large fruit tree—the same fruit she saw everywhere. In the branches was a brown bird with lines of orange and red along its wings. The first sign of life since she walked into this labyrinth.

"Well, hello there," she said with a smile. Then a brown squirrel scurried under some bushes near the other side of the ledge.

She sat for a moment looking out at the view. Then she saw something else: straight down the cliff was an orchard with a waterfall. Her lips were parched having not drunk anything for the longest time. She quickly made her way down the rocky cliff to the orchard. There were enough winding dirt trails to make the descent relatively easy.

Along the stream, under some trees, she cupped her hands and drank. She let the cold water run down her face.

She sat on a rock by the cascading water and glanced back up at the cliff now towering above her. She considered crying again, perhaps from the small bit of joy she felt over such a paltry thing as water, but she thought better. Besides, the sound of running water soothed her. A little. Then she thought of Lalaina, Sandra, and Engel. Would she see them ever again? How about her mother and father? Or Uncle Henri?

"What a fool, Casey!" she said to herself out loud. "Stupid! First poor Sandra! Now ... now you. Why, you don't even know where you are. Why are you so curious? Almost being eaten by a lizard beast! Then nearly drowned! Stupid! Stupid! Stupid!" She hit herself in the arm—the right arm, where her wound was. The pain forced her to fight off tears again.

"Now, don't cry, princess. We mustn't do that. It's not proper. Don't cry." She laughed bitterly, thinking she sounded like her mother. "They will never find me." A single tear ran down her cheek. She looked back up toward the cliff where she had climbed down, barely making out the dark cave, and shook her head. "Never."

2 2

BUSINESS AS USUAL

Queen Avva rushed to Henri's guest house. It was an ancient dwelling sitting on the outskirts of the palace. It was in the gardens but hidden like the castle zoo, surrounded by thick trees. The house was famous. Once it had been Nefertiti's residence. Legend said that when Nefertiti returned to Azure, shunned by her people, she abandoned her nymphs in the palace and lived alone, for a handful of moons, in this house before leaving her homeland entirely for Egypt. So the home stood as a memorial to the nymphs.

Avva had given it to Henri. Not because of its past, but because its architecture was so much closer to the homes of the Hinterlands, his home. And Henri visited Azure Blue often.

It was a hot day. As she winded down a path between blue trees and shrubs, she sweated a little in her thin gray peplos, even this early in the morning.

A lovely cobblestone path led from the side of the castle to Henri's house through a canopy of blue and red trees. Red roses and green bushes, foreign to Azure, lined the path to the entrance—planted at Henri's request. Green grass from Adelain had been planted in the front yard too. And a wooden fence at the entrance led to walls of simple white stone with a thatched roof.

Avva knocked on a wooden door.

"Come," a voice said.

The simple furnishings were similar, Henri had said, to his home in Shadow Forest before he had moved to Castle Cove—the home where he had raised Sol when her husband was a boy. There was a wooden floor, a stone hearth, a soft couch (brought from the palace by Avva), and various wooden tables lying about. And wooden shutters covered the holes that served as windows. There was no glass on these windows.

Henri lay on his side on animal skin, in the den by the foyer, writing on a scroll. This was the way people sat in the far South and outside of Atala. He wore a long brown tunic. His white beard was trimmed and short. And, when he looked up, his wise eyes seemed to sparkle with his smile as she walked in.

Old Henri was now a fixture in the kingdom. Known by all the nymphs as an eccentric but kind old magi, he was extremely popular. Many Amazon liked him and visited him often. Some came for healing, others for magic spells or charms. In fact, Avva wouldn't be surprised if he was expecting another nymph to visit. He was kind, jovial, and friendly to all. But most importantly, like Engel, he was always available to Avva for counseling.

"Your Majesty," he said, getting up from the floor and kneeling.

She ran over and, ignoring all formalities, leaned down and hugged him.

"Oh, how I missed you. How come you didn't tell me of your arrival last night?"

"It was late. I didn't want to disturb you."

Avva could smell eggs. She saw them cooking by the hearth.

"Have you had breakfast?" he asked, gazing at the eggs with her. "I've got plenty left over, although it's not what a queen is accustomed to. But the bread was a gift freshly baked by ladies from your kitchens."

"I'd love your eggs, Henri."

They walked to the kitchen area. The windows, shutters half opened, looked out upon Henri's new garden. Apparently, Henri had tried to make the garden look like home too. He had brought plants and bushes from Gaia and Avva, and he had even painstakingly removed all the purple and blue soil, replacing it with brown.

He brought Avva a metal cup of something warm. She sipped it. It was delicious, with a cinnamon and clove taste.

She sat on a wooden chair and looked out his window. Then she turned to him with a smile. "Henri, I thought you loved my kingdom. Why plant these things? Why visit so often, yet do everything you can to make your house look like home in Shadow Forest or Azerban?"

"My eyes burn after a few days from all the blue." He pulled up another wooden chair and sat down. "I can only take so much of your beauty."

Henri smiled, but he didn't seem like his usual self. Usually he was almost bounding with energy. Today he seemed unhappy—even anxious. That worried Avva.

Then he got up and started sorting through scrolls strewn about the room.

"Make yourself at home, Anna."

He placed a stack of scrolls on a shelf. Then he ran over to the hearth, put some eggs on a metal plate, and handed it to her. But the moment she took it, he busied himself grabbing more parchments from another stack on the floor. She absentmindedly sat at the table playing with her food; then she finally slapped her leg to get his attention.

"Oh, Henri. Tell me."

"What do you want to know?" he asked with a laugh.

"Everything. How's Sol? How is the front? When you look uneasy, it makes me uneasy. Is everything all right?"

"Your husband walks and breathes, my lady."

"I'd think so. If something bad had happened, you would have told me when I first entered."

He nodded and put the scrolls down, though it seemed like

he didn't want to. Then he sighed. "We have some quiet. The king suggested I spend some time back home with you. It's been hard. But the idea of getting away from the violence sat well with me."

"Sol just took back the Sun Kingdom. Why are things not better? Why do I keep getting letters of more trouble?"

"This war may be at a turning point, but if he leaves now, we could lose ground."

"What war?" Avva sighed and shook her head. "What sort of progress? Where is this war going? Solinair has united my father's kingdom. What else do you all want?"

"I think…" he said. He stared at another parchment for a moment. Then he finally sat beside her again. "Well, Anna, you know how dangerous it is. Your husband fights for safety. Let him do it. If he fails, you will have to play a nasty game of strategy like your mother, which you told me many times you don't like doing."

Avva nodded.

"As it is, at least only your husband sees killing. No Amazon fights anymore. Why not be happy with that?"

"Because he's not here."

Henri smiled and nodded. He jumped up and got more eggs. Then he handed her another plate, but she pushed it away.

"I knew your royal tastes were too much for it," he said with a shrug.

"Oh, stop, Henri! You know why I don't care for your eggs right now. Tell me more."

"Then eat. Perhaps the food will … ease your mind."

Avva started eating again. "Fine. Umm. Very good, Henri. Wonderful eggs." Then she put the plate down. "There. Best eggs I've had in ages. Now. Tell me. What's happening? Is it Morteus?"

"Aye. Always. And King Philipp of Kitheria. And the Fox King. They all hide Morteus."

"Crystal Lake?"

"It's ours, Anna. After a short battle, Morteus ran. As always."

"The legendary lake of Harmonia." She thought of that with pride for a moment. But then she saw Henri's look of disdain. "Well, Morteus always runs. Let him. But the Crystal Kingdom is ours, then?"

"Aye. The borders of King Darius are safe."

"Then we are safe. And everything is well. So why is my husband not here?"

Henri nodded as he sipped his brew from his silver mug. "I can't say I disagree, Anne. There's good news. Some peace and quiet. But Anna, man foolishly believes that the threat of violence and the sacrifice of life holds peace. There is a great flaw in this logic. But the problem is, advisors like me don't lead men. It seems the cowards of the world are destroyed by the brave." He shrugged. "Seems true with Morteus and your husband, anyway. All follow the sword."

"Please, don't speak in riddles," she said, shaking her head, "and philosophy." She looked him over. But she softened. The old man, she loved him so, looked so tired and worn. "Please be direct. Why do you look like you haven't been sleeping?"

"Your husband and I had a fight." Henri put his cup down. He ran his hand through his unkempt white hair and shook his head. Then he pointed at her. "You can't change your husband. Neither can I. I tamed a lion. And you married one."

"Please Henri. No more riddles."

"Let the lion hunt."

"That's a really big riddle."

"He's a big man."

"Please," she snapped. "Be direct with me."

He chuckled and shook his head.

He got up and grabbed more of his hot drink from the stove. As he poured it he looked out at the garden with her. Avva finished an egg. He took her plate. Then he motioned for her to rest on the couch in the adjacent room.

The house was small, and all the adjoining rooms were

open to each other. She accepted, not because she cared for comfort, but because she wanted him to get on with his story. Here there were two more wooden chairs. He sat on one beside her. She sat on the couch staring at him. When he looked away from his garden back at her, he laughed, seemingly at her impatience.

"Anna, the Crystal Kingdom is ours. The battle was bloody, but brief. Only maybe two regiments and the royal cavalry were needed. It was a surprise considering that the empire has survived centuries. Not even your father had ever overrun the Mangus kingdom. But my bitterness has more to do with the price."

He paused. The pause was painful.

"Afterward, there was great celebration. People drank, made love, fought with fists, and did all the stupid things men do. We're told through history of the victors, but few speak of the fallen. But the losers, those in the Crystal Kingdom, and even Solinair's enemies from the other empires, survived. Except Morteus's lead generals. They were executed in front of the great lake. The rest were taken. And the castle was burned.

"But the celebration was short lived, Anna. Your husband was determined to find and kill Morteus. He's obsessed with that after what he did to your father."

"As he should be."

"Aye. Sol sent spies, now unimpeded, throughout the Crystal Kingdom searching for the coward. Incredibly, it was discovered that the king had not only fled his castle, he had fled his entire realm. We suspect he's in ancient Caravia: Telaria or even Jedithian. We believe the Caravians protect him there. Somewhere far from our grasp. But some fear he's even run across the sea to Egypt."

Henri paused and looked out a window again.

"And?" she snapped. "And?"

"I'm so happy to be back in your kingdom, Blue."

"Great. Now tell me what happened."

"Do you really want to know? Perhaps you should throw me

off your shores like your ancestors did. I've already tainted your garden, as you said."

Avva didn't say anything.

"Well, the border of the Crystal Kingdom, now our kingdom, is shared in the south with King Philipp's marshlands along Kitheria, and the oldest city in all the lands, which sits between Caravia and Kitheria, Logencia. And the most ancient Caravian mountainous kingdom in Teleria. These are sparsely populated dead lands with few threats. Much of the land is marshlands and cannot be tilled, except the very south of Caravia and a few ports. This is why your father never bothered with the South. But perhaps you remember that your husband was born in Harkist? Well, I was born in Kitheria too, living my childhood in the great harbor city of Arbor Dunn. But you probably don't know King Philipp, eh? And why should you? The Azures are a good week's journey away from those lands. A little further south and you'd sail across the Strait to Egypt."

"I know my geography, Henri. I've been informed of all the kings by Imada."

"Of course. Philipp is a Kitherian king. His tastes involve living in tents. His people are nomads. They have no place to call home."

"Sounds like Sol."

"Indeed." Henri nodded, then he raised a finger. "Ah. You're not far off there. In a strange way, that's why I'm here."

"Go on."

"King Philipp is not a friend. Nor is he a man. He's an animal. Yet Sol needed an ally. Someone who could tell him the inner workings of the southern realms, continue to hunt for Morteus, and help achieve enough of a peace for Sol to return and live with you and Casey in Azure Blue. And, for the first time, someone who could possibly do the killing for us. Perhaps even get Morteus's head on a silver platter, as you once joked with Sol and me. Well, the only way to get this was a sacrifice."

"What sacrifice?"

He nodded but didn't speak. Rather, he seemed to be scowling at the ground.

"Tell me," Avva said impatiently.

"Anna, what would a nomad want? How can you convince a nomadic people to fight for you, to die for you? What could you possibly give them?"

She shrugged.

Henri squinted at Avva and hesitated. Then he took a deep breath, leaned forward, and said, "Did Sol ever tell you about his childhood?"

"Only that you raised him in Shadow Forest. What does that have to do with it?"

"Before all that?"

"He said he was born a prince. That in Harkist, nomadic tribes surrounded his father's castle and killed his mother and father. He witnessed it. They burned his small village when he was younger than Casey."

"Did he tell you what happened before he met me? After he witnessed his mother and father being cut down in front of his eyes. He was maybe six or seven. It took me many moons to find out, but I think you should know. Do you know what happened to any child without a home? Even our resourceful and brave Solinair?"

Avva shook her head.

"Slavery. He was taken into slavery. He was beaten and abused by nobles. Had he not run away from *them* and learned how to live off the land like an animal, he would surely have died."

"What's so shameful about that?"

"His back, Anne. His back."

Sol had never told Avva the source of his scars, but they were terrible. His back was battered and clumped and horribly disfigured. Avva suspected it must have been a scourge, a whip with blades or rocks, to cause such a terrible disfigurement.

They grew silent.

"What's his shame in that?" Avva asked. "It's an achievement to have survived such torture."

"Indeed. Only my son will never respect his origins. Because he hates his true father for not protecting his mother and his brothers and sisters from the surrounding tribes. He told me once that he would die before being a slave again. And he would bring any man down with him if they threatened him and his family. Such a disgrace, in his eyes, would never be livable again."

"What's this to do with your news?" Avva said, shaking her head. "The Far South is nomadic, Henri. I know all this. The tribal kings are brutal. There was no hope for his father to remain safe. It wasn't his father's fault, and Sol shouldn't blame him. But tell me what's going on now."

"Sometimes we don't agree with the decisions of our parents," he said, lifting his brow. He needn't say much more for Avva to understand the hint.

"All this has a great deal to do with what's happening, Anne. Imagine what Darius's sons thought of his adopted son when Sol removed his shirt. Now you can understand Torinth and Ansel's disgust with him. And why they never would have accepted his ruling over anything. Only a man as great as Darius could turn away from such a past. And I knew that when Darius died, Sol would either fight his brothers or wait to die. Sol never told you about his back, did he?"

"I suspected he was a slave."

"But he never told you." Henri nodded. "Sol's family and home were burned. It is why, I believe, he never will be. He can't lose. You witnessed what happened at the Valley of Polis. Sol will fight to the death before accepting such dishonor. None of the other rulers in Atala, except perhaps Torinth, have the courage to do that. Sol does what he needs to do to survive. And because of that, I sided with him not only out of love, but because I, and so many others, knew he would be the final Sun King in this war."

"But what does all this have to do with now?"

"Success and power can change us. He made a final sacrifice, to give us peace, that I will never stand for. It is completely anti-thetical to what he was and what we fought for."

"What? What is it. Tell me, Henri."

"Slaves. Sol is selling slaves, Anna. People. He's selling people. And selling people is something I'll never stand for. People who work for you, who cook and clean for you, who will do what you ask them to do at the price of their life. Now Sol is doing this. I never agreed with your father over it, and I shall never be a part of it with Sol."

"Slaves?" Anna's eyes opened wide. "Henri, you know what my people think of slaves! We don't allow slavery in Azure. Freedom for all has been instilled deeply in all of us since Queen Nefertiti."

Henri turned from her. Somehow, this made him get up and grab more parchments from his stack and sort them more furiously than ever.

"Henri, our people live for freedom and the freedom of others!" Avva stood up. "My … my people even died for men in the name of freedom." She was beside herself. "Because when I helped Sol in battle, Henri, it wasn't only out of love, it was out of trust in his values. Sol is selling slaves? If I had ever thought he believed in slavery …" She walked up to Henri and knocked a scroll from his hand, "I'd never have sided with him! What's the matter, Henri? Do you hear me? I would never have been his queen if he had believed in that! Do you understand?"

"I don't believe you," Henri said, shaking his head. "I don't. Bear witness to the palace you live in. How do you think it was constructed by Nefertiti's mother for you Amazon?"

"Henri!" she said. "Henri, by the gods, explain." He was completely ignoring her. He just bent down and started picking up the parchments. She walked over and pushed it out of his hands. "What did my husband get in return for this sin? Tell me!"

"A fighting force. Strong enough to keep order, using King Philipp. A loyal nation that will do whatever you or he requests of them. Philipp, a puppet that our king can control."

"Who were the slaves?"

"Does it matter, Anna?"

"Who, Henri!"

"The conquered people of King Morteus's realm. Anyone siding with the Mangus line in the Crystal Kingdom. A twisted piece of justice, aye?"

"I thought you told me he treated them fairly."

"No, I said we spared them. King Morteus murdered your father. So Morteus's royal family, his trusted guards, and the workforce within his palace were enslaved by Sol. Does that sound better?"

Avva sat back down on the couch. She drank the remnants of her drink from her cup. "I love him, but I don't agree with this."

"I love him too." Henri got up and poured himself more of his warm, steamy drink. "The world is hard. But I'm afraid that's not all."

"I'm not sure I want to hear any more," she said, cocking her head back.

"Oh, good, Anna. Now we have an understanding. Forget the whole thing."

"Tell me."

"Once you taste the fruit, you will take in its pulp and swallow its seeds. But perhaps you've eaten myrle berries already, when you flew over the Strait."

She wasn't looking at him. She walked to another nearby open shutter. This "window" looked out at her beautiful kingdom. She gazed at the blue-green fields surrounding her palace between the windowless shutters. The sparse purple-blue trees and the forest by the shore. And, in the greater distance, beautiful Mount Ambitus towered like a wall to the west.

"Tell me," she said again, staring outside. She looked back and Henri returned to his chair. He gestured for her to sit back down.

"A week before I left," Henri continued, after a deep breath, "we met with the nomads of King Philipp. There was a large celebration. A great bull was sacrificed, beheaded, and eaten raw.

I watched barbaric rituals. Things we think of as unclean and uncivilized—debauchery, acts witnessed only in the Underworld, I'd thought. After a long night of barbarism, I sat leaning on my elbow, drunk, with Sol and Milo watching with amazement as the evil one, our archenemy Hades himself, arrived with a small group of Eruboi to join the festivities. We were quite drunk, Anna. But inebriated or not, we were disgusted at the sight of the Dark Lord. You may recall that Hades was once Ansel's greatest advisor. And I'm sure you remember Sol's defense of your throne.

"Sol and Milo jumped up with their short swords, but quickly sheathed them as King Philipp and Hades embraced one another. I sat there with my eyes wide open in shock. Here was our number one enemy, of all our enemies, Hades, god of the Underworld, breaking bread with us. I left. I headed back to my tent.

"Well, late that evening, Anna, as I left my tent to water, the Dark Lord approached me in the shadows. He wore all black, reminding me of a burial shroud. He's a fearsome shadow. *'It is a twist of a tale that now I join your son, Henri Untair,'* he said. *'Is this because of your clever trickery? Know that such trickery does nothing to please my brother and sister.'* I didn't answer, standing silent. Honestly, I was terrified. Then he smiled his sardonic grin, put a hand on my shoulder, and replied, *'Be comforted. I want nothing more than any god. Libations. Sacrifice. We shall have our sacrifice, Henri. One trick for another.'"*

"And that was all. He was telling me something terrible. What it was, I didn't know."

"And Sol?" Avva asked.

"Sol and Milo enjoyed the party the rest of the night. The next morning your husband, still drunk, had a very nasty fallout with me. You see, I agreed with Nefertiti regarding slavery. Then..." He rubbed his eyes and took a deep breath. "I mentioned his back. You know, I might have been gifted with wisdom, but I can act like a complete idiot. You know I love him more than anyone. He is ... my son. But, like you, he has a terrible temper. My disagreement over the price was one thing, my comparing it to his own shame was quite another. Needless to say, it is very possible he won't ever speak to me again."

"Why would the Dark Lord show himself?"

Henri seemed amused by Avva's ignoring his last comment. He shrugged. "I don't know. He enjoys those sorts of parties. My argument with Sol only opened up his own feelings. But he wanted nothing of me afterward. And … well, who knows? Perhaps he's right about the whole thing? Perhaps I'm being unfair. I argued with Darius far more than I ever did with Sol. I'm an advisor, not a king. But I tell you, Anne, I'm getting too old. I can only take so much mud and filth before I need to return to your clouds along your shores. I hope to live the rest of my days here."

"Henri," Avva said, leaning forward and taking his hand, "I'm sure Sol will come around. I'm sure you both will forgive one another."

"It's not just us. It's the cost. I tell you, I will never agree with this arrangement. Whether we make up or not."

"So it isn't quiet, Henri? You lied to me."

"I didn't want to disturb your peace."

"Perhaps he needs me. I'll speak with him. I'll tell him to break off all ties with King Philipp and end this treaty."

"He won't do it." Henri shook his head.

"Then I'll remind him of his back."

"You don't understand," Henri said, chuckling. Then he smiled sadly. "If we do not work with slaves, the war will drag on. He won't ever come back home. Not for you or for Casey. True, his pride nearly caused a row with me, but the real fight was over the treaty. He won't yield. He'll never break it, not over pride, but because it would mean not seeing his family and your lands again. Because, you see, my lovely nymph, he does not live an immortal life. He doesn't have time to continue the fight."

Avva furrowed her brow. But then she nodded in understanding.

"Well, it's not so bad, is it, Henri?"

"What do you mean?"

"Well, he enslaved Morteus's people. Is that so bad? I hear slavery is commonplace in the—"

Henri laughed, shook his head, and turned back to the window. "Perhaps the king and queen of the Sun Kingdom won't fight at all."

"What do you mean by that!"

"Perhaps this will help, particularly for an Amazon. Many of the slaves were women. The women were sold for sex, Anna. And children, very young—babes really—were sold for household labor, likely to be whipped like your husband." He shook his head and chuckled bitterly. "They didn't need the slaves to help us fight. They needed them as spoils of war."

He jumped up and walked back to the kitchen, angrier than ever. Then he went about cleaning the table with his towel. He seemed to be attacking things. He threw a mug in a pot, metal clanging against metal. Then he washed the pot with a wet towel. He seemed to be scrubbing so hard that the metal would rub off. He threw the pot on the ground.

"I think we should meet later, Your Majesty," Henry said, stopping and looking down. "Seems I'm still upset."

"Tell me about this party. Did Sol enjoy the women?"

Henri turned in surprise. He stared at her for a moment and then tried to smile. "Ah, how could he after looking in your eyes, Blue? His mind's not well, but his love for you is eternal. All he does is speak of you."

"Then, Henri, all is well."

A knock came at the door. Then a bang.

Henri ran over and opened the wooden peephole. He opened the door. It was Cambria in full hoplite scarlet armor. She even wore her helm. And when Avva saw her expression, she jumped.

"What is it, Cambria?" asked Avva.

"My queen," Cambria fell on a knee. "I'm afraid it's the princess ... your ... Casey's gone."

"Where's the brat gone to now?"

"They have been missing since last night. With Engel, I figured they were all right, but then—"

"She told me she was at your house?"

"No."

"Is Lalaina okay?"

"Yes, my lord. Lalaina's home now."

That made Avva feel terrible. Why would Casey be the only one missing after going with Lalaina? Cambria nodded as if reading her thoughts and said, "At dawn, Naya and Inghorn were spotted from the towers walking alone in the fields before the palace. It was so queer, I immediately dispatched monokera and flew from the tower stables. I didn't notify you yet as … well, they've gone missing before. I found a green light flashing by the Mount. Engel was holding up a mirror outside Hermes' cave to help us locate them. When we got there, he told me there had been a struggle. I didn't think anyone had been in there in over a century. And now …" She paused, looking down at the ground. "We have yet to find her."

"You'll find her." Avva shook her head and sighed. Then she turned to Henri. "This happens all the time." But Henri's look of worry made Avva nervous.

"No, Avva." Cambria shook her head. "No. I'm sorry, this time we won't. Engel told me where she is. There was a struggle with an Amphiuma. He saw the serpent. When he tried to fight him off her, the creature grabbed Casey and threw her down into the abyss."

"Where's Engel now?" Henri asked.

"Sandra's in such a terrible state," Cambria continued to Avva. "She fell on Naya from high up on the Mount before all this happened. I've had her escorted home." Then she turned to Henri. "But Engel—"

Engel barged into the room. Then he fell to the ground before Henri and Avva shaking. "My queen," Engel said, sobbing. "My queen."

"*Where's Casey!*" shouted Avva.

"Gone. She's fallen. No, not fallen. She was grabbed. It was a trick. A creature was expecting her. She wanted to go there for many moons. She had told me that a morning star sang to her. I … I thought she was playing. When we stayed the night for shelter, an Amphiuma grabbed her and dragged her down the hole. But we heard her voice. It was faint, but she's made it down to the bottom alive."

"Where's this hole!" cried Avva. "Take me now."

"It's at the entrance to Hermes' cave. It's in Mount Ambitus."

"Take me!"

But Engel refused to rise. He just shook his head. "I've failed you. First you and now your daughter. I've failed in protecting all of you. Every one of you!"

"Take us to this chasm, Engel," said Henri with a remarkably calm tone, gently touching his shoulder. "Please."

2 3

MANGORNIA

Cassandra awoke to laughter. It jarred her awake from a deep sleep. The view around her was unaltered, unfortunately, when she opened her eyes. She still lay in the cursed underground valley, but the yellow light above was a little brighter. Under the earthen brown canopy, the effect was like a bizarre afternoon with sunshine radiating from everywhere.

She heard voices. She searched around her and found the source through the branches of a bush under a fruit tree. She could not make out the words, but she was certain they were distinct voices. She carefully rose to her knees. The talking stopped. She slowly made her way back to her waterfall to drink. After she'd had her fill, she listened again. Voices. Even laughter again. But it was remote, beyond the trees. These orchards consisted of the same yellow and green-leafed trees she had seen through the caves, but they now surrounded her. Then she saw movement through some branches. Some sort of animal standing upright … no people … three people were carrying baskets.

Cassandra quietly moved closer. Crouching behind some green shrubs, she got a good look at them through the leaves. They were small. Plump. All little with blue skin and beards. Two wore brown leather hats. All wore the same dull gray tunics. And they had pointier ears than she did. They looked like cave dwarfs, the famed creatures Engel had told her about in fairy tales since she was a little child. They didn't appear threatening. They were even laughing and joking with one another.

Cassandra checked her belt. She still carried her camping dagger. This was enough to give her the confidence she needed. She came out.

"Hello."

"Who are you?" asked one, jumping back. The tone of the question was more of a demand. The man in the center glared at her and looked down at her knife. He was old with thin white hair. The others' hair was brown. He signaled for them to put their baskets down.

"My name is Cassandra. I'm a princess. Who are you? You look like children." She laughed. But judging from their expressions, that was the wrong thing to say.

"Children?" said one. But the eldest man, the one in the center, put up his hand. He squinted and seemed to examine Cassandra. Then the other dwarf came over and touched her arm near her wound.

"Ow!" she said, backing up.

"You look more like a child than we do," said the old man, gently touching her hand. "And you're hurt?"

His hair might have been thin, but his beard, though white, was thick and bushy. He had gray eyebrows. His features were striking with his deep blue skin. Particularly his eyes, which were a bright blue like hers.

"It's nothing," she replied, pulling her arm back. But it still bled a little.

"Your palms are blue. And there's a faint shade along your ears. You're a nymph."

She nodded.

"Young girl, you're far from Napea. What business does a young nymph have in Mangornia?"

"I fell."

One of the companions laughed.

"I got lost with some friends." Then Casey lost all her feigned courage and fell apart. "Now I want to go home. Can you help me? I don't know the way. I don't know what to do. Can you help me get back?" She wiped her teary eyes on her sleeve, but that made her eyes burn from dust. She turned from them and patted her eyes to remove the dirt. Her clothes were so filthy from all the cave travel.

"This is Enerita and Keif," said the elder gently. "These are my friends. I am Intar. We have no king or queen or princesses here, but we live and breathe. Far better than many Outworlders." He turned to one of his friends. "Get some bread and meat from your pack, Keif. This *princess* looks hungry."

"Yes, Intar."

Intar touched her wound as his friend had, gently, with one stubby finger. "This is a bad wound. It's red and festering. I'm also a healer. That arm needs tending. How'd you get like this? It looks like a bite."

"It is a bite," Casey said. "It was the animal that took me down. A red and black striped thing."

"Probably an Amphiuma, Intar," said Enerita.

Intar nodded. Then he said, "A nymph, eh? Do you know Nephrea?"

Casey furrowed her brow and shook her head.

"Young girl, it's been a long, long time since we assisted nymphs," Intar said. "But your people are as welcome as my brothers. You'll make quite a stir in the village. Come. I'll tend to that arm at my home, and then we will try to find you a way back. If there is a way. Don't be afraid. Azure nymphs are our greatest friends."

"The witches," said the man named Keif. "She might try the witches."

"Maybe." Intar nodded. "I was thinking that."

"The shrine is best," said Enerita. "You should take her to the shrine. If she's who she says she is, it's hers anyway."

"The wound first," Intar said, shaking his head. Then he offered a large jovial smile, but Cassandra didn't smile. She looked down at her shaking hands. She was so tired. Afraid. But this small man, whoever he was, seemed kind.

Enerita walked up to the princess and offered her his bag. She unfastened a rope and looked inside. There was dried meat and stale bread. Cassandra eagerly grabbed the jerky and relished every bite. Then she bit into the hard bread. She hadn't realized how hungry she was. The fruit had not been enough.

"Thank you," she said with her mouth full. "Thank you so much, sirs."

"You're welcome, princess," Intar said with a smile. "There is a man who might help you. And if not him, three women. Come."

The dwarfs gathered their baskets. Then they walked with her further down into the valley, through the orchard, to streams and rivers surrounded by tents.

Cassandra spotted hundreds of these little men further down the valley. The area was so vast that she hadn't noticed how many of them there were when she first entered. Many walked along trails, strangely dug into a shelf on the earthen walls. Then she recognized red curtains and saw some dwarfs walking in and out of them as if they were doors. And she saw boys and girls, even tinier then the dwarfs, running by the tents laughing. The boys and girls wore simple gray leather cloths around their waists. Their chests were even bluer than the older people.

When they crossed a long bridge, these dwarfs seemed to go mad upon seeing her. Everyone stopped what they were doing and rushed her. Intar and his friends had to walk in front, guarding her from being trampled.

"Get back!" Intar said. "Stay back and leave her alone."

Cassandra was so confused. So many were clamoring to touch her. And they all smiled like Intar.

Then came a very old man with a white beard. She had spotted him earlier, by the bridge, hoeing fields behind a wooden fence. As they had walked over the bridge, he had hollered to someone and then moved as fast as he could. As this old, wrinkled blue-skinned man walked through the crowd, the crowd made way.

"Nephree?" he asked in wonder, approaching her.

Cassandra shook her head.

"She sure looks like her," Intar said. "Yes, she does. An incredible resemblance." The eldest man shook his head, but he still gazed at her, as if inspecting her. "She says she's an Ambrosia princess, Pangrin. She's family, if what she says is true."

"She's hurt," Pangrin said, examining her arm. "Tend to this, Intar."

"Yes, Pangrin." Intar bowed his head.

"What brings you here, young girl?" Pangrin asked.

"She says—"

"I'm asking her, Keif."

"I ..." Pangrin stared at Casey so intensely that it made her nervous. "I ..." Then she remembered them laughing at her when she said she fell. "I lost my way. I am Princess Cassandra Ambrosia of Azure Blue. I am Napean."

At the word Ambrosia, many of the dwarfs cheered. Some, oddly, fell to their knees.

"Can you help me get home?" Cassandra asked, looking down at them. So many surrounded her now. "Please. Can any of you help me? I just want to return to Azure."

"So young," Pangrin said to Intar. Intar nodded. "But this is terrible." Then Pangrin sighed. "Do you know where you are, child?"

Cassandra shook her head.

"This is Mangornia," Pangrin said. "This is the land of the Mandrigel. Once we lived above with your people in Napea. And I'm old enough to have known the dark heart of your founding queen. I warred with her. But I also learned of the kind bright light of her daughter, Queen Nephree. And wise enough to have learned the difference. Looking upon you, Cassandra, I ask you: Are you Harmonia the butcher or Nephree our savior?" Then Pangrin smiled, looking at his people surrounding her. "It appears my people believe you are the latter."

Cassandra now recognized those names from Engel's schooling. She reasoned that when they spoke of "Nephree" they were referring to Queen Nefertiti, the second queen of Azure Blue and the great pharaoh of Egypt.

"I am an Ambrosia, sir. Who I'm like, I'm unsure."

Pangrin smiled at that. He nodded. "Perhaps you're too young to know." He turned again to Intar. "But this is so terrible. This is no place for a child. We must get her home."

Those words gave her hope. And she was sure that this old man, who seemed like their leader, would find a way. If there was a way.

"We thought of the witches," Intar said. "Could the Stygian Witches help?"

"They might. It seems a bit more than a coincidence for an Ambrosia to be wandering the Underworld, though, don't you think?" He lost his smile. "Not a good omen, Intar. Tend to her wound. Then, when rested and fed, bring her to the witches. But not yet. She looks exhausted." Then Pangrin turned to the crowds and suddenly raised his voice. "Enough! Everyone back to your business. You've seen the nymph. Bid her a fond farewell and leave her be."

A few shouted and raised fists to her before leaving. Many cheered. Then, slowly, they dispersed.

"You have many friends here, Cassandra," Pangrin said. "Go with Intar. He'll make you well. You may stay as long as you like. Like Azure Blue, this valley is your home. It is the home of all nymphs since the great Nephratee Ambrosia's sacrifice."

"Come, Casey," Intar said.

"I just want to go home," Cassandra said to Pangrin with a nod.

Pangrin became very serious. "I don't know why you're here." He sighed deeply and patted her hip. "I'll do all I can to help you."

"Thank you."

LIKE IN THE tunnels Cassandra had traveled, the yellow light of
the fake sun rose and fell twice. Two "days" passed, if you'd call
them days. Then when the yellow light on the dome far above
her dimmed for the third time—probably nightfall—Intar took
her to a special hovel, larger and more distinct than the rest of
the dwarf homes. It was far from the others' dwellings along the
cliff walls.

Intar did some strange things at the entrance. He left food
and wine by a red-curtained entryway. He told Cassandra that
they were offerings to her ancestor.

As he stood by the curtain, Cassandra stared at a mural
painted on stone at the center of the entryway to this cave. It was
prominent with fading black paint splashed across the rocky wall.
It appeared to be some sort of emblem. It was in the form of a
large black bird with colorful rainbow wings. Cassandra recognized it. It was her people's standard, a phoenix. She had seen it
on the armor of the guards back home. But why was it *here*?

"Come," cackled an old voice from inside. "Come inside,
Intar."

Intar lifted the red curtain, and the princess walked into a
large empty stone hallway. In the center water ran on the
ground, leading to a marble fountain lit by surrounding candles.
On a wall hung colorful rugs in random designs. It was surprisingly vibrant in the darkness, perhaps because all these colored
tapestries lay in such a drab gray-brown hovel. But the room was
dark. The only light shone from under the curtain of the front
door and these candles. There were three stone chairs by the
central fountain.

Intar signaled for Cassandra to kneel beside him facing the
chairs and fountain. Then he lit more candles.

"What is this place?" she whispered.

"A shrine," Intar said quietly. "A shrine for your ancestor, the
great Queen Nephratee. Now also a shrine of the Graeae."

Intar hobbled up and grabbed a silvery metal stick and metal shield hanging from a rope from the earthen roof. He struck it. Then he returned to kneel beside her, waiting some more.

"What's this about, Intar?" she whispered. She didn't know if she was supposed to whisper, but it seemed like the right thing to do.

"The Graeae can help you," he said quietly. "I believe they are the only ones who can."

"Why?"

"They have the sight. They'll know why you are here."

"I just fell."

"No, Cassandra. No one just falls into the Underworld."

"That's true," she whispered in the darkness. "I was attacked, I suppose. A light on Mount Ambitus beckoned me. It sang to me and drew me there. I suppose it could have been a trap."

"How is the arm?" Intar asked with a nod.

"Better. Thanks to you. You've been so kind."

"I owe your family much more."

"What did Nefertiti do that was so great?"

He didn't have time to answer. Three human women, crouching and leaning on staffs, slowly entered the hall from a very dark corner. Cassandra hadn't noticed the corner before, but it seemed there was another dark room inside the chamber and, perhaps, more rooms deeper inside. They were old, very old, even older than the elders back home. Their pale faces were wrinkled like prunes. They wore drab, dusty gray robes. Their white hair was curly and unkempt, running down their shoulders.

Intar bowed to the women and then motioned to Cassandra to do the same. They raised their heads as if to sniff the air in Cassandra's direction, but their eyes wandered. Then something flickered, reflected in their eyes, and Cassandra lurched back. Their eyes shone pearly white.

The women sat in the three stone chairs under flickering candlelight. Intar signaled to Casey to remain on her knees facing the Graeae.

"What did you bring? Hmm?" said the one who sat closest to

them. "Hmm? Intar? The whole village is excited, but we don't care. We're hungry. What offering do you have?"

"It's by the door."

"Troubled you too much to walk it inside?"

"It's not for you, but you'll eat it anyway."

"Hmm. Great way to start begging for counsel. Tell us. What's the little ewe's name?"

"What's the girl's name?" another repeated, her eyes roaming about the room.

"What's her name?"

"Allow me to introduce Cassandra," said Intar. "*Princess* Cassandra Ambrosia, of the royal Azure family."

The three women nodded. Then they gave wide, creepy smiles and aped a bow.

"You were sent to bring fruit from the Endlands, Intar," said the one sitting closest to Intar and Cassandra. "Did you do that? Hmm? We need more than Nephratee's offering, you stupid little monkey. You starve us. You know we don't care for the outside. You've been late and we're hungry."

"He brought an ewe instead," said another old woman. They burst out laughing. "Fresh mutton from the Isle of Napea!" And they laughed harder.

"Be kind, Enyo," said the one closest to them. "Be kind. She's young. We mustn't frighten her." Then she leaned forward, and her pearly white eyes seemed to run up and down Cassandra. "We won't eat you." Casey's skin crawled even more when she said that.

"Why are you here, child? Are you an idiot?"

"It was an accident. I ... I fell."

All three burst out cackling again. Cassandra had forgotten their reaction the last time she said it. She decided she wouldn't say it ever again.

"We came for your help," snapped Intar. "If you—"

"Why don't you ladies tell me *your* names," Cassandra said, throwing her hair back and sitting up straighter on her knees. "Now you know mine."

"Impetuous and impious. Impetuous and impious. An Ambrosia, indeed. I am Pemphredo, this is Enyo, and this is Deino. We've presided over this world longer than anyone. We are so old we remember living in the stars. We have lived so long that we remember when the queen of the Underworld was younger than you. We are the Graeae."

"They're the gray witches," added Intar.

They didn't look like people who could help her. But they did look like witches. Indeed, they were ugly and they smelled putrid like rotting meat.

"Tell us what happened, child. You fell? How did you fall? Are you blind too?"

And that sent the witches rolling into uncontrollable laughter again. But then Pemphedro raised a hand. They quieted. They couldn't see but, somehow, they followed her command.

"I was wandering about a cave," Cassandra said, "when I came upon a bright hallway. It was a brilliant gold hallway."

"Hermes' lair."

"I walked around the golden hall. Then I realized I was being watched."

"The messenger god once guarded the entrance to the Underworld. It was abandoned after the grain goddess destroyed the pyramid. What sort of creature watched you?"

"A snake or a snake-like man."

"An Amphiuma, we think," Intar said.

"Shut up, Intar," Pemphedro said. "No one cares what you think. If your thoughts mattered, you wouldn't have summoned us. Particularly, you wouldn't have neglected to bring us a meal."

And the lead witch leaned over again, waiting for Cassandra to continue.

"He attacked me," Cassandra said with a nod. "He grabbed me at the entrance and dragged me down. I fell far below, into a pool of water. Then I walked through purple—"

"The Plum Caves," Pemphedro said with a nod, raising her skeletal finger. "You took the Outworld path."

"Of course, the Amphiuma's home," said Enyo. "The beast could withstand the fall."

"But how did the girl survive, hmm?"

"He must want her in one piece."

"For now?"

"Yes. For now."

"Honor shall destroy her."

"The young grain goddess said that. Yes, she did. When she was younger than the ewe."

"And then the goddess shall cause the destruction of the world."

"She said that too. Yes, she did. She will do it."

"We should have the nymph for dinner."

"Shut up, Enyo. Don't scare the poor girl."

"I kind of like her."

"She's warm. Yes. It's been so long since we've felt an Amazon."

"For later, perhaps."

All three laughed again.

"Must you ladies amuse yourselves!" cried Intar. "I gave you an offering. Now no riddles. Tell us how she can leave."

"You don't know," Pemphedro snapped at Intar. "It doesn't matter how. But you don't know. What matters is why. Sometimes knowing why you're trapped is more helpful than how."

"Why?" Intar asked.

"Shut it, Intar!" Pemphedro snapped. "Offerings indeed. We're starving and you give us ceremonial leftovers."

"Ceremonial scraps," echoed another.

"Tell me what we ask or I'll never give you a thing again," Intar said.

Pemphedro flashed a sly grin at Cassandra and pointed her skeletal finger at her again. "Oh, pretty, pretty, pretty girl, there's no riddle. I speak common sense to a Napean."

"You probably noticed," said Enyo with a wicked chuckle, "that your path led one way. The Outworld path goes only one direction, and now the way back is sealed."

"Is there another way then?" Intar asked.

Pemphedro nodded and appeared deep in thought. She stood up, hunched over, walked closer, and reached out to touch Cassandra's face. Cassandra lurched back.

"Let me touch you."

Intar nodded, reassuring her.

The old woman touched Cassandra's face, slowly groping along her cheek. Cassandra withstood it only out of hope that Pemphedro could tell her how to leave this forsaken place. But her bony fingers disgusted her. Then the witch reached into her pocket. She brought out what appeared to be a human eyeball. Cassandra shrank back as the witch stuck it in front of one of her white eyes. She seemed to use it to scrutinize Cassandra.

"Incredible. A little Azure child. She even looks like Nephratee."

"Let me see!" yelled Deino. "Give me the eye!"

"No, let me!" added Enyo.

"Perhaps a taste?" said Enyo, standing up with a cackle.

Intar stepped in front of Cassandra and pulled out his dagger. Pemphedro laughed. "Back off," Intar said, brandishing his weapon. "We gave you libations. If you can't give us information, we'll go. For good, I swear it!"

But Pemphedro handed the eyeball to the witch beside her. Thankfully, this witch didn't get up and touch Cassandra's face. But they each took a turn with the eyeball, gazing at her.

"I need to go home," Cassandra repeated, shaking her head with a long sigh and looking at the dirt ground. "Can it be done?"

Deino squinted at Cassandra with the eyeball and then shook her head and said, "We won't eat you, little girl."

"Princess, once the Underworld was bountiful," Pemphedro said. "The dwarfs slaved under our god. A glorious time. Hades needed workers to mine gold and then trade for the riches above. And the fire fields cooled the Underworld. It was livable before the young grain goddess destroyed the pyramid. And then Hades betrayed us."

"He betrayed us," said Enyo.

"Betrayed," added Deino, nodding.

"Yes, yes." Pemphedro stared at Cassandra again. "Your great ancestor, Nephratee Ambrosia, took away the fires. She freed your Mandrigel friends after destroying Ambitus Pyramid —after taking away *our* freedom."

"She freed you three, too," objected Intar.

"More like chained us," Enyo said, shaking her head.

"Can you help her or not?" asked Intar.

"Can you feed us or not?"

"She can't return on the Outworld path, so you say?" Intar replied. "What of Avernus?"

"You see, child, Nephratee was a queen and a fierce warrior," Pemphedro said to Cassandra, ignoring Intar. "Why, she even battled Cerberus, a three-headed dog beast who guarded the entrance. And later, with the Mandrigel, she battled Eruboi. She gave Intar and his people a will to fight. She told them that freedom was more important than immortality. She told them the meaning of life can be found in the risk of losing it. And the Mandrigel loved all that nonsense. As the centuries passed, people called her the fire queen. She was represented by her phoenix, the immortal firebird, that same bird you see on the entrance to our shrine. Because she single-handedly mounted a rebellion against Hades and freed all the Mandrigel."

"Is that why you are helping me?" Casey asked Intar.

"I help you because you're a young lost girl," he said, shaking his head.

"The toadstool helps you because he likes you, child," Pemphedro said, shaking her head. "I needn't be a seer to know that."

"Tell us how to get her back home," said Intar. "Not for me, for the little girl."

"He doesn't know how his favorite heroine, Nephratee, left," Pemphedro said. "Now he doesn't know why another nymph appeared. You don't know anything, Intar. That is why when

Nephratee left the village, you stayed back—letting all of your friends who tried to help Nephrea down the Mount die."

Intar's eyes narrowed and his face turned violet. He squeezed his fists tightly, shook his head, and jumped up in fury. "Enough! I swear it, tell me now. The Outworld path was blocked after the quake. We know that. What of Avernus? Nephrea didn't go through Elysium that way either, right?"

"Because she would have ended up in Etruria if she had done that, you idiot," answered Pemphedro. "And then, after she damaged the pyramid, there's no way Poseidon would have granted her passage by sea to Azure Blue."

"And she was blocked by the gods, right?"

"Stories," Pemphedro said, shaking her head. "Myths. Why would Zeus block Nefertiti in Elysium? Zeus would have loved banishing her to Etruria. No, instead Hades killed your little friends, throwing them down a crumbling pyramid."

"What of Lerna?" he snapped. "Or the cave in Tenarus?"

"Myths. Stories."

"So how did she end up traveling home?"

"Let me touch your face again, child," Pemphedro said. Cassandra knelt again while the others giggled. "Let me see and perhaps I can help."

"No," she said, shaking her head.

"Leave her alone," said Intar with a sigh.

"Let me touch you, child. Then I will prophesy. Let me touch your face and I will tell you if you leave, or if you are destined to stay."

Cassandra turned to Intar. Even in Intar's anger, he quickly nodded.

Pemphedro reached over again and felt the contours of her face.

"What do you see, sister?" asked Enyo, leaning forward. "What do you see?"

"Hmm? What is it?" asked Deino.

"I see," Pemphedro said, shaking her head. And then the strangest thing, tears fell from Pemphedro's white eyes. Casey felt the sadness as if it were her own. "Poor child. You poor child. Poor girl. Afraid. Frightened."

"Tell me, please," Cassandra said, choked up. "Please help me." She felt Intar put a hand on her shoulder.

"You shall be free," Pemphedro said with a nod and a smile. She took a deep breath and threw her head back almost violently. "In time. I see ..."

Freedom comes by sacrifice of one you love.

All the candles went out. It became dark and the only light shone through a crack under the curtain by the front entrance.

Cassandra cried uncontrollably, but she didn't know why. Nothing had changed. But somehow, when the witch had prophesied, her predicament had come back to her. And then, the strangest thing was that the evil witches who had been laughing were crying now too.

In the wind, she heard the words of prophecy again:

Freedom comes by sacrifice of one you love.

The candles lit. She heard the sound of the fountain. And she found herself still on her knees near Intar in the same spot as before.

The witches were silent, their eyes wandering about the room as if they had turned disoriented; as if the effort of prophecy had drained their power. Then Pemphedro turned in their direction, looking somber.

"Queen Nefertiti," she said very sternly, "left the Underworld with the help of her daughter, Persephone. Seek her. Seek Kore. Go to Tartarus. Ask for an audience with the king and queen. Only by konabera rising through the flume of Thyra will you leave. It is the only entrance to Mount Olympus and the only way home. That is how Nephratee returned home down the Mount."

"The flume of Thyra?" Intar said, jumping up. "You can't be serious? This is madness. An audience with Persephone and Hades?"

Intar's anger seemed to wake Pemphedro up, and she gave that infernal smug grin again. "There's no other way, dwarf."

"What's the flume of Thyra?" asked Cassandra.

"It's what the Dark Lord uses to ascend to Olympus in his flying chariot."

"Yes," Pemphedro said with a nod. "But rejoice, child. I foresee that you shall leave. But be warned. The course of time can change. Prophecy is not always certain. Go to Tartarus and petition Lord Hades and Persephone. But, most importantly, I advise you to find out why you are here. Then after your sacrifice, you may leave."

"A sacrifice of one you love." Enyo raised a finger and nodded with a stupid smile.

"How does this help?" asked Intar. "Damn you, witches! We can't petition the Dark Lord for his chariot and fly up the flume. He'll kill her, especially being Nephree's descendant."

"There are stairs," said Pemphedro. "You needn't only fly by chariot. The craterous flume is the only way I foresee. Perhaps Persephone can help. Perhaps Cassandra was sent here to finally get the goddess home? I don't know. I know that the young grain goddess never wanted to be left down here either."

"Can we get around Hades?" Intar asked. "Is there a way to evade him?"

"Why ask that, stupid? The flume lies in the center of his kingdom."

"Then it's impossible. Hades will never help her."

Pemphedro turned away from his gaze and shrugged. The fact that the blind woman even knew where Cassandra's friend was sitting was creepy.

"So your wisdom leads us to this?" Intar asked, jumping up again. "You'd like us to seek an audience with the king of the Underworld, who will then kill us on the spot."

"He nearly killed your hero," Pemphedro said with a nod and a laugh. "And Nephratee was a fierce warrior. I wonder how a little girl will fare?"

"I think we should try Avernus," Intar said.

"Then she'll never get home," Pemphedro said, raising a skeletal finger. "Poseidon will not allow Cassandra to travel back to Napea. That is why Nefertiti preferred the flume. Sorry, the only way back to Azure is to seek the god's help."

"The only way she'll leave is by Avernus." Intar lowered his head.

"You doubt my prophecy? How will she pass Cerberus? And Charon? And Nyx? And the great chasm to Elysium, without Hades' attention. Nephratee was a hero doing these things. You think a child can? But what does Pemphedro know, right, sisters? I'm just a starving old witch."

"Pemphedro's an old fool."

"An idiot!"

They all laughed.

"And why, Intar?" Pemphedro asked. "Why is the girl here? Perhaps you should ask *why* instead of how, you fool. That is far more important."

"Why, then?" Intar asked. "Tell us."

But with that question, they rose. Apparently, they were done. They got up and crept slowly into the dark chamber on the other side of the cave until they disappeared into the shadows.

"I'm sorry, princess," Intar said, shaking his head and touching her shoulder. "They're terrible. I felt like if I warned you, it'd only frighten you more."

"What have I done?" Cassandra looked down and nodded. "I trapped myself under the earth."

24

HOPE

Engel sat close to the exit of their tent, quieter than Avva had ever seen him. He dared not say a word. She'd said she didn't blame him for Cassandra going missing, but her emotions were quite different than her words. Whatever she had told him, she couldn't help but hate him for losing her daughter.

Avva sat on a wooden chair and stared through a crack between the curtain and the doorway, gazing at white moonlight. It was late. It would be another long, sleepless night.

"I've given up," Avva said with a tear running down her face. "There's no comfort I can ask from anyone anymore."

After a long silence, she heard him reply quietly, "Me too."

Avva looked down at Engel. The poor man put his head in his hands, leaning against the tent pole. He wasn't crying. He had probably cried too much already.

"Engel, I'm sorry."

"Why apologize? I failed you. I was with her. I should have stopped her."

"I don't blame you."

"I failed you when you were young," he said, choked up. "Queen Delia wanted to run a sword through my stomach when you crossed the sea. I should have let her. Not stopping you from landing in the Hinterlands after the death of your father was idiotic. You were my responsibility. But, more so, I've failed all of you. Even Delia with your father. And Dainya before that. I—"

"Have you heard from my husband?" She was trying to change the subject.

"No."

She wouldn't comfort him. Apologize for cruelty, perhaps, but comfort him? No.

"Sol hasn't slept," he said. "He's spent every effort in the caves, every man on trying to find her."

"Of course," she said quietly. Then she smiled sadly, "This is the first time he's visited me and I haven't even said hello. He came and asked for me. I..." She fought back tears again. "I couldn't bear it. He must hate me so much for losing her."

"He understands, Avva. He loves you."

"How? How could anyone understand this?"

"He doesn't sleep. He doesn't eat. He's been torn apart. So has Henri. They're both doing all they can at the chasm to rescue her."

She jumped up and walked to the curtain. Indeed, along dirt paths in the forest, a row of tents were propped up. Overnight, the kingdom had quickly set up a base the size of a small town along the Stratos in efforts to find their princess. And she saw many nymphs, and many men, rushing back and forth. All in search of her daughter.

"Engel, so many times in the past you held back telling me things about Ambitus," she said, turning to the shadow of a mountain wall above her. "You talked about your Nephrea. You told me your loyalty to my people was because of her. You said how brave she was. But you never told me what she did to survive. You met her in the Underworld. The place where Casey's trapped."

She looked back into the tent and Engel hadn't moved. But he didn't have his head in his hands. He was staring uncomfortably at the ground.

Avva walked over to a large wooden chest by her bed. It had

been brought over from the throne room. Inside was her golden scepter, and buried underneath the rod was rolled papyrus. They were ancient scrolls and maps. Like the maps of the Imada.

"This is Ambitus Pyramid, isn't it?" she asked, pointing to a figure on the papyrus. "My mother once told me about these maps. They're ancient, given to us by my great ancestors. Kept by Ambrosia, not Imada. On the back lies information regarding the pyramid's interior. I need to find my daughter, Engel ... I'll do anything to find her, even fall down the hole myself. You need to tell me about this place and how to reach her."

Now she was glaring at him. He was still leaning on the beam. He took a deep breath and reluctantly got up and hobbled over.

"I have memories," he said, looking at the scrolls. "I remember you as a baby. I remember your mother. And her mother. And I remember my joy at seeing Nefertiti return from Egypt, though briefly, with her daughter. Many of those memories are cherished. But Nephree..." He looked down and put his head in his hands. "I dreaded what she asked me to do."

"What, Engel? What did she ask you to do?"

Tears streamed down the poor dwarf's blue-tinged face. He swallowed and struggled to speak. It seemed like a terrible question.

"She asked me to care for her daughter. She said that Dainya couldn't be raised on the Nile. She said that her mother had been right all along. Her mother, Harmonia, who she had always chastised for leading our Amazon into war against man and the Mandrigel. She said that Egyptians would never accept a nymph child. Her husband had been hunted for being different. She knew the Egyptians would do the same to her and Dainya. So she asked to leave Dainya under my care where Dainya would be safe. She said that ... by the gods..." He struggled so and it made Avva tear up too. "She said that she only trusted me. She said she trusted me more than anyone in the kingdom. The man who failed you and everyone in your family.

"I don't deserve to care for you anymore." He fell prostate

before her. "Please, Avva, take this responsibility from me. Take it now. I've failed all of you. Take it away or strike me down now, as you should. Your child was my responsibility. I didn't protect the immortality of Dainya. I tried to make things right, I failed her. Then I failed your mother. Then you. And now, the worst thing of all, I've sentenced your child to the fate of Nephrea herself! By all rights, your family should take my life and end it now!"

"Oh, Engel ... please ... Please stop. Not now. It's not your fault. You're making things worse."

"If Nephrea were here," he shouted. The shouting shook Avva. She had never heard him cry out like that before. "Nephrea would have killed me! If not her, then her mother. I ... I am nothing. Nothing to my people and nothing to yours."

He sobbed on the ground.

"Oh, Engel, I can't take away your burden," she said, looking down at him. "I have enough to deal with." But, though she was still mad at him, she put her hand on his back. "Engel, you said once that this great Nephrea of yours demanded that you would always be free. Why is it that now you bow before me?"

He rose wiping his eyes with the sleeve of his brown tunic, but he didn't look into her eyes.

"You're not nothing to me, Engel. Of all people, you are more important than anyone tonight. You're the only one who can tell me about this place."

"It's dark. Cold. Or hotter than a furnace. It is everything painful and miserable."

"I need details. I need to know everything Casey faces."

"I've told you. I told you many times in ways you can accept. In fairy tales, ever since you were a baby."

"Fairy tales?"

"It was the only way you could face it, Blue." He looked down at a map. "Avva, what you see here is a horrible place. One which I, or anyone, would be happy to forget."

"But you've said in the past that you longed to be home?"

"Of course. But if you knew where my home was, you'd understand."

"Tell me, Engel. Tell me everything. You said you're nothing. You know more of this horrible place than anyone in the kingdom. You are everything to me right now."

Engel turned from the scrolls.

"Please, Engel, for Casey. Tell me."

"What good will it do! I'm the only Mandrigel from the Underworld who escaped and lived."

"Yes." She knelt on the dirt floor beside him, looked at him, and held his shoulders. "Yes. Exactly. That's why you're the only one who can help me."

"What can I tell you?"

"How did you leave?"

"The dark demon let us go through the dry flume. After Nephrea gave my people freedom for the price of yours, the demon claimed to allow free passage. He did, but he tricked us by not helping us. When we climbed to the top, near Mount Olympus, there developed a great storm. The same storm that nearly killed Sandra. We could barely stand, and we had to climb down all the way from the top of Ambitus. My people are expert climbers. So was Nephrea. I'd argue, we climb even better than your people. But we lost everyone climbing down the Mount to Azure. It was a pyramid, Blue. We used the crumbled ruins as steps but most of it was a sheer drop. Of course, Nephrea would have sacrificed herself for us. She was that way. But my friends did everything, including tricking her, to keep her alive.

"That's how we did it. I lost so many friends climbing down Ambitus. Some of the leftover wall crumbled under our feet. Hades knew the sentence he had given us. And Cora couldn't help, for she was imprisoned by him. I watched so many fall from the edges of the cliffs. And it wasn't only the mountain, it was the clouds. Only someone as stubborn as your great-grandmother could weather the storm of the gods.

"Only the two of us left, teetering on a precipice with the wind trying to knock us down. I thought that was the end of my life. Indeed, at one point, I had given up. But not Nephrea, no, not her. She was the most willful, stubborn, resolute woman I had ever known. She grabbed me and looked into my eyes and…" He paused, fighting tears again. "'Help me, Engel,' she said. 'Help me. I need to return home to warn my people of the Strait and their mortality. I can't make it back to warn them without you.' You see, even then, Blue, it wasn't about me or her. It was about the welfare of you and your people."

He fell to sobbing and Avva waited.

She got up and sat back in her chair, put her hands in her lap, and just waited for her friend to stop crying. When he stopped, she said simply, "Is there anything, any possible thing you remembered, that could get Casey back?"

"Hades rules those lands. Cassandra is a child. Nephrea was a seasoned warrior. The snake will take pleasure in hurting her. And, in so doing, I suppose, hurt you and me."

Avva shook her head.

"Oh Blue, I guess, if anyone could escape, it'd be Casey. She's an Ambrosia."

"I need you to go through these maps with me tonight, Engel. However long it takes. Comb through them, tell me everything you know. I want to know every step, every piece of the domain that my daughter has stepped into. We will pore over it, even if it's useless, as you say. There's nothing else we can do."

Engel shook his head.

"You must!"

"An order, my queen?" asked Engel solemnly.

"Order or curse, perhaps punishment, however you want to view it, but you must help me. I need your help."

"Like Nephrea once before. Look where my help always leads us."

THE GREEN SUN brightened through the crack in the tent. It was a clear, beautiful day. Avva and Engel paid little attention. They still studied the map and drew new ones. Only by late afternoon did Avva allow herself to lay her head over her arm.

She awoke to the tent opening. Cambria in her red armor walked in somberly and whispered to the queen.

"Guests, my lady. The king and his counsel."

Avva looked up. She had been sleeping on the dirt near the maps, which were strewn all over the floor. Engel still slept on his side beside her.

Her husband walked in. She hadn't seen Sol in many moons. He looked like a different man. No battle had ever seemed to do what this abduction had done to him. His face was pale under an unkempt beard. His step was labored. This was the bravest and most energetic man Avva had ever known. And now, for the first time, this boy did not look like a young man. He looked old.

"Anna," he whispered, offering a hand to help her rise from the floor.

"You look so sad, Sol."

Her husband forced a smile. Then he offered her a hand again.

"What time is it?" Anna asked, getting up.

"It is near sundown, Blue."

"Don't bother to tell me what you've accomplished. I can see it in your face."

Sol nodded. Then he motioned to Henri by the threshold. Henri walked over and bowed. Henri looked tired and worn too. They both wore their weathered outdoor clothes and blue leather armor. They were battle clothes, cleaned from the savagery of war but still dirty, likely from their wanderings in the cave. They had obviously just returned and had not bathed.

"Is there anything that can be done, Henri?" Avva asked.

"We've done all we can as mortals," Henri said. "There is no way down the chasm without the loss of life. No one has survived the fall. We did manage to kill an Amphiuma, though. Possibly the fiend who grabbed your daughter. I hope."

Avva caught a glimpse of the outside through a crack in the

tent. The sky was turning a dark jade. It would turn twilight soon.

Henri walked over to a wooden table full of parchments. They had drafted some maps of their own from Engel's memory. Henri thumbed through them with interest.

"I will return soon, Anna," Sol said. "We will continue our search."

"There's no way down the cliff?"

"No." Solinair gnashed his teeth. "Many of our men perished trying to climb down with ropes. But the ledge is metallic, as sharp as a sword. Our spikes won't hold. And there's no passageway down. It's as perilous as the Stygian Hole. I can't understand how Casey survived the fall. Enchanted, perhaps? I don't know."

Aviva looked at Henri, who still thumbed through the parchments. "How can I get her back?" she asked him. That finally made him raise his head from the stacked sheets. The words seemed to echo in the tent, cutting at everyone's heart. Even worse, no one answered. Sol turned away and, for a moment, she thought he would cry. Could her husband cry? Then, indeed, he quickly rushed out of the room.

"There is a way, Henri," Avva said, pointing at Engel, asleep again on the ground. "There is! Look there. There, old man, is proof that one can travel through the mountain and survive. Engel did."

"I see." He nodded.

Engel woke up suddenly, shouting. It startled them.

"You're an oracle, Henri," she persisted. "Can you … at least give me prophecy. What do you see? What will happen to my Cassandra?"

"I don't know," Henri said. "I honestly do not know, Blue." He plopped down on a chair by the scrolls and leaned his chin on his hands.

There was great silence. Engel stirred on his side again, but he fell back to sleep. Then the Mandrigel whimpered with his eyes closed. So horrible was the little man's plight that he cried in his sleep.

Sol walked back in, nodded to his wife, and stood by the entrance. He folded his arms and gazed out at her blue world, now turning dark. For a moment, just a flash, she loved him again.

And then …

Henri started chuckling. It was so weird. Everyone in the tent turned. He was examining one of the parchments. Perhaps the stress had made him go mad?

"What, by the gods, is so funny, Henri?" asked Avva.

"What is this? Now hold on … What is this? What's this?" He picked up the parchment and waved it toward her.

Avva came over and grabbed it. It was a drawing among many drawings etched by Engel in red ink. It was the royal bird of Queen Nephratee aflame. The bird was in flight, with flames surrounding its wings.

"It's a phoenix," said Avva.

"Aye. Your phoenix," said Henri with a big smile. "Your people's standard."

"What is it, Henri?" asked Sol.

"That bird. That is not just a bird, Sol. It is the original mythic bird on Anna's royal standard. It is their immortal phoenix. Didn't you tell me long ago of the firebird and its connection with your royal family, Anna?"

"It's Nefertiti's bird. Harmonia's before that. Yes, it was adopted on our flag. What of it?"

"But what Engel drew is not a flag. He was drawing the *actual* bird, wasn't he? Why?"

"The bird helped save my people," Avva said. "Engel was telling the tale. Nephrea called on the phoenix to burn Cora's shackles. Engel drew it to explain how, after being freed by the phoenix, Cora ran and used the scepter to freeze the fire lakes. It helped free her."

"Aye," Henri said with a nod. "Aye. Don't you see? That bird is still in your palace, isn't it?"

"How could it be?" asked Sol. "Nefertiti lived centuries ago."

"Of course it's alive," said Engel, stirring. He groaned and sat up. "It's an immortal bird. It will always be here, Henri. It can't be killed. But what of it?"

"Quite right. It can't be killed … Praise the gods! Don't you realize, Engel? All this work the two of you dredged up, it was worth something, indeed. For the love of your daughter, Anna!"

"What is it, Henri?" Anna asked.

"No human, or Mandrigel dwarf, or Azure nymph can travel into the Underworld and return from Hermes' lair. The walls were created as slick as iron. We've tried. But a bird can. Especially an immortal bird. The bird is immune to Hades' hold on life because it is eternal. And if it dies, it is simply reborn. We can use your bird to go in and out of the Underworld. The legend is that Nefertiti told the bird to burn Cora's chains so that the goddess could destroy the pyramid. Don't you see? Nefertiti *spoke* to the bird. The phoenix listened to her. Why can't we use it to message Casey? To see where she is and, if we're lucky, help her!"

"Are you sure of this, Henri?" asked Sol.

"Why not? The journey is perilous but if the bird dies, it's reborn. It can enter the Underworld and return at will. It is the only thing I know that can. Assuming of course, Engel, this phoenix of yours is indeed the bird of legend and not just a symbol."

"I've witnessed it falling to ashes and being born with my own eyes, Henri. I saw it free Cora myself. He's kept in the aviary in a cage in the zoo. He's lived as long as Queen Harmonia. He's as real as you and I."

Henri gave a great big grin. Then he rushed over to Engel and hit him hard across the back, nearly knocking him on the ground. Henri turned to the king.

"I must try to speak to it. I can speak with some fowl, Sol. I can try. If I fail, perhaps it will speak with you nymphs. Alas, it … it's the only chance we have left."

"Anna," Henri said, walking up to her and touching her

shoulder, "you asked me what can be done. This. I can't tell you what the future holds. She's far beyond my sight now. But the bird offers us a chance to watch her. And, perhaps, even speak to her."

"Cambria!" Avva shouted and ran to the tent door. "Cambria!"

The guard rushed over and bowed. Cambria smiled at the sight of their excitement.

"Fetch me Mainax from the aviary. Quick. Mainax, our sacred bird. Get him for me from the palace zoo!"

"Of course, Your Majesty."

2 5

THE RIVER OF LIGHT

Cassandra prepared with the Mandrigel for her great journey. She slept in Intar's room, said to have once hosted Queen Nefertiti herself. She was even given the queen's clothes. She had only simple brown traveling clothes that were too worn and torn, by rocks and the snake's fangs, over her perilous journey. Amazingly, Nefertiti's red scarlet military uniform had stood the test of time. It was a little big, but it fit well enough. The princess's height was now almost six feet, like her mother and, apparently, like the fabled queen. The old scarlet chain mail armor was similar to Cambria's, but it was less shiny, and glistening emeralds and rubies were embedded in some of the leather and gold lace that held the clothes together. On the metal chestplate was the emblem of her people. The phoenix.

Pangrin and Intar helped her with the armor, and they stood by a mirror admiring the uniform.

"It was kept to be admired," said Pangrin. "We asked her for it in order to remember her. She had no qualms about handing it over. I never thought it would be worn by an Ambrosia again."

Cassandra turned to the side and looked at the dark red metal chestplate, red pteruges, and chain mail. And a web of metal chains ran down her neck. There were matching red shoes too. With the helm on, she looked just like Cambria.

She unsheathed the queen's ancient sword and thrust it in the air.

"Careful, Casey," Intar said with a chuckle. "That's Mandrigelian. It's a special enchanted blade."

Indeed, it shone red at one angle and blue at another. She had seen these swords wielded by her guard.

"Her armor has been enchanted by us as well," said Pangrin. "That is why it has not turned to dust over the centuries. It will protect you. It is said that no arrow or blade can penetrate the chest. Only another Mandrigelian sword. Wear the clothes to protect you on your journey, princess."

"It's magnificent," she said, turning again to her side by the mirror.

"You look menacing, princess," Intar said.

"Not menacing enough," Pangrin said, losing his smile for a moment. "What useless knowledge from the old hags. For everything we do for them."

"To Avernus we go," said Intar with a nod. "It's the only way. They weren't a waste of time telling us that."

Cassandra nodded, but she didn't like hearing that. The witches had said that the caves of Avernus would lead her to Etruria. And then Poseidon would never let her get home.

"We will travel together with a group of fifty men," Pangrin said to Cassandra.

"Fifty?" Casey snapped, whirling around. "Ridiculous. This is a death mission. Save yourselves."

"They've volunteered, Casey. We owe you and your family."

"Then gather ten. Not fifty. Let the sacrifice be light."

"Don't talk like that," Intar said solemnly, shaking his head.

"Are you coming?" she asked Intar.

"Of course. I wouldn't miss it for the world."

"And me too."

"You, Pangrin?" Casey asked opening her eyes wide. "You must be joking."

"Excuse me, princess, I might be old, but I can still walk. And I've been to Tartarus. Intar hasn't. Besides, I owe Nephree."

Cassandra sighed, looking back at her red armor. This time, she didn't like the look. She looked like she was going into battle. That made her nervous. "The plan's tomorrow?"

"You've slept well?" asked Pangrin. "You haven't needed anything?"

"You've all been so nice. I just don't want to wait anymore."

"We'll leave in the morrow then," Pangrin said with a nod, patting her back.

THE LIGHT above turned a faint white, the light of morning in the Underworld. Cassandra and the Mandrigel rode small albino horses, smaller than monokera and horses of the Hinterlands. More like the size of ponies. They carried supplies on their backs, and her companion dwarfs wore the ancient white painted armor of the Mandrigel army. Their exit was like a parade, and many from the village surrounded them, bidding them farewell.

Then they all followed a dirt trail, meandering along a small creek, until the village and farmlands were no longer in sight. As the orchards dwindled to a few lonely fruit trees among bushes and reeds, they approached the giant arched exit.

Soon the walls and earthen ceiling tapered into a smaller tunnel again. It was midday. The white leaves now shone their brightest along the walls and ceilings of the smaller caves.

As their small horses walked, Cassandra noticed a stream. The water seemed to appear from underground, running parallel to their dirt path. It was surrounded by mud and black, leafless bushes, covered at times by more of those strange fruit trees. The water had a strange pleasant brightness to it, but it was shallow. She liked the sound of it running over stones.

"What a beautiful brook," Cassandra said.

"Careful," replied Intar, shaking his head. "I wouldn't call anything for the rest of our journey beautiful."

But it was beautiful. Its light captivated her. Along its shallow edge, the current ran slowly over large rounded black rocks that were lit more by the water than by the yellow leaves on the ceiling. And an array of glowing waterfalls trickled down from nearby rocky walls as the caverns widened over another valley. Soon the valley became larger and even brighter, hurting her eyes. But the glow gave warmth, and she liked the light.

"Poison!" cried a nervous Mandrigel riding behind them. His name was Corisin. "Don't drink. Don't even look at it."

"Its brightness is tiring," said Cassandra, nodding, with a yawn. "Yes … it is."

Some of her companions yawned too. Intar, who rode beside Cassandra, looked down at the stream and shielded his eyes.

"Drink from its waters and you'll forget where you are," cried Corisin. He rode in front of Pangrin. "We must blindfold the others."

"Yes," Pangrin said. "Who should lead us, Corisin?"

"I can."

"No," Pangrin said, yawning again. "I will. I'm too old to be lured by such beauty. I can resist. I won't look."

"Are you sure? Perhaps we should take turns?"

Pangrin shook his head.

Then they all stopped and tore scraps from their clothing, using them as blindfolds. But the light was so bright that it even shone through the cloth. It reminded Cassandra of the light of Ambitus, which had drawn her to this accursed place in the first place.

"Casey," Intar's voice said. "The cloth won't shut out the light completely. Close your eyes too. Just whatever you do, don't look into the light. These are the waters of Hypnos."

"All right, Intar."

After letting the horses seemingly lead themselves for a while, Corisin spoke again in a panic. "Pangrin, we must pick up speed! I fear we're falling under the water's spell. Are you sure you can lead us? Walk as fast as you can and lead the horses away from the water's edge."

"Cassandra, are you awake?" asked Intar.

"Yes. But I feel so tired." She yawned. Then she opened her eyes and that was worse. The light through the cracks in her blindfold made her eyelids heavier. And yet it was so pleasant that she wanted to take the blindfold off.

"Nephrea blindfolded us to avoid its curse once," Intar said. "It is a hard temptation. Keep your—"

Cassandra leaned on her horse's neck with her head down. She took a deep breath, opening her eyes as wide as she could to take in the beauty of the yellow light. At the upper edge of her blindfold, she could see flowing bright water. Hypnos. It was the most beautiful river she had ever seen.

SHE BLINKED HER EYES. Her blindfold was off her face, and she had awoken to a burning yellow light surrounding her. She heard galloping. Then she felt herself being pushed forward. Horses were in full gallop splashing over water.

"To Lethe!" cried a voice. "Hurry. Pangrin's fallen. So have Orius and Nimny."

"Ride, to Lethe!" shouted another.

"My king!"

Then she heard faintly, though shouting, "Casey! Casey!" She got up on wet knees and looked out at a lake of gold. It was breathtaking. The water flowed over her legs, soothing her skin as if she was in the most relaxing water of her life. Had she fallen off her horse?

"*SPEED THE HORSES!*" yelled Intar's voice in a panic. "*Everyone, ride! Ride! Let's go forward and away from the water. Wake up your neighbors! No one sleeps!*"

Strangely, Cassandra was no longer on horseback. She

looked down and her boots were ankle deep in lovely bright gold. She leaned down and splashed her fingers along it.

Why was she here? Where was here?

"Do not look upon the water!" yelled another Mandrigel, yanking at Cassandra's elbow and grabbing her. Cassandra turned and a little man wearing a gray blindfold was desperately tugging at her. But he wanted to draw her away from the lovely light. Why?

"It feels nice."

"*Gather the horses! By the gods, they're walking into the river too!*"

Cassandra's horse was now in the water. Further to her right, toward deeper waters, a group of horses, maybe ten to fifteen, were swimming, wandering deep into the lake. A few slowly submerged under the water. Then they didn't rise. They didn't even struggle.

"Casey, wake up! Wake up!" shouted Intar's voice.

He was tugging at her arm. She heard a splash and realized her eyes were half closed. When she opened her eyes, she noticed that she was waist deep in the bright water. It felt as if she were in a warm, comforting bath.

"*Shield your eyes!*" yelled Intar. "*Close your eyes and take my hand!*"

Then she heard him splash. She looked at him and a brown cloth was still tied over his eyes. She giggled. He dragged her until she was only knee deep, but the yellow still shone over them.

"Pangrin! My god, Pangrin!" cried another. "My king! He's drowning!"

"Pangrin!" Intar's voice was so panicked that Cassandra opened her eyes as wide as she could. Much further out, with only his head above water, was Pangrin. Pangrin turned for a moment as if barely hearing them. Then his head submerged.

He never rose.

"The king! The king's drowning! Everyone help the king!"

Intar let go of Cassandra and ran with Corisin back into the water. They searched everywhere but could not find Pangrin. And although Cassandra felt such extreme fatigue, she felt a faint flutter in her heart and a terrible sadness. Why?

Pangrin is dead.

Cassandra was neck deep in water now. She looked at Intar and Corisin curiously, then realized they were the only ones awake. Their eyes were still covered with cloth, and they were holding each other by the arm. Only a couple of stragglers were by the shore, most crouched on the ground with their arms covering their blindfolded eyes.

Now Cassandra felt the water touch her lips. It tasted incredible. Sweet. Soft. And …

"*The princess! Get the princess out! All is lost if she goes under. Pangrin's gone, Intar. Leave him. Help me save the princess.*"

She felt someone touch her. Then she felt the burn of a slap across her cheek. And then a jab on her wounded arm. She opened an eye for a moment and saw a couple of Mandrigels, blindfolded, wading and dragging her back to the shore. Somehow, all who had covered their eyes had come to get her.

But as Cassandra fell onto the shore, she thought of Pangrin. She thought of his height and how they had found her but not him. Because she could still stand, being taller.

Pangrin's dead.

There was weeping.

"What's happening?" Cassandra asked sluggishly, mostly to herself, with her eyes half opened.

Intar quickly covered Cassandra's eyes.

"I've turned your back from the water. But still, don't open your eyes."

"Our king!" someone wailed. "Our king is dead! By the gods, he's dead!"

"He's drowned!"

She felt another Mandrigel. Then another touch from behind. It seemed all who were left were now dragging Cassandra away from the shore. They pulled her onto her knees further down a dirt path. Light turned to darkness. Then dark to light again. All the while, people kept pulling her.

By a tree they sat her up. "You can look now, Casey. You're

facing the wall. The water will dry and you'll feel better. Just don't turn around."

But even the wall looked bright. She yawned.

"What … what happened?" She blinked her eyes. He sat beside her and pulled his cloth from his eyes. He was drenched in bright dripping water. She looked down at her armor. So was she.

"They're gone. Most of them … Pangrin, our king, has left us. We weren't ready. We weren't ready. We hadn't left Mangornia in so long. We just weren't ready for this. I'm so sorry, princess."

He put his head in his hands and cried. Others were crying too.

"Our first trial and already half of us and all the horses are gone," said Intar, shaking his head. "And our king is dead."

"He died for her," said another Mandrigel. "Let his death not be in vain, Intar. Let's leave this place and move on."

"I'm sorry," Cassandra said. Then she started crying too. "I'm so sorry."

Intar put his arm around her. "Shh. It's not your fault, Casey."

"But your king, Pangrin."

Soon she could no longer cry. She felt too tired and afraid. And now, instead of shivering with pleasure, she shivered from the wetness in her armor. And as the light faded, she felt sick and afraid.

Her companions were defeated. The remaining men, maybe a quarter of their party, with no horses or supplies, walked with her, still blindfolded, away from the bright light. They walked quietly with their heads down for the rest of the day. And, even worse, occasionally they had to stop another companion from wandering back.

By nightfall, if there was a nightfall in the Underworld, when the light leaves had faded to a dim glow, the group set up camp. Finally, the light was too dim to bewitch them. But still no one spoke.

They snacked on food, brought from their village, from their drenched pockets. They all said nothing. Then they tried to sleep. When Casey lay down with the men under a withered black tree, she cried. And Intar held her.

"It's all my fault."

"No. All of us knew the risks. Pangrin was too old to resist Hypnos."

"But why did your king sacrifice himself? Why did he even come along with me?"

"Because Nephrea would have done the same for him."

WHEN THE MANDRIGEL AWOKE, gathered their things, and prepared to move on, they didn't get far. A large party of armed Eruboi mercenaries on large beasts—giant black horses with red eyes and smoke pouring from their mouths and nostrils—konabera, the witches had called them, were waiting for them near the black river Lethe. And so her quest with the Mandrigel was over before it had begun. What was left of her party were only seven Mandrigel. And all of them, including Cassandra, simply offered their wrists to be tied by rope.

THE CITY OF DARKNESS

THE FURTHER THEY RODE THE MORE SHE SWEATED UNDER Nephrea's armor in the ever-increasing heat. Cassandra was sitting on a konabera behind a huge Eruboi warrior, and her hands were tied. She and her companions were granted full admittance by Charon across the River Styx. Then they passed a terrifying but chained Cerberus. And finally they passed a coastal valley of sandy black terrain.

It was dark and dead. A few traces of red plumes, not much taller than a person, glowed along a dry black desert. These seemed to provide most of the light in the blackened valley. And small plumes, the size of her hand, erupted here and there under blackened dead bushes. But there were no leaves. There weren't many small animals, either. But there were birds—black birds matching the blackened volcanic soil.

The konabera frequently crunched over dry rock or even passed over a few smoky black cracks. At one point on the dark dirt trail, she even saw a hoof fall into flame, but the steed didn't appear hurt. These creatures had thick hooves seemingly created just to withstand this terrain. So their journey was swift across the smoldering volcanic desert.

They rose over another cliffside and saw a valley nearly as

large as Mangornia. A fortress, behind a huge broken wall of volcanic stone, stood in the center. And in the center of that, through cracks in the walls, Casey could make out a tall glass tower. This tower of crystal would have been beautiful, like her Azure Palace, if they hadn't reflected the valley's fire and blackness. It looked like a shard of an onyx stone.

Her entourage rode over a giant cliff bridge to the gates of Tartarus. Beneath her was a dry moat similar to the moat back home, but this one was ten times deeper with smoke rising from below. And Casey had to cover her nose due to the stench of sulfur.

Inside the fortress, their party made their way up a circular cobblestone road that turned into a central street. A line of carts and vagabonds walked this street. They moved to the side of the road for Cassandra's caravan of black-armored soldiers. It seemed like the entire city had been created for this one road leading up to the dark tower.

Cassandra saw naked people embracing in public. And thieves being stretched on racks before tents and broken-down cottages. The Eruboan that rode with Cassandra laughed at these people. And then laughed harder at the sight of a man tied to a stone being stabbed in the head. No one hid their sins. And many smiled. Their grins were full of evil, mischief, and deceit.

"Welcome to Tartarus, little girl," said her captor.

And even the Eruboi on the patrolling roads joined the violence. There was no order. So bad it was that Casey felt safer with her captor.

Then she saw the strangest thing she had ever seen in her life. Some of the strangers had transparent companions. Ghosts.

She entered the dark tower and found herself descending dusty steps with these black-clad soldiers, as if entering a crypt. This led into larger torch-lit hallways and, eventually, a giant earthen hall. It looked like her throne room, but it was nearly empty, with walls of rock instead of windows. At the far end of the room a raised throne sat atop three marble steps. And on the golden chair was a tall man wearing black pants with a rippled bare chest. He was bald and had a short goatee. He sort of dangled his leg to the side and glared down at her while holding a crystal glass of red wine.

"Welcome," he said, gesturing to the giant cave. He sipped some wine. "Welcome. Welcome, Casey. Welcome to my hovel, gifted to me from the bottom of my bastard brother's heart."

Two Eruboans, on either side of her, held her arms and walked her closer.

At least fifty torches lit the room. And there was a gilded table to the side where a downtrodden man in rags poured red wine into crystal glasses. A satyr sat on animal fur to the right of the throne. It reminded her of Engel, who often sat by her mother's throne.

"I ... I'm afraid I don't know you, sir," Cassandra said, shaking her head.

"Ah, well, I know you. I know you very well." He jumped up, placed his glass on the top step, and bounded down the stairs. "Princess Cassandra Ambrosia, of the royal Napean nymph family of Azure Blue. Descendant of Avivae Ambrosia. Descendant of Delia, Dainya, and Nephratee, all the way back to the great Harmonia Ambrosia. I am so happy that you have finally come to visit me."

"You are Hades, sir?"

A group of men in black armor to his right laughed.

"Aye," he said with a wink. "Smart girl. Smart like your mother."

She bowed before him. That made the guards by her sides and near the door laugh even more.

"I am delighted by your respect."

She stood up, with as much pride as she could muster, and addressed him with shaky legs. "Your Majesty, I come to ask safe passage for myself and my companions out of your kingdom. You see, I lost my way. I traveled to Mount Ambitus in Azure. Then I fell ... I mean, I came down a cave into your realm. I followed a path to Mangornia. There I met these great friends..." She looked back and saw Intar with the others by the door. All the Mandrigel, including her close friend Intar, just stared at the ground. "These men. I mean, they swore to help me find my way back home. All I've wanted, since that day, was to find a way to return home. Can you help me?"

"You don't like it here?" he asked, walking back up to his throne. Then he sat back down. "It's disrespectful to Harmonia to wear that uniform. That's armor she and I made. Why, she probably sewed the seams on that one. I'm sure she did. It is Nephrea's. Right? But you are not an Amazon warrior like her, are you?"

"No, sir."

"Harmony was a great Amazon. In some ways, your mother reminds me of her. Obstreperous and insubordinate. Not at all subdued or wistful like Delia. But you, of course, you never met your grandmother, did you?"

"No, sir. Never."

"Not like the sycophant Dainya? Or your prig of a great-great-grandmother, Nefertiti, either?"

"What do you—"

"They were all good Amazons. All of your ancestors. But not with heart like Avva. I detest and adore her all the same." He leaned forward. "What of you? Tell me, why did you come to my lair, Ambrosia princess?"

"I told you, I came down—"

"Why did you come to Mount Ambitus?"

She had been beckoned by strange music. But would she tell him? She didn't trust him. He seemed shifty and cruel.

"Sir," she said with a half bow. "Can you let my friends and me go?"

She looked back at Intar. Intar looked up for a moment and gave Cassandra a comforting glance, but then his gaze quickly fell back to the ground.

Then she noticed something else. Someone that looked completely at odds with this earthen crypt. And when the Eruboi by the door saw her, they fell to their knees. It was a woman with a strikingly beautiful pale face, long golden hair, and bright blue eyes. She walked, no, glided, across the room, in a bright red peplos. The peplos was tight around her bosom but flowed down to her sandals.

"Would you care for something to drink, sirs?" the elegant lady asked the Mandrigel by the entrance. Her voice was like honey. "Poor souls, you must be very thirsty after traveling through our pit."

One nodded. The others dared not move their eyes. Intar just stared at the ground.

"Get them refreshments, Litvius," the lady said to one of the Eruboi. He looked surprised. His glance shifted to Hades, and Hades merely nodded.

"We have a special guest, Cora," Hades said.

Cora made her way to the other side of the throne room. Her husband stared at her. She turned and looked at Cassandra. Then she covered her mouth and giggled. "Oh, my dear. Look what you're wearing. You're so young. What brings you here, child?"

"I was just telling the king, my lady." Cassandra curtsied.

"*My lady*," Cora interjected. "And listen to her voice. So young but so formal. Why, she's cute, Hades." Cora giggled again. Cassandra didn't like that.

"Does she entertain?" Hades asked, leaning forward.

Cora put a hand to her mouth and yawned. Then she said with a shrug, "Anything beats the boredom of your kingdom."

"But I've come here by mistake," said Cassandra. "I fell … I mean I went down…" She paused for a moment. This lady squinted, peering deep into her eyes. "You are Persephone? Queen of the Underworld?"

Cora nodded.

"Your Majesty," Cassandra said with a bow. She cringed when Persephone giggled again. "I went down into a cave by Hermes' lair while exploring Mount Ambitus. I've been trying to find a way out since. The Mandrigel have come to help me. And it … it was terrible. Most of our companions and supplies perished by Hypnos."

"Why, she looks like a little kid version of Nephree, Hades!" Cora blurted out with a laugh. "Of Nephrea. Oh, oh, Hades, she's so cute!"

"That's what I was saying, woman," Hades said with a grin. "Now, if you don't mind. She was in the middle of groveling."

"I wasn't groveling."

"Why did you come to Mount Ambitus, little girl?" Hades asked again.

"I…" Cassandra instinctively backed away. "I … I don't know. I…" For a moment, Cassandra could have sworn Cora gave her a look of encouragement. "I heard music," she said to Cora. "I don't know how. But when I looked at Mount Ambitus, I heard music. And I saw a lovely glow, not much different from Hypnos. That's why I went there."

"Well, now that you are here," Hades said, "I wouldn't advise you to beg to leave."

"But I protest. I wasn't begging. I was only asking that you permit me and my friends to be on our way. I would very much like to go home. Can you help me go? And release my friends so they can return to their home?"

"But maybe your home's here."

"It is quite remarkable, husband," said Cora, examining her. "That this girl survived as long as she has. That deserves respect."

"I helped her," Hades said. "But she shouldn't be permitted to leave."

"You once let Nefertiti escape," Cassandra said, shaking her head, "through the flume of Thyra."

He furrowed his brow. Cora uncomfortably fluttered her eyes.

"You think you're like her?" Hades asked Cassandra, leaning forward. "Perhaps with her armor, there's a resemblance. When she wore those clothes, she had something to trade me. What do you have to trade? She had your nymph race. You have nothing."

"I'm of no use to you. There's no reason to not let me and my friends go."

"But that's not true, little girl." He shook his head with a big grin. "I have plenty of reasons."

"Cassandra dear," said Cora, looking up at Hades with a scowl, "you don't know my husband. He enjoys causing suffering."

"Not true," he said, raising a finger. "I enjoy watching suffering. I never cause it."

"Well…" Cora shrugged and stood up. "Seems like this is a situation you delight in."

The witches said Cora might help me. She keeps looking as if she wants to. Why? She doesn't even know me.

With a sly smile Hades squinted at Cora. Then he rested his chin on his hands. He crossed his legs and pointed toward his wife, but before he could say anything, she turned and walked off.

"Where are you going, Kore?"

"Since your mind's made up, husband, I shall retire. I like to pretend that this time of day is night. And then, perhaps, I can dream of the lands I once roamed. The sweet fields which you took from me. Anyway, you showed me your spoils. I don't approve."

But before she walked through the cavern exit, she froze when passing by Intar. It seemed she hadn't recognized him before.

"See, Casey, that's my wife," Hades said addressing the princess quietly. "She always sneaks and lies. It's just that way with women. And Persephone excels at it. Frankly, it excites me."

"She seems like a harmless young girl," replied Cora, now standing by the door. "Let her and her friends go."

"This nymph violated my law, Kore," Hades said, shaking his head. "She passed into the Underworld in Gaia." He turned to Cassandra. "*Gaia*, yes *Gaia*. By the way, Casey, Mount Ambitus is outside of your borders. I have every right to keep you now. Your snooping around like your mother dug you your own trap."

"Perhaps you should ask your brother why the trap was set before you harbor an Amazon nymph," Cora snapped.

"What are you insinuating, Persephone? That she's here because of your father?"

"You know damn well why she's here."

"Hmm," Hades remarked. Then he stared down at Cassandra. "Isn't it interesting, Kore, how she resembles your fabled heroine. Ah, Casey, if only you had met your great-great-grandmother. Nephrea was a remarkable woman. Don't misunderstand me. I might have despised her, but I had the utmost respect for her. It was because of her that my family has kept their hand away from you Amazon. Until your mother, Avivae, and that gorilla, Solinair, sarded the whole thing up."

"I'm proud of my lineage, sir," Cassandra said.

"Of course you are. Well," he said, wagging a finger at her, "you and your parents don't realize a little secret. Would you like me to tell you?"

"She's too young, to deal with your—"

"Don't interrupt me, wife!" he snapped. "I warn you. And don't leave. Or I'll have her and the rats for dinner! Or breakfast. Or lunch. Or whatever sarding time it is. Do you know the time, Pan?"

"It is whatever time you'd like, sire."

"Casey," he said, "I've always been fascinated by your family. And this brings me to the point of our meeting. I shall dictate my terms, since you obviously have nothing else to offer me."

"Be gentle," Cora said.

"Don't tempt me to be wicked." He took a deep breath. "Casey. Casey, Casey, Casey." He took another deep breath, looked at Cora, and stroked the goatee on his chin. Casey noticed he had sharp, ugly fingernails. "For violating my edict, I sentence you to imprisonment. You shall remain here forever."

Everything turned black and there was a sensation of falling.

WHEN SHE BLINKED her eyes open under flickering torchlight, Hades was still gazing down at her from his throne. He hadn't moved. But Cora's face was gazing down at her too. The goddess was holding her.

"I'm not finished," Hades said.

"You've said enough!" snapped Cora. Her blue eyes turned a terrible, frightening red. "I warn you, husband. Watch the games you play!"

But with Cora's eyes now turning a bright red, she looked more like a monster than Hades. Cassandra pulled from her embrace. Then she cried. And behind her, she heard the Mandrigels cry too.

"Why!" Cassandra asked. "What have I done to you? I only ask to return home. Why keep me here?"

Cora shook her head and looked up at Hades with those terrible red eyes.

Hades walked down the steps from his throne. Then he knelt down and said, "Because it will hurt your mother." He walked over to the table and grabbed another crystal glass of red wine. "Allow me to explain—if you won't faint. Before your mother, no one traveled outside of Azure. That kept the peace. But when Avivae stepped foot on the Hinterlands, your mother broke the peace. She angered Zeus. Then came her marriage to the barbarian. Ceremonial marriage is forbidden between men and nymphs. Their union is a necessity at the games, but an actual ceremonial union is forbidden. It's been that way for centuries." He drank more wine standing by the table. "And now, your father, the husband of a nymph queen, is conquering Atala. That upsets Zeus and Demeter more. So someone must be sacrificed. That someone…" He took a drink from his glass and closed his eyes, seemingly relishing the drink. "That someone, young girl, is you. Princess Cassandra Ambrosia. But you shall not die. I wouldn't dream of that. I will let you live to entertain my wife."

Then he put the glass down and looked all over the chamber. "Where did she go? Guards, where did Cora go? Pan, do you know?"

"She left the hall, sire," said the satyr with a yawn, still lying on his side on animal fur.

"She never had the stomach for this. Ah, well. Anyway, Cassandra, let me explain further."

He walked back up the throne steps and sat back on his chair. Then he leaned forward.

"Centuries ago, girl, when you weren't born, Queen Nefertiti met me in this same chamber. She wore the same battle armor you wear now. She offered me a deal. She sacrificed the freedom of her people for that of the Mandrigel. Do you have any idea, little girl, what Queen Nefertiti's people thought of her when she returned?" Cassandra said nothing. She turned and gazed at her friends sobbing by the entrance. "Do you! They despised her. But with the scepter restored, Imada didn't dare rebel. And when the kingdom was bequeathed to her chief guard, Jaida, for the second time, there was peace. And Nefertiti left for Egypt.

"Well, you and I and your stupid sobbing friends by the door know better, don't we? Queen Nefertiti was a hero. And she deserved their praise. See, she gave sacrifice. Life is full of sacrifice. It is what makes us live. Our suffering. Our sacrifice. And you, dear girl, are your mother's and father's sacrifice. They take the continent of Atala, I take you. Do you understand now?"

He stopped and leaned forward in his throne.

"But you can just let me go," Cassandra finally said.

"Your Ambrosia blood will fight and fight until there is no longer a mechanism driving your muscles and bones. Even at this age, you're an obstinate nymph. Actually, I adore it. I tell you what. I know just how to explain this better. I haven't finished my decree."

He looked over at the Mandrigel and then his guards. He gestured to the dwarfs by the door. "Kill them."

Cassandra stared in disbelief. Then she stared at Intar. Intar didn't look up.

"What say you to that?" he asked, laughing.

The guards raised their swords and rushed the Mandrigel.

"*Wait!*" cried Cassandra. "*Allow them to mourn! Their king just died.*"

"What?" Hades asked. He raised his hand to his guards. "King Pangrin?"

"Their king went with me to Hypnos. But he's old. He thought he could help us pass. He went into the water and died trying to save me."

"Pangrin? King Pangrin?" Hades furrowed his brow. He fell solemn for a moment.

"Yes. Please allow his comrades to mourn."

His men stopped and looked at Hades, waiting.

"But what good would it do them now to mourn?"

"Please. They helped me. I—"

"Young lady, I am the filth of the world," he interrupted. "I am a vile serpent, repulsive gorgon, king of worms, and butcher of all that is righteous. Do you think that I hold compassion for the leader of the rats who tried to kill my only true love? Your Ambrosia cleverness will not save them. Not this time."

He nodded to his guards again. They grabbed her friends.

Cassandra started screaming. She didn't even know what came out of her mouth; she just cried out senselessly.

"Take me!" Cassandra shouted. "Don't kill them! Please! Please! Take me!" She ran to Hades and bowed. "You want a sacrifice, kill me! That'll be enough for my mother and father! Kill me, but please don't hurt them!"

"Ambrosia, indeed. But your death would upset my wife. I spared a Mandrigel once. My wife used him to abet a prisoner. A little man who raised you. Engel was his name. Never again, princess."

"Please, I beg you! Do with me what you will. My companions are innocent. Spare them!"

"*Leave them!*" shouted a voice by the door.

It was Cora. With incredible speed, she flew around one of the guards who had raised a sword over Intar. She grabbed the guard from behind, took his blade out of his hand, and held it by the guard's neck.

"Welcome back, Kore," Hades said, rolling his eyes. "Come

to save the downtrodden? Now who's the one putting on clothes like our fabled fire queen, Nephrea?"

Cora held the guard, threatening to slice his throat. The man was three times her size, but the goddess's strength seemed far greater.

"*Don't tempt a fight with me!*" Hades shouted, standing up. His eyes reddened for the first time, and he pointed down at her. "*I warn you, Kore.*"

"She's just a little girl. Now she's ready to give her life for your forsaken family too! Imprison her, fine. But keep the guards away from her and her friends. I warn you, you coward."

"*Call me a coward on my throne!*"

"Take the girl prisoner, Orcus, but, by god, don't kill her friends in front of her! I shield her from your horror. And your accepting your brother's will without a fight disgusts me. It is, *yes*, cowardly!"

Persephone shoved the guard away, and the force made him slide across the stone floor. Then she raised the sword over her head and shifted into a fighting stance. It was an Amazon fighting stance, which shocked Cassandra. The pose looked so odd in her flowing red peplos.

"You mutant whore!" cried Hades. "You have no home! You don't belong here and you don't belong with nymphs. Perhaps you should live with the rats. What do you intend to do with that sword? Kill your own guards, Kore?"

"If they cross me."

"*To entertain!*"

Hades took a deep breath, closed his eyes, and dropped his head in his hand. He shook it violently. Then he fell back in his chair. "There will be no killing by my wife. Stand down, men."

Casey looked at Cora, but she did not break her red-eyed glare at Hades.

"I forfeit, Kore. Happy? Alpha, beta, to nothing. You win. Drop the sword and stop acting like a nymph."

But she didn't.

"Drop it! You think me cruel? Your father will think differently about this sentence. They should be killed by order of Nephrea's own edict." He sighed and signaled to his guards. "We mustn't upset the children, boys. Take the princess to the first-floor dungeon. She can be imprisoned like her mom. Bring the Mandrigel to reside under her. Let them all pass through a slow death under the queen's new decree. Then we shall all suffer for her usual sentimentality."

One of the guards came over and grabbed Cassandra, but he glanced at the goddess first. Cora remained in her bizarre nymph fighting stance, still shielding the dwarfs.

By the exit, as Cassandra was escorted past Persephone, Casey said, "Thank you." Cora glanced over, then quickly averted her red eyes.

Cassandra was led through dark corridors, alone, by the giant black-armored men.

She heard an explosion. Then shouting. It sounded like Hades and Cora yelling at one another and throwing things back in the hall.

27

MILDEW

Avva glanced at her palace garden through the glass windows of her throne room. The chartreuse sky was clear. Purple and red birds landed beside the walled glass along blue trees. And a stream trickled through the garden. The light shone through the dome above, adding a green glow to the dust in the air. It was all beautiful. Precisely the opposite of Avva's disposition.

The double doors opened and Cambria announced, "Menilda Eulalia arrives, Your Majesty." Then she hit the stone floor by the door twice with her staff.

Milda was adorned in gaudy gold necklaces over a very long, ugly gray peplos. The peplos was wrinkled and worn. Her messy white hair hung limply over her shoulders. She walked down the central aisle, looking uncomfortably at Avva, who glared at her from atop her throne. Engel stood up, out of respect, by the bottom step. Milda bowed to Avva, but she couldn't resist scowling at Engel.

"Queen Avivae," Milda said. "How may I serve you, Your Majesty?"

"Milda."

"You asked for a private audience? This is highly irregular."

"Indeed," Avva said with a deep sigh.

Avva let Milda stand uncomfortably in silence for a while. Then she said, "I need information."

"Of course. But I hope this doesn't involve Imada. I can't reveal our secrets here. Especially…" She looked down at Engel with a wrinkled nose. "In front of him."

"Engel is my chief advisor." Engel smiled. He hated Milda as much as she did. "My daughter's missing, Milda."

"The whole kingdom knows that, Your Majesty." She put her hand up. "Forgive me. I don't mean disrespect."

Avva sat up straighter, straightened her long blue peplos, and brushed back her long black hair. "When I was crowned, I met with your friends. You women told me that you were given knowledge by the gods. I've called you to tell me if you still have contact with them."

"I can't speak about this here," Milda said, looking around the hall.

"There's no one else in the room."

"I'm sworn to secrecy."

"There's no one here, Milda. Your secrets are safe with me. Now tell your queen, do you still have contact with them?"

"I am not the only one in the room, Queen Avivae." Milda nodded down at Engel again.

Engel nodded and rose. "I'll take my leave, Blue."

"No, you won't. Sit down."

"You've refused our counsel," snapped Milda. "Now you ask me to give it in front of a Mandrigel. I don't think you understand this insult."

"Upon the throne of Harmonia."

"Indeed. Imada was created by Queen Harmonia to defeat these Mandrigel. And I can tell you, she never deliberated in the throne room."

Avva looked over at Engel and nodded. "All right. Please leave us."

"Yes, Your Majesty."

Engel got up, bowed, and hobbled down the main hall and through the double doors. When the doors closed—

"I must protest. No Azure queen has ever asked Imada to meet in the throne room. No one doubts your power. This hall was built by blessed Harmony. But my words are not secure from prying ears."

"I won't meet with you in a dungeon."

"But that is where—"

"Unlike me, Engel is too civil to tell you to your face what Nefertiti once said behind your back. I'll tell you now, though I think you can guess. Nefertiti spared you after your rebellion. I've learned a lot about you from Engel. Harmony once called you *Mildew*. Our founding mother treated you like a dog."

Milda didn't deny it. She simply looked up, narrowing her eyes.

"You may act high and mighty," Avva said, pointing at her, "but I am on to you."

Milda still didn't respond. Nor did she avert her glare.

"It was hard to get secrets of the past from Engel. But I did. I squeezed everything out of him. But I love him. I warn you, Milda. There's no telling what I might do to get information from someone I don't like. Especially a traitor against Nefertiti."

"How dare you assert that," Milda hissed in a whisper.

Oh, I'm not finished.

"I might have been an innocent girl when we met after my crowning, but now, after my daughter was kidnapped, I've been forced to grow up. I am a woman and your queen. And I have little patience for the likes of you." Avva was breathing heavily. Her heart was pounding. She looked at the garden again, but something about it, something about its beauty, reminded her of the liar now standing before her. All this beauty was more painful in the midst of her suffering. "Tell me. Tell me quickly. The room's empty. How does Imada get its information? If you don't speak, I can find ways to make you. There are ... from Harmonia's time, when Nefertiti was a child, ways I've learned from Engel—and the records reveal them as well."

But Milda stood silently staring at the window.

"Engel said you swore allegiance to my family. He said you were about to be banished after your rebellion, but you swore service to my family for your life. It was public and was meant to last for centuries, at least while Nefertiti's daughter was in power. Now *my* daughter needs your help. Did you lie to Nefertiti?"

"You take counsel from dwarfs!" she snapped back. "You call Nephrea *Nefertiti* because you know nothing about what a traitor *Nephrea* was to her own people. I didn't hate Nephrea for her edict. Not for jailing us, puerile queen! I hated her for abandoning us! Upon my rebellion, at least I intended to rule. She got up and left. And the Mandrigel? The Mandrigel, the man who gives you counsel, were treated as vermin by your ancestors. Whatever nickname you hear of me, Harmonia treated Engel's people as rats that simply needed to be exterminated!"

"Queen Harmonia Ambrosia? The leader who teased you, calling you names?"

They both stewed, and the silence was filled with their heavy breathing. But Avva wouldn't stop because forcing Milda into discourse was torture for her. And Milda didn't dare leave because it was forbidden by law—but it sure looked like she wanted to.

"What did I expect from you?" Avva said dismissively, waving a hand. "You were barren and never had a daughter."

"I will tell you what you want to know," Milda snapped. "But from this day forward, Avivae, consider us enemies."

The double doors opened again. It was Cambria. She crossed the threshold and bowed. The noise of their fight must have stirred her. Avva waved her hand dismissively. When the doors closed again—

"We were never friends," Avva said. "Now answer me. Word around the palace is that you women still have contact with the gods. Is this true?"

"Yes."

"How?"

"They come to us. We provide food and wine as tokens of respect."

"You violate one of Harmonia's most sacred edicts? You provide libations?"

"Yes. Because this respect for Olympus brings the gods. Especially when the offerings are by us. No Amazon is known to submit to a god. This sacrifice is more meaningful to them from us than from any other being in Gaia because of that. In return, Hermes sends us word."

"From Hades?"

"Once," Milda said. She got up and walked to the window and looked outside. Then she said softly, "No more."

"Who?"

"The information I give you now not only makes you and me enemies but turns you into an adversary of the gods. This is not only Imada's secret but Olympus's. Is this information that important to you, Avivae?"

"For my daughter, yes."

"Apparently your favorite Mandrigel has told you our history," she said with a nod. "But there are many things he doesn't know. Hades once loved Harmonia."

"I've heard this. Nefertiti must have told him that too."

"Hades adored Harmony. They used to reside together in the palace. I saw them together often. It was before Persephone. Back then, there was no need for messengers. The sacrifice was unnecessary too. The information given to us from Olympus was out of love. This changed after Harmonia's death. When Harmony died, the only way for us to get information was through offerings on the Stratos. But perhaps, due to his rage over Nefertiti's influence and the damage she did to his kingdom, Hades and Persephone abandoned us.

"Soon Hera learned of Imada. She visited Dainya. Hera is not one to visit anyone. Dainya was wise, malleable, and true to the law. Not only did she obey Hera, she followed our edict to the letter. For peace. If your mother had done what you did, stepping foot on the Hinterlands, your grandmother would have run a sword through her. Dainya was not foolish like you and Cassandra. Or even Delia. And we had peace."

"So your information comes from the queen of the gods herself?"

"No." She pushed herself from the window and walked back to her position before the throne. "It comes directly from Zeus. After we sacrifice on the Stratos."

"I see."

Zeus is Imada's informant? How strange. That means that the Amazon kingdom all the way down from Dainya to Delia has been advised by Mount Olympus … I suppose this makes sense, in a way. Hades has always rebelled against them.

But then the snake abducts my daughter? Why? Why support us and take the princess?

Imada has changed sides? Since Nefertiti, Amazon Imada has been an instrument of Zeus? Aligned with Olympus and Hellena. Perhaps I can align myself with them to get my daughter back?

"Milda, can you send word imploring Zeus to help get Cassandra back? I'll give them anything they ask."

"Why would Zeus help you, Avivae? King Solinair has taken nearly all of Atala. Caravia, though once the greatest empire on the continent, is now weak and ready to be conquered. And Kitheria is full of tribal warlords. Zeus has lost the continent to you and Solinair. By a Crescent king, a shameful defeat, and by you, an Amazon nymph. The god of Olympus doesn't favor you. He enjoys your suffering. He wishes it."

"And you?" cried Avva. "This isn't just about me, it's about an Ambrosia princess! My daughter. Even if you don't care about me, don't you care about Harmonia's lineage?"

Milda quickly shook her head. "The Underworld is under the power of Hades and Persephone. Even if I could petition Zeus, he does not hold power over that realm. He couldn't recover his own daughter, Persephone. And I told you, I no longer communicate with Hades."

"I see," Avva said with a long sigh. She turned to the outside window and felt the same desperation and melancholy she'd felt for many moons. "I see."

"I can ask, Avivae."

Avva nodded. "I … I'd even be willing to set up temples in Napea for this. Anything."

"Your Majesty! I must object."

"Why? Your Imada does this."

"In secret. In public, it would be a major affront to your lineage. It will damage our reputation. This … this is why you should be advised by us and not an old dwarf."

"Find out if there's anything that can be done," she said, waving her hand. "Go. Ask for a trade. Send advisors to the Stratos now and communicate with the gods."

"Yes, Your Majesty," Milda said with a bow. "I'll try. By your order."

"You're dismissed. And … thank you."

"You're welcome. But for forcing this information, you have now publicly dishonored me. We are enemies now, Avivae Ambrosia."

No different from before, Mildew.

28

HOME

"Tell me more about Azure, Casey."

"I miss it, Cora," Cassandra said with a shrug. "I miss it so much."

Cassandra stroked the soft feathers of her bird as she sat in a wooden chair beside her barred window. She wore a simple, drab brown tunic, pants, and sandals. Cora sat in an chair next to her. The queen had just entered, but it wasn't the first time. Cora had visited her many times.

Her cell was small and dark. The light shone through the one small window, blocked by metal bars. Beyond the bars lay the outside courtyard with leafless black trees and bushes. Gold shone throughout the walls of the cell, which was odd. Cassandra had never seen so much gold and silver, but it was everywhere in Tartarus. It lined the walls and reflected the outside red glow, lighting the room a little more. But such wealth brought no comfort. During the "day," or the brightest time, it was hot and she sweated terribly; during the "night" she shivered with cold. Even Cora suffered. A bead of sweat glistened on the goddess's forehead as she smiled, waiting for more morsels about her home world. She seemed to love any word of Azure, for some reason.

One desk, a bed, and a dresser filled the small room. The furniture was made of the finest oak. The bed was just as comfortable as her bed at home. But she never slept—not well, at least. She was miserable. In body and mind.

"Tell me, dear. Please." Cora's eyes opened wide with excitement. "Go on, tell me. Go on about your lands." Cora smiled. "Tell me of this Azure Blue of Napea. Maybe if you tell me more about where you're from, you won't miss it so much."

"How's that?" Casey asked, looking up from her bird.

Cora shrugged.

"There's a chasm in the fields east of the palace known to my people as the Stygian Hole, Cora. I've been there a few times. It's so deep you can't see the bottom. Legend is that you were taken there. Is that true, Cora? Are you from our lands or Hellena?"

She had tried to use a neutral tone, but she couldn't hide a hint of suspicion in her voice. She didn't trust Cora. She liked her, but she didn't trust her.

"Don't tell me about holes, Casey."

Cassandra laughed.

"Tell me of the forests. The blue trees and purple wheat fields you were talking about. And bright red leaves. The glowing blue waters of the rivers and streams. And of Mount Ambitus. I was on Mount Olympus, that's true, as a little girl, but I haven't been down in your lands. Tell me of your flying unicorns. Tell me about all these strange and wondrous things, won't you, Casey? I like it when you talk about it."

Cassandra shrugged while petting her bird's head again.

Cassandra liked Cora's dress. The goddess had on a long bright red, almost scarlet, peplos that went all the way down to her sandals. It was similar to the dress she had worn when they first met, but this one draped so far down that it dragged as she walked on the floor. Her face was painted in thick makeup too. Her long blond hair was perfectly combed. And her blue eyes shone in her pale face. She looked lovely. Cassandra not only loved her company; she liked seeing the wonderful things Cora wore. The goddess must have spent hours dressing and smelling nice. It was almost as if she felt like if she was lovely, her world would be lovely. And sometimes Persephone even loaned Casey some of her clothes.

"Well … I miss the sun. A bright green sun shines during the day. I can't tell day from night very well here. And the—"

"A green sun," Cora interrupted, closing her eyes dreamily. "Green? My memory of Gaia was of a yellow sun. Like we have in Olympus. Have I been away so long?"

Cassandra laughed. This made Cora laugh too.

"It's yellow in other lands, Cora. But I've not been to many other places. It's forbidden, you know. Daddy says it's yellow in his realm. He says the rest of Atala has a yellow sun. When I flew among the clouds toward the summit of Ambitus, I saw a yellow sun. I think I saw Mount Olympus."

"Ah, yes. You're not permitted to step foot outside your lands."

"From your husband's edict, Cora."

"Yes. Tell me more. Go on."

"Well, our land is blue. Everything is blue. The bushes. Trees. Some are green. Some are even a bright red. But most of it is blue." She put a finger to her chin and felt a smile, a foreign thing she hadn't felt in a long time. "But the sand on the beaches is purple. There is blue everywhere in our lands. It is so beautiful."

Cora opened her eyes wide. "Sounds enchanting. Magical. I wish I could visit one day. They say Azure Blue was created by Poseidon, the god of the sea. Perhaps that's why your land is so blue?"

"It's home," Cassandra said with another shrug. She resumed looking down at her bird and stroking his rainbow feathers.

"Tell me more."

"Must I?" asked Cassandra. She yawned. "I'm so tired. Perhaps I should just sleep."

"But you just slept the night, Casey."

"Well … I know, but I'm tired. I told you I can't get used to the time."

"You will."

Those words stung a little.

Cora looked out the barred window, and Cassandra gazed out with her. Behind the courtyard fence, she saw many merchants walking back and forth in drab black clothes and standing morosely in line. This was the line going out the main entrance to the dark tower. Few spoke. And most had expressions of a deep melancholy, staring down at the ground. It was the same melancholy Cassandra felt and saw in Cora. Some got into fights. Some did nasty things, displaying themselves naked or stabbing and cutting each another. But Casey stopped looking at the people. She did what she figured Cora did now. She gazed beyond their little black garden and beyond the city walls of Tartarus into the black volcanic fields. Although her cell was on the first floor of the tower, the tower was still at a high enough elevation that she could make out the volcanic valley, in the distance, surrounding Tartarus. There was always a dim red glow out there, even during "nightfall."

Cora got up and walked to the window. She ran her fingers along the metal bars and said, her voice surprisingly somber, "These bars, Casey, you know … these bars on your window, I've spent an eternity behind bars."

Cassandra nodded and a tear rolled down her cheek. But she felt like it was really a tear for her friend.

"Tell me more, Casey," she said without turning. "Please. You must tell me about Azure. You must. Won't you?"

"Why?"

"Because it makes me happy."

"Well," Cassandra said softly, now choking up, "there's my unicorn, Inghorn." She struggled to speak. "Inghorn is my monokera. A beautiful, magnificent creature. Inghorn can fly. Only in the Azures can the horses fly, Cora."

Cora covered her eyes and leaned on the bars. Casey saw the goddess shake. Persephone was crying.

"Much like my bird here," Cassandra continued, "you know, an animal can provide some comfort."

Cassandra lost control of her tears too. She wept bitterly with the goddess.

After a while, Cora walked by her and touched her shoulder gently. She said, "I think I should go."

"No," Cassandra snapped. "Wait. I didn't mean to make you cry. Please don't leave."

Cora gave her a solemn nod. "How old are you, dear?"

Cassandra looked at her with confusion. "Almost thirteen, after being in the Underworld, I think. Thirteen. I find it hard to keep time."

"Casey," Cora said with a smile, "I ask because I wasn't all that much older than you when I fell. Things will get better."

"But Cora, I … I don't want it to get better. I want to go home."

The magnificent bird hopped on the windowsill. Cassandra got up and grabbed her bird again.

"You know, Casey, that bird is forbidden. A phoenix is forbidden. Don't ever tell my husband he is here."

"Is that what this bird is? A phoenix?"

"Yes, of course it is," the queen said, surprised.

"He's magnificent."

"He's a phoenix," Cora said, petting his scarlet head. "Don't ever tell my husband about him."

"He seems to have taken a liking to me. And I think he likes you too, Cora. I call him Firebird. I used to visit one of these birds in our zoo. This one looks like him."

"Well, they're very rare. And they are enchanted. Did you know this bird is beyond immortal?"

"No." Casey shook her head.

"The phoenix can't be killed. It sheds lives like a snake sheds skin. At the end of its life, it bursts aflame. Then it is reborn from its ashes. It can never be destroyed. It will live forever."

"Didn't Nefertiti have one?"

"Yes, she…"Cora turned from her. She seemed to want to rush out of the room.

"What is it, Cora?"

"Don't mention that name." Cora shook her head violently. "Don't ever mention that name again."

"Why?"

"You …" She flashed Cassandra a very ungenuine smile. And, for a flash, her eyes turned red. Casey had learned to stay far away from the goddess when her eyes became red. "You've meant a lot to me since you came here. I don't want anything to come between us. But, Nephree … Nefertiti … your Azure people … Well, I've always thought of you nymphs as my enemy. That is, until you came here. Now I view the nymphs differently. But, please, don't mention her again."

"Your husband confuses you."

"Just never mind, Casey. Don't mention her again."

"All right." Cassandra nodded and petted her bird. "I'm so grateful to you. You're my only friend here."

Cora's eyes turned blue again. "And you are such a very great comfort to me, child." Cora ran her hand along her back. "A great comfort. Whatever I can do to ease your pain, my dear, I am here."

Cassandra nodded.

And then, after a long silence, Cora said, "Tell me more about Azure."

"Cora, why can't you leave? You can travel to Azure Blue. You're a goddess. Haven't you tried?"

"Shh. Never mind. Just tell me about—"

"The doors are closed," Casey continued quietly, cocking her head back and looking at her. "No one's around, Cora. You can tell me."

"My husband has eyes and ears everywhere, child. Anyway, I've tried. I've tried many times. Forget it. Just tell me more about your home world."

"You'd like the Azures, Cora. But I think you would find the winters there the strangest. Here, it is hot and cold. But I don't see rain or snow. But in my home, in winter, it turns white and snows. Then everything is emerald, not blue, reflecting our green sun."

"Ah, I remember snow," said Cora.

"Well, the myrle berries ripen come springtime," Cassandra said, suddenly changing the subject.

"Spring," Cora said with a smile. She closed her eyes and sniffed the air as if it had arrived inside the room. "Yes, spring I miss very much. Especially the fields. I love spring the most. And you don't know how much I miss the wheat fields."

"Spring is beautiful. Is that tale about you and the seasons true?"

"Myths," she said, shaking her head. "Lies. Of course it isn't. I wish I could return springtime. You know that, Casey. Would you like to go to the courtyard today?"

Cassandra turned excitedly. "Oh, can I, Cora? Can I?"

"Of course," Cora said with a chuckle. "You need fresh air, child. We can go today."

"Shall we go now?" Cassandra turned to the bird again. "Oh Firebird, have you heard? We can be in the courtyard today. Outside! How wonderful. You and I can be in the gardens."

"I can accompany you as well," Cora said, "if you'd like?"

"Oh yes," Casey said, stroking the bird's tail. "That would be so nice. Please, Cora, don't leave me. Come with me and keep me company."

"Of course, Casey."

29

NEWS

Sol sparred in an outdoor courtyard within the walls of his Castle Cove with Prince Gavin. Gavin was Torinth's son and held the same wild eyes and temperament as the mad king. But Sol had adopted him and loved him in the same way Darius and Henri had once adopted the lone wolf Solinair. Now Gavin was Sol's son.

They fought shirtless with pants and silver armor on their chest and legs, dueling with heavy longswords. Blood trailed down Sol's right shoulder. He was drenched with sweat. The younger prince was tiring too, but being wild, he was constantly on the attack.

Gavin struck and missed Sol, hitting a white marble column hard enough to damage the blade. But the boy had so much energy that he pulled it from the stone and struck again. Gavin tried blow after blow, but Sol blocked every strike.

"What's the matter, boy? Fight me!"

"You …" Gavin said, breathless. "You win because—"

"Because I never give up. You are stronger. Younger. Faster. Now raise your sword and fight."

Gavin shook his head. He brushed the sweat from his long

black bangs. Then he looked up with a sly smile and lunged again.

Sol heard the courtyard gate opening and in walked an old man in a long brown robe. As Gavin looked over, Solinair stepped forward and thrust his sword toward the prince's neck. He stopped short of cutting his throat. Gavin dropped his sword and raised his hands.

"Don't be distracted, boy!" admonished the king. And Sol hit the top of Gavin's head with the dull side of the blade.

Henri laughed and, for a moment, Sol felt happy as he embraced Henri. But then he remembered his daughter.

"My lord," Henri said with a nod. He looked at Gavin. "How's the prince faring? Hasn't he beaten you yet?"

"He cut my arm. That's something."

"Could have cut off your head," said Gavin. "Had it not been for Henri." Gavin sat on his knees, winded. He turned toward the magi. "But I stopped my throw. Sol has a god-like will."

"He never gives up," Henri said with a shrug. "That is why he will never lose, boy."

"How do you fare, friend?" Sol embraced him again.

"I've been sleepless." Henri lost his smile. "And the trip to Castle Cove is an arduous one. Even within your boundaries there are brigands. Perhaps you and the prince should simply travel alone in the forest for sport."

Solinair grabbed a towel and wiped his face. Then he took off the heavy silver chest shield. Gavin jumped up and helped carry a pile of armor, placing it under a tree.

"It's good to see you," Henri said. Then he looked at his shoulder. "He wounded you good, son. Let me take a look at that."

"It's nothing. Never mind. Tell me, tell me everything, old friend. I want all the news. Come. We'll talk inside in private."

"Goodbye, Sol," Gavin said. "Good fight, sire."

"Aye, boy," Sol said with a nod. "You'll win yet. Go and fetch word from Milo. Perhaps it's better at the front than in Azure."

Henri forced a smile and nodded. Then he and Sol walked under a white stone portico and through the halls of the castle, in silence, toward the central throne room.

Castle Cove was empty. It was a beautiful day—hot, but the sky was clear. Many subjects were outside fishing, hunting, or just enjoying the hillside. Few were indoors.

They entered the large white-columned stone throne room. Sol made his way to a raised stone chair at the center and sat down. Then Henri formally bowed to him. Sol's eyes ventured to the open windows of his throne room. These windows were not glass as in Azure Palace, but the view opened into outside gardens. He gazed at a mossy green garden, and the lovely sounds of the castle streams surrounded the room. Castle Cove may not have been a dreamscape like his wife's palace, but King Darius had done his best to copy it.

Sol sat sweating. His fingers tapped impatiently, then they gathered into a fist and he pounded on the arm of the throne as Henri stared outdoors.

"Damn it, Henri, get on with it. Tell me news. Good or bad."

"Perhaps we should be outside, Sol. It's the first clear day in a while."

Sol's energy from his sparring was over. Now he felt a familiar heavy weight over his body. He was exhausted.

"Philipp's army—"

"Sard Philipp and his army, Henri. I don't care. Tell me of my daughter."

"Mainax returns," said the wizard with a nod.

"Good. But I don't like your look."

"It's not all bad. Your daughter is alive."

"Thank the gods!" And Sol leaned back in his chair, running his hand over his forehead and long wet hair.

"Aye, the bird's taken a liking to your daughter."

"He's a phoenix. Of course he has."

"Aye. He's become her pet, Sol. And Casey knows no better. She has no idea that the fowl reports to me. Or that he's the same bird as the one in her palace. Oh, I so wish I could tell her. I'm able to see many things that transpire, but I can't talk to her. Casey lives at the bottom of the Dark Tower of Tartarus. She's well fed. And she has company."

"Does Anna know she's alive?"

"Yes. I retrieved Mainax in her kingdom, at the Stratos. I told her."

"She's been so worried, Henri. Does it ease her?"

"A little." But he didn't like Henri's forlorn expression.

"Go on."

Henri looked at the king, then paused. He dragged a heavy wooden chair from across the hall. They had chairs like Azure, too, but the wood was three times as heavy as Mandrigel-constructed furniture. It was so empty in the Hall that the sound of the legs sliding over stone echoed. There were two guards outside the entrance, but otherwise it was empty. And unlike the throne room in Azure, this one had no aisle of chairs.

"Anna needs this news, old friend."

Henri nodded and sat down. "I'm afraid Casey's ... locked up, Sol. She's imprisoned."

All Sol's joy left him. He looked down and put his head in his hands.

"But she's alive."

"What good is living like that? But what did I expect? Of course she's imprisoned. She survives, but of course the fiend jails her."

Henri nodded. "It's not all bad. She's being well taken care of. The hardship is just the confinement."

"I see."

"And she has help. It's been miraculous. The Mandrigel helped her. Engel's race thrives down there in a kingdom called Mangornia. And she has someone else. The bird told me a woman sees her and has become her good friend."

"A woman?"

"Yes," said Henri with a nod. "A goddess. Persephone."

"Persephone?"

"Aye. Persephone. Persephone cares for Casey as if she were her own daughter."

"Persephone! That beast's wife?"

"Aye, my lord, but you don't understand. Persephone's provided for her where her husband has not. If the viper doesn't give her food, Kore, as the bird calls her, feeds her. If the snake doesn't provide enough shelter, Kore sneaks in blankets for warmth. She's taking care of her, Sol."

"A whore comforts my Casey?"

"Things are not all well, son. True. Things are very hard. But she's cared for. That is not bad."

Sol looked at the garden through the holes in the walls once more and squeezed his hand tightly. He watched a man gathering water by a stream. And another child running down a grassy hill with his mother. A child. Seeing a little girl with her mother hurt him more.

"Do you remember the story I taught you when you were a boy? About the goddess Persephone?" Henri asked. "Persephone, daughter of Zeus and Demeter, was abducted and raped as an innocent child and then taken down into the Underworld. Do you remember that famous tale?"

"What of it?" Sol's bearded chin rested on his hand. "Why should I care about fairy tales now?"

"You should care a great deal. Kore feels compassion for your daughter because your daughter was once her. That goddess could very well be our savior, son. Just as Mainax is our messenger. Shall I remind you of the tale?" Sol said nothing, so Henri went on. "On a clear warm morning in Argos, much like the one we have today, the innocent virgin Kore was running along the fields picking lilies when she heard a sound from the sky. She looked up. There among the clouds was the shadow of a dark chariot with four black horses. It was the chariot of Hades. The devil flew down and swooped the poor girl from her fields. Then the earth opened, and they both fell straight down the hole into the earth. Some say she fell into the fields of Argos. Others claim it was the crater in Avernus. And even the nymphs lay claim with their Stygian Hole.

"Demeter, her mother, searched the ends of the earth for her daughter. Not finding her, she made the earth turn cold. There was a terrible snow. Winter. This is why we have the seasons. Then down in the depths Hades tricked the young goddess into eating myrle berries—the Napean name for the seeds of pomegranates. That locked her in the Underworld forever.

"Persephone's mother, Demeter, met with Hades. They agreed on an arrangement. Persephone was to be allowed to roam Gaia during the spring, but then, come winter, she would return to the Underworld. This part of the myth accounts for our seasons. Of course, from what I can see, Persephone appears to be imprisoned for an eternity. There was never a way back. And, as far as I know, Persephone has never returned to the surface of Gaia since she fell."

"Why tell me this?" Sol's eyelids closed. He felt so tired.

"Their attachment seems to make a great deal of sense. Their tales are similar. Casey is innocent and young. She wasn't abducted by a god, but we know she's been taken."

"She was abducted, Henri. Engel saw her pushed. So why are you so happy?" asked the king with a yawn. "She's still trapped. Are we to make some agreement with that evil demon to see my daughter every springtime?"

"I think we have a chance with this goddess. A chance." But then he turned quiet. "We have a chance. I think between my bird and her very powerful friend, along with your daughter's courage and cunning, she has a chance. That's all."

"What can you do with the bird?"

Henri smiled. "He is not only a phoenix, Solinair. He is an *Azure* phoenix … Do you understand what I mean?"

"No."

"I think I can help Casey escape, but she will need Persephone's help. She is too young to leave alone."

"That harpy will only hurt her, Henri. By the gods!" Sol

slammed the arm of his throne and gnashed his teeth. "You should have let me scale down the wall."

"Believe me, Sol, I wanted to go in and get her too."

Sol nodded. "What ... what about Engel's people? Do they help her?"

"Mainax saw Persephone help a few return home after journeying with Casey. They helped her get to Tartarus. Maybe trying to find a way out for her? I don't know. Many died, I'm afraid, helping your daughter."

"Tell me that snake didn't make my daughter see that!" he snapped with a scowl. "By the gods, Henri, how can you smile at all when my girl is in so much trouble?"

"I love Casey," Henri snapped back. "I smile because there's a chance. And, as far as the death of her companions, well ... all I can say is that your daughter has likely seen things now that even your eyes have never witnessed."

Those words really hurt Sol. He had a sudden urge to dismiss Henri.

He sank in his throne. The hard wooden throne felt particularly uncomfortable now and he shifted on it, then turned and looked at the courtyard again. Birds sang. The leaves swayed in a gentle breeze over a stone promenade. It was tranquil. Utterly contrary to his feelings.

"Perhaps we should continue the rest of my report later," Henri said with a sigh.

"Whatever can be done, Henri, do it. Do it ... do it. It's just..."

"What?"

"All our hope is in a bird and a witch. You've warned me so many times not to go after her but I'm afraid, old friend, if you can't free her, I swear, sheer cliff or not, in the face of the ferryman, I will slide down those walls myself. Even if by my death. I'll travel down the cave and see my daughter."

"You've seen how many have died trying. The fact that Casey survived the fall is a miracle itself ... or a part of this whole mystery."

Sol took a deep breath and nodded.

"Anna told me the same," Henri said.

Sol turned to him.

"Now I'll tell you what I told your wife. Give me more time. Please, Sol, I beg you, a little more time."

"I shall give you a few weeks. That is all. If you can't give me news of a rescue, then foolish or not, I'll go down."

"I know you will, Sol. I know it. A few weeks. I'll let you know as soon as I hear word from Mainax."

Sol nodded and got up. "In the meantime, Henri, rest. At least stay the night in Castle Cove. But I must hear the news of my enemies later. I can't deliberate over politics right now."

"Yes, my lord," he said formally with a bow. "But no, my lord. I came here to deliver the good news. I will tell you of the front when you are ready. Afterward, I'll make my way back through Shadow Forest to Napea. At least now you know your daughter is alive, praise the gods. There's hope. And with hope, I return to Mount Ambitus to continue sending my messages through Mainax."

"I'll be there soon. For Anna."

Henri nodded and, with a broad stroke of his arm, gave Sol a deep bow.

As he approached the exit, Sol said, "There's no mystery, you know, Henri. I don't have to be an oracle to know this is the work of the gods. Olympus took my daughter the moment we made our agreement with King Philipp. You told me you spoke with Hades yourself."

"It … it's possible," Henri said with a nod without looking back.

There was silence and Henri stood still for a moment. Sol gazed out at the courtyard. He spotted his son, Gavin, rushing through the grassy fields on horseback. Gavin would return to speak with Milo and his army.

But his army would have to wait. As much as Sol meant his threat to jump down the chasm, he knew his wife meant it far more. Sol would have to return and see her. And stop her.

Henri remained by the door, as if waiting to be dismissed. Then he cocked his head back and said sadly, "Sol, whatever our disagreements, this war with Olympus is not your fault. It did not begin with you. It began when Anna stepped foot on your shore and fell in love with you. But had that not happened, Cassandra would never have been born."

30

FILLING COFFERS

The next few weeks were even tougher. Cassandra's firebird left her. Persephone grew busy. The novelty of Cassandra's presence in Tartarus had seemingly worn off for her bird and her goddess. She felt extreme loneliness, more loneliness than she had ever felt in her life. Her mother had told her many times of her imprisonment under her grandmother as a child, but at least her mother had friends visiting her.

She started writing. On days when she was permitted to enter the courtyard outside, she'd spend most of the day writing hymns with a feather over a scroll, though she knew it was probably a waste of time. Who would ever read it?

She had given up on leaving. When she was first imprisoned, she had looked for ways out of the fortress, examining her environment, watching guards, and marking their movements. But soon it dawned on her that, even if she found a way to escape Tartarus, she'd have no idea how to leave the Underworld.

The absence of time soon drove her mad. She lost any notion of night or day. Only a dim red hue brightened or dimmed a fake earthen sky in which, if she squinted hard enough, she could see the dirt dome.

Today, Casey sat by her barred window drafting a poem.

Light to dark, darkest night

Words of flight, words of fancy, to each a feather

"No, that won't do!" She crumbled the parchment in her hand. "Sounds like an incantation."

Cassandra heard tapping at the bars. She turned. It was her firebird standing outside the window.

"Firebird! Oh, Firebird!"

She had not seen him in so long. And as he often did, he squeezed through the wide metal bars of the open window and landed on Cassandra's lap. Casey stroked the feathers of his wings. "Oh, I've missed you! I'm composing a poem." Then she gently put the bird down on a wooden table beside her. "Would you like to hear it?"

Mainax cooed.

She leaned her chin on her hand and read the scroll aloud to the bird.

Dark bloom, blue bells, stone of alabaster

Coral red

What ensnares?

Morning dew ripples

From dog fangs? Or viper? A kiss from a man?

"Hmm. Not sure where to go with that." Cassandra giggled. "A kiss from a man, eh Firebird? Hmm. That's good … How 'bout—"

He might go and dance for a while.

And she laughed again.

Along the lands of Azerban.

"Do you like it, Firebird? Hmm?" She laughed as the bird seemed to nod its head. She ran to Mainax and picked him up again. "I thought you would. I hope Cora will. Here's the rest." And she read it to her firebird:

Mount Ambitus, blue and green corsets fill my coffers

A tall order for me to live? Or to see what coins the demon offers.

From the blue-green Stratos to Shadow Forest, I yearn.

To be free. Far far away from kings and queens.

A leaf sails a stream. A babe fades
We might go and dance for a while
Betwixt and within the lands of Azerban.

She checked to see if her bird was listening. He simply sat on her lap, leaning against her stomach.

Light to dark, dark to light
Heat upon a candle light
Between flame, the smoke adrift
The liquid stained by … flame—

"You do like it, Firebird, don't you?"

Casey looked around, surprised. Being attentive to reading her poem, she hadn't noticed her phoenix had left her. She spotted him at the windowsill hitting the bars with his beak and seemingly prepared to squeeze through the bars again.

"Well, don't go. I haven't finished—"

The iron bars caught aflame and exploded, blowing smoke at her then filling the room. Cassandra coughed terribly. She ran toward her door, fearing she would be trapped in flames. She was about to bang on the door, for fear of asphyxiation, when the smoke cleared. It gave way to a light red mist. She could see the window. To her amazement, two bars were blown open, giving her enough room to squeeze through. There was enough room for her to escape!

She looked at the wooden door behind her. No one approached.

The window frame was very hot, but she confirmed that it was wide enough for her to fit through. She turned back one last time. Then she took a lovely saffron peplos lying near her bed—another gift that had been Cora's—and used it to cover the rough edges of metal. When the borders were cool enough, she started to squeeze through the frame. She had gotten halfway through when she noticed ash on the ground outside the window. Then, to her amazement, the ashes spun up like a dust devil and coalesced back into her firebird. The phoenix looked up at her as if nothing had happened.

"Oh Firebird," she said quietly, squeezing her waist through, "you did it! You want me to be free? Hang on while I try to … nudge … through this escape route of yours."

She pushed her body all the way through. Then, in horror, she heard a voice inside her cell.

"Casey? Casey?" It was Persephone. She must have just entered. Cassandra turned and looked inside her cell.

"Casey, what's happened?" Cora coughed and waved her hand, pushing away smoke.

"Oh, Cora, I'm free!" Cassandra said in a forced whisper. "This is my chance. I have a chance to escape … I shall miss you. I will miss you so much, Cora."

"Wonderful, child! Go as fast as you can. Run across through the garden courtyard, cross the fence, and enter the city streets. The main streets circle down to the main bridge. It's easy. Run as fast as your feet will take you over the bridge. Try not to look back."

"Thank you. Oh, thank you for everything, Cora!" She hugged Cora tightly through the window.

"Your company has been a gift, dear girl. Hurry. Go quickly! You can do what I've only dreamed of."

Cassandra nodded but froze for a moment. Cora smiled reassuringly, but it seemed strained. Then Cassandra turned and ran as fast as she could.

She headed through the garden courtyard and paralleled the main road to the entrance of the dark tower. Mainax followed her from above.

She passed the people walking solemnly in line, waiting for admittance to the dark tower, pushing carts or standing alone. Many turned with blank expressions at the sound of her feet, but many more kept their heads down and ignored her. One ghost rushed toward her and passed through her. It didn't impede Cassandra. She ran as fast as she could.

She turned from the dirt path and ran toward a field of dead bushes and trees. Here there was another metal fence. Cassandra searched along the worn metal and the hedges, covered with blackened branches, for a hole to exit through. When she found a way out, she felt dread again. Two large burly guards in black armor stood beside the hole, which opened into the main street. How could she pass?

"Why are you running, girl?" a guard with a bushy beard asked. "From whom?"

"I … I have…"

She had been so stupid. She had dreamed of escaping for weeks, but she had no plan.

"You need to let me pass." Cassandra stood up straight, attempting confidence.

"Who are you? Where are you going?"

Then a beardless younger guard said, "Look at her palms. They're blue. And look at her ankles. She's a nymph. She must be the nymph Lord Hades and Persephone have staying at the palace."

"I'm in need of assistance, sirs," Cassandra stammered. "The queen's been burned. I'm her close friend. Yes, I'm a nymph. My friend Persephone and I were in the courtyard, when she was burned by my firebird. You see that bird above." She pointed up to her phoenix circling over them.

"So?" asked the guard with the beard. He laughed. "You could probably burn our majesty to ashes and she'd revive herself."

"No, you don't understand." Cassandra shook her head. "That's an enchanted bird. It will keep hurting her if you don't help her."

The two guards looked at each other.

"The bird exploded in her face! You must help us!" It was the best thing she could think of at the moment. "Can you help me?"

"She is Cassandra Ambrosia." The bearded guard nodded. "The nymph princess."

"Please, help the queen," pleaded Cassandra. "The phoenix keeps coming down and burning her. There's no time. Hurry, she's hurt."

"I'll go," said one of the guards, shaking his head. "You stay and watch this girl."

"No, you don't understand. The *queen* is hurt. She can't walk. She needs to be moved back into the tower. I tried to lift her, but I'm too small. You two are strong and can carry her together."

The two guards looked at each other again.

"Then you come with us."

"Of course," Cassandra said with a smile.

The two guards left their post and walked with their backs toward the courtyard. As they walked, laughing at her story—thinking they were simply returning the "little girl" to the tower—Cassandra bolted. It was foolish, but she had no other plan.

She escaped their grasp and ran across another black dirt field of thorns and dead trees. She paralleled the broken main stone road.

Cora had said that if she followed the main road, she could find the fire moat. She ran between some thatched-roof homes to ditch the guards and turned back onto the broken stone road again.

She looked back and thought she had lost the guards, but then they chased her near another house.

She spotted a small orchard of leafless black trees. The shrubs below had dark violet leaves and seemed thick enough for a young girl to hide in. She ran to the bushes, did her best not to be cut by the branches as she dug in, and hid.

Looking through a hole in the bush, she was surprised to see Persephone walking—no, gliding—elegantly as always, in her draping red peplos. She didn't appear rushed at all. She nonchalantly approached the guards.

She's delaying them!

Cora turned and looked at the bush. She seemed to look right at Cassandra. Surely, she couldn't see her through all the leaves?

She waited for them to leave.

Two large gloved hands probed the thick sharp branches. One contacted Cassandra's shoulder. She had been discovered!

At that very instant, Cassandra came to a terrible realization. She felt more alone than she had ever felt in her life. Cora had feigned helping her then told the guards where to find her. There was no way the guards had seen her in the underbrush.

31

LOST

Except for an occasional sliver of light under the door, Cassandra's new prison cell was completely dark. After a while, as her eyes adapted, she could make out her mattress and the filthy gray stone ground. She was robbed of light and sound, but far worse, she was robbed of company. It could have been days, weeks, she didn't know. Hades had assigned her to a terrible prison cell to teach her a lesson. Whereas before her cell was more like a simple room with bars over the window, this was a dungeon. Hades claimed it was the same room where her ancestor Nefertiti had been locked up centuries before. And he made Cassandra wear the legendary nymph's hoplite armor.

But Hades didn't starve her. First guards threw open the metal door and tossed stale bread and bowls of water on the floor. Later someone snuck in delicious-smelling real food.

At first, she let the feast sit in a corner refusing to touch it. But the smell drove her mad. In time, she crept over. It smelled like pheasant, something wonderful. And there were freshly baked cakes and an amphora of liquid that tasted like some sort of tea. Everything was warm, which she surmised was to keep her warm in her cold prison cell. She devoured it. It was one of the best tasting dishes she had ever had. And how strange to eat such a wondrous dish in the middle of her horrible plight. The next day there was more.

Of course, she knew who had sent her food. It was her Underworld "friend." Her perfidious goddess, the most conniving woman she had ever known. Such a friend. After she had been caught, Hades told her, during another fight in his throne room, that her "friend" had caused her to be taken into the Underworld in the first place. Of course Cora protested. Then Cora screamed and threw things at him. It didn't matter. This is what her royal meals in the dungeon were like. They were like Persephone. A goddess so kind and sweet and lovely, yet the cause of all her suffering. Although Hades was terrifying, her "friend's" guile in some ways scared her more.

After forever—she didn't know how long—the door creaked open to a familiar voice and a very bright yellow light. It was Persephone, holding a blinding lantern.

The betrayal was forgotten in a flash. Cassandra ran into her arms.

"Oh Casey," Cora said, choking up. "I'm so sorry. Can you forgive me?"

"No. I can't. But I've missed you a lot, Cora. How can I forgive you? I can't trust you."

"I know."

Cora shone the light over Cassandra. Casey squinted.

"Have you been eating?"

"Yes," Casey said with a sad smile. Then she turned from Cora, returning to her mattress, which under the light was filthy and torn. "But I shouldn't have taken your gifts. You're a monster."

"I am a monster. But I'm *your* monster. And I've sworn my immortal life to protect and serve your family."

There was silence. Cora put the torch in a sconce on a wall by the entrance and sat on the cot beside Casey. Even here in the prison, Cora wore a beautiful flowing red peplos of lovely sparkling materials Casey had never seen before. She glowed. Her long hair was a perfect gold, and she had accentuated her lips and face with makeup. She looked amazing in the dark dungeon.

She smiled. Why smile? Cora had betrayed her and sent her back to this dungeon.

"I've brought you something else, Ambrosia princess. A gift. I've never given you anything."

"That's not true. You gave me your peploi. Many of them."

"Stop." She laughed. "That was nothing." She looked sternly at Casey. She seemed to be examining her. Then she nodded and patted Casey's leg. "It's time. I've learned to cope as best I can. I've accepted my lot for the promise of things to come. I've waited. For you, Casey. But long ago, just like now, I couldn't stand to watch your great-great-grandmother wither away. I certainly won't watch you suffer. I want you to run. You must move quickly. I'll help you get out."

"I don't believe you."

"Do you see this?" Cora patted a silver battle helmet under her arm.

She nodded.

"It's not just a helmet." Cora placed it on her lap. "It's my husband's cap. It's enchanted. Whoever wears the silver helmet is rendered invisible. You'll need this for us to pass the guards. This is my gift." She looked away in thought and nodded almost to herself. "First I aid Nephree and now you."

"I thought you hated Nephrea?"

"I loved her." Cora shook her head. "I loved her more than anyone. I asked you not to mention her because it hurt me every time you said her name. It hurt me because of what happened to you and what happened to her. I loved her, Casey. Nephrea was my mother." Cora smiled and ran a hand along Casey's bangs. "My husband's right. You look so much like her."

"You stood in an Amazon stance. That wasn't Greek."

She nodded. "I was trained by Amazons, Casey. Your family." Then she touched the leather over Casey's arm. "Her armor fits you. It's yours. Wear it with pride as I take you back home."

"How, Cora? How can I leave? I can't pass through Elysium. I don't know the way."

"There is only one true way. It is how Nephrea left."

"The flume."

"Yes. How did you know?"

"The witches told me of it in Mangornia. And they predicted you'd help me."

"Mangornia? I see. Yes, the Mandrigel are a good race."

"That isn't what you thought when you killed my friends," Cassandra snapped. She pushed away from the goddess in sudden fury. The memory of what had happened to Intar and her other friends suddenly filled her with unbearable disgust. Cora's kindness only made it worse.

She jumped up and moved as far from Cora as she could.

"Quiet," Cora said, looking back at the cell door. Then she shook her head. "Shh. I helped your friends get home. They're fine now."

"I don't believe you."

"Oh, Casey, I can't prove it, but it's true. I set them free and helped them home, where they're now safe. How could I let Hades hurt Intar? Intar saved Nephrea's life." Cora shook her head almost violently. "There isn't enough time to explain all this. You have to come with me. Put the helmet on and see for yourself. You'll turn invisible and I will take you home."

"But why would you tell the guards where I was and then help me escape?"

Cora sighed. Then she looked at the metal door again. "Because it wasn't the right time. My husband is away for business in the fields of Nyx now. I stole his helmet before he left. He can't pursue us. If I had let you go, you wouldn't have made it past the bridge."

Cassandra smiled sadly then shook her head. "Cora, even if you're telling the truth, there's no telling what your husband will do to you if you help me escape."

"Shall I tell you a secret?" Cora asked, permitting a faint smile. "I prophesy that one day you will free me from this forsaken realm and destroy the hold Olympus has over all humans and nymphs. You, Cassandra. I don't know how, but I've prophesied this. And I've waited here, all along knowing that I must remain to play a part in freeing you and freeing my husband and myself. My husband knows the prophecy. He knows that when that day comes, he and I will gain great power over the world. That's the reason he keeps you here. Not to punish your parents. He couldn't care less about them. He wanted you to remain here to free us. And Zeus favors you remaining here too. But it's time. I must help you get home now."

Cassandra nodded.

"Casey, I've wronged you only to find the right time. You must believe me. When your friends sent the bird, it was the wrong time. Now Hades has left Tartarus."

"My friends sent him?"

"There's no time to explain. Come take the cap and go. I don't blame you for not trusting me but, tell me, would I give you this helm if I didn't mean for you to escape? I want to help you. I've wanted to since you fell."

Cassandra didn't trust her. And yet if it meant even the possibility of leaving this dark cell, even for a moment, she'd do it. She came closer to Cora.

"I need you to be brave," Cora said, taking her hand. "Think of home. Think of Lalaina. Think of your parents, Avva and Sol. Think of Uncle Henri. Think of everyone you love. The thoughts of your loved ones will help you down the Mount. It's a perilous journey, but we can do this together. I know you have the strength, girl."

"Will you go with me?"

Cora nodded.

"Can you stay with me in Azure?"

"I must see this through to the end," she said, narrowing her eyes and staring at the wall. "There was another time when I could have left, but all of this is about Olympus, not me, or Hades, or even your blessed people. It's about stopping my family." Cora sighed. Then she looked back at the door anxiously.

"There's no time. Just know that even when you're home, I watch over you. Your family's all I care about. Take this cap. No one will see you, not even the gods. Not even me. You'll be as unseen as I was when I entered your room, blinding you with this lantern."

"All right, Cora."

Cora stood up and gently placed the helmet over her head.

Cassandra didn't feel any different. Then the goddess reached for her hand and brought it up to her eyes. It was invisible.

"You can go home now, Casey."

3 2

THE GREAT ESCAPE

Cassandra found it hard to keep up with Cora. The goddess had boundless energy and seemed to leap up the steps of her dungeon. Then, in a hall, she groped for Cassandra. Cassandra gave the goddess her hand, and Cora practically dragged her through the halls of the fortress. But when they had climbed one more flight of stairs and opened a metallic door to the outside, Cora stopped rushing. She turned and looked around her, searching the stairway. "Casey, are you here?"

"Yes, Cora, I'm right here," Casey replied, panting.

"Don't speak. When I'm stopped by the guards, simply stand aside. No one will see you. We have to walk another quarter of a league to the outer wall. The streets will take us there. Inside the flume, we'll use my husband's chariot to escape. Just remember to be quiet. They can't see you, but they can hear you. Okay?"

"Okay, Cora."

Cora smiled, even though she didn't meet her eyes. Indeed, Cassandra was invisible even to her.

When she opened the metallic door, the goddess shifted the fabric of her red dress back and walked regally down the main street of Tartarus, just as Casey had seen her do many times before. Bystanders from the city—beggars, vagabonds, and even ghosts—gave her a wide berth, terrified at the sight of their queen-goddess. She walked slowly in public, and it was easy to keep up with her now.

They followed the broken main cobblestone street until they veered from the line of people and entered a side street. Then they made their way through many more broken roads. Villains did some of the most heinous acts she had ever seen—maiming, burning, and stabbing. Cora didn't seem disturbed. Perhaps she had grown accustomed to it. But even the most unscrupulous looking person quickly averted their gaze or ran from the mere sight of the goddess.

They walked down an even darker and seedier alley. They turned once more. Here she spotted the shadow of the earthen stone wall that rose from the city all the way to the rocky ceiling. She hadn't noticed the wall being this close to the city before. She figured it was because all the light in the city came from the occasional fires lit in the fire fields on the other side. This area was simply too shadowed.

A garrison of black-armored Eruboi stood at attention by the sidewalk on the opposite side of the street. There must have been a hundred soldiers lined up, in formation, coming from the end of the street.

Cora walked faster. It seemed like Cora didn't expect soldiers here, but Casey dared not say anything.

There was a door that seemed to be attached to the rocky wall. It was silvery metal and reminded her, with a shudder, of the metallic door that had opened into the cave, which had drawn her into this cursed world in the first place.

A guard opened the door for Cora. Inside were more turns and long rocky hallways. Eruboi lined the halls of these labyrinths. They traveled down another dark corridor until they faced a similar silver door as outside. Cora turned but still did not meet Casey's eyes.

"Be very quiet," Cora whispered. "The guards are all over the base of the flume."

"Yes, Cora."

Cora smiled and put a finger to her lips again. Then she opened the door.

Inside was a very bright circular hall surrounded by rocky walls. But what took Cassandra's breath away was what lay above. A hole that seemed to rise forever, and at the top was a brilliant yellow-white light, flooding the hall. The brightness made her and Cora squint. In the center was a huge chariot with four winged konabera.

At the sight of the light, Cassandra felt more elated than she could remember. There was finally hope that she could leave this forsaken place and go home. She realized this light was the sun. It was brighter than any artificial light she had seen in the Underworld.

Then, what a strange feeling to have all her euphoria crash. Her eyes fell on a rider atop the chariot. It was Hades, wearing a dark hooded cloak, facing them with a nasty sardonic grin.

"Going somewhere?"

"What … what are you doing here?" Cora asked. "I thought you told me you were on your way to Elysium."

"I was. Then I realized that in my sleep I had misplaced my helm. Would you happen to know where it is, Kore?"

"You won't need it in Elysium."

"No." He shook his head, chuckling. "No, I won't. But someone else might need it here."

"Whatever do you mean?" Cora cautiously walked toward him. She flashed an open palm behind her back, gesturing for Casey not to follow.

"You never stole my cap before. Why would you do that now, Cora?"

A few soldiers walked through the door where Cora and Casey had entered. Cora's eyes narrowed at their approach.

"I don't know where your helmet is," Cora said.

"All right, dear. Then tell me why you're here?"

"I roam where I please. I grow bored in our home. I've told you that many times."

Another ten soldiers entered the flume.

Hades jumped down from the chariot and approached Cora. He ran a finger along Cora's cheek. "Where is she? Tell me, wife."

"Who?"

"You know. Where is our nymph daughter?" Hades looked around the hall. "I don't see her. But then she'd be invisible, wouldn't she?"

"Really, husband," Cora said with a laugh. "I have no idea what you're talking about. I like visiting the flume because it's bright. It reminds me of Gaia. As far as your cap, I honestly don't know. And as far as our nymph, you, bastard, imprisoned her."

"Liar." Hades stared into her eyes. His eyes were now glowing red. "Let's be straight, Cora, for once, shall we? She's here. Where?"

"She's not."

"Casey?" Hades said, looking all around him. "Oh Casey? Casey, darling, take the helm off so I can see your pretty blue face. Did you know, dear child, that I let your mommy, Cora here, save the dwarfs? Did you know that I could go back and just as easily slay them for breaking the treaty? Particularly Intar. He's Engel's brother. Did you know that? Would you like Engel's brother to live? His fate can be changed. It is my mercy, after all, that allows them their safety in Mangornia. The treaty is a farce."

"You swore an oath!" cried Cassandra.

Cora spun around and looked more afraid than ever.

Hades took a deep breath as if enjoying the fragrance of her voice. "Ah. That's it. Very good, Cassandra. Now take the cap off and show your lovely nymph face before your wood nymph mommy, Persephone."

"Run, Casey," cried Cora, searching the room. "Run! Go through that door and up the flume. I'll catch up."

There were only two doors in the hallway. The door that they had walked through to get in, which was now blocked by Eruboi, and the one Cora pointed to. So there really wasn't any other choice.

Cora rushed to Hades, lifting her fist, ready to strike him.

"Go, Casey," Hades said. "Run. Go on. Up the stairs. It leads to the outdoors and your home. That's how Nephrea did it."

Cora stopped her arm from striking him. "You're letting her go? You're letting me take her home?"

"Of course not, traitor. I'm letting her go up the flume by herself."

As Cassandra threw the door open and gazed at bright steps rising—but this staircase led to only a sliver of sunlight through the ceiling—she heard Cora shout, "Wait, Casey! Come back. It's a trick. You need me to make it down the mountain."

Cassandra ran back to the bottom steps and again peered through the open door.

"She'll go," Hades said. "She'll go *alone*, Cora. That's what you told me. Your prophecy stated that the nymph princess would free us after she was imprisoned like her ancestor, Nephratee. I returned her to prison to fulfill your vision. Or should I say, you did. But I always wondered how she'd end up here in order to satisfy the Graeae's prophecy of the flume. How amusing that you arranged that when trying to help her escape. We work better together, wife, than you think."

"Viper! No foretelling is certain! You'll kill her if she goes alone!"

Hades shook his head. Then he nodded to the Eruboi behind her, who grabbed Cora.

"Unhand me!" Cora cried.

Casey leaned against the dirt wall, hesitating, unsure whether to somehow help Cora or ascend.

"Fiend!" screamed Cora as she struggled with the guards. "She'll die! I won't let this happen again!"

Then Cassandra couldn't believe her eyes. Cora dragged five soldiers on her back, but another ten jumped her. Then Hades grabbed her wrists. Finally, soldiers threw her on the stone floor and tied her with thick ropes to the chariot so that the konabera held Cora in place.

"No!" cried Cassandra, removing her helmet. "Leave her alone!"

"Stop resisting, Kore," Hades said. He looked right at Cassandra. "You're upsetting the wood nymph."

"Get off me!"

The flume turned pitch black. Soldiers in the shadows gazed up—even Hades did. Then a torrent of water crashed down. It was as if a dam had broken and the entire ocean was pouring down the flume. It became so dark and stormy that soldiers scrambled to light torches—or tried to—but were thrown to the ground by the water in the shadows. Casey put her helm back on, now using it as shelter, then covered her head and crouched to the floor to protect herself from the waves of water. Then lightning struck and flashed the chamber with light. Between the bolts, the chamber alternated between pitch black and bright white.

"Calm down, Kore!" Hades cried. "You're flooding the flume."

"This will be the end of us!" Cora cried, in tears, struggling against the konabera. Another flash of lightning filled the chamber. Casey saw Cora, incredibly, dragging all four of the beasts and the chariot. "I swear, Hades! I will never forgive you! Don't lead a child to her death. So help me, you'll regret it! At least let me help her down the Mount! I don't care what our family thinks of me! I'm not afraid of them, you coward. Release your guards and let me help her! So help me, Hades! Let me help her. I ask nothing more from you!"

"I didn't plant the Amphiuma," Hades said. "This isn't my fault. I can't have your father see me or you helping her survive. But I can let her go alone. That fulfills the prophecy."

"Fight them, coward! Fight your brother and my cursed mother! Don't let an innocent girl, the descendant of your true love, die at the top of the Mount!"

"But she won't die, Kore," Hades shouted. "That one was

prophesied by the Graeae. One who loves her will sacrifice her life to save her. That can't be you—you can't die. She will live. And with her life, according to *your* prophecy, you and I will be free and reign supreme on Gaia. I'm not sending her to her death. I'm sending her away for our liberty."

"You and I are through!"

With another bolt, soldiers threw more rope over her torso and even hammered ropes to the ground, through the storm, as if trying to anchor a ship. She was finally immobile, but she still bucked and shook, violently trying to free herself. *"You hear me! Not only because of what you've done, but because you're weak. I curse you and hate you. From now on, I play your wife no more!"*

"Goodbye, Cora," Cassandra said by the door.

"Don't go, Casey!" Cora shouted in tears, dragging soldiers behind her. "Please! Don't leave me!"

But those last words gave Casey the resolve she needed. *Don't leave me.* This wretched goddess seemed to do everything simply to appease her own selfishness. Her needs were more important than anyone else's.

Cassandra ran up the steps.

There was a scream below. Casey thought it was Cora, but she wasn't sure. Whatever it was, it was followed with more water than ever. Then the men screamed below. She wondered if they were drowning.

The light was snuffed out and waves poured down the steps. She ran up more stairs and the stairway widened. Then Casey pressed herself as close as she could to the cave wall as a torrential wave raced down the steps. At one point, she tripped, but she regained her balance on a stone step. The water rushed so heavily as to make her consider rushing back down to the flume. But then, looking down, she saw water was rising below her. She had no other direction to go now. If she went down, she'd have to swim.

It would be pitch black if it weren't for a flickering flame above. As she advanced up the steps, fighting the water, she saw a single torch still burning on a wall.

She waited for it to dry enough to climb further. The water calmed. Sunlight appeared through a crack in the ceiling again.

She ascended but it took forever. After resting and climbing endlessly, she saw another metallic door under an open roof. She opened the cold metal door and found herself outside atop an icy cliffside. Above was a brilliant clear blue sky with a yellow sun. But it was frigid. She could not see the ground, for a sheer rocky wall fell under her into the clouds. And there was another cliff, perhaps a few hundred yards up a sheer rocky wall, reflecting golden yellow. Mount Olympus? She caught a glimpse, barely visible in the glare, of white stone columns. She wasn't sure. There was no way to climb up.

The only way was down. A snowy trail, leading down, was to her left. As she looked out to the horizon, she expected to finally see her home. She didn't. All she saw were thick clouds.

Then she was startled by a screech. Soaring in the blue sky above was her firebird. Apparently, her phoenix had been freed too.

33

A LEAP OF FAITH

Avva heard a knock on the pole outside her tent. She almost missed it with the sound of rain pummeling the fabric above the tent. She pulled the cloth open and a very wet white-haired Henri, wearing a heavy gray chiton and carrying a coat over his head to shield himself from the rain, rushed inside.

"Avva." They embraced.

"Henri, what news? Strange to have this sudden storm."

He nodded.

"What is it?"

"Casey." He looked down, forlorn.

"Is she close?"

"Aye. Closer than ever, Anna." But he had a look of profound sadness. That made her nervous. He walked over to a wooden chair and sat down.

"Forgive me, Anne. I told your husband first."

"Told him what?"

"I told him about Casey. Your wonderful daughter. She was spotted by Mainax near the summit of the mountain. She's climbing down."

"She's out!"

"Aye." He nodded.

"But how will she get down the Mount?"

"Aye. That's the problem."

"She can't climb down the Mount. Not even our best climbers can do that."

"No." He shook his head. "No, she can't, Blue."

He turned from her. Avva looked through a crack in the tent fabric and saw rain pouring outside. The storm was getting so bad that Cambria had told her they might have to return to the palace due to the water flooding the tents. She had never seen Napea rain so hard before.

"Hanna has gathered the best climbers in the kingdom," replied Avva with a nod after some silence, "who have volunteered to travel up the mountain if commanded. Many brave men and Amazon. They can climb to the top. I mean, it's never been done. But I think it can be done. No one has ever had a reason to try it. It's … I think with enough … I mean we certainly have a reason to try now, right, Henri? Perhaps they can go tomorrow when the storm clears."

Henri looked at her. She did not like his expression. "There's no time for tomorrow."

"We have to try."

"Exactly what your brave daughter thinks, Anne."

"Well, what else, then?"

"This is what I was just talking to the king about."

Avva walked over to her desk, where she had been writing. She pushed the scrolls to the side and put her head in her hand. "So close," she murmured to herself. "I can't believe it. She's free. Now this. … you're so close to being home, Casey."

"The tales told by Mainax are incredible. Your daughter is a hero in her own right. You should be proud. She traveled through Hypnos. She faced Hades. And now, she journeyed up and out of the Underworld itself. To think that any girl could go through the trials she's endured. She is an amazing girl. A true Amazon. Somehow, she traveled through the Mandrigel lands, through Tartarus and up and out of the mountain."

"I thought you told me Mainax helped her."

"No. The phoenix was my eyes, but he did little. Our little heroine did the rest."

He got up and stood near the hole outside the tent. It was small and had a canopy outside keeping the rain out. Avva could see the rain pour so hard that it limited visibility much further out.

"I think we shall have some finality at last," Henri added. Avva didn't like the sound of that.

"I was rummaging through legal work. About one lady's farm and another. It's not important. So? Tell me. What do you think about our team of climbers? Should I order them out there now?"

"Anna, I don't think you understand what I'm trying to tell you."

"What do you mean?"

"She walked down some of the way. As she continues, she will find a wall. Then she will have to use ropes. She has no one to stand by her, no one to help her. She's a good climber, but hardly an expert. And Mainax reports that it is storming just as bad, if not far worse, up there."

There was a long silence. Then Avva said quietly, mostly to herself, "She'll fall."

He merely nodded.

"No one can climb Ambitus," Avva said. "I'm not so sure Nefertiti ever did. I'll not have my subjects die on the cliffs. But I—"

"I don't know of an Azure girl who's passed through the gates except, perhaps, the great Pharaoh Nefertiti. And that may only be legend. Casey was even chased by Eruboi. She is the bravest and strongest girl I've ever known. I am so proud to have known her. An Ambrosia for sure. She will be remembered in song for all time."

"*Remembered!*" Avva snapped. Henri jumped. Avva hadn't intended to shout at him, but she couldn't believe Henri's words. "Remembered? ... What do you mean *remembered?*"

"Aye. Well—"

"Is that a prediction? *Remembered!*"

"Hmm? What, Blue? Prediction? No. We discussed—"

"You're joking."

"Hmm?"

"How can my daughter have gone through all this? Suffered so much? For what?" Her voice was rising. "To be remembered?"

"Anna," he said, putting his hand out.

"She can't fall down the mountain!"

"What else can be done?" he asked, shaking his head desperately. "You're right. You can't send climbers. Even without the storm. I went through all this with Sol. I've told you—"

"Told me what? I think you do know. Sometimes, I think you know quite a lot more than you say." Then, enraged, she swiped her arm across the desk and toppled all the scrolls over. She started shouting, almost screaming, in hysteria. She didn't even know what she was saying. Then she sifted through a chest and pulled out her scarlet Amazon armor—the same armor she had worn when she'd helped Sol in Crescent Blue.

"Anna, what are you doing?"

He put his hand on her shoulder, but she yanked it off.

"You and my husband have no plan?" She grabbed her scepter. She changed in front of him, not caring for impropriety. He had been right. There was no more time.

"Anna!" he yelled.

"You both do nothing?"

She grabbed a coat hanging against the wall. She ran over to her belongings, and then started sifting through them in a mad rage. She threw the contents all over the room.

"But what can be done?" he asked incredulously. "Think. What can be done, Anna?"

"*Remembered?*" she repeated in disgust. "What good is your stupid bird now, Henri? Hmm?"

When he didn't answer, she made her way past him, knocking her shoulder against his as she stormed out of the tent. "How about this, Henri? I shall be remembered too!"

"Anna, wait! Where are you going? What are you doing?"

"I'm going to help her."

He stared at her and, judging from his expression, she figured she must have looked crazy. Then she ran into the storm.

She could barely see a few steps ahead of her, the storm was so bad. The wind and rain raged so hard that she fought to move forward.

"Cambria! Cambria!"

The general ran out from another tent. Cambria wore a simple tunic and pants. But Henri was closer and caught up to Cambria first, pulling her aside. Avva could not hear what he said, but Henri's eyes were bulging and he kept pointing at her. When the queen kept yelling for her, Cambria ran and knelt on the mud under the pouring rain.

"Your Majesty," Cambria said, staring at the ground.

"You are to remain here. That is an order. I do not want anyone to follow me. Do you understand?" She was talking fast, and Avva saw Cambria's expression. They all thought she was crazy.

"Whatever is your order, I obey, my queen," she said with a nod.

Henri ran as fast as his old legs could take him. He headed straight for her husband's tent. Then he ran harder as Avva started whistling for Antilus all over the compound.

Solinair came out in a thick coat. Henri grabbed him, shouting, "She's mad, Sol! She intends to fly to the top of the mountain to get Casey. She'll never make it. Speak with her, quick! She'll die!"

Avva answered by whistling even more. It was late, and many people walked outside to see the commotion. All the while, the rain poured.

Solinair caught up with Avva and grabbed her arm.

"What's going on?" Sol shouted in the rain. "What is this?"

"This doesn't concern you." She turned her back to him whistling some more.

"By Hades it doesn't!" He pulled her toward him again. "What's this all about, Anna?"

"Stay back. Guard the camp. If I perish, you have my kingdom. As king, husband."

"What are you talking about?" He grabbed her arm once more.

"*Unhand me!*" she yelled, yanking her arm back.

Hanna ran over from her tent wearing a heavy coat over a nightgown.

"What's the matter, Avva?" Hanna asked.

"I've been told by my husband's counselor that Casey's climbing down the mountain. She can scale a wall, to be sure, but a mountain is suicide. She needs my help. She'll never make it."

Avva whistled again. "Antilus! Antilus!"

"What are you going to do, Blue?" asked Hanna.

Avva whistled frantically again. Hanna grabbed her wrist hard. Avva turned and, with wild eyes, yelled, "I told you! I'm going to get her! Leave me alone and don't follow me!"

"You don't intend to *fly* to her?" Hanna asked with her eyes wide.

"Why not?"

"That's how Casey got into trouble in the first place. Hasn't she proven what will happen? You'll fall. And how will we help you?"

"You won't," she said as if the facts were as plain as day. "Keep away from me. It's too dangerous."

"Then why are you doing it?"

"Antilus and I will jump to the summit ... and ... and then ... get her." Avva started whistling again. She ran about the tents, whistling and waking everyone.

"Then we'll follow," Cambria said behind her.

"No!" Avva yelled, turning to her. It was the only thing that finally stopped the queen's crazed whistling. "You won't follow, Cambria. That's an order as your queen. I won't allow it. I go alone. It's too risky for you. No unicorn can fly over the mountain."

"Then why are you attempting it, Anna?" This time the question came from Sol. And his voice was oddly calm.

"I have Antilus," she said, addressing her husband. "She is … Where is she! … *Antilus!* … She … is the only one who can make the jump. She and I can make it."

"Why not wait until the rain stops?" said Solinair. He spoke so calmly. "Think this over."

"Our daughter may be dead then."

"Stop her, Sol," urged Henri.

"I can't allow this," Sol said. He grabbed Anna's arm and she tried to yank it away, but he wouldn't budge this time. Then she spun around, knocked his hand off her arm, and faced him in an Amazon fighting stance. Cambria stepped between them.

"I'll call my men," Sol threatened.

"Stand back from the queen," Cambria said. "You are outnumbered, sir."

"I'm the king of this land, Cambria!" he shouted back. Cambria backed up but remained between them. Sol ran his hand over his face and through his hair. Then the queen turned from him and resumed her mad whistling.

"Avva, even if you fly to the summit," said Henri, "How will you fly back with our daughter? It'll be hard enough to make one trip. Do you think Antilus can carry both of you back?"

"Why are you all trying to stop me!" she yelled. "Antilus! Antilus, can't you hear me? What cruel demon brought on this storm?"

A whole group now circled Avva. Sol looked as if he was about ready to throw her down.

"Anna … please," Sol said calmly again. He pushed Cambria aside. "Please, Anna. Please. Let me speak with you for a moment alone at least. Then go."

Antilus flew down from the skies. Avva clapped in excitement and ran to her unicorn, petting her mane. "Oh, I've missed you, girl," she said, cradling the unicorn's head.

Solinair touched her arm and spoke into her ear. "For a moment. I beg of you, my love. A moment is all I ask."

She kissed her unicorn's head and clutched it tightly. Then she turned to him. She felt tears falling down her face—or was it the rain? A large group of nymphs and soldiers had now formed around her.

Avva nodded.

Sol led her to a nearby tree. When they were alone, Avva spun around. "Do I embarrass you in front of our friends? Is that it?" But she saw the concern in his face, and she softened. "Henri thinks I'm mad."

"You're not mad, Anna."

"I can't take it ... It's ... it's been so long. And now, she's here. I have a much better chance of jumping the mountain than she does of climbing down. Don't you understand?"

He turned from her. His face was drenched in water. His night robe was drenched too. Perhaps she was mad? But when he looked back, his dark eyes seemed so tormented that even though she was angry at him, she wanted to comfort him.

"I have to do this."

"I don't want to lose you, Anna. I can't lose you, Blue."

"Ah," She forced a smile and ran her hand along his wet beard. "Ah, if only your enemies knew your heart. Sol, you once called yourself nobody. But I am the true nobody. Don't you understand? I'm a ghost without Casey. I can't live like this."

"I feel the same."

"Then you understand why I have to go."

"I understand why you *want* to, but I'm not sure you have to."

"You'd do the same if you could."

"Aye. I'd indeed kill myself for her. And you'd do everything to stop me too."

"So," she said with a sad smile, "at least we understand each other ... for this quarrel, anyway."

"I understand. But—"

"I can't live like this." She violently shook her head. "I can't, Sol. And neither can you. We have to do something." Then she gazed at the others. "Why don't they understand?" She grabbed his elbow in desperation. "Sol, If I don't do this, there's no more life for me. Nothing's left for us. I swear, if you, myself, or anyone stops me, it will never be forgiven."

"Without you, there will be no life for me."

His forlorn, defeated expression amused her, for she had never believed this man could be defeated by anything. In battle, he would kill himself for his cause. But this was different. He seemed defeated for he couldn't bear to let her go.

She took his hand, "You know, it's not just me, *we* won't survive. Casey's death will finally defeat both of us. You'll lose me either way. But if there's justice in this cruel world, Sol, someone or something that looks down on us, to see all we've been through, all Casey's been through, then my success will be granted. God willing, husband, I will rescue her."

"Can you make it?"

"Yes. I'll make it because I have to."

"Is it even possible?"

"I don't know. But I know she won't make it down alone. If I don't try, our daughter will die."

"Let the others go with you."

"I won't risk their lives."

"They can help if you fall. Engel saved Sandra."

Avva thought for a moment. She reluctantly nodded. "All right. Have it your way. Cambria may hover, but far below. Do not have her enter the main storm."

Sol fell silent and looked at the ground. This great king would never cry, but crying would have been a merciful release for whatever tormented his heart now. She lifted his chin. She ran her hand along his beard again and kissed his cheek. Then his lips.

"I love you," she said.

"Come back to me," he said finally with a sad smile and a nod. "Do not fail or you'll finish me."

They embraced and kissed each other. Then tears fell from her eyes. But the rain pounded on them so hard that she didn't know whether he was crying too.

"Cassandra won't be *remembered*, Sol. Not yet. Not *remembered*.

And neither will I. I've watched you do this so many times for us. Let me do it this time."

He nodded.

She leaned into him and closed her eyes in his embrace for a moment, kissed him one last time, then pushed him away and ran to Antilus.

She had her unicorn hover in the air as she raised a fist before the crowd.

Hanna ran to her yelling, "You can't do this, Anna! I can't let you!"

"Remember Hanna. Promise me. Don't follow. That's your Azure queen's decree. Do you understand?" Then she addressed the camp. "Do you all understand?"

"Let us go with you!"

"No," Avva said, shaking her head. She rose higher into the air with Antilus flapping her mighty wings. "You may follow but don't enter the storm. As Amazon, queen of Azure, descendant of Queen Harmonia, it is my edict that no one follows me into the storm. Those that do disgrace our revered Harmonia. I go alone." She hovered for a moment. Then she shouted, "When I return, you'll greet me and the princess!"

Then she shot up in the pouring rain.

Her subjects bowed before her. Then, in deference, Sol's men bowed as well. Then the rest of the camp ran to see her go up into the dark sky.

THE CLOUDS SURROUNDED HER. The air grew thick and dark. At a great height, she could only see a semblance of the camp deep in the valley below the clouds. She held on to Antilus's mane, ducking her head and using her helm to ward off rain as she ascended the mountain. The turbulence from the storm shook her and tried to throw her from Antilus. She flew through it blindly, closing her eyes and letting Antilus navigate.

Of course, the abduction was her fault. She shouldn't have

waited for disaster to rummage through the ancient scrolls with Engel. She should have known all these things before Cassandra was born. All the hardship and fears of the past year came crashing down like the pouring rain as she held on tightly to her beloved Antilus. Everything that had happened had been building to this point. She would either climb the Mount and save her daughter or die.

Antilus stopped soaring upward. She stood hovering, resting for a moment in midair. But Avva knew there could be no break.

"Go, girl! You can do this!" Avva yelled. Antilus labored. "You're the finest steed in Azure! You can do this! Now climb! Climb! Climb!"

Avva invoked this order as her great ancestor Harmonia once had. She wanted to gently touch her unicorn but, in the violence of the storm, she struggled to stay on the slippery, moving steed, so she yanked at the horn hard. Antilus squealed and groaned, kicking her head about in the pouring rain. Then she dove. Avva felt a surge of terror thinking that she was going to plummet to the ground, but then Antilus used the momentum of the fall to shoot up further against the rain.

The gray clouds blackened further. Avva began having difficulty distinguishing up from down, and she feared the same for Antilus. As some clouds dispersed, she saw the moon—fortunately above—and pulled Antilus's neck up toward the moonlight.

Antilus groaned.

"Oh, Antilus," Avva cried, rubbing her slick, feathery hide, "We can do it! We must. For Casey, girl! For Casey!"

She passed close to a vertical wall. The Mount was becoming steep here and the trees sparser. Antilus dipped and rose again. She did this several times and slowly they made headway climbing up.

After more frantic climbing, Avva searched desperately for a landing site, thinking Antilus must rest. When all hope was nearly lost, Avva spotted a large broken rock jutting out from the wall. The surface looked wide enough for her unicorn to land, but treacherous enough to possibly collapse under her weight. But Antilus had labored so much Avva had no choice. They hovered until Antilus's hooves slid onto a wet gravel-like surface.

Avva cautiously got off. She tried to not look over the precipice. Her legs quaked as she stood beside her unicorn and stroked her head. Within an arm's reach, the fall was straight down—worse, between the clouds, she caught a glimpse of the ground, which was now so high that the camp wasn't even visible and the river was only a dark line.

"Rest, girl," she shouted through the storm, petting her soaking feathers. She brushed more water from her face as it poured over them. "We can do this."

Avva crouched near the horse with shaking knees. She waited as Antilus panted under the storm. Then she shivered. She had on a cloak, but it was too light and wasn't made for this storm. Under it were her pteruges and bare legs. It was freezing cold. The horse shook too. Carefully, by the ledge, she examined Antilus's wings.

"Antilus, you're the only one who can do this," she whispered into her ear. "You've always been there for me. Be there for our princess! Help the princess!"

Antilus threw her head back and gave a high-pitched whinny. But, in a moment of panic, Avva feared the excitement would throw them off or break the ledge.

She wiped the water from her eyes again. Then she took her scepter, tied at her waist, and tapped the horse with it. Avva carefully mounted her.

"Back, girl," Then she raised the scepter over her head. "We rise higher. For Harmonia!"

Antilus neighed and nodded her head violently. They fell from the ledge.

Hard granite walls appeared by their side as Antilus flapped her wings against the storm. Avva noticed the climb led to yet another summit. And then another. How high did this Mount go? It seemed to go on forever.

It grew dark. Then the rain became ice flurries. Ice stabbed at her face and body.

Things became desperate. Antilus could no longer rise despite flapping hard against a torrential wind. The storm was like a hurricane now, and Avva not only shielded her eyes, she struggled to not be thrown off.

"Antilus! Antilus! You have to climb! You have to!"

It was no use.

Avva shouted. No longer was it encouragement; it was chastisement. She would not fail. There would be no failure. She loved Antilus, but she loved her princess more. She would climb the Mount or they would die.

"Climb! Climb, Antilus! Do it now! I order you!"

She hit the monokera with her legs. Antilus tried again, but it was no use. For a moment, Antilus shut her eyes, and Avva feared her unicorn would fall.

In stubborn desperation, Avva leaned her whole body against the horse's neck and pushed herself upward, putting all her weight on her left hand. With this maneuver, most of her body was midair, tempting a tragic fall. Balancing her body while holding the scepter outward, she shouted with all her might into the wind:

Eneich Aneu Loriaan!

Eneich Aneu Loriaan!

And with those words, icy tracks appeared before Antilus in the air.

Eneich Aneu Loriaan!

The monokera walked up the ice. Avva did it again and again, creating icy shelves in midair for the steed to tread upon.

Eneich Aneu Loriaan!

And, whereas Antilus had been about to dive in exhaustion, the appearance of these icy steps seemed to rejuvenate her. Her hooves leaped on the glass shelves, shattering them while using them to propel them higher and higher.

Eneich Aneu Loriaan!

And so it was that every time Antilus was about to falter, Avva formed steps and solid ground.

They rose higher.

After what seemed like forever, the cyclone ended. The flurries died and the air cleared. Most of the clouds were beneath them now. Avva landed on another ledge. She hopped off. Here there was a light snow. And yet there was still a wall of mountain above them.

Avva embraced Antilus's head. Antilus moaned and struggled to stand. "I'm so sorry, girl! So sorry! But I never doubted you. Look what you did. I knew we could do it!"

The horse neighed weakly under Avva's caress.

Then Avva squinted before a bright white light piercing through the white clouds above them. And then a strange sight. A yellow-white sun like the yellow sun of Gaia blazed over them.

"You're the best monokera, Antilus! The only one who could have done this."

She took out her backpack. The bag was enchanted and held a great many things. But most importantly at the moment, it held a small towel. She wiped her unicorn's face. Then she wiped her own. She kissed Antilus.

"Oh girl, but we have to move. We have to find Casey."

Antilus seemed to understand and even nodded her head.

As the sun crept behind another cloud, Avva mounted her unicorn again. Antilus still labored, but all Avva could think of now was her daughter.

It was at this time that Avva realized a stupid error in her plan. To her, Mount Ambitus had always been a single mountain. And in climbing any mountain, one traverses a tangible distance. But many mountains comprised the Mount, and it was so vast that its size, even close to the summit, was beyond her comprehension. How could she find her daughter?

As she flew around the summit, she panicked, looking everywhere for Casey. She was so close and yet impossibly far from rescuing her. She searched the sides of the mountain, but could see no sign of Cassandra. But she didn't give up. They flew and rested, flew and rested, shivering and beating off the cold while repeatedly combing the side of the Mount.

Then she heard a screech. Above her, above another break in the clouds, a silhouette of a bird soared under the yellow light. It was a large black bird with rainbow wings. Mainax!

The phoenix flew close to Avva.

"Mainax!" cried Avva. "Mainax. Oh, Mainax, I can't talk to you like Henri, but you can understand me, right? Can you? Where's Casey? Where's the princess? Find her for me. Find her? Show me where she's climbing."

Mainax at first soared in a circular motion. Then he glided downward on a more orderly route. Avva followed, though the prospect of heading back into the black clouds terrified her.

The clouds thickened. It stormed again. At times, Avva lost sight of Mainax, but Antilus still followed.

Finally, the phoenix circled over an icy, rocky ledge with a thin stone canopy. Avva got excited thinking her daughter would be there, but she didn't see anyone. She clutched Antilus in the freezing rain.

"Firebird!" another voice yelled through the storm. "Oh, Firebird! Come here. You come to keep a stupid fool company?"

It was her daughter's voice! But where? She couldn't see her. Was this simply a hallucination? Another fiendish trick of the gods? Or perhaps a deception of her mind out of desperation?

Mainax flew to the ledge and under a stone sheltering him from the storm. Avva focused her eyes on a clearing in the packed ice and snow. The phoenix did not touch ground but perched in midair.

"Antilus?" someone asked. It was her daughter's voice again. And then, "*Mother?*"

"Casey! Casey, yes, it's me! It's me! Where are you?"

A figure materialized, removing a silver helmet. But this person looked like Cambria, wearing Azure scarlet armor. Avva winced and squinted to see through the flurries.

"Casey, step back! I'm landing."

There was just enough room a little higher up a trail, outside of the shelter. Avva landed carefully with barely a foot to spare. Then she dismounted.

Her daughter stood staring at her in disbelief. Her face seemed otherworldly, her eyes glassy, as if Avva were not really there, as if Cassandra thought this was a dream. And she shook violently.

Avva gathered her in her arms. "I'm here to take you home."

"Momma?" Cassandra asked. They both shook in each other's arms. "Oh, Momma."

Avva pushed her back, gazing at her daughter's face, and ran a hand over her cheek, brushing back her wet hair. She barely recognized her. They were the same stature now, but Cassandra had lost a lot of weight. And her face had seemed to age years. Her daughter was no longer a girl. She had grown into a woman.

"I'm so sorry, Momma," she said, falling into her arms. "I'm sorry. Can you ever forgive me for what happened?"

"I've forgiven you long ago. Let's go home."

But when she turned to Antilus, the unicorn was leaning against the icy wall, groaning, with her eyes closed.

"Oh, Antilus," Cassandra said. "Mother, she's hurt."

"Antilus," Avva said, rubbing her face. "We're going home. Can you take me and the princess home?"

The unicorn opened her eyes and weakly nodded.

The journey back seemed not so terrible, for Antilus no longer had to climb. But the storm still raged. Casey held her mother tightly as the monokera nearly threw them off while swerving back and forth at the mercy of the wind. And once again, a few times, they could not see. But they kept descending.

Soon Avva spotted the encampment along the river through the clouds. Thousands of soldiers stood looking up. As long as the climb had seemed, it had not been that long after all. All the men and nymphs were still there waiting.

"We've been at the foot of the Mount by the Stratos for many moons waiting for you to come back, Casey," Avva shouted, pointing down.

"Thank you, Mother," Cassandra said close to her ear, clutching her tighter.

Oh Casey, you sound so weak. Not only have they imprisoned you, they hurt you. Hurt by the gods. I shall never forgive them.

The rain mercifully fell to a drizzle. Then a green sun shone forth. Dawn? The storm had ended in Napea.

All couldn't be better. Until Antilus's wings suddenly folded. They were close to the river when, all of a sudden, they dropped like a stone. Cassandra gripped Avva tightly from behind, holding for dear life as Avva clutched the unicorn's neck as hard as she could.

"Antilus!" cried Avva.

Avva looked down and her unicorn's eyes were closed. She had fallen unconscious. Avva pulled at her mane. Then she hit the unicorn with her fist. They would have flipped if it weren't for the unicorn's eyes slightly opening and her wings opening into a glide once more.

"Oh, Antilus!" cried Cassandra, petting her feathery hide. "Momma, she's so hurt! She's hurt badly."

It seemed Antilus was fighting as hard as she had when ascending, just to keep her wings straight as they glided down.

She heard cheers. Many soldiers, Amazon and men, ran under them as they descended.

When they landed, everyone in the camp surrounded them. Sol ran and grabbed Cassandra from the unicorn and held her tightly in his arms. Avva weakly dismounted and Hanna and Cambria came to help her.

The shouts and jubilee made Avva feel happier than she remembered having felt before. She grabbed her daughter in her arms again and Cassandra cried. Then Sol caught her in his arms.

But all the shouting and jubilee stopped when Henri cried, "*Anna, come quick!*"

Avva turned and saw her beloved white unicorn, Antilus, lying on the ground. Everyone turned. Cassandra fell on her knees before the unicorn.

"Antilus! Antilus!" Cassandra cried. "Momma, she's not moving." Casey pushed her torso and ran her palm over her head. "What's the matter? She's not moving, mother! Oh, Antilus, not you! Not for me. I love you!"

Avva crouched beside Henri. The Magi touched the monokera, stroking the unicorn's soaking head on the ground.

"She couldn't take it, Anna," he said sadly. "She's dead."

"Is there anything you can do?" Sol asked Henri, standing over him.

Henri got up from his knees. He shook his head.

Avva kneeled beside Cassandra and took her in her arms again as they cried together.

"Momma, she died for me!" cried Cassandra. "For me! It's not fair! The witches said that someone would die when I was freed—someone I loved. And I do love Antilus! I do! How could she die?"

"It's okay, Casey. It's all right. You're home now. Nothing else matters."

3 4

RETURN OF THE KING

MANY MOONS PASSED AND IT DIDN'T TAKE LONG FOR SOL'S daughter to become the girl everyone had loved once more. She had the same courage and daring that Sol loved in Anna. And she had grown into a teenager. But her journey into the depths had made her grow old and wise at too young an age. Something dark had fallen over her. A melancholy. A sadness. A deep sadness that she seemed to have carried out with her from the Underworld. And there was nothing anyone in the kingdom could do about it.

Sol had remained in the palace until he felt things had returned to "normal." Now that it was nearly normal, he had to go.

He found her at the top of the north tower, wearing one of Avva's long azure dresses, staring out at Mount Ambitus, the mountain that had imprisoned her, the Mount that Sol had learned to despise. Sol hated the mountain so much now that he averted his eyes from the mountainous wall. Her long black hair was tied back with a glistening silver band. The elegant blue peplos covered her wrists down to her fingers. Her blue-tinged fingers, nearly the same color, gripped the balcony railing. Like her mother, she was lovely. And when she cocked her head back and smiled, he was struck by her resemblance to Anna.

"Casey. You look beautiful."

"Daddy," she said with a smile. She turned and embraced him but then lost her smile gazing at his clothes. He wore a dark brown coat and pants. It was his simple travel clothes. She touched his arm. "Where are you going?"

"I have to return to Castle Cove. I've been away far too long from Azerban."

"Mom will miss you."

"Hmm. I was thinking *you'd* miss me, Casey."

She laughed and hugged him again. "I will. So much. Take me with you."

"You're like your mother. She would have said the same."

"Didn't she?"

He walked to the ledge and cast a quick glance at the mountain wall he hated. There, up in the clouds, the gods had done this to his daughter. They had cast a shadow over her.

"Take care of her, Casey, will you?"

"Mother can take care of herself."

"That's true," he said with a smirk. "Well, goodbye then, princess. I will miss you terribly."

But she snatched his wrist. "What's wrong, Dad? Did you two have a fight?" She searched his eyes and he couldn't help but laugh. "What was the fight about?"

"What makes you think we had a fight?"

She smiled slyly. "Your face. You always look terrible after you fight with Mom."

"Then I must look terrible often," he said with another chuckle. He didn't want to tell her. The last thing he wanted was to leave after fighting with her too.

"What is it?"

"Nothing. Don't worry. Look." He rummaged through his pockets and handed her a small contraption the size of his palm. "I almost forgot. I've got something for you. For next time you get lost."

"A compass," she said with disinterest. "Wow. Thanks. I shall cherish it always."

"You get the point. Don't ever get lost again. Actually, this one is very valuable to me. It was my first. Your uncle gave it to me when I was a little boy. I carry it around always. You never know when you will need to find your way back home."

"I didn't need one before."

"No." He suddenly became very serious. "No, Casey, you didn't. You came home all by yourself."

"You know I'm not a child anymore."

"Why would you suggest otherwise?"

"Tell me what the fight was about then." And she gave him a sly smile that reminded him of her mother. "Tell me."

"It was nothing that time won't heal. Only a difference in opinion."

"What? Tell me. If you don't, I'll get it out of Mom anyway."

She was right about that. She stared at him, waiting.

"Your mother doesn't agree on policies in South Atala. I'm afraid these differences ruined our excursion the other day. And, yes, it was a very big quarrel. It's things we didn't talk about when you were away. Things we couldn't until now."

"Is it really her business?"

"My home is her home. Her lands spread beyond the Azures. They are all hers too."

"Even if she doesn't live there?" Then she laughed. The laughter caught him off guard. She had the same laugh as her mother, and he cherished it.

"What does she not agree with?"

"Forget it, Casey."

"You never can tell. I might agree with you, Dad."

He paused. She stared into his eyes.

"I'm so happy you're home," he said, as if that answered her. "Tell me."

"All right." He gave another sigh and gazed into her bright blue eyes. "Over the last few years, we've allied our kingdom with King Philipp of Kitheria. In exchange for slaves. Philipp's people have fought and defended our southern lands from rebellion and the outer empires. It's kept things quiet. These slaves, *slaves*, Casey—that's what your mother is so sore about— are what has kept things in order while you were away. I argued that even your grandfather King Darius used slaves from King Gunther's kingdom to keep peace with King Morteus long ago. But she is disgusted by slavery, learned from your people and from the revered ancient teachings of your ancestor Queen Nefertiti. That's all, dear. I don't want to discuss it anymore."

When he was finished, she surprised him with a laugh.

"Never mind, Father. Mother always feels dreadful when you go. She'll miss you. She loves you too much. Give it a few weeks and she'll forget the whole thing."

But Sol wasn't so sure. He squinted and gazed at her. Then he shook his head and said, more to himself that to her, "I'll never understand women."

"She'll come around."

"Hmm. Well, your spirits seem a little better. That's all I really care about."

"I've suffered," she said, looking down with a nod.

There it is. That sadness. A terrible sadness. Aye, her laughter doesn't hide what lies inside. What, by Hades and Persephone, did you do to her!

"I'm happy to be back, Daddy." Then she shrugged. "And now sad that you're leaving. I guess I understand things better. You and Mom shouldn't fight. Life could be so much harder. You should be happy for what you have."

"What do you think of my actions in Kitheria?"

"I think they're human," she said, putting a finger to her chin. "Flawed. I understand why Mom's upset. But I also understand why you did it." She touched his hand and nodded. "And that is why she'll forgive you." Then she laughed heartily, with the laughter of her people, and hugged him.

"You're so wise, like your uncle. Take care of her, Casey. I love you and her dearly."

"Take care of yourself, Daddy. Return home soon."

WHEN KING SOLINAIR returned to battle, things had changed. For years, King Philipp had stolen the power of his empire and claimed the Sun King's flag as his own when fighting, trading, or bullying neighbor states. The nomad king even brought excursions into the ancient Caravian empire, claiming the ancient town of Logenus, passing over the Cliffs of Zonoch, and invading Teleria. He even threatened the southern border of Atala, by the ancient harbor town of Jedithian. But King Philipp didn't take land. He was a nomad. Rather he used Sol's golden flag to plunder and terrorize. Then he left. All the while, the Sun King had done nothing. Until Cassandra had returned.

Now Sol and his army fought again by the border of Sinteria, a town on the border between Kitheria and ancient Caravia. There was hope that Morteus had fled there, but it was a rumor. Yet this drove Sol to fight to take Sinteria from King Philipp's enemies in the East.

The castle was a small run-down stone fortress run by a feudal lord. The lands around it were marshlands and poor for growing crops. It was a poor kingdom, one that Sol's father, Darius, had never bothered to fight.

By nightfall, a terrible fire surrounded Sol's blue-armored soldiers. It burned the castle and the surrounding village; ash, dark smoke, and the smell of burning wood, oil, and flesh permeated the air.

Henri rode quickly. His white hair flowed behind him as he approached Sol near the gates.

Sol was exhausted. His blue armor had turned red like Anna's. He fought only to try to find Morteus. But it was not enough to ward off pain and exhaustion.

"We can't find him in the castle, Sol," Henri said. He panted heavily. "I'm sorry. We now have word he was never there. I think it was a ruse created by Philipp to get your aid and take the city."

Sol nodded. Then he looked around at the chaos. He turned

and, only a few yards away, two knights were still fighting a desperate battle with sword against sword. One of the men was gravely injured in the arm, but he fought on. Above him, on a burning tower, a score of other warriors were fighting hand-to-hand or blade-to-blade. A hundred bystanders, men, women, and children in simple tunics and pants, carrying bags, were running from the walls trying to escape. Yells and screams of battle and the smell of fire and iron surrounded him.

He looked toward the entrance gate. There soldiers were gathering townspeople before they could escape. All were simple farmers, women, and children.

"Ride to the gate, Henri. Tell my men to spare all the women and children. Gather them up so that they may be liberated."

"Liberated?" Henri looked back at the king in surprise. "They're claimed by Philipp, Sol. The victory's shared. The prisoners are now forfeit to Philipp, by our treaty."

"Do it, old man," Solinair snapped. "Free them. By my order."

Henri nodded. He hesitated for a moment in thought, but then rode off.

Solinair rode to the aid of his nearby soldiers. Everyone now fought hand-to-hand. What had started as a volley of arrows and fire was now close combat. Many soon breached the castle wall, but many more did not know that the battle was over.

Solinair had lost his horse somewhere along the way. He ran toward the entrance to meet up with Henri. But as he ran, he had to fight his way across a burning moat.

He coughed and struggled to breathe. Then he passed the gate and witnessed something he had never seen before. His soldiers, in sky-blue armor, were fighting each other. They were not enemy soldiers; some of his own soldiers had rebelled. Henri was shoving some of them and getting between others, knocking down swords.

"You have the king's orders!" shouted Henri. "Stand down. Gather the women and children! Let them be freed outside the castle!"

A young soldier shoved Henri to the ground. Henri pulled out his sword. Then another soldier hacked at his wrist guard. If the blow had landed with more force, it would have sheared off Henri's hand.

At the sight of this, Sol removed his royal Mandrigelian sword, now covered with blood, and hacked his way through his own men to save his beloved counselor. A few swords splintered upon contact with his enchanted blade. Other men dropped to their hands and knees at the sight of the shimmering red-and-blue blade of their king.

Sol charged Henri's attacker. His blade met the attacker's blade. This freed Henri, who quickly left. Then Sol began to fight his own soldiers. He shouted while jousting with them and pushing them. But they were bewitched by the madness of mutiny.

The king would have slain his own men if it hadn't been for the sudden arrival of Milo. The general was accompanied by the cavalry. Upon seeing the king in trouble, Milo jumped down and joined the fray. He fought and quickly subdued the rebels. But some of them wouldn't relent. When Milo threatened to stampede a group of them, the fighting finally stopped.

Milo helped Solinair back upon a black horse.

"What is the meaning of this!" shouted Sol. "We take the castle and now you wish to kill each other?"

No one said a word. Many of the traitors had been gathered up, on orders of the general, and their hands were tied behind their backs. Sol glared at them.

"Speak!" Sol raged, looking down at them. "Speak before I order you killed! Why raise your swords against me?"

"We had a disagreement on how to treat the defeated, sire," said the man who had attacked Henri. This was Visus, one of Philipp's most trusted officers. He was a young man with a short mustache and long greased-back hair. He had a sinister smile. His hands had been tied behind his back too. Visus bowed.

"There's no disagreement, Visus," said Milo. "The king's word is law."

"I beg to disagree, sir. Some of the men wanted to free the prisoners. Including the king's own chief advisor. I had to remind them of our treaty."

"What treaty?" asked Sol angrily.

"King Philipp has claim to all prisoners won in battle, sire. You know this."

"This is more important than your king's orders?" asked Milo.

"Visus," said Solinair, shaking his head, "the treaty held for the Crystal Kingdom, but we are now deep in the Hinterlands."

"Liar," Visus said, looking down.

Sol stared at him in astonishment.

"How dare you!" yelled Milo. He then signaled for his men to throw Visus to the ground. "Bow down before the Sun King."

"I have bowed many times, General," replied Visus. But looking up with that same sly grin, he said, "I meant no disrespect. I state fact. You lie. You know my master's treaty. You threaten to not pay your dues. If you do not pay, then *you*, sir, emperor and Sun King, in fact, are a liar."

Solinair dismounted and pulled Visus up by his breastplate. Visus met his gaze with a rebellious glare. Sol struck him hard in the face with his fist.

"If you weren't Philipp's emissary, I'd cut your throat. But, as it is, you're under his rule." The fiend smiled wickedly again. "Take your traitors and return to your king. The treaty is fulfilled. You've stated your case, but I owe Philipp no more bounty. For fighting my men, you are banished. Don't ever stand with our ranks again."

"Thank you for my freedom, King Solinaray," he said with another infernal grin. "It seems you delight in it. But, forgive me, Lord Philipp will not see it your way."

"No more families will be torn apart to feed your people's greed. I won't take part in slavery."

"We've sacrificed our lives for you!" shouted a man beside Visus. A few others yelled in support.

"You had our help in fighting King Morteus," said another. "Now you break our agreement!"

"I will not enslave people," Sol repeated.

"Then what is your payment, Crescent King?" Visus asked, still on the ground. "What do you have to offer us for the battle we just waged?"

"Let me run a sword through him, Sol," said Milo. "Please, sire."

"Gather up the women and children, Milo," Sol said, shaking his head. "Line them up. Tell them they are all free. Their Crescent king frees them. No longer will they–"

Visus said, "You will—"

"I've heard enough from you!" interrupted Sol. "You're free too. Get out of my camp and take your friends with you! This rebellion's over. Run back to your king and stop your talk or my anger might change my mind."

"You may have earned an enemy."

"Better to lose an enemy than aid a fool," remarked Henri.

"Little disrespectful rats!" cried Milo. "Please, sire. Three of your guards died by this villain's vile hand tonight. Let me slay him."

"Free Visus, Milo," said Solinair. "And the rest of his men. Let them return and tell their king that we are no longer in need of his services."

"Sparing us will not repair this betrayal," Visus said.

Sol kicked him hard and the man rolled on the ground. "Get him out of here before I lose my temper and kill him myself, Milo!"

A group of soldiers grabbed him and hauled him up. Visus spat at Sol.

The army gathered all the women and children and lined them up by a wall. Sol looked upon them with pity. None of them looked up. They all assumed they would be enslaved and traded. The only thing that lifted his heart was their look of hope when he set them free.

"You've done the right thing, Sol," Henri said. They were

both on horseback, side by side. Henri patted him on his back. "Avva would have agreed, son."

"Aye, Henri, she would," Sol replied, but he spit on the ground in anger. "Aye. But at what cost?"

"They all feared being sold, enslaved, or killed by my lord, the emperor and Sun King," Henri said to himself. "But my Crescent king freed them all."

35

NEETERU BELOK DISPIN

Henri's peace with Sol could not be enjoyed for long. It was only a couple of moons later that Sol asked him to do something he had vowed he would never, ever do again—ride to an enemy camp, as his chief advisor, and seek peace. Henri was sent personally to Kitheria to try to repair the damage done in the battle of Sinteria.

The trip was madness. But Henri rode knowing that he had finally turned Sol to his side. And for that, along with a life of eternal devotion, he rode for the true king of Atala.

It took Henri two days to cross the wastelands of Kitheria before finally entering an open grassy valley. The journey was full of vagrants and robbers lurking in decaying forests and bogs. Henri hadn't been in these parts since before he had counseled Sol's father. He finally headed down grassy hills to a harbor town, Arbor Dunn, once the wealthiest and greatest ship port on the entire continent. This had been Henri's home when he was a boy. The town was situated close enough to the Strait of Aethiopia and the East Mediterranean Sea to have served as a port, over the centuries, for the Phoenicians and Egyptians. Now, under the rule of the tyrant nomad king, Philipp, the trees withered and the stone roads and buildings decayed. In fact, Henri could scarcely recognize his hometown. It seemed to reflect his somber mood.

Rain fell so heavily that Henri could barely make out the muddy road before him. He stopped by the side of the road, dug into his travel pack, and put a heavy coat over his tunic. Then he walked his horse along the broken muddy road until they reached the gates and walls of the town.

From the outskirts, he caught a glimpse of broken-down thatched-roof houses and torn-up roads. A man shaking in rags passed the main gate, staring at the ground, with a cart hauled by an ox. Poverty weighed heavily on the people.

Henri meandered through an unguarded gate along another muddy trail, which had once been a road, across a few rickety bridges, and past dead branched-trees toward Philipp's "Court" by the sea.

When Henri was a boy, Arbor Dunn was a grand harbor full of ships and trading merchants. Now the only thing that reminded him of his childhood was the shore. All else had been abandoned. Under a full moon that sent beams through dark clouds, the sea was the only thing of beauty. This was Hazindae Port. But most of the stone houses of his childhood had been abandoned and replaced by rows of simple tents.

The rain stopped but it was still bitingly cold. The moon, along with scattered torches, welcomed him. Then Henri caught sight of a bright complex near the sea. A huge brown tent was lit up by a hundred torches. And beside it were a hundred smaller cloth tents.

Two guards in long dark coats, patrolling on horseback, approached Henri.

"Hail, sir," said one of the guards, raising a hand. "State your business."

"I am Henri Untair of the great Emperor Solinair's counsel. I've come here to speak with King Philipp." He showed him a scroll with Sol's seal. It had been buried in his coat, but the rain had been so fierce that it was damp.

"We've been expecting you, Sir Untair," the other guard, a toothless man, said with a nod and a smirk. "Follow us."

They rode along the beach to the large tent. It seemed the whole town was here. Now, even this late, there were many merchants selling things under cloth canopies. Surrounding the merchants were many homeless families begging. But each tent bore the black-and-white standard of Philipp's kingdom: a black star surrounded by a white flag.

The guards helped Henri off his horse and walked him into a grand tent.

What he saw was a direct contrast to the outside. The large tent shone with torches. Henri had to squint in the bright light. More merchants stood by the entrance. They rushed toward Henri, selling ampullas of wine and meat. Another brandished a board full of swords and knives. Many of them had been pilfered. These merchants were more affluent than the ones outside. And yet even here by the entrance, men, women, and children were begging.

Toward the center of this great hall were dancers. They maneuvered over men and women lying on their sides under a large wooden stage bearing a throne. Many dancers swayed, wearing transparent violet cloth. They seemed unsteady. Drunk.

Henri was led to the stage, where a man sat on the throne, elevated above the dancers and guests. King Philipp. The king wore a long draping saffron robe. He had a thin mustache and onyx eyes, his eyebrows were bushy, and he squinted and glared down at Henri as he approached. Directly under the stage at least fifty of his subjects lay on their sides. Many shirtless women and men surrounded Henri, drinking from silver cups, laughing, or holding one another.

The man closest to Philipp lay on his side on a purple carpet on the stage. He had a mustache, like the king, and held a suspicious gaze. His hair was slicked back into a ponytail, similar to the Egyptians of the South. He wore a long fur coat. He stared at Henri. Henri realized this was Visus, the fiend who had struck him during the siege of Sinteria.

"Henri Untair, sire," one of the guards beside Henri said.

Many of the bystanders surrounding Henri moved, giving him space to approach the throne.

Henri bowed low, "Your Majesty. A great honor."

King Philipp smiled. He gestured to a man placing a silver tray of fruit on the stone floor beside Henri. Henri nodded graciously and sat on the ground.

"Where from this time, Magus?" Philipp asked. "Hmm? Napea Or Sinteria? Did you leave our lord Solinair's camp, or did you come from his Amazon girls' isle? Hmm?" Then he gestured to the topless women on the dirt floor, in the arms of men drinking from silver cups. "Personally, I prefer to sard the ladies by my feet."

"Aye! Aye!" Many of the men around him shouted like the barbarians Henri knew them to be. Henri didn't answer. Instead he grabbed a cluster of grapes.

A dog barked. Henri hadn't noticed, but a small brown and black dog with hairless patches was sitting on Philipp's lap.

Henri turned and looked back at the entrance. Many guards in blue armor were now by the exit. Their armor was painted sky blue, the blue that—Henri noted in amusement—he and Sol had invented for their "Crescent" kingdom. Once a color of weakness, it was now a color used to intimidate and impress enemies on the battlefield.

Henri propped himself up higher on his side near his food tray.

"So?" asked the king. "Where did you travel from? Hmm?"

"Azerban."

"A long journey?"

"Aye. Five days, sire."

"Five days. Hmm. No doubt you took the route around the lake? By Crystal Lake? Morteus's old realm."

"What's left of it. Yes, sire." Henri eagerly grabbed some jerky and tore at it with his teeth.

"Your ways of the North are such a mystery. It seems foreign to you that we sleep under different roofs, but for us, Sir Untair, your ways are unnatural."

"These lands were once settled," Henri replied with his mouth full. "But whether the body journeys or stays in one place, it is the head that needs to stay true, King Philipp. Anyway, our people get along well enough."

He pulled at more meat with his teeth. It was bland and tasted spoiled.

"Well, we used to." He looked down and petted the mangy dog on his lap. The dog barked. Then Philipp shook his head. "But I'm afraid recent events changed things. We've been slighted by our lord, the Sun King. It becomes difficult for me to keep the peace."

"We are only interested in peace, my lord. My mere presence tonight attests to that."

"True," said Philipp, stroking his bushy beard. He petted his dog again. Then his eyes suddenly lit up. "I tell you what: allow me to present a gift. You've traveled long and you deserve plea-sure after your pain."

He pointed at a group of ladies. "Allow me to introduce my wives."

The guards led them, by ropes tied around their necks, toward Henri. They were naked. They looked down and trembled.

"You may pick one," the king said with a big smile. "Con-sider it a conciliatory gift."

"No thank you, sire," Henri snapped. But then he raised a hand. "But I do thank you for the offer. I do."

"I see," continued Philipp. He looked offended, but it seemed fake. "You know, Henri, that reminds me of the situation with our beloved Sun King."

"How so, my king?" Henri looked up again.

"Well, old man—please don't take offense—King Solinair Solinaray reminds me of a renegade. An upstanding pimp."

Henri stopped eating. He slowly pushed his plate from him. Then he got up.

The insult was intolerable, even from a king of these lands, and everyone within earshot turned and stared at Philipp. It grew silent. No one dared laugh except Philipp.

"I'm afraid such words do not bode well, Your Majesty," Henri snapped. Then he stroked his white beard and stared at the nomad king.

"Would you like me to explain?"

"No. I'd like you to apologize. Publicly in front of your Court."

The king squinted at Henri. "I'm free to speak as I choose about your bastard son, Henri. My lands have not been taken by him *yet.*"

"Now you've slighted my king twice," Henri said, straightening. "First you call him a pimp, and now a bastard."

"I only speak the truth. Do I not?"

"You do not. You are in the wrong twice. The great King Darius made Solinair his son. He is not a bastard. And he is hardly a pimp. I've never seen Solinair sell anyone for pleasure."

"*In* pleasure, Henri?" King Philipp asked heartily. "Or *for* pleasure? You've never seen Solinair like selling anyone, you mean. That doesn't mean he didn't do it. He may not have liked it, but he did, Henri."

His men finally laughed.

It gave Henri a chance to finally consider his predicament. Guards were circling the entire tent now with their hands by their scabbards. It was Philipp's entire guard. Henri held his sword by his waist. There was only one exit that he could see— the way he had come. He was an old man, but skilled enough to fight and kill many of these ill-trained barbarians. But there was no way he would make it out alive with so many surrounding him.

"My dear fellow," Philipp said, slapping his knee, "Your king provided those exact services to me. Why, the women I just offered you…" He burst into even louder laughter. "Were once a part of a royal family. Since, of late, his supply of the poorer stock has dried up and I've needed to gather more of the upstanding ones. Anyway, it's a more fitting gift to the emperor's favorite counselor, is it not?"

"Unlike your people, we're not accustomed to trafficking women," said Henri quickly. "I believe you've been in the slave trade much longer than I have, for I believe you don't realize the offense—"

"Please go, ladies," Philipp said to the women, twirling his fingers in the air. "Rumor is that Henri does not care for women, not because he's old. He never did." Then King Philipp turned back to Henri. "Why would Solinair send you alone? Is he stupid? Does he want you to die?"

"He trusted you. Should he not? My king values trust. Trust and honor. My presence shows his trust. Does your kingdom lack honor? Even King Ansel, under the guidance of the Dark Lord himself, never violated the common laws of war."

"Oh, I see. I see. So we are at war then, sir? Are we at war, Henri? He's a brave man, isn't he, Visus? Aye, he's been brave since advising lies with Emperor Darius." Then he turned to Henri, looking serious. "Do you not fear death?"

"We are not at war. But your speech has been provocative. I can look away, of course, if you—"

"Tell me your king's terms." The dog barked on his lap. Then Philipp fell silent.

"King Solinair wants nothing more than friendship," Henri replied, bowing again. His legs twitched. The act of bowing before this beast disgusted him. "You claim in your letter that we've violated the treaty, but Solinair disagrees. The treaty involved the initial occupation of the Crystal Kingdom. Now, years later, we are not bound to traffick with you at borders."

"That isn't the way I see it," the king replied. "I lost three thousand, six hundred, and forty-two souls in your battles within the Crystal Kingdom. I count each and every one of them. And I'm not referring to years ago. I'm referring to the fighting over the past few moons. I haven't tallied that with the original charge. It is enough bodies to fill this tent, I can tell you. Not only that, my friend Tolimus and even my nephew Mitus were killed. And not only that, I have been pitted against King Morteus, once a very good friend. I'm forced to fight a two-front war. All because your conceited Sun King made friends with me. Now that friendship…" He started to raise his voice. "Was based on trade. Now, your arrogant king suddenly claims to be above such practices. But here, in the South Hinterlands, you are well aware, Henri, that people are worth more than their weight in gold."

"Yes," Henri said, placing his hand up to protest. "I know, sire. And we are so grateful for your sacrifices. But we've provided you with a sizable number of slaves. And we have promised you our defense and—"

"Your defense!" he yelled and spat on the ground. "Your defense! Are you joking? We've fought this battle for him while his army's enjoyed cooked meals by nymph whores! You hypocrite! As far as I see it, your king does nothing!" He stood up. "I fail to see any attack on Morteus. Nor even you lifting a finger to aid in battle."

"We've sent advisors to help with the borders. And in Sinteria—"

"*Liar!*" Philipp shouted and stood up pointing down at him. Everyone turned throughout the Court. "Liars!" Then he grabbed a silver cup of wine and hurled it at Henri. Visus looked over with a wicked smile. Henri began to object again, but every time he started to speak, Philipp put his hand up.

"Visus," Philipp finally said. "Enough of this. Bring in our guest. Show the old fool so that he understands."

Visus's smile became wider. He rose and bowed. Then he walked behind the wooden stage.

With a sudden instinctive response, Henri pulled out his sword. The minute his glistening silver was brandished, guards surrounded him and did the same. King Philipp sat back down on his throne and, for the first time, a look of fear fell on him. Then the dog barked wildly.

Visus walked back from behind the throne with another man.

A short, weak, broken man with thin gray hair walked to Philipp. Henri recognized him immediately. King Morteus Mangus. Then his archenemy was given a wooden chair to sit beside Philipp.

"Meet King Mort—"

"*How dare you!*" cried Henri in astonishment. Henri forgot all royal etiquette and even pointed his sword at Philipp. It didn't matter anymore. "How dare you shelter that rat! This means war. King Solinair will break all ties with you! You know this insult is unforgivable. He will break you!"

"He may do more than that," replied Philipp with a smile, "after I have my way with you."

Henri looked at the king. His intention was clear now. He would not be captured. He would be tortured and then killed.

He turned and looked behind him again. He was trapped. There was no way out.

The guards came closer. But as he held his sword, they approached cautiously, likely knowing his renowned expertise with the sword. All the while, Morteus and Philipp smiled with malice and laughed at him.

"*Neeteru Belok Dispin,*" he said quietly. People looked at him bewildered. Some backed up, fearing it was some kind of Magi incantation. But nothing happened.

"What does that mean?" asked King Philipp.

"It's a final message of love to my king." A guard grabbed an arm, and he yanked it away and pointed the blade at him. "It shall stay for my family. And with it, a wish that they feel no regret, remorse, guilt, sorrow, or pain. For such is the curse of our loved ones when we die."

"*I swore pain to Solinair!*" yelled Morteus, jumping up. "And he shall have it, Henri! He will, Henri! And you will suffer for him! Just as I hurt King Darius, I will make you suffer until you die. You will—"

No more words could be spoken.

With great swiftness, Henri jerked out of the arms of another guard and swung the sword masterfully. But he did not aim at the surrounding men. Their deaths would mean nothing. He swung the blade at himself. It flew around his body until entering deep in his stomach.

Henri fell to the ground. He closed his eyes and slowed his breathing. Then he let his body go.

$$36$$

THERE ARE NO WORDS

SOL HEARD SOMEONE APPROACH HIS TENT. THEY WERE CAMPED along the marshes near Logenus. It was late. Sol had been up all night, waiting for word of Henri. The delay was grave news. Now he sat on a chair, staring out the tent window. He already had terrible suspicions.

A boy ran into the royal tent and bowed. It was his son, Gavin.

"Father." Gavin bowed low.

When Sol looked upon Gavin's face, it seemed the whole world crashed down on him. Time slowed. He felt a desire to escape to anywhere. And the boy's face, for the first time since the king had known him, reflected sadness too.

"I have news of Sir Untair."

"Do not speak of him so formally!" Solinair shouted. "He was your grandfather. And my father as well!"

Gavin nodded. The king turned back to the window.

"King Philipp sent a messenger with a package for you and a letter. I have not opened the letter. The package was … well …"

Sol put his head in his hand.

Gavin paused. He was fighting to speak. "King Philipp refuses us the body for burial, my lord … Only … the head."

Gavin handed him the parchment and Sol squeezed it tightly in his fist.

The silence festered. Not a sound. Until Sol heard wailing, but it was not from the tent. It came from all over the camp. The distinctive sound of pain from his men. The news had spread fast. It seemed the whole camp had broken out into cries of mourning. Their cries were his, but Sol sat completely frozen.

"No act goes unpunished, son," Sol finally said quietly. He stared outside again. "We will mourn. Then they shall have what they wish."

"War, Father. I would like to lead the—"

"Please leave. Leave me alone now."

CRESTFALLEN

Cassandra had told Avva that Sol was mourning in Henri's home outside the palace. It was an odd place to be and she didn't want to go there. Going back to that small Hinterland cottage would remind her too much of Henri. That was too painful. But her husband hadn't been seen for nearly a week, since the funeral. She was worried about him.

It was raining. The shutters were closed, but thunder struck with flashes of lightning around the garden. It shone over the Hinterland daffodils, sunflowers, and roses that Henri had planted so long ago to remind him of his home.

It was midnight. The queen knocked on the wooden door but there was no answer. But the door was unlocked, so she cracked it open. She saw his silhouette by the hearth. He was still. The sight of him sitting by the fire made her jump, for he sat on a chair often occupied by Henri and his posture and long hair were exactly like Henri's.

"Thank you," she said by the threshold. She tried to put on a smile when he turned.

"For what?" Sol asked after a long silence, turning back to the fire.

"The ceremony was lovely."

She pulled up a wooden chair and sat beside him. They both stared at the fire.

"How long do you intend to sit here, my king?" Avva asked quietly.

"I don't know."

"Do you mind company?"

"Whatever you'd like."

She gently touched his hand. He didn't pull away. She would give him her hand, or anything, to help ease his pain. They sat like that for the longest time.

"I keep thinking he'll rush into the room, Anne," he finally said. "It was his way. He would leave for so long. Then one day, when you least expected it, he'd charge in, excited about something. Usually it was some strange thing I didn't understand in the slightest, or even care about … but seeing him was all that mattered. He loved this place, you know, your home in Azure. He loved it perhaps even more than Azerban. So I can understand why he wanted to be buried here."

"It's our home."

"Aye," he said with a smile and a nod. "That it is."

More silence. Just the crackling of the fire.

"You know, Anna, I can't do this."

"Do what?"

"Sit. I cannot sit here. I can't just sit, Blue. I never could. I've lost too many friends and family in my life. But I … I could never just do this. Just sit. I never could do that."

"He was your father."

More silence. Then she felt his pain. She didn't squeeze his hand, but she kept his hand there. The tinder crackled and popped, and they watched the flames. She had a lump in her throat and she wanted to cry. But she didn't.

"I suppose he was all of our fathers," he said. "More than Darius." He started shaking his head and repeating, "But, I can't do this. Just sit here. I can't."

"It's my fault." He surprised her by jumping up. He hesitated, looked around the cottage, then merely sank back into the wooden chair and put his head in his hand. Then he resumed gazing into the flames, looking as if he had forgotten what he had said and why he had risen.

"It's okay, Sol. But it wasn't your fault. Sit."

"I can't," he said, shaking his head.

"Sit."

"Anna, I never knew my real father. I was too little. You know that. And I haven't grieved like this since the death of yours."

"Our two fathers have been so important to us. It's like we've had the same fate. We were born together."

"Aye, a strange union, indeed."

"Yes, but together as family. You have me, Sol."

She leaned into him. Then she started to cry. They sat quietly as she shook. She cried for him because she knew he would never cry in front of her. And yet the sobbing shamed her. She had come to the house to comfort him.

She managed to shake off her grief and straighten. Then she rummaged through a pocket in her black peplos. She took out a letter and placed it on his lap. He ignored it, staring at the fire.

"It wasn't your fault, Sol," Avva said again. "Before his death, Henri wrote this letter to me. The letter spoke of you. He said you had changed. He said he had regained his respect and love for you, not only as his king but as his son. This is why he did what he did, Sol. Because he believed in you. He wanted to help you. He could just as easily have left you and come back here to live here in the Azures. He had threatened it many times. He changed his course and sacrificed because you did. And he was perfectly willing to risk his life. He knew the risks. It wasn't your fault. You can grieve, husband, but don't think that."

He said nothing.

"He always wrote to me when he was away, you know." She shrugged. "And, when you were gone, he came here often. I think I liked him best because he reminded me of you. It was like he brought me a piece of you when you were away."

"Aye," Solinair said sadly. "But I'm afraid it seemed he no longer trusted me."

"No," she said, shaking her head. "That's just it. I have the letter. Read it. Read what he says about you, Sol. It's all there."

"There's no reason to read the letter," he said, handing it back to her. "You just told me what's in it. It was meant for you. But I cherish your words."

She shook her head and put it on his lap again. "Read it. It's a father's pride in his son, and a counselor's pride in his king. You can miss him, but don't feel bad for what happened. Read the letter and you'll understand."

But Solinair pushed it back to her.

"Please, Sol. He knew the risks. He doesn't blame you."

They were silent again.

"Anyway, truly, it was my fault," Avva said.

"What do you mean?" Solinair turned and looked at her.

She met his gaze. His bloodshot eyes flickered in the light. He had cried, but not in front of her. Probably not in front of anybody.

"It's my fault," she said. "My ideals, Sol. That's what drove him into danger. Had you never listened to me, he would never have visited King Philipp in the first place. I got to you and you got to him. It's all there in the letter. Please, read it now. I can't get rid of your grief, but I can take away your guilt."

Sol furrowed his brow. He finally accepted the letter from her hand. He opened it and she looked it over as she leaned on his shoulder.

Dear Anna,

Don't fear these words. Actually, I write them for your comfort. The news may sting, but hopefully it will serve as medicine later.

Anna, this is my last prophecy. This one is not foretold in any book, star, cup, or ash. It lives and breathes within me. I wish I could tell you in person, but I'm afraid there's no time.

Dearest Anna, I'm dying. On this final errand, Philipp will slay me. He will do this to hurt you and Sol. Terrible? It is our fate. Do not fear. I am old. I've lived a long life. I go with pride. I leave this earth without any regret. In a day, it will be done. I do not know how, but I know it will come.

But think of my life, Azure Queen. Do you know my story? My world is simple. At first, alone. Then one day a stray wolf landed on my doorstep. I was fortunate to take him in: the true Sun King, as great as—no, greater than—your father. Made even greater because of you. Once this wolf met a wondrous, beautiful nymph—you, Anne. And along came the greatest wonder of all, your daughter Cassandra.

In my life, it was only when I thought I lost Casey that I felt complete despair. Even upon seeing my death now, the fear is not so great. But when Casey returned, Anna, I felt young again. After you returned her. You see, I've lived all my years for your family.

I know the fear of emptiness, darkness, nothingness. Our lives are diffi-cult. The end is difficult. But do not make things harder with confusion. Sol did everything for you. Whether it be slavery or war, he repents for the higher good. His heart has grown. He risks more ... and the secret, Anna, is he did it all for YOU.

Do not let the horror that befell Casey destroy us. Take this as a request from father to daughter-in-law, if you'd permit me such an honor. Love Sol, for, Anna, Sol loves you more than himself. Honor your king and daughter. Honor our family.

But, Anna, if I fail to bring you peace with my words, perhaps you may find peace in the words of your great-grandmother. Once in my Azure home, the same home that once belonged to Queen Nefertiti, I happened to stumble upon some of Nefertiti's late writings, before she left for Egypt, while rummaging through a desk. I believe she discovered something in her strange disappearance. I found great strength in her words. It reminded me of you.

Allow me to part with them in the Egyptian ancient tongue —
Neeteru Belok Dispin
(Behold, I see nothingness never was)
In eternal love, Henri Untair

When Sol finished the letter, his head fell in his hands. He jerked. Anna held him, but she failed in strength, too, and cried with him.

"Oh Sol! I'm so sorry. I'm sorry."

"Blame me or not!" Sol cried when he finally got a hold of himself. He jumped out of her embrace. "I should never have sent him! And he should never have gone."

"Sol, I'm sorry. So sorry. After reading the letter, I rushed messengers to you, but it was too late."

"Aye. Henri knew. He knew our love. Our family. My love for you, Blue. But how could he do this if he knew he'd die?"

"Because of what it represented. Because of its atonement for you and the kingdom."

He turned from her and banged his fist on the wall.

"I miss him already, Sol."

Slowly he returned to his chair, sat back down, and just stared at the fire as if nothing had changed. Avva sat beside him but didn't touch him.

Soon it became eerily quiet. Avva looked around her. Then she thought of Nefertiti and the dead. Ghosts. She didn't like those thoughts.

"Sol, I don't like being in this house. Can you go back with me to our own room? Our own bed? Stay with me tonight. Please."

"All right, my love."

She stood up. Then he surprised her with his apparent weakness. Usually he bounded with energy and strength. Tonight he rose slowly and, as Avva helped him up, a flower fell from his tunic. A fluorescent blue flower. The same bright azure flower she had given him when she showed him the palace gardens for the first time so many years ago.

"It's still alive," Sol said with a sad smile.

"I'm surprised it looks fresh and new. We're growing old, husband, but our love is eternal, I suppose."

"Ah, you sound like him, Anna."

"I guess he visited me too often," she said with a wry chuckle.

Her laughter seemed to brighten Sol's face for the first time. He nodded. She held out her hand and walked with him out of the cottage's courtyard.

As they walked, the wind stirred. It was late and cloudy. The wind seemed to howl as they made their way back into the palace. And in the air, Avva seemed to hear distinctly, blowing in the wind:

"*Neeteru Belok Dispin.*"

She turned to Sol and he seemed to hear something too. He furrowed his brow and searched the palace grounds. Had he heard the same words? Then the air spoke again:

"*Neeteru Belok Dispin.*"

"He's not gone, Sol," she said with a smile, holding him closer. "He's not." Avva searched the area again, now listening for the wind. "He lives. He lives in the wind now."

"And in you, Anna."

"And in you, my love."

They embraced and Sol finally squeezed her hand.

3 8

ACCEPTING THE SNARE

Cassandra was in her room dressing for the meeting. It had been over a week since the funeral. But she was late—very late. For what? She didn't know. Engel had told her that it had something to do with Henri's estate. But Henri's possessions were already hers and her parents'.

"Princess Cassandra!" Someone was knocking on the door. "Princess!"

She gave no reply. She was too busy slipping into undergarments.

"Princess! You're needed now."

It was early. The green sun had begun to shine through the curtains of her room and Cassandra, like her mother, was not an early riser.

"Princess!" the voice said again, now shouting. She didn't recognize this voice. It was a man's voice. He banged repeatedly on the wooden door. Then it swung open.

The princess darted behind her dressing curtain. She was not fully dressed.

"Sorry, madam."

"Don't you knock?"

"I'm sorry … but … but we're late."

"Who are you?" She asked as she pulled on her dress behind the curtain.

"My name is Gavin. Prince Gavin Solinaray. Your *brother*, my lady."

She glanced around the curtain. Gavin was a young, strong, and athletic man, but he had a boyish face—it was made more youthful by an attempt to grow a beard. He was dressed as a knight, in leather painted blue, bearing her father's yellow sun standard on the chest. His eyes were bright green and wild. He seemed to survey everything with those fidgety eyes. His dark hair was long but not as wavy as her father's.

"Everyone's waiting, princess."

"Do you usually storm into a lady's bedchamber, Gavin?"

"Only when I can."

Under the purple curtain, she watched his feet shuffle in his boots as she changed.

"Can't see why I'm needed." Cassandra draped a blue peplos over herself. "I don't need an escort anyway. I know the palace like you know your sword, sir. I suppose this mystery meeting's in the throne room?"

"No, princess. It isn't. That's why I'm here. It's in a secret location."

"Secret?"

"Aye."

"Just a minute. I remember you. You're the obnoxious one. King Torinth's son. Why, I bet you planned to catch me half dressed."

"I was fortunate in timing, unfortunate in the view. No, I didn't see a thing. All I saw was a blue blur."

She laughed. Then she came out from behind the curtain.

Gavin stepped back. She wore one of Mother's dresses, usually worn to the Court: a short azure dress. She had worn it a week ago, with pride, around the many guests from Gaia during the funeral ceremonies. She was too sleepy to think of anything other than the business at hand. But the sight of it made Gavin look timid. And the last thing she would have guessed about this boy was that he was ever shy.

"Do I look all right?"

The handsome prince nodded with a stupid smirk.

"Shall we?" he asked, reaching out his hand. "I'm afraid the king may kill us. He's been waiting. And, although that's a very fine dress, I hate to tell you, but no one is dressed up for this occasion."

Oh, that's why he was staring at me. Idiot, Casey!

"I'll change," she said, running back to the curtain. "Who else is there?"

"The king. Your general. Our general. No, princess, there's no time. We have to go."

"So it's about war?"

He nodded.

"Mother's there?"

"Of course she is."

"Let me change into something less formal."

"You can't," Gavin said, raising a hand. "Sorry, but everyone's waiting. They'll understand."

They walked quickly together through the halls. He seemed to know the way even though he had probably been a stranger to the palace until the funeral. She remembered that the last time she had seen him was as a child running with her around the gardens at a harvest festival. But he couldn't have spent much time inside the palace.

They headed to the south tower. Then in a hallway with a series of doors, he took out a set of brass keys.

"I never knew what this door led to," Cassandra said.

"You're not supposed to."

They descended a dusty stone stairway into the basement under the castle. The walls were lined with sconces holding lit torches. They reached another short hallway. At the door at the end of the hall, Gavin knocked. The door opened.

A large, dusty wooden dining table, reminding her of the one in the great dining room, stood in the center of the room. The walls were made of similar wood. Only flickering torches lit the room. Sitting on one side of the table were five elders, wearing azure robes with high collars. Gavin was right. Only she and the elders wore formal clothes. At the head of the table was her father. And beside him was her mother. The two generals of the Atala empire, Milo of the Sun Kingdom and Cambria of Azure Blue, sat across from the elders. There were two empty seats beside the door.

Her father gave Cassandra a warm smile. Mother didn't. Avva stared at the wall across the room brooding. She merely nodded as Cassandra sat down. Her mother didn't look sad, she looked furious.

"All is accounted for," Avva said. "On with it." Then she turned to Milda with a look of disgust. If Cassandra hadn't known any better, she would have thought she was disgusted over Casey's tardiness. But her mother had always told Cassandra of her deep hatred for Milda.

"Welcome," Milda said with a big fake smile. "Welcome, princess," she said, tipping her ugly white curly head at Cassandra.

"Welcome," echoed another elder. "We may proceed."

"We have a letter to open," Solinair said quietly. He pulled it out of his tunic. "I'm afraid this is a bad time, but there really isn't a good time. This letter was sent personally by King Philipp's couriers. It has remained unopened until now. It came with Henri's remains. I decided I would leave it unopened until I could gather my most trusted friends together. That is all of you. You are here to decide our next course of action. After all, my chief advisor is now dead …" Even that simple statement seemed to disturb him and made Cassandra choke up. "So I rely on all of you to act in his stead." Then he nodded to Milda. "Including Imada. Times are so dire that they've agreed to join this meeting."

"We are here to provide counsel," Milda said.

"Let me read it," Avva said, reaching for it.

Sol hesitated but passed the letter to her.

"Before Anna reads it," Sol added, "understand that everything we say within these walls is secret. You are to tell no one. I'm afraid we've entered difficult times, and until we end this war, we need complete secrecy."

Avva pulled the scroll from a silver ring and read it out loud:

Dear Crescent King,

Take this warm gift from a king to a thief. You've stolen my lands. You've pillaged my castle. You've enslaved my family—fortunately for us all, the great King Philipp has found it in his heart to return them to me. I have sent you in return …

Avva paused for a moment. Sol quickly gestured for her to hand him the letter, but she refused. She continued in a broken voice:

Sent you Henri Untair's head on a silver platter. It's been rumored in the realm that your wood nymph wife wanted my head in a similar fashion.

When you stole my home and, more recently, burned my lovely castle to the ground, I swore one thing. To hurt you. To hurt you and your family. And so, what a great plan. The illustrious King Morteus, your new friend and ally since my treaty with Philipp, agreed to fulfill the role.

Allow me to teach you something, boy king. You've stupidly angered every surrounding nation of Gaia. And, as powerful as you are, you have no friends. No doubt, you make a worthy adversary as a soldier, Solinaray, but your policies are idiotic. Well, boy, I have friends. I've spent a lifetime making friends. And I will see to it that they side with me on one simple goal—to hurt you.

Think, child king. Think hard. As you plan your revenge, don't do anything foolish. I have over five nations surrounding your golden empire. And all of them are willing to fight you.

But if you wish to chase me, I welcome it. In fact, I desire it. For everything you do, I will see to it that you suffer more. Do not think my terror ends here. Henri was first. Others come later. I will continue to whittle away your pathetic family. And you will not only be alone in this world— you will live the rest of your days in darkness and fear.

With love,
  King Morteus Mangus of the Crystal Court

Avva added, "There is a notation at the end of the letter in different handwriting":

Enjoy the gift,
  King Philipp Bruefield

Avva scrunched the parchment in her hands and turned to the dark wall again.

"Speak," the king said, looking at everyone. "I didn't have to read this to know its contents. That's why it wasn't read till now."

"It is accurate regarding the state of the world, Crescent King," said Milda.

"*Address my husband as the Sun King!*" hissed Avva with wild eyes. Her mother's rage made Cassandra jump. "How dare you."

"I apologize. But it is rumored that your husband doesn't mind that title and, in fact, reveres it, as it came from your father."

"This is true." Sol raised a hand warily and rubbed his eyes. "It's okay, Anna." He looked so tired—more tired than Cassandra had ever seen him before.

"No, it's not okay," Avva said. "She doesn't have respect for me or you or anyone but herself."

"But she's here, Mother," Cassandra said.

She said this only to keep the peace. It worked. When her mother looked at her, she sighed and nodded dismissively.

"You know what must be done, *Sun King*," Avva said, looking into Sol's eyes.

Sol turned to Milda. "Speak, madam. Please. You're right. Titles are nothing more than something used in mockery or flattery, as the great King Darius once taught me, and I have no problem with being reminded of my upbringing. I asked you here for help."

The old witch seemed to soften.

"Our enemy's words are true," Milda said. "Imada is aware of a grand canal and port being constructed by the Egyptians at the lower Nile. It is a new port city named Thonis. Further from the water gather lines of soldiers who we've watched train regularly. But most concerning is their ship building." Milda untied a scroll and handed it to Cambria, who passed it to Sol. "We believe their intention is clear. They will cross the Strait and attack when Atala is weak. But we also believe they wait, like King Lanius, to see the victor. If things remain as they are, the Egyptians will do nothing. If you take the rest of the continent, they'll do nothing. But if you lose, King Solinair, these men will invade. They don't side with us nor our enemies. Actually, out of all the outsiders, the Egyptians are most likely to befriend us because of their past ties with Nefertiti. Like here, their people still praise Nephrea in song."

"If they're ship building, seems they bet on us losing," Milo said. "How sure are you of this, woman?"

"With my life. We are Imada. We've seen it with our eyes."

"How?"

"Imada," Milda said dismissively. "And I am not called *woman*. I am an Amazon nymph, sir." Then she turned to another elder. "Tell them of the East."

A younger elder with thinner long gray hair and the same shifty eyes addressed the table. "Unlike the battleships of the South, we believe there are no current threats from the East. We watch Colchis and Nineveh with great interest, but they are not in the business of ship building—they are more interested in defense. The only ports in this region are meant for trade. Nevertheless, the port at Adelain that you've rebuilt, sire, is of some concern to them. The construction of our navy may force them to build their own."

"How can we believe all of this information?" asked Milo.

"Any information from the elders is from Imada," Cambria responded. "Any secrets from Imada is either gifted by the gods or shed by Amazon blood. Everything is trustworthy, sir."

"Our biggest concern is not the East or the South," Milda said, raising a finger. "It is the West. The ancient Phoenician power is waning. We believe the greatest threat on the horizon now is from Hellena. The Greek Isles, though broken up into city states, are the greatest force we face. They call our continent Atlantis. They hate us, our culture, and our ways far more than Babylon or Wasset. When you look at the three great empires, it is the Greeks I fear the most. Like the Egyptians, they are building ships, but their triremes are powerful—the strongest in all of Gaia. And even without their ingenuity, they have Lord Zeus and Olympus on their side."

"Seems the greater our power, the bigger our problems," Sol replied.

Milda simply nodded.

"So what do you suggest we do?"

"Attack," Milda said with a shrug. "Attack now. War is inevitable."

"I'm shocked," Avva said. "Of all of us, I thought you, Milda, would be the most against war."

"Usually, yes, but not now. This is the last fight to take the continent. The longer you dawdle, the stronger our enemies become. We must fight and we must defend ourselves from these outsiders. Imada supports this because we know that the fates are now sealed. If King Solinair fails to unite the kingdom, it will be torn apart by the outsiders. First Hellena and then Assyria. We've come to this point, ironically, because your father united the lands. The unification has weakened our defenses against our surrounding enemies. And if the Hinterlands fall into pieces again, this time foreigners will invade Azure Blue."

"I would never allow that," Sol said.

"Apparently," Milda said with a nod. "Unfortunately, it is your very love for my queen that has locked man's fate to our future."

"Milda," snapped Cambria.

Milda shrugged again.

"You've heard Imada and our external challenges," Sol said. "Now we discuss the army within." He nodded to Milo.

"My lord." Milo nodded and addressed the whole table. "We are far outnumbered in the South. Morteus speaks the truth. Likely his forces are greater in number, but trained soldiers are few and far between in the Hinterlands. Our army is the most powerful in Gaia."

"Imada indicates you have overrun most of their forces in the Crystal Kingdom," Milda interjected. "And Caravia is weak now."

"True," Milo said with a smile. "The Crystal Kingdom is ours. Although Morteus speaks with confidence, we believe the snake hides in the ancient land of Logencia. But my suspicion is the five nations he speaks of in his filthy letter is also truth. We are surrounded, just like this Amazon state in Napea. King Philipp's lands in the south, the Greek Isles in the far northwest, and of course the tiny but independent Fox Kingdom of King Lanius in the east. Some of these lands are so distant that we know little of them. Their allegiance is suspect—with anyone. I believe you, Milda, that they will side with the victor. Remember the great battle of Azerban, Sol. King Lanius was not our friend, but he certainly wasn't Philipp's or Morteus's either. He came simply to destroy and pillage."

Milo paused. He drank from a crystal glass of water by his seat, but he didn't sit back down.

"Everyone at this table wants a fight," Milo said. "I loved Henri too. I knew him longer than any of you. But..." He addressed Sol and Avva, shaking his head. "Well, Henri was the one who always drew your plans. You know that. And what I learned from him is that we should weigh all our options and act carefully."

"Speak," said the king impatiently. "Speak your mind."

"Our success is our challenge. Morteus has weaseled his way into alliances with border nations. They don't care of such things as righteousness and honor. They care for their skins. The only area that remains truly neutral, thankfully, is Egypt. How he got Hellena and Assyria as allies is beyond me. And yet, these friends might think differently of him if we were to use our power to threaten them.

"I propose three options. One is that we do nothing. No one here will agree to that. The second: war. We have the know-how, armaments, and power to strike a grave blow in Kitheria, perhaps Caravia, and annex the rest of the continent. The third choice is an interesting one. We could simply demand Morteus as ransom—demand Morteus be given up on the threat of war. Philipp would consider giving him up if it meant averting a fight with us. I believe he aligned with the beast to get even with us, not to—"

Avva hit the table with her fist. "And what of Philipp, Milo? He helped kill Henri. No, both must pay."

Milo merely sighed and nodded. Solinair looked wearily at Avva.

"Can we win this war, Milo?" Cassandra asked.

All turned and gazed at her.

"Yes," Milo said. But then he shook his head. "But it will cost us dearly."

"We are at war," the king said. "A war which Anna and I inherited but didn't start."

"Not true," remarked Milda. "You could have ended all this after Azerban."

Avva hit the table again, but before she could respond—

"What is the cost of fighting Kitheria and Caravia, Milo?" Cassandra asked. "What sort of terrible cost?"

"Thousands of lives, princess. And just as Morteus said— pain. This will inflict pain on all of us." He ran his hand along his bushy beard. "Forgive me, but we owe it, ironically, to Henri to be forthright. I must bring up something that none of us wants to discuss." He took a deep breath and said, "I've heard objections in the past to the king's policies regarding slavery. But the context must be understood."

"This is not the time," replied Sol.

"Don't misunderstand, Sol. The point is that you acted wisely for Atala with your truce with King Philipp. You have been wise ever since I met you, and that is how we have survived. But now we tread dangerous waters. The war drums are sounding. I fear we are about to slip. Everyone here wants to get Morteus's head on a spit. Good. Perhaps I want that even more than you do. But I advise … no, I beg you to consider: he's provoking us. I believe he can only gain from war. At the moment, he is a poor and lost king. So he has Philipp kill Henri and break from us. He takes from us a saint of a man, a man who deserved to pass away in peace in this wonderland. A man who our king loved more than any other man. Morteus takes him, then performs this grotesque act. And what does Morteus think we will do? He knows damn well what we will do."

"I understand all this, Milo," interjected Sol, "but—"

"Sol, it's a trap. Morteus sat back watching you fight your brothers. He trapped you with Torinth, he trapped you in Azerban, and he's trapping you now. He's dragging you into battle. He will get you to fight Philipp. Then he will draw in the rest of the world and run away like he always does."

"What do you propose then?" asked Sol. "Even Imada advises we fight."

"Time," Milo said with a nod. He finally sat back down. "Do not fight, king … not yet."

"If we fight now, will we lose our kingdom in war, Milo?" Cassandra asked.

"Hmm, not to barbarians," quipped Gavin.

"No, princess," Milo answered.

"How can you be sure?"

"Our men are better trained, better equipped, and better fed. I don't speak of victory. I speak of the cost. And what you all must think of is not our final victory over Atala, but what the cost of such a victory will mean to us and the surrounding nations *afterward*."

"And to the gods," said one of the Imada.

Milo sat down and drank some water, forcing it down as if it was a bother. All eyes were on the general. He looked concerned, but he seemed just as angry as the rest of them.

"Will you need our services, general?" Cambria asked.

Milo shook his head. "You're immortal. Why curse yourselves?"

"For Henri," Avva said. "For Henri, we'll do it."

"Do as you wish, my queen," Milo said with a sigh. "But I'd prefer you leave foolish fighting to man."

"What is needed shall be done," Avva said.

"Do not send your people unless your lands are threatened, Anna," Sol said sternly.

"She will not," said Milda. "We are bound."

"We will do what we must do," Avva snapped.

"Imada will not support another incursion on foreign soil, Ambrosia," Milda said, shaking her head. "Keep soldiers in the air if you wish, but we will not ready the army to fight on the northern border of Egypt. Harmonia herself backed down there because her fight brought Zeus down upon us. Our presence on the ground will force Zeus to turn against Azure. I'm sorry, but so long as I breathe, queen, I will not allow—" It looked like her mother was going to jump across the table and strike the old hag.

"Do we agree on war?" Sol interrupted. "Hmm? No one will take Milo's first option. And it does not seem as though anyone wants to barter for Morteus; though I agree, general, it's possible the rulers in the south would give up Morteus for peace. But Anna's right, Philipp is our sworn enemy now. Does everyone here agree to fight?" Then Sol looked at Milda with a nod. "Amazon excluded, *gladly*, my lady. No Amazon shall touch down." Then he turned to the rest of the group and struck the wooden table with his fist. "If we win, we can unite Atala and promise long-lasting peace."

No one said anything. Cassandra figured all their minds had been made up, anyway, even before the meeting started.

"Milo," the king said, "it's settled. We fight. We will be cautious, as you've warned, but I will avenge the death of Henri. And I will finally take away the beast's life."

"Our first job," Milda said, "should be to find who our

friends are. Perhaps not all the nations of the outside world are our enemies."

"I've already sent emissaries to sea to investigate that very thing, Milda," Milo said with a nod. "But, please, if your Imada has information, enlighten me."

"We'll do what we can." Milda nodded. "But I warn you. You must realize that Zeus is against this war. With Hades' abandonment after Harmonia, and now this final war, we are truly estranged from Olympus and all the gods. I fear for the future of Azure Blue."

"Damn the gods who took my daughter, Milda!" The king shook his head. Milda's words seemed to stir up more rage in her father than her mother. But he quelled his rage looking at Casey. He took a deep breath and addressed everyone. "We are strong. Not because of how we fight or what we hold, but because of this very table. We survive for each other. And we will help and care for each other as one family. We shall not accept foreign soldiers upon this continent. We shall finally secure our lands in the South. Then we shall finish construction of the navy to defend against the outsiders that surround us. We are one Atalan continent, and in the face of our Greek enemies of Gaia, one Atlantis."

He rose. They all stood and bowed before the king.

"For Henri!"

They all repeated, "for Henri!"

"And for my ..." Sol looked at Avva. "For *our* father, Darius."

The meeting adjourned.

LOGENCIA

THE FIRST BATTLE WAS NO SURPRISE. IT WASN'T MEANT TO BE. Sol gathered a handful of regiments and, with no effort at concealing his intentions, marched straight across the bogs in the south to Logencia, along the northern border between Kitheria and ancient Caravia. He was brazen and loud. His men could be picked off as they marched, but their large presence was meant as a signal to the barbarians of the South that the emperor had arrived.

The river bridges were small and outdated. So, to speed their progress, his army constructed a bridge, the largest bridge ever built in the known world. As the military built the bridge, Solinair sat on horseback, spotting many families fleeing by boat. Every family was spared and given safe passage. And, the next day, when rumors spread of the king's mercy, what had started as a small handful became a flood of thousands.

Sol had expected his army to be stopped by the river. Milo and Sol had predicted soldiers would try to ambush them there. They didn't.

Then came the threshold of the fabled city. His father, King Darius, had never fought in Logenus, but for many years, Sol had lived there. It was more a settlement than a city; thousands of fences and tents with various farms but nothing of permanence. And now everything had been abandoned.

When the bridge had been built and Sol had transported only half his sky-blue hoplite soldiers across a grand overpass, he was finally met by a line of silver-armored soldiers, some with black star flags, on the other side. They hadn't struck by the river; they had waited for them to cross.

"Seems we won't be lodging in Logenus on our way to Teleria, sire," said Milo with a smirk.

Sol nodded. "Gather the troops. Arrange them in line. Prepare the phalanx. Then gather the cavalry. I ride with you, friend, to cut down these weeds."

"Yes sire," Milo said with a bow and rode off.

Milo organized quickly. There was no way to get all the foot soldiers in line as they were still passing over the bridge, but those regiments that had crossed quickly lined up and held the rear, with shields and spears, in rows.

Sol removed his scope and saw a messenger in silver ride down a hill, splashing through the bogs, toward Sol. Solinair broke tradition and rode to greet him himself.

"Ho," the stranger said. Then he gave a shocked and frightened bow. "Emperor Solinaray." He stammered his words. "The illustrious people of Logencia demand you return your army and leave our blessed city. We promise to forgive this intrusion if you simply turn back."

"Tell your people to bring me the heads of King Morteus and Philipp," the king replied, quietly gazing at the town. "If you do this for me and forfeit your lands, I shall gladly sheath my sword."

"Emperor Solinaray," the messenger said, bowing again. "We are but a merchant town. Those two kings aren't here."

Sol did not respond; he merely shifted his horse's position with his reins. He gazed at the inner-city dwellings. Lines of carriages crowded filthy roads as the townspeople desperately tried to escape. A motley crew of soldiers, missing helms, shields and spears, were trying to gather along the dead marshes.

"I shall spare all that I can," Sol said, finally looking at him.

The messenger waited for more words, but the king said nothing. After some time, the messenger bowed, confused, and rode quickly back to his men.

The king returned to his men, now organized in blue rows. He raised his hand and his men cheered. Their roars could be heard throughout the valley. Then he cantered slowly across the land, paralleling his men and preparing for another speech. But his heart yearned for no words—only revenge.

"We stand before barbarians," Solinair shouted atop his horse, "We are here to teach them. Some will die. Others will return home. Those that survive will tell the tale. Tell your families that you fought to brighten a wasteland. We will brighten the coldest region, which I call Hades. For this is as dark and dead a world as the lands beneath that harbored my daughter. Be brave. We come to brighten them."

He fell into a slower trot, looking at his men, many young, many with the familiar look of horror before battle. One young soldier couldn't help himself and vomited before the king. Others stood frozen with eyes wide. In the past, Sol had felt their fear, and he had felt pride as he marched before his soldiers. Not now. Now all he felt was a sickening, festering rage.

"We will do what no one has dared do before," he cried, stopping before them again. "We will take these lands and cleanse them. Then we will move on and shine our light. We will do this to spread our way of life. A way of peace and liberty.

"Many of you argue that you fight for a king's loss of one man." Some jeered and shouted objections to this. The king held out a hand. "No, no. I know what's said. But tell me this—you all know the tale. Tell me, how should we right what was wronged? For a man was killed by these animals before you. A man who forfeited his life for you. Because he believed in a world of independence, peace, and freedom. And he would have died, without a moment of hesitation, for any one of you."

He stood silently struggling with emotion as many shouted his name and banged their shields. He cocked his head back and saw the enemy's incompetence as they continued to attempt to gather together. This only gave him more resolution. Then he caught a glimpse, in the sky, of a horse in the clouds. Her wondrous monokera were here in support too.

He looked down and shook his head.

"My fathers, two of the greatest men to ever walk this earth."

Perhaps spoken too softly.

He raised his head and shouted, "My fathers … fed upon with deceit by our enemy." His soldiers cried in rage. "Invited by lies. By whom? King Morteus and King Philipp. Enemies of the people who now stand in these wastelands."

The soldiers thundered in their own rage. They banged their shields and stomped their feet.

"Have we avenged him? No. But we will. Glory will be our crescent as it brightens like the sun over Atala. As it shines from the mystic lands of Azure all the way down to Egypt."

Further shouts rang out. And Sol was satisfied as their fear seemed to fade.

"Take your anger! Take your rage! We shall crush them. Stomp them. Snuff them out. Show them how civilized men live and breathe! We will take these lands and free all who remain. Atala will be one kingdom. In memory of Darius and Henri. Or else, I promise you, surely, I swear it, I will gladly die by your side now!"

Further yells, now loud enough to be heard by the enemy. He paused for a moment. Then he galloped along the blue line of hoplites as he had once done as a boy king in the Crescent Kingdom and before Castle Cove.

"Follow me! For justice! Follow me to die in honor for Henri and Darius, better men than have ever lived. Follow me. Follow your Crescent king!"

There was a great roar of support with the metal clang of swords against shields as he rode back to his line.

He did not wait. Follow him, or not, he would die alone if need be. For the pain of a childhood of slavery tore at him. This, along with the sadness over the death of Darius, his misery at the loss of his daughter, and now the death of Henri, his true father, seemed to all come to a head now. He felt it all in his charge straight into the heart of the silver-clad soldiers, a brazen attack aimed to strike fear in them.

The strike created the intended chaos. Before the battle had even begun, some of Logenus's best soldiers had been slain on the field. Unfortunately, the city's archers were ready too. As Sol charged, a volley of arrows fell upon them from wooden towers surrounding the walls of the city. The act was callous as some fell on townspeople still trying to escape, but such was the extent of his enemy's barbarism.

The battle ended quickly. Sol was filled more with disgust than joy. He watched as the enemy, just as in Sinteria, torched their own ancient city.

When the battle was over and Sol walked the smoky fields of the dead, Kaios ran and bowed before the king.

"We've taken the city!" Kaios said. "Praise the day!"

"The death of so many doesn't please me, Kaios."

"But our goal, Sol," said Kaios. "That makes it worth it."

"What goal?" he asked, crouching down and digging into the sack he carried. He placed coins on a fallen soldier's eyes.

"To take the rest of the continent, sire."

"Aye." Sol rose and stared out on the smoky field. The brilliant fire was so large that it warmed his cheeks. Then he looked at his chief officer. "Take the continent? That was not my goal."

Sol's scouts saw Morteus's chariot running from the city. Sol followed and gave chase, but they never found him.

4 0

———

THE UNINVITED GUEST

Avva sat on her throne leaning her head against her wrist, staring at the empty throne room. It was midday. Engel had suggested that she join the princess and him for a walk. "It will do you good, my lady," Engel had said. She was in no mood. She was so worried about Sol. Word from Imada and her scouts was not enough. She just sat and worried.

She had done the same the day before. And the day before that. Occasionally, Cambria would introduce one of her subjects. They would walk in requesting something, and she'd try to pay attention, as part of her job as queen, the part she hated the most.

Meanwhile the outside was lovely. The green sun shone through the glass dome above, shining green on the sapphire, garnet, and lavender vines sprouting over tall vases along the aisles in the throne room. Her eyes wandered inside and then outside, at the beautiful gardens. But all the beauty in the world could not be appreciated when one's mind was chained. Cassandra had caught her twice in the stables ready to fly to the battlefield. Her level-headed daughter had stopped her.

She heard a knock on the double doors. Cambria rushed

inside. Her lovely complexion of faint blue had turned a ghostly white.

"Your Majesty, I couldn't stop him. I didn't have time to ask and—"

Five men wearing black armor, one in the center with his face shrouded under a hood, barged into the room. The one at the center she recognized immediately with his sly grin and dark goatee.

"I tried to warn you, Your Majesty," continued Cambria, "They flew by chariot."

"Do you know why I'm here, Avivae?" Hades asked, removing his hood and black leather gloves.

It was only when Avva leaned on the arm of her throne that she remembered her disrespect. She had not bowed.

"No," she said.

He nodded and walked down the aisle. He headed to a window by the throne and peered out admiring the view, just as she had.

"Do you refuse chairs for your guests like your barbarian husband?" Hades asked, still looking outside. "Should we pull them from the rows ourselves? Or lean on our sides on the floor?" A few of his men laughed.

"Bring chairs to the throne, Cambria."

"Yes, my lord," Cambria said with a bow.

A few other nymphs ran in and helped arrange chairs for the men to sit on. Hades didn't sit. He walked over and just stood by his men. His guards seemed very amused by their leader. One with a long bushy beard had a huge grin Avva wanted to wipe off.

"I'm a little upset," Hades said. "A little angry, Anna." She was surprised by his use of the Kitherian pronunciation of her name.

"What can I do for you?"

"You know damn well what you can do for me. But we shall play. I seem to be missing two things dear to me. My helm. And —" He stuck his finger to his chin. "Hold on. Explain to me why you aren't in Amazon armor aiding your husband? I'm shocked that you didn't fly there yourself."

"Your edict forbids it."

"What edict?"

"Anything that is yours, I'll give back to you, sir. If I have it. I'm unaware of a helm, but if it's in this palace, it's yours."

"Avva," Cambria interjected with a deep bow, midway down the aisle, "shall I bring the Eruboi refreshments and—"

CRASH.

Hades swung a shining Mandrigel sword against the floor with a shout, cracking the stone underneath. The sudden violence shook Cambria. Another Azure guard ran to the front of the throne room, pulled out a sword, and stood in a fighting stance.

Hades laughed. He sheathed his sword and came closer to the throne.

Both guards now stood, with swords drawn, at the sides of the room, while the Eruboi remained in their seats laughing at some misunderstood joke.

"Do you have any idea, Queen Anne, how hard it is to travel to Azure Blue? My brother bewitched the sea. My most omnipotent sea brother, with the help of Hephaestus, created a pyramid as tall as the clouds. One you are thoroughly familiar with, aren't you? The Mount is an impasse you, arrogant nymph, tried to fly over. First you used the scepter to freeze an army, an offense so heinous as to make Zeus ask me for your crown. You don't know, can't know, wood nymph, what it took for me to stay Demeter's hand from destroying Azure. Do you know what stopped her?" He paused for only a flash of a moment. "Not you, Anne. Believe me. I couldn't care less about you. *My* Azure. *My* Napea. Sara nearly destroyed this land centuries ago, and I wasn't about to let her do it again. But then your obstreperous blood wouldn't stop, would it? Only three times worse—" He lifted three fingers. He was pacing now. Avva turned to her right, and Falena was still standing in a battle stance awaiting her command. For what? A suicide charge at a god and his mercenaries? "The minute your daughter was seen on the Mount, you took a monokera and tried to fly over Olympus. Do you have any idea the height of that supercilious hubris?"

"What would you have me do?" snapped Avva. "Let her die?"

"*Yes.*" He turned and furrowed his brow at her, looking at her as if she were stupid.

"You imprisoned her," Avva said, standing up. "What do—"

"*Sit down, wood nymph!*" thundered Hades with his eyes shining red. "Sit down before I sit you down! Isn't it enough that you don't bow before me?"

Hades walked over to his men. Then he waved his hand before them. "Leave us!" he snapped. "All of you. Get out!"

Avva still stood in rebellion. But when she looked down at her hand, covered by a violet lace sleeve, it was shaking violently.

"I waited a few moons," Hades said, oddly docile. He sat down on the chair as his soldiers got up and walked down the hall to the exit. Then he folded his hands and looked up at her. "A few moons," he said more gently. Then he opened his red eyes wide. "Sit. Sit now, or so help me, I shall lose patience and turn mean."

Avva sat down.

He looked out the window at the garden again, seemingly enjoying the view as much as Avva had earlier.

"Dismiss them," Hades said, gesturing to Avva's guards. The guards looked at Avva and Avva nodded.

When the double doors closed and they were alone, he said quietly, "That act was glorious, Anna. You humiliated my family. No nymph had done that since Harmony. I could have kissed you. But this went beyond disobeying the edict over the borders of Gaia. You passed the border of mortals."

Avva's heart was racing. There was a brief uncomfortable silence.

"What do you want?" Avva asked.

"I want my helm back."

"I don't have it."

"And I want your daughter. Ask her where it is. You know the edict. Does it mean nothing to you? Cassandra needs to return to the Underworld. I gave you time to mourn. I know your grief over the death of your beloved Henri. That bought you an extra two moons by my grace. Now I ask for the princess. Not to be brought to the Mount. I ask for her sacrifice. Perhaps then, my brother Zeus and sister Sara will be satisfied. But even then, your affront could be irreparable. I don't see how Amazons can ever live on Gaia again. I've tried exhaustively to deal with Ambrosia blood. As much as you hate me, I've been your spokesperson and the buffer between you and a far more evil god. I'm not your enemy. I come here as a messenger. So, what will it be? Will you come with me like your mother before you, or will you give me back your daughter? Either way, Olympus shall have sacrifice."

"You will never have her."

"Then be like your mother. Come with me."

"No."

"Then hand me your scepter," he said with a shrug. He shook his head and looked at the ground. "Your reign is over. So is your people. This is the end of your race, Avva. Without the sacrifice of your daughter, I ask for the life of Avivae. Without the sacrifice of either of you, Olympus shall destroy Azure Blue."

"You abducted my daughter!"

"She fell."

"She told me she was grabbed."

"She fell," Hades said, shaking his head. "And one day you will learn that when a god tells you what's occurred, you will accept it."

"Are you seriously asking for this? You want me to give up my daughter? When I just saved her?"

"If it means following the will of Zeus? Yes. Why is this so…" His eyes widened again. "Sit down, Anna!"

But Avva didn't sit. She walked down her steps and opened a chest. She took out a golden rod, her scepter.

"Here," she said, offering him the golden scepter. "I don't

care about my crown. I only care about my family. Sol, Casey, and myself."

"And Henri," Hades said with a smile and a nod. That sly smile made her angrier.

"You come here and act as if you're a messenger!" Avva cried. "No, you're the instrument of our pain. You killed my mother. You kidnapped my daughter. You even kidnapped your own wife. You are worse than a serpent. You belong buried in the ground your family's given you. As far as I see it, you gods are the ones with hubris. Always asking us to bow—"

"*Sit down, Avva!*"

"I won't." But she nearly did, faced with his thundering voice. "No. I won't."

"When life began, it was Zeus, Poseidon, and me who formed the world, little girl. Not King Darius. Not your Crescent king. You point to me as evil? What of you? What of your constant never-ending desires and conquests? You don't follow the simple laws of nature. You whine and throw tantrums. You shall see the consequences of these complaints, *Blue*."

He turned away for a moment, looking out at the gardens through the windows.

"A lovely world, Anna Ambrosia," he said, almost to himself. "Too bad it must freeze. *Any Outworlder who steps foot on Gaia will come to me*," he said. Then he stood up and walked to Avva, his red eyes staring down at her. She shuddered.

"I know the edict," Avva said, forcing herself to meet his gaze. "I told you long ago I don't agree with it."

"Any Outworlder who steps foot on Gaia will come to me," he repeated. "The law is more than a simple monostich. It means you will lose your life when you try to touch the gods." He touched her chest with a single finger, pushing her back. "It means that you may struggle and scream at the heavens." She walked backward as he advanced closer. She found herself pushed all the way to a window. "But you remain a puerile little girl. And you have touched far too much for any mortal."

He said no more. He stared deeply into her eyes. "What's your decision?"

Avva's eyes opened wide and she shouted at him, "*You will never have me or Casey!*"

The outburst made Cambria advance into the room, but one look from Hades' red eyes and the guard stepped back against the wall. Others ran to the entrance, including Engel.

Avva raised her scepter between them.

"Put that weapon down," Hades warned.

"Get out," Avva said.

"Give me Cassandra," he said, wagging a finger. "Think about it and think hard. You know I can take her, and you can live many, many more happy days in this selfish paradise of yours. I will even forgive your excursion into the Hinterlands. How's that for a deal?"

"Get out."

"Consider my warning. It comes from Zeus and Sara, Amazon queen."

She waved her great scepter by his face, "Be gone, demon! Leave now!" Then, pointing the scepter at Hades, she screamed: "*Eneich Aneu Loriaan!*"

Nothing happened. The air before her didn't even turn cold.

He struck the scepter from her hand. The gold rod landed a few feet from them, rolling and clanging along the stone floor.

"*How dare you!*" Hades thundered. She fell on her side. "You raise my scepter at me!" His voice not only echoed but literally shook the throne room. His rage stopped Avva's heart, and she involuntary cowered before him. "Not only Prometheus! Pandora! Not only countless other gifts I've given, but to the nymphs, to my dear Harmony, my scepter! You raise it against me? You raise my scepter to hurt me! Just as you'd raise an army to attack me! You don't know who your enemies are, you fool. Harmonia's scepter? Do you know whose scepter that is? The trident was forged by Hephaestus for Poseidon. The staff of the thunderbolt for Zeus. And the Scepter of Hades, not the Scepter of Azure, lowly wood nymph, the Scepter of Hades, that you just pointed at me, was forged for *me*! Only by my grace did I bequeath this gift to your people. *And now you try to use its power against me!*"

"Forgive me," Anna said, shielding her eyes.

The doors swung open wider and Hades' men ran through the entrance. Cambria and Falena, beside the door, turned and faced them. Two of the Eruboans pulled swords of their own. Then another Azure guard in red armor ran in.

"That staff doesn't belong to you, you dog!" Hades raged on. Avva remained on her side, shaking on the ground. "Do you, infant, think you deserve it? Do you know what Harmonia sacrificed? *My sacrifice!* She died so that Nephrea would live. So that *you would live!* My lover died for you! I didn't care about your people, I cared for her. And she died for you!

"You fly atop a mountain? *So what!* You used a monokera, the best monokera, *my monokera.* Your family killed her! Your family killed my lover. And now you fly her monokera, given to her by, guess what god? *Me!* And you killed her too!

"You aren't Harmony! Ah, but if it wasn't for her, so help me, I'd tear you in half on this stone floor right now. No. You remind me of my childish wife, Cora. You are puerile like little Persephone. But so help me, for her sake and Harmony's memory, I won't strike you down now! But I will abandon you. I shall leave you! I leave you and your people forever!"

Avva said nothing. She couldn't stop shaking.

"Do you like cold, Queen? You like freezing things?" He turned again and bowed to her in mockery. "You might even be unrulier than Harmony, but your dullard mind lacks her cunning. Very well, wood nymph. Watch your lands decay under Sara's wrath. I give these lands back to Poseidon. I no longer protect you. Go play with the goddess Demeter alone, bantam nymph. Until you succumb, you'll suffer the cold you so cherish, but know that even now, as I storm away from your profound disrespect and hubris, *even now*, I of all the gods favor you."

"*You took my daughter!*" Avva shouted between tears. "*You monster!*"

He leaned down to her ear and said, "Sara will take far more."

He threw his hood over his head and walked swiftly, with his soldiers, down the aisle and left the throne room.

There was an odd silence.

Anna whimpered.

"Are you … all right, Your Majesty?" asked Cambria over her, oddly docile.

Avva heard Hades still raging with his men outside the great hall.

Avva sat on the floor with her head in her hands and wept. She cried, not only because of Hades, but because of the weight of all of her stress over everything. Everything from her mother, to this god, to the entire weight of the world that she had fought since she was born. She had never seen so much rage. And all that evil and rage had been directed at her.

She heard the throne room doors slowly close. And then she wept alone.

THE CLIFFS OF ZONOCH

Solinair sat in a large tent with maps and battle plans strewn before him on his desk. He was busy rummaging through a pile of scrolls. Some, brought from Azure, had been drawn on ancient papyrus, possibly by Harmonia herself. The plan had been laid out. They would fight by the Intec River then capture and kill Philipp. It was hoped that Morteus would follow.

Legend claimed that this was the famed border where the Amazons were finally stopped in their attempts at conquest of the continent. A wall stood before the southeast and the legendary city of Teleria, a city that resided atop the mountains. This final cliff border was the most difficult militarily to take. But if Sol won this, he could take the rest of Atala. And so, with great irony, he faced the same obstacle that his wife's great ancestor, Queen Harmonia, had faced before.

It was late. Sol had not slept. It looked as if he would not sleep again.

He heard a knock on a wood pole by his door. His weary general, Milo, walked into his quarters. He looked exhausted as he smiled and bowed.

"News?"

"Aye, my lord. I've secured the border of Trintz. General

Cartazen and the rest of Philipp's elite guard was captured or killed in the raid. Philipp is now an unguarded king, much like Morteus. But he and the Caravians are still willing to die by the border."

Solinair got up and hugged his general, then patted him on his back hard.

"Well done, Milo!"

"Aye. It was a brutal strike. Much of it was fist to fist. These last soldiers were specially trained. But when we trapped them, many were trampled by horses on both sides."

"Brave fools. Likely Philipp's last order."

"Aye … I also have some grave news, though nothing unexpected. The army gathering by the base of the mountains is sizably growing. It's the largest I've seen since Azerban. We may have hurt Philipp, but that doesn't mean that he and the Caravians or the outsiders are going to give us Teleria."

"They send everything," the king said with a nod and a sigh.

"Seems so. I don't advise that we go on the defensive. We must strike back and lead them to retreat to Jedithian now. Then chase them to the sea if need be, sire. We shouldn't wait much longer."

"Did any of their men indicate plans for a counterattack?"

"There are whispers of it, but I doubt it. They wait for our strike."

The king rose. "Good." Then he walked over to his bed and gathered the sheets of parchments. "Time to move and finish this."

"To Trintz."

"Trintz. Let's proceed with the plan and lure them to the river."

"A close fight."

"Aye."

"Aye," Milo echoed with a heavy sigh.

Milo walked over to the desk and picked up a flower over some parchments. A blue flower. An azure flower.

"It is like what you carried with you into Azerban," Milo remarked.

"The same flower."

"The same?" Milo asked spinning around.

"It's enchanted. And it reminds me of Anna."

"Incredible. Would you like me to give her news?"

"I'll send a letter."

"Very well. Oh, one more thing. I have mail for you."

Sol smiled. His smile felt foreign. "Anna? But she just wrote to me a day ago?"

Milo shook his head. "No. This one's from your daughter."

"Did you read it?"

"Aye. Here."

Sol sat down at his desk and unrolled the parchment.

Dearest Father,

I didn't want to bother you. I know you're on the verge of victory, but this is urgent. It's frigid — the coldest I can remember. It ruins all my fun. But, oh well.

Without jest, I'm very worried. It's known to be icy this time of year, but never like this. Ice seems to be freezing everything. Worst, it's freezing our harvest and even our winter stores. Mom, being proud as always, refuses to send for your help. But we need you.

If the weather turns, as it should, I won't bother you again. But if it continues, I will send a messenger again your way.

Please consider my concerns. And please take care of yourself. Stay safe.

Love,

Casey

Princess Cassandra Ambrosia of the Sun Kingdom

Solinair placed the letter down and ran his hand through his long hair.

"Did you read this, Milo?"

"Aye," he said with a nod and a smile.

"You never had children?"

"No, Sol. Never had time. Perhaps Gavin's one, like he is to you."

"I miss her so," he replied with a nod. "Casey's gone through so much. She means everything to me."

Milo nodded.

Sol got up and started packing again. He grabbed his bags and pushed a pile of shirts and pants into one of them. Then he grabbed items from his desk. He carefully tucked the bright blue flower into a pocket in his tunic. Milo just stood watching him.

"We have many soldiers guarding the North, my lord. We can spare some and make a journey up to make sure Napea is safe."

"We need everyone on guard." Sol shook his head. "No, we can't afford a turn like last time through the Strait. Not now. We must keep the soldiers around Crescent Blue and Adelain. I'll send Gavin."

"The prince, sire?"

Sol ran his hand through his long hair again and sat on a wooden chair for a moment. "Oh, I'd go if I could, of course. Believe me. Gavin is the only one I can trust, aside from you. Obviously, old friend, I can't spare you. Send Gavin. If need be, he'll return and I will come as soon as I can."

"Perhaps you should tell him yourself. He's lived his life wanting this fight. He hates Morteus as much as you, perhaps more. He wants revenge for his grandfather. He won't be happy leaving the front."

"He won't listen to me. He'll listen to his general." He got up and resumed packing. "Is everything else in order?"

"You never know. Napea snows. It gets cold this time of year."

Sol shook his head, "This is Cassandra. Casey's been through more than you and I. If she's worried enough to send me a letter, it must be serious. I trust Gavin the most. And I trust Casey's judgment the most—perhaps more than Anna's. Though I love the queen more than anything, I don't trust she'll be thinking straight. Not before this fight. We must have the prince go and check on Azure Blue."

"I understand, sire."

"Of course. Are the units ready? Will we be ready for this fight? Are we—"

"We're very ready, Sol. All the men stand by you. We won't fail you, my king."

"Very well then. The next time I see you, it will be on Trintz. We shall move over the cliffs into Teleria."

"No drink to celebrate?" he asked with a grin.

"I'm sorry," Solinair said, shaking his head. "But it's late. And I have a lot to prepare. Let's postpone our drink until our victory in Caravia, friend."

"In Caravia then." He bowed and left the tent.

The minute his friend left, Sol sat at his desk. He unrolled a piece of parchment and wet a feather.

Dear Anna,

I hope all is well. I miss you and Casey terribly. You've asked me to keep you informed.

We're preparing for battle. It will come in a matter of days, and I think it will be the most terrible fight I've faced since taking the Sun Kingdom. Or perhaps the battle where you saved me. Word is that there are tens of thousands preparing by the border of Caravia. They surround us not only from South Atala, but from the outer empires. I don't fear defeat. I don't fear death. But I do fear the possibility of not seeing you again. Aye, this alone makes me tremble.

Don't fret. We will triumph. I'll avenge Henri and your father. All intelligence tells us that the two demon kings will be there. I only hope that I can slay them with my own sword.

I've recently received a peculiar correspondence from Casey. I hesitate to tell you because I believe it was meant to be in confidence, otherwise it would have been sent by you. I'm sending Prince Gavin to visit in my stead. Please allow him to help you with whatever ails Azure. Believe me, I'd come myself if it were possible. I care for Azure Blue over all else. And you, my love.

Enjoy your wondrous lands. I hold your flower close to my heart.

Love,
 Sol
 Solinair Solinaray, The Crescent King
 Emperor of Atala

He was about to set it to dry, but then he scribbled one last quick message out of desire for less formality.

Oh Anna, I love you. Whatever happens, through life or death, I'm yours always. Be happy in peace, my love.

Sol's army gathered by the Black River in the Shivera Valley of Trintz, bordering the base of the Cliffs of Zonoch. Sol and Milo believed it was these very cliffs that had given Philipp the courage to kill Henri. His enemy had never believed, nor did Milo completely, that Sol would actually chase them all the way over these mountains.

The dark river was aptly named "black," as a canopy of trees and drab shrubs along the shore shadowed everything. The water was opaque. The air was clouded by mist. And the surrounding fields were leafless dead bogs. This blackness contrasted with a range of colors seen across the water.

Sol led his horse slowly along the shore, gazing at the collage of painted armor under torchlight. The hoplites and flags of various colors were practically a stone's throw from him, across the river. All these colors proved Milo's fears to be true. Philipp and Morteus had seemingly managed to align the entire world against Sol. Apparently, they believed that, like the fabled Amazon queen, Sol needed to be stopped.

Milo had played a cat-and-mouse game with the enemy for weeks. His aim was to exhaust and confuse them. Straw- and dirt-filled barges were being used as decoys. Sometimes the cavalry even rode halfway across regions where it was shallow enough to cross. Soldiers would move out and watch as the enemy across the water panicked and ran in formation, only to find the boats completely empty or the cavalry retreating across the river. Sol had accompanied them many nights, to confuse and deceive the enemy. From these false advances, Milo was able to ascertain their weaknesses. They had learned that Philipp had been given absolute power in this defensive, not only over his infernal black-starred nomadic barbarians, but over the emerald-flagged Caravians, and even over the Greeks, the Assyrians, and all the other outsiders who had joined them. No soldier advanced without the Kitherian nomad king. Only Lanius the Fox roamed free. He was an outlier and, thereby, the most dangerous. Indeed, today, Lanius's silver-armored hoplites lined the shore atop their dreaded elephant beasts.

Despite the numerous feints, the actual time of the invasion had been carefully planned weeks before. Sol had picked the anniversary of King Darius's death. His men knew the anniversary well, and the enemy across the water surely dreaded this day too.

It was midnight. The fog and rain had cooperated with him. Visibility was scarce and that was perfect for their true advance into a close-range fight.

Sol rode to the general one last time. "It's time," he said quietly.

"No turning back?" said Milo with a smile.

"Follow me closely," Sol said, squeezing his reins tightly. "Philipp and Morteus owe me vengeance, and I will take it. If he strikes me down, join me. We shall meet Charon together, friend."

They clasped their gloved hands.

"It's been the greatest honor of my life to serve you, Lord Solinaray," Milo said with a bow on his horse.

"For my fathers, Milo," he said with a nod.

"No, Sol," Milo said with a toothless grin. "No one's ever gone this far. This time, it is for Emperor Solinair Solinaray."

"If you wish. Or an emperor and his general."

The two turned and looked at the shadows of their soldiers, who now stood in perfect formation, in the darkness, under scattered torchlight. Some in the flickering firelight showed fear, but every man showed determination.

Sol gazed up at the clouds that passed over a crescent moon. He smiled at the omen.

"Let us live through battle. I mean *really* live," Sol said, looking back at Milo. "They shall sing our songs. And if Zeus and his infernal family have their hands in my defeat, let us stand before him in Trintz with the courage of Harmonia and her Amazon. We fight Morteus, Philipp, the gods, and the whole world tonight, Milo."

"Ah," Milo said, lifting his head and closing his eyes. "I'm glad at least you were able to give *me* one of your great speeches, Sol. I only wish you could have said it to the men."

"Are my speeches that good?"

"Aye." Milo nodded and smiled. "We shall have victory, sire." And they clasped gloved hands one last time.

Sol nodded and turned to a group of riders in the darkness. He raised his fist three times as a quiet signal and then readied himself by the shore, clutching his reins tightly. The water had been tested by scouts and was shallow enough tonight to cross.

And so it began.

Barges crossed the deep parts of the river first. As many times before, they were met by the enemy's arrows, but Sol's line of archers threw arrows of their own. And this time, the crossing barges did not hold dummies; they held real men.

The enemy had mobilized, but it seemed like they were not orderly, wondering if the attack was real. Anniversary or not, Sol had tricked them to the point of exhaustion.

When far enough across the stream, Sol drew his Mandrigelian sword, glistening red in the darkness, and ordered the cavalry beside him to charge. They raced forward with the same fierce discipline as the foot soldiers.

They met the first line of defense by the opposite shore. Many of the black-and-white hoplite enemy tried to mimic the menacing phalanx of Sol's army, but their lack of discipline could not hold their men in line. The initial line of soldiers broke, but then a line of green hoplite Caravians rushed to reinforce Philipp's meager defense. The Caravians were renowned for fighting with knives, and Sol fought many who leaped from their horses and piled into the fray. By now, he had succeeded in subduing most of Philipp's remaining army.. Indeed, if Philipp was alone, Sol would have already won. But just like the legendary Amazon queen centuries before him, Solinair was outnumbered by the Caravians and outsiders. And for the first time since Azerban, he saw dark bronze hoplites under torch fire carrying the flags of Assyria. These outsiders did not form in a phalanx, and some of their weapons were weak and easily broken like the weapons from centuries ago, yet they fought fiercely.

Sol jumped from his horse and sloshed in the mud fighting, a band of soldiers sword-to-sword. The Intec, another stream closer to the cliffs, was his prize and he pushed forward in that direction. If he could fight through the foreigners and Caravians beyond this last river, he could begin climbing the cliffs to Teleria. Thereafter, according to Imada surveillance, the enemy fortress did not hold enough defenses to stop him. But he couldn't move forward.

Kaios and Simeus came close to protect him. His lead officer, Kaios, shot two soldiers that threatened his king with arrows. But then Kaios was wounded by a knife in the back thrown by a green hoplite soldier on horseback. As another soldier ran to help Kaios, he received a mortal wound in the chest by a spear.

Many Assyrian soldiers in bronze closed in now, so close that they fought with fists. These were not the long fields in Azerban. The battle was in close quarters, with soldiers body-to-body all the way up to the Intec and, in the chaos, Sol's left arm was cut by a sword. The cut was sharp but couldn't hinder him.

Sol rose, fighting to ignore the flashes of sharp pain in his left arm, and found an opening to the Intec. He shoved through friends and foes back to mount his horse to try to charge through. Fortunately, Milo's foot soldiers arrived to reinforce the decimated first wave of Sol's cavalry. Sol's horses moved aside as his phalanx advanced.

The sun began to rise over the bloodstained bogs. This was a foreign marshland, drab, desolate, and dead, which many of his soldiers had never seen, but Sol had seen it as a wild, wandering child. With the light of morning, Sol could see the cliff's base towering close to the Intec. But as Milo cut down the green-armored Caravians and bronze-armored Assyrians, Lanius's silver foxes arrived. With the blowing of their salpinx, men rode on the backs of their dreaded mastodons once again. The huge beasts charged at Sol's beaten cavalry and Milo's phalanx, trampling them. No matter how brave and strong they were, they could not stay together under this charge. But Sol was ready this time. Sol's foot soldiers fought the beasts with a row of spears, burned the animals' feet, and threw flaming arrows at their legs. It slowed their progress, but just as before, the elephants trampled hundreds of men.

Sol met up with Milo on horseback.

Milo was staring at the Intec River before them, watching as more silver hoplites from Lanius's army poured over the Intec, with renewed excitement, in the wake of his mad offensive with the beasts. They looked at each other, and Sol sensed defeat in Milo's eyes. He knew his general well enough. Sol made his decision then: advance or die. And so, brave or foolish, he turned with a raised sword and charged into the water, headlong toward Lanius's fresh batch of silver hoplites. Some of the enemy laughed at Sol's bravado. Milo shouted something inaudible.

Lanius had a few elephants left. He directed them all at Sol.

Sol realized this was his end. A stampede of a dozen elephants rushed unimpeded toward him. But just when Sol believed his death was nigh, a volley of arrows fell from the sky. His men raised fists and cheered. Sol looked up and saw the Amazon nymphs soaring over him. Once again, Anna's nymphs had come to rescue him. The mere sight of Amazon fighting again drove some of the enemy soldiers to retreat. The nymphs' arrows buried the elephants intending to ride over Sol. And the rest of the elephants were now raging and stampeding over some of Lanius's own soldiers, running from the arrows.

Milo caught up with Sol again. They rode across the Intec together. Milo laughed and pointed at the enemy running.

Exhausted and in severe pain, Sol jumped from his horse and stood upon a fallen elephant. The mastodon was covered in arrows. Sol stood straight and shouted to his advancing men.

"Watch them run!" Sol shouted, pointing at his retreating enemy. "Killing their own, now they run from us!" He paused for a moment as a shade of blackness rose over his vision and he teetered from pain in his arm. Kaios, though wounded, rushed to help him, but Sol raised his hand. Sol shouted again, "You who withstood their might and fought their unholy monsters! You tire? Aye, we all tire. But we will not stop until we reach the cliffs!"

Shouts and cheers rang above from the scarlet-armored nymphs as a flock of them strafed the Crescent army again. And with them came echoes of cheers from his men all over the valley.

"Come! Follow me into the heart of Caravia. Do not let your friends die a needless death! We can and will take the lands that are rightfully ours. Then our grave losses will not be in vain. Do not falter! Let us end this war now with victory!"

They cheered. And hearing their shouts and cheers, despite all devastation, Sol knew they had struck fear into the hearts of those few enemy soldiers who still remained fighting.

It was midday. Milo had men arrange barges from the Black River to move more of their equipment over the Intec. Other men trudged through the shallow waters along the river's edge under cover of the king's archers. They all crossed this last river. Then they entered the valleys under the cliffs.

As his army crossed the dark marshland and began climbing the gray rocks of Zonoch, they were ambushed. The fight wasn't over. Now the infernal enemy had turned to guerrilla warfare.

Sol gathered his remaining cavalry and pushed into the

dangerous narrow paths of the mountains. But there another force lay in wait. Greeks. They had hidden along the sheer cliffs, and when Sol was close enough, these wily outsiders in shiny bronze hoplite armor marched in orderly lines to meet them. They imitated the phalanx invented by Harmonia, holding their spears forward and shielding their brothers in a turtle formation. It was as well ordered as Sol's army.

The surprise was enough to force Sol and Milo to regroup back along the Intec. The Greek forces were meager, but their men fought with great discipline and skill. And, like the Caravians, their fighting impressed Sol.

Milo regrouped his men into a phalanx again. Then the clash between these two formations was horrible, far worse than engaging the Caravians had been. These foreigners would not yield. And yet, Sol's army was bolstered by the continuous rain of arrows the Amazon were firing from above.

Then the worst of tragedies struck. General Milo was struck in the head by a spear. The wound was instantly fatal. Milo fell from his horse.

"Milo!" Sol yelled, pulling his reins. He lurched back. "Milo!" He turned his horse to help him.

"Leave him, my king!" yelled Kaios, who rode beside him. "We must move with the phalanx into the cliffs! We can't abandon them!"

"But he's been hit, Kaios! Milo's been hit."

"We must move ahead, sire!" Kaios pleaded. "We must!"

Sol was spent. And now he felt it. His body moved automatically, but his mind was still back watching Milo fall.

Then, all of a sudden, by the base of the cliffs, Sol's cavalry was ambushed again by Philipp's remaining black-and-white-armored horsemen. They had not fled. It was likely they had hidden with the Greeks.

"My king!" Kaios cried. He grabbed Sol's reins and tried to push his horse forward. "Solinair! We must move forward! Milo's dead. You can't stay here or we'll be finished!"

Kaios moved closer and pulled Sol's reins. It was only when

the king saw more of his men struck by enemy arrows, cut down by their swords, or speared that he woke from his daze. Dizzy and sick to his stomach, he grabbed his reins back from Kaios.

"Take half the men!" shouted Sol, pointing. "Turn and ride as swiftly as you can back toward the Intec. I'll stay and stop Philipp's advance. They will think you are fleeing. Cross the river and join me on the West side. That is our final advance."

"Sire," Kaios said, shaking his head. "I won't abandon you."

"Do as I say! No phalanx. Race back and around with the horses and ride into the enemy. Show them the way my father Darius did things in Atala. Ride through the Greeks and break their line."

"Aye … aye sire," he replied reluctantly.

Sol had nothing left in him. These Kitherians and Greeks were fresh soldiers, and they battled as well as his own. And yet he raised and swung his sword and yelled, "For Milo!" Those who knew their general had been slain shouted in support.

Sol and his cavalry pushed in on the enemy's line once more, clashing shield-to-shield. The armies faced each other along the narrow valley, close enough to spit at each other. Soldiers were now choking or beating each other to death.

This was the hardest advance of his life. His left arm stung terribly. He had dropped his shield long ago. Many fell to his prowess with the sword or the protective arrows from the sky above. He hacked and stabbed, no longer even knowing who he was fighting.

Then came a vision, almost as if in a dream, of a king in royal green armor under a black star flag. King Philipp? Or Morteus? The royal king was within a javelin's throw. The enemy king was hurt too, with his green armor now stained red.

There was a guttural cry and Sol was unsure if it came from himself or his men. The enemy king met his gaze and turned his horse to flee.

Someone among Sol's ranks shouted in triumph that King Lanius lay dead. Then there were cheers and the sound of a salpinx again.

King Morteus. Morteus.

Was it a whisper or a voice in Sol's head? Searing pain crippled him. Then blackness again.

Sol saw his father, King Darius, lying on the rack being stabbed and whipped. Was this imagined, or had Sol been somehow magically transported to the dungeon to witness his adopted father's death? Or was it his own death now? Had he been taken prisoner?

Sol opened his eyes and found himself on his knees with his sword raised over a king's head. He did not know how he had gotten here, but he was here. And under him was a king with long wavy black hair and a short mustache. But this was not Morteus, this was King Philipp. Philipp looked around wildly, trying to squirm out of Sol's grasp. Sol had pinned him. But before Sol thrust his blade down on him … Cheers rang out again with another sound of the salpinx. The sun began to set, and he heard his name being shouted repeatedly by the multitude around him.

"Get it over with, butcher!" Philipp said, gnashing his bloody teeth and staring up at Sol's red-and-blue blade. "Do it! You betrayed my people. But you believe me to be evil?"

"Aye, I know you to be." Sol thrust his blade through Philipp's neck. Philipp's eyes met Sol's gaze one last time before losing that flicker of life that Sol had seen end so many times. Then Sol fell on the king's body and all turned black.

"Victory, my lord!" he heard in darkness. It was a young soldier's voice. Kaios? He was too sick to be sure. But then he recognized the voice with his eyes still closed. It was young Carnaus. "Kaios ordered me to send you news. There will be more ambushes, for sure, but we will win now. They have no chance, sire. Victory!"

"Where … where is he?"

"Who? Blessed day! Is that King Philipp under you?"

"Where is he?" Sol muttered.

"Who, sire? Officer Kaios?"

"Where … Morteus? Is Morteus dead?"

"Blessed news. Lanius is dead. The captains of all the Greek and Assyrian armies are captured or dead too. The war is over."

"But what of Morteus? Did you get Morteus?"

"Morteus? He hasn't been found, sire. Scouts have been sent upon orders of General Kaios. We believe the coward is hiding alone in the cliffs now."

"I shall give chase."

Sol finally forced his eyes open. It was blurry, but he recognized young Carnaus holding him up. Sol ran his gloved hand over his eyes and shook dripping blood from his glove. His forehead was bleeding.

"Sire, let me help you. You're hurt."

"He went alone?"

"Morteus could escape more easily, sire, with few men."

"Where was he? Does he flee to Teleria?"

"No. Morteus was last seen running south. Deep into Caravia, we think."

He felt his body propped up and leaned on something hard and cold. A shield?

Sol forced his eyes open again. "I hunt my spoils, Carnaus. This time, he has no one to protect him. This prey is my right. Take a regiment and scout … along … the southern border of Zonoch. Tell the men to not let him escape. Do you hear me? Do not let Morteus escape the mountains. I hunt him, but the army guards the base. Don't let him escape."

"You go alone?" The boy opened his eyes wide.

"Aye." Sol nodded.

Sol gathered his thoughts in deep meditation, as he had been taught by Henri. It helped his aching head … a little. But then his arm burned. He got up leaning on a knee.

He was surprised to see a dark valley now empty of soldiers. All that was left was fallen bodies. He had been so sick that he had fainted. For how long? He was unsure. But the battle was over.

"At least take this, my king." Carnaus tried to pour something from a purple ampulla into his mouth. It was an ancient herbal remedy for pain.

Sol knocked it from Carnaus's hand. "I need my wits, lad."

"It's a blessed day. With this victory, word is Jedithian and Teleria have already sent messengers announcing surrender. Caravia is ours. And with it, the entire continent of Atala, emperor!"

Sol forced himself to stand, but he couldn't fully rise without Carnaus's help. He looked toward the cliffs and smiled at the sight of a hundred monokera still overhead. But as he looked back on the fields, he saw that some of the immortal nymphs and unicorns had fallen. Aye, the continent was his, but at what a terrible cost! Milo had been right. The cost was grave. Even at the death of his dearest friend, Milo.

"Help me up on my horse, Carnaus."

"But I must protest, sire. Forgive me…" He gave a quick bow and held him by the arm again. "But I fear for your life. I do not think you can ride."

"Help me on my horse. I order you. If Morteus was seen, I will capture him. If he flees down the cliffs, kill him. Don't let him escape. If he escapes, all is in vain. I killed Henri's slayer, now I am going for Darius's. Send every man to stop Morteus, even at the expense of guarding Trintz."

"But sire! We should protect Trintz."

"All their kings are dead," Sol cried, shaking his head. He moaned from a sharp sting in his left arm. Then he touched his aching head. "All are dead but one. I will get Morteus."

"Yes sire." Then Carnaus smiled and said, "But rejoice, you are lord and emperor of all Atala now."

"I didn't come here for that."

THE CLOUDS OPENED and rain poured over Sol's eyes. He nearly fell off his horse as he let go of the reins and wiped them. He had already camped for three days. His left arm was too painful to lift. And yet he rode every trail of Zonoch, chasing Morteus. He tended to himself as he had been trained to do all his life. And yet, though his wound did not fester, he yearned for bed and shelter. But he wouldn't yield. He would find Morteus. For the coward would not be guarded by soldiers this time. Indeed, he would be Sol's prey.

Just as Sol had done as a boy, he let his horse go free (the trails were becoming too narrow, anyway), and slept alone in bushes and under trees, hunting fowl and living like an animal. And yet, through his pain and exhaustion, he searched on, knowing there was still a chance he could find Morteus. Because Morteus would not do these things.

By the fifth day, he finally found a trail where bushes had been trodden upon. Bringing the leaves to his nose, he smelled the resin of trodden ground. The rain fell again, but it was under enough undergrowth to be dry. And nearby there was the slightest hint of mud along a dry log. It could be one of his scouts, but then he saw something else. Pieces of meat strewn under a tree. The meat was old but, more importantly, cooked. Only dry and salted meat was regulation for a soldier in the army, and even that was scarce. Cooked meat was far too expensive. Only a rich, fat, and spoiled king would travel eating that. He followed the trail.

As he climbed rocks, the rain worsened. It poured so heavily as to limit visibility. Looking back toward the Intec, far below, he could see nothing from this height, but he figured his men probably were still gathered, searching the slain and tending the wounded—such was the horrible extent of bloodshed and death.

It was not long before he reached the summit. Here, away from the main trail, the trek became treacherous. One slip could throw him off the side. But he figured the danger made it the perfect hiding place for his slithery archenemy.

Fortunately, the rain slowed to a drizzle. Along the plateau, visibility increased as the clouds dispersed.

He heard voices by nightfall. He crouched down by a shrub and surveyed the area. Further down a slope, among trees and shrubs, a short man sat on a rock by a cliff. He was a stone's throw away, yet far enough to be a treacherous jump. Sol quietly made his way through bushes down to the ledge. When close enough, he stealthily unsheathed his sword and crept up to the man from behind.

"Morteus?" Sol said. "Could it be? Alas, I've never really spoken to you." The man spun around on the granite in surprise. He appeared to almost faint. And what a sight Sol must have been. He had not bathed or changed his armor since the battle. He was covered with dry blood and mud after days of camping in bushes. His face was probably coated by enough mud to look as if he had fur. Indeed, he probably looked like an animal. "But we once met over the false treaty with my father at Azerban. You were just as small and feeble then."

"I don't think I know you, sir. Who are you?"

"I am Solinair Solinaray, son of King Darius."

Morteus's eyes opened wide, but there was deceit in his gaze. The light of the half-moon shone on his face, illuminating his dirty jeweled emerald-colored clothing and his sweaty bald head. As Sol got a better glimpse of the king, Morteus stumbled over his words. "King Solinair?"

"I've come for you."

"Ah," Morteus said with a sudden smile. "I am so happy to hear of your victory."

"I've waited a long time for this."

"Indeed. Perhaps we should talk?" Then Morteus looked behind him at a sheer precipice below.

A flash of a blade ran across Sol's periphery. Sol spun around. A man had tried to leap on him but missed. Then he rushed back, meeting Sol blade-to-blade. His foe had a greasy mustache and sweaty, slicked-back black hair in a ponytail. It was Visus. And his sword was as enchanted as Sol's.

"Ha, Crescent King!" yelled Morteus laughing. "I am not alone!"

With great speed, Sol sliced Visus's hand from his wrist. As Visus looked down to nurse his bleeding stalk, Sol kicked him off the cliffside. He watched as the body plummeted down the side, his screams finally silenced after careening against a wall. Then Sol spun around to Morteus.

The cowardly king wasn't there. He was crawling down the rocky cliffside down a narrow trail. Sol jumped down a few feet and landed right in front of him. Morteus threw his hand out to protest.

"Please!" Morteus said, panting, "Please! I won't fight. Perhaps we can make some arrangement?"

Solinair debated whether to throw him off the cliff as he had Visus. Morteus took out a dagger with a shaking hand but looked as if he were unsure how to use it.

"Why did you kill my father?"

"What?" Morteus furrowed his brow.

"Why did you torture him?"

"Who?" he said, catching his breath.

"My father."

"Darius? Do you mean King Darius? You can't mean Darius. He wasn't your father."

"Insult me to your disadvantage!" Solinair shouted, gesturing to the drop to their side. "Why torture him? Why inflict pain before his death? Do you deny it? Hmm? Why? He was a better man than you could ever be!"

Sol was pushing Morteus toward the ledge. Morteus raised his hand in protest. Sol fought the urge to plunge the blade through his throat.

"What do you want from me?" asked Morteus, looking repeatedly behind him. They were at the ledge again.

"Why did you kill Henri Untair?"

Morteus tripped over a large stone and would have met his end had Sol not caught his arm. Sol had believed his left arm was lame, but apparently his rage was enough that he felt no pain holding his enemy.

"Was he your father or Darius?" Morteus quipped with a nervous chuckle. Sol was surprised at Morteus's sarcasm. He advanced his blade, nearly pushing the dirty, bloody sword into his throat. "Sun King, what do these questions mean? Do you wish to talk, or are you simply torturing *me* before you slay me?"

"I'm judging you."

"What makes you think you have the right to judge anyone?"

"What sick pleasure did you take in torturing him? Tell me."

Morteus looked at him, perplexed. Then he seemed to hold back laughter. "Who cares?"

"I must know."

Morteus examined Solinair. There was a brief silence, which seemed to drag on. Then Morteus said, "You hunted me. I never hunted you. For years. You enslaved my family. What of yourself? Judge yourself, butcher. You robbed me of everything. Now you point a sword and ask me why I tortured Darius? Do you think, had the opportunity arisen, that Darius would not have done the same thing?"

"*I do not!*" Sol shouted. "*He would never!*"

"You will never hold a kingdom, because you don't understand the world. You can conquer, but you will never hold it. Your father was not a king either. He knew how to fight, but neither of you knows how to lead."

Sol squinted and, for a moment, pulled his blade back from the weasel's neck.

"Or perhaps you're a nymph?" Morteus remarked with a laugh. "Was Queen Delia your mother? Then your sister is your wife? You dare judge me!" He shook his head. "Oh, it's easy to pick at you. I take Henri's life, but look at me, I'm a weak old man." Morteus gazed into Solinair's eyes. This time, instead of showing fear, he grew angry. "What do you want! Kill me! Do it. I can't stand you standing over me like—like some kind of stupid monkey!"

"Insult me as I hold a sword over you?"

But Solinair sheathed his blade and sat down on a rock. Morteus looked at him oddly, though he still kept throwing glances behind him at the precipice below.

"You could let me go," Morteus said. His tone sounded oddly conciliatory. "That'd be justice. Think of the compassion. That would be a good thing, Solinair. You are, of course, a *good* king?"

"I'm not an idiot."

"Of course not," Morteus said dismissively, raising his hand. "How could a general as powerful as you be stupid?"

"Or ignorant. I question you as I had hoped there was something to you other than just plain greed and barbarism. It must have occurred to you that I'd kill you after the death of Henri."

They fell silent. Solinair was feeling exhausted again. His hand twitched at the handle of his sword. It took all his strength to not swing it down on him.

"You will never be king," Morteus finally added. "A general, fine. But … frankly … you're not personable."

Solinair laughed. His own laughter surprised him.

"Not personable?" asked Solinair. "All right then. Don't worry. I'll slay you here. I debated on capturing you, taking you down the cliff, and having my people tear you to pieces…" Morteus tried to interrupt, but Sol kept talking. "Instead, you'll be thrown off a cliff. You are my spoil and I have the right to take my prize. You're so conceited that you can't stop insulting me even as you beg for mercy."

Solinair lifted his sword, but as the little man shook, he sheathed it again.

"Better," Morteus said with a hesitant smile. "Come … let's talk this over. I could be of use to you in your dealings with the other monarchs. The Greeks are strong. I can advise you regarding them and the other outsiders, emperor."

"Do not think that just because I lowered my sword, I've changed my mind."

It began to rain again. Morteus shivered a little in the cold. Sol might have shivered but he didn't care to notice. He stared at his prisoner. He didn't kill him—yet. He rather liked making the man wait. Torture? Perhaps. Perhaps it was to torture him? His hatred ran so deep that he didn't know how to end this.

"You sent Henri's head to me," Solinair finally breathed. He spoke quietly almost to himself.

"Is that not what you threatened to do to me!" Morteus objected, practically spitting at Sol. Morteus pointed a finger at him. "Spike him on a stick!" Then playing a woman's voice, he said, *"Bring back his head on a silver platter, dear."*

"Is that supposed to be Anna?" Sol asked, unsheathing his sword and standing again.

Morteus opened his eyes wide and lifted his hand. Then he looked back and saw that he was at the cliffside once again. One more step back, and he would plummet hundreds of feet to his death.

"I beg for my life, sir," he said, shaking and holding his hand out again.

"Your method is not very *personable.*"

"Do what you will!" Morteus yelled with a flash of rage, staring into Sol's eyes.

"Deserter. Leech. You left your general to die. You ran from your land and your people to save yourself. You're a coward without honor. You *strat-e-gize* for your stomach. Indeed, I judge you. If men consider you a king, I gladly forfeit any such title."

Morteus looked behind him again, teetering on the edge.

"I will throw you over the rocks," said Sol.

Morteus lifted a hand in protest one last time. But, as he scrutinized Solinair's expression, he simply nodded. "I hurt you. For that, I am satisfied. Goodbye, bastard Kitherian."

Morteus straightened his arms, closed his eyes, and simply fell backward off the ledge. Sol jumped to the cliff wall to catch him, but he couldn't grab his tunic in time. He watched as Morteus's body fell like a sack, crashing against the walls as Visus had. But unlike Visus, there were no screams.

The rain stopped. It grew calm.

Sol closed his eyes and lay on the stone, finally giving in to nausea and exhaustion. He realized that his arm still hurt. He wondered if he'd lose it due to lack of care. But his fatigue went beyond the pain.

He dreamed of Morteus still clamoring along granite rocks, running from him. Then he saw Henri, even Darius, speaking to him on the ledge.

The morning sun shone over him as he opened his eyes. A beautiful yellow-red splashed across the cliff vista. He stood up. On one side, he could see the Intec like a faint line far, far below. On the other, he saw blue on the far horizon, as blue as the clouds. The Strait of Aethiopia. The sea. Sol had conquered all the known world, from Azure Blue to Egypt. A Crescent king. A nobody. It was a war that had lasted his entire life. Even as a child, his parents were killed in Kitheria because of the disorder of this lawless land. And now, after meeting his archenemy, he had found King Morteus to be nothing—nothing at all. A true nobody. A nothing king.

Sol turned again and peered as far north as he could toward his beloved lands on the island of Napea. But he was nearly a hundred leagues from home. He could not see his Azures. Nor could he see his wife. But he longed for her. Now, he thought only of Anna.

4 2

ICE

"I must inform Father."

Those words had been said by Prince Gavin a week ago to Cassandra and her mother. He told Casey his intention was to take a raft and ride alone to Crescent Blue. Then he was going to ride back to Kitheria and tell his father of the plight of Azure. He had waited for the snow to stop for safer travel. It never did.

Now Cassandra escorted her brother to the West Harbor. It was a small harbor in Napea, on the shore, near the base of Mount Ambitus. The princess rode upon Inghorn while Gavin preferred a horse from the Crescent Kingdom. They wore long heavy furs. Cassandra could not remember a more terrible winter. Gavin's horse and her unicorn trudged through ankle-deep snow along a normally purple sandy beach.

The view frightened her. The Strait of Azure was gone. The sea was no longer full of raised isles of ice; it was one long sheet. She could not see the ocean, only this white ice spanning from the trees of the nearby forest to the far distant hills of the Crescent Kingdom.

Because of the thick ice, the usually short journey along the shore to the West Harbor took them nearly the whole day.

Gavin was quiet. Solemn. He had been worried about the army all week. Now this.

They stared with open eyes and mouths by the harbor. The docked wooden ships were locked in shards of white ice. Green rays of light reflected off the white as the green sun set upon the distant horizon. The ice had trapped all her father's ships.

"You may not need a ship after all," Cassandra said morosely. "Perhaps you can walk to Caravia?"

"Has this ever happened before?"

She shook her head. "It is something I haven't seen since the Underworld."

Gavin angrily jerked his horse toward the main gate.

The gate was bustling with blue hoplite soldiers in thick coats. Two guards met them and one raised his hand. Cassandra gave them a scroll, and the guards looked at them suspiciously. Then they laughed.

"Do you mock us, sir?" asked Gavin angrily.

"No, but I'm afraid you're not going anywhere. There is no ship in the world that can sail through this. You could try to walk, but I wouldn't recommend it—in case it thaws, you know."

"Do you know who I ride with?"

The burly guard looked at the princess and nodded. He fell on a knee. And he turned to Gavin and bowed to him as well.

"It is a great honor," he said with a smile and a deep bow. "My lady. Sir. Forgive, I meant no disrespect. I guess this bad omen has taken my senses. My name is Unter. Prince Gavin, I fought with your father in Azerban. Aye, I even helped free your lands from King Ansel. And you, you likely don't remember, you fought with me. But you were just a boy then. Aye, I know you. It is a great honor, prince and princess."

"Then you must give us a ship," Gavin said.

"I cannot." He quickly shook his head. "Sire, this is not out of disrespect but due to nature. I tell you, there's no way a ship will sail."

"If the snow stops," asked Cassandra, "how long will it take before the ships can be sent out again?"

"I don't know. We've never had our ships locked in ice before. Not in our lives, not in our fathers'. I think it's a very bad omen, princess."

Cassandra looked at Gavin and sadly nodded. She put a hand on his shoulder.

"I'll be back," he said, shrugging, trying to be cheery. Then he turned to the princess. "Seems this day is not so sad. I won't be leaving you after all, Casey."

"When you return, prince," replied Unter, "the first ship freed will be ready for your service."

Gavin mounted his horse. He tipped his head to Unter. Then Cassandra followed. They headed back to the palace.

FOR THE FIRST time since her coronation, ages ago, Avva's power had been challenged. Hundreds of nymphs stood before the doors of the palace and behind the windows in the castle gardens. Some threw eggs, even stones, at the glass. They were desperate, begging for food. And last night, their shouts and screams had been heard all the way to her bedchamber.

Cambria stood with three other guards beside the door of the throne room. Avva sat on her throne wearing her black hair wrap like her mother—she simply didn't want to bother with her hair —while leaning her chin on her fist. And Engel sat on the floor below, as he always did.

Engel said nothing. He stared at the ground.

Avva stood up and walked to one of the great windows. The garden was still beautiful, but beyond the flowers and neatly manicured green-purple shrubs, a long white coat covered the horizon for as far as the eye could see.

Then another rock was thrown at her.

"I'd stay clear of the windows, Blue," Engel finally said.

"I will not sacrifice my daughter."

Engel slowly nodded. "Your mother once faced the same predicament. The gods' ways are very hard. Too hard. It was terrible for her. I know you never forgave her, but she jailed you to protect you. Then she sacrificed herself."

"Are you saying I should do the same?"

"No … no. You know I don't want anything to happen to you. I don't think I could take it."

Avva placed her hand on the glass window, almost defying her subjects to throw another stone at her. She jerked it back because the glass was frigid.

"Perhaps I should tell you what she told me." He chuckled bitterly. "It is what I told her when Dainya, her mother, had passed. I said it to her as a child to make her feel better. Would you like to hear it?"

Avva didn't answer. She just stared at the mounting snow.

"I said you might as well ask why the sun sets, or why there are stars in the sky, or why clouds form. It seemed to—"

"You're an old man, Engel. My mother was heartless. She imprisoned me. And all I can remember is the witch mocking me, through my entire childhood, in front of the Court."

"Yes. But she saved your life."

"I know what she did. You don't have to tell me how wonderful she was." Avva backed away and climbed back onto her throne. She placed her head in her hand again.

"Everything will be all right," he said.

"No, I don't think so."

Engel climbed the steps and placed a hand on her shoulder. At first, she looked at him crossly, but then she melted before the Mandrigel's smile. His eyes were watering. "Oh Engel, you're the best friend anyone could have. I love you so much." She leaned her head toward him, and he hobbled up the last step to the throne and embraced her.

"I'd be a hypocrite if I told you what to do," he said. "I've made the worst nurse and protector for you and your family."

"You've been the best," Avva said, shaking her head. "And I think I'm not so bad a mother as mine was. I am merely the worst Azure queen."

The two of them jumped as they heard shouting outside the

double doors. Cambria and the other guards barricaded the door.

"What now," Avva said sadly, letting him go. "What are they doing now? I wish Sol were here. He'd know what to do. It seems he's never here when I need him."

"Your husband has always been special."

"Aye … but never here."

"Casey's here."

"Yes. But Henri's gone."

Engel sat back down on the steps under the throne.

"Maybe I've lived too long," Engel said. "I witnessed the end of your mother and your mother's mother. And even her mother Nefertiti's disappearance. I've seen too many leave me."

"Nefertiti. There she is again. You admire her so."

"Everything she did, she did for others."

"It's because of her decree that we suffer, Engel."

"No. It's the gods' will. Nephrea did everything she did for others. She even traveled the depths to save Persephone."

"Persephone imprisoned Casey, Engel."

"Casey said Cora tried to save her. I met her once. Cora's bad, but there's good in her. Yes, but Nephrea was the greatest Azure queen there ever was. … I can tell you, Avva, that if Nephrea were here today, she would do everything she could to right what's wrong. She would—"

He stopped. And she knew the reason. He was about to tell her that she needed to sacrifice herself.

"It was her way, Avva. She was very honorable."

Avva didn't feel honorable. She looked out the window as green reflected off the snow, turning her kingdom turquoise. "I'm a selfish child, Engel. And I am very scared."

"But Avva, I see Nephrea in you. You saved Casey from the Mount. Even Nephrea didn't do that. I know you'd sacrifice everything to make things right, only you have Harmonia's stubborn rebelliousness. I understand. I love both of you. Just as I loved your mother."

"I'm nobody." She chuckled and dried a tear with her sleeve.

"That's what my husband called himself when he met me. But no. *I am* Nobody." There was a crash behind the door. The guards had their staffs raised, ready to fight anyone barging through the doors. "Perhaps being nobody is better. I can't take any more of this. I'm no queen. Look at what I've done. You mistake me. I'm not your Nephrea."

"You are Avivae Ambrosia. I love you. And I know you will do the right thing. Maybe I understand you better than you understand yourself."

43

THE REBELLION

THE DOUBLE DOORS TO THE THRONE ROOM BLEW OPEN, AND A hundred nymphs rushed in. Avva was sitting on her throne nearly dozing off, having been unable to sleep all night. As the crowd poured into the room, stupid old Milda with her long curly white hair led the charge. Cambria and the other three guards tried to block the nymphs with their staffs, but there were too many. And behind them were a hundred more, crowding the inner halls of the palace.

They rushed up to the throne but then stopped as if held by an invisible force—a tradition so strong—as if the ghost of Queen Harmonia protected Avva and held the rioters at bay. Cassandra and Gavin were in the crowds, shouting at the nymphs trying to keep them back.

"What say you, Avva?" cried Milda. "How do you plan to feed your people?"

"*Leave the Court!*" shouted Cambria. But Avva couldn't see her in the thick crowd. "You all break the law barging in here!"

"None of you," cried Gavin, "have been granted admittance—"

"Admittance?" Milda bellowed with laughter. "Ha! You're not even a nymph."

"Step back from the queen," shouted Cambria, "or you'll be charged with treason, Milda!"

"No one permits you to speak in the throne room!" thundered Gavin.

"Avva rules with men," Milda continued, pointing back at the crowd. She made her way onto a wooden chair in the front row. "You see Atalan soldiers along the beaches and now roaming Harmonia's Court. If our founding queen were alive, I tell you she'd crucify them. And see that boy, Gavin of Torinth, that's the Tiger King's son. He and the Crescent king run the Azures while our nymph queen does nothing. Nothing to feed us. Nothing to lead us."

Milda stopped there and stared up at the queen, challenging her. Many others in the throne room looked to Avva. They waited for her response.

"Get out."

Avva spoke in a normal tone, but it sounded like a shout in the chaos. Then she reached back behind her throne and grabbed her scepter. "If you wish cold in the throne room, I can oblige you."

"You swore to Jaida you'd never rebel against an Ambrosia again!" shouted Engel. He stood up on a chair in one of the back rows. "Nephrea spared you. Now you go against—"

"She and you, little man, will starve us with your incompetence," Milda said. "There's no time left to be ruled by fools. All the food stores are frozen."

The crowd jeered.

"Get out of the throne room," Avva repeated to Milda. "Take your followers with you. I'll excuse this offense if you leave now. When the time comes—"

"I will not," Milda said.

The crowd cried in fear as Hanna flew Inghorn through the double doors over their heads. The crowd dispersed when it seemed Hanna intended to land on them.

"Back away! All of you!" Hanna said. The unicorn was now trotting near the throne. "This is the queen's unicorn. The beast has more rights in this chamber than you animals." Then Hanna dismounted and guided Inghorn's head toward Avva.

"Her friend threatens to trample us!" Milda stormed. "And the queen wishes to freeze us with her scepter! Is this what has become of Napea, Amazon? Well, we have swords. We have shields. And we have arrows! We can fight."

"*How dare you!*" Avva rushed down the steps. Milda lurched back. "You threaten the crown? You should be banished to the ice! All you traitors should! Are you cold?" She waved her golden scepter and her subjects fell back in terror. "Cold, hmm? So am I! Hungry? I haven't eaten in two days! Ask the guards who you knocked over by the door. Concerned you'll starve? Maybe we will. So we'll starve together! As Amazon."

"Not true," replied Milda. "We don't starve together, Avivae. It's common knowledge that you hoard food."

"I've ordered our food stores be given away," Avva said. She nodded to Cambria.

But Cambria shook her head. Avva squinted at her.

"Cambria? My edict for the famine?"

"I'm sorry, Avva, I couldn't give away your royal stores. I must protect your life."

The crowd roared in rage. Many took out swords and daggers. Their rage rattled the windows and shook the glass dome above.

"My daughter sleeps hungry!"

"Baceus is sick! She's sick!"

"There's no food left!"

"My roof caved in under the ice!"

Milda raised her hands and quieted the crowd. "You all should know the selfishness of your queen. I do not care whether she offered food, because any such compassion won't absolve her anyway. Because *she* is to blame for the winter." Then she looked at Avva. "Perhaps, if you truly are just and honorable, you'll tell the people why."

Everyone stared at Avva waiting for her words, but she said nothing.

"I thought not," Milda replied with a triumphant smile. The crowd quieted listening to their rebel leader. "Imada finds our struggles, our pain, sisters, stem from Queen Avivae. Let me explain how."

"You accuse the queen!" yelled Hanna, still cradling Inghorn's head before the throne.

"Perhaps even you, Hanna, shall be charged for abetting her. Allow Imada to explain to you, nymphs, why we are in this predicament.

"Avivae was visited by Hades. Hades demanded that she return Cassandra to the Underworld. He made it clear that the refusal of this sacrifice meant a winter not seen since the winter of Persephone. Now…" She smiled smugly at the queen. "Avva could have sacrificed herself as payment, like her mother. But she didn't. Or she could have given the Dark Lord her daughter. But she didn't. So, this ice and snow stems from her refusal to yield to the gods. Such a queen does not deserve favor. She would rather starve us. This is what the Ambrosia family gives you. This is who you follow. Avva does not care about you."

Cassandra looked at Avva in disgust. She had never told her daughter, because she knew her too well. If Casey found out, she'd sacrifice herself.

The people shouted in fury and nearly charged the throne again. Cassandra turned and rushed out of the room.

"Casey!" Avva yelled.

"Grab her," yelled Milda. "Don't let the princess go. She can help end this famine!"

Avva rushed Milda with her scepter, and the old hag fell from the chair and covered her face and body with her arms. But Avva, even with all her bitter hatred, couldn't strike the old hag. Instead she turned from the witch and mounted Inghorn.

"I swear, Milda, if I return, I shall banish you and all your wretched Imada who follow you. Watch yourself, or that sentence could change to a hanging."

Inghorn flapped her wings and Avva rose.

"It's her fault!" shouted Milda, still lying on the ground, pointing at her.

The people burst out in protest, shouting at Avva. Avva rose high, nearly touching the glass dome above. She saw Hanna nod below her as she hovered over everyone.

"There is no proof that Avva's act led to this storm," cried Gavin.

"Avva's innocent!" cried Hanna.

But Avva's heart sank—because it was her fault.

The people advanced under Avva. Gavin swung his sword to keep them back. Then Avva hurled her scepter to the ground. That made the people finally scatter.

She tugged on Inghorn's neck and spoke near her ear. "We shall fly away from here like I did with Antilus when I was a little girl, Inghorn. To the depths of Hades to all of them. I hate them. I hate them all." Inghorn whinnied. Then they soared over her people toward the exit. The crowds ducked and crouched to the ground as the monokera's hooves came close to their heads.

"Your queen runs!" screamed Milda, pointing. "She runs away like Nephratee Ambrosia before her! She abandons us! An Ambrosia abandoning us again!"

"The king will hang you for treason when he returns, witch," Gavin answered. Avva was satisfied when she looked back and saw the hag seemed to fear the prince's words.

The throne room was large enough to house a flying horse, but not the hallways beyond. That's when she saw her friend's method. Hanna had crashed through a window.

Avva galloped, dodging more nymphs in the halls, and burst through the same glass hole. Then she ascended over the palace.

She felt a rush of rage and sadness. She had heard her best friend and son defend her. But she knew in her heart that it was all her fault. And yet so many of her people had abandoned her. Even if they saw the truth, told by that infernal Mildew and Imada, how could they blame her? How could they expect her to sacrifice her daughter?

The fields of purple shone green in the dim light reflecting off snow-covered grass. Threatening clouds loomed overhead.

She soared past a crystal tower and approached the central drawbridge. Then she looked at her husband's beloved lands across the Strait. The ice had become so terrible that it had frozen the entire sea.

She swooped around past another tower. Few of her subjects were on the icy cobblestone roads. But some were crouched over their children, trying to warm them from the cold. It reminded her of beggars on the streets she had heard of in the poorer kingdoms of Gaia. This was not the kingdom she had known all her life. And Avva thought once more—*it is my fault.*

"Inghorn, this shall be our last flight, girl," she said close to her ear, petting her soft feathery hide. "Like Antilus before you, you and I fly from the palace. Let's make this last flight memorable. Just you and I. Not for your Azure queen, but for Anna. Huh? And for Antilus. All right?"

Inghorn neighed and bucked her head up and down.

Avva turned her unicorn toward the Stygian Hole and finally accepted her fate. But as she passed over a stable tower, she saw a nymph mounting a monokera. It looked like her daughter.

"Let's go," Avva said, reaching down to Inghorn's ear again. The unicorn whinnied and rushed past the palace walls, in the opposite direction of Mount Ambitus. Behind her, a nymph on a unicorn was following her.

44

THE FIREBIRD

The Stygian Hole, or the Stygian Crater, was an abomination rarely mentioned in the Azures. It was a bottomless chasm, and few knew how it had come about in their beautiful lands. Some said it had been created when Hades abducted Persephone. Others said this was myth and that Persephone had been taken in Argos in Hellena. Whatever the case, no one visited it out of superstitious fear. The chasm lay on the far southeast side of Napea, in the opposite direction of Mount Ambitus, in the midst of a grassland. It was at least an hour's journey by foot, but close by air.

Avva and Sol had thought of this passage many times when searching for ways to save their daughter. In fact, many Crescent soldiers had lost their lives attempting to descend the great chasm with ropes. Yet the bottom was shrouded in mystery. No one knew if the bottom truly was a gateway to the Underworld or if it simply dropped forever. But most believed it led there.

Avva did. That was why she now stood alone over the chasm in the thick white snow.

She shivered, still wearing her simple blue dress. She had not had time to grab a coat during her escape, and the icy air had numbed her face and body. At least her hair had been wrapped in a black cloth in the tradition of an Ambrosia queen. That provided meager warmth.

Cassandra landed her unicorn hard, practically skidding along the ice near her mother. Avva cocked her head from the pitch-black chasm and saw more monokera in the sky, behind her daughter, giving chase. They would be arriving shortly. She wouldn't be sure if they sided with Milda or her until they landed.

Avva looked down again. She saw sharp rocky edges, possibly climbable, but then nothing. Just pitch blackness. Was the Underworld below?

"How dare you not tell me, Mother!" Cassandra rushed over. "Why did you do this? How could you? You had no right! I'm not a child who—"

"Casey!" snapped Avva. "I won't lose you. Never! Never again! Do you hear me? Never! Your father and I—"

"You already lost me," Cassandra said, turning from her. Her look of shame broke Avva's heart. "All the people hate us now, rightfully so. I can't respect what you did, and I never will. I don't know who you are anymore. You've changed."

Avva pulled her daughter's arm and spun her around.

"Listen to me," Avva said. Casey's eyes were bloodshot. She had been crying too. "If I weren't here, you'd be right. But look where I'm standing. I will right my wrong here and now. This hole leads to the Underworld. I shall drop down now."

"What?" Cassandra's eyes opened wide. Then when Avva nodded, Casey's eyes bulged.

"There's no other way," Avva said. "You don't understand. I was asked to sacrifice you. No mother would ever do that. Even at the price of her kingdom. But I will die if there is no other choice. I made a mistake. You're right. Now I'm here to correct it, Casey. I'll jump and sacrifice for you and the people. Then the snow will end. The gods will give us harvest. And all will be well. And you will be queen."

Cassandra gazed at the approaching monokera and then the dark chasm beneath them. She seemed to fight with her thoughts. Then she looked at Avva and violently shook her head.

"No!" Cassandra said. "No, mother! No!"

"Yes," Avva said sadly with a nod.

Casey grabbed Avva and shoved her down on the ground away from the hole. In the far distance, Avva heard people approaching. Casey wrestled with Avva on the snow, but Avva didn't want to hurt her. She just wanted to be free of her. "Let me go! What are you doing?"

Her daughter wouldn't let go. She held her with all her might, refusing to release her.

"What's the matter?" Avva said, finally stopping Casey from grappling with her. "First you hate me for not sacrificing myself, now you fight me to stop me from doing it?"

"Why is it so hard, mother!" Cassandra said, letting go, sobbing. "Why is everything so hard! How could you want to do this? Why do you have to do this?"

Avva thought of her memories of her childhood. Of being imprisoned by her mother. Then she thought of the day she had lost her daughter to the Underworld. Her life seemed to be full of pain and suffering. Why was it so hard, indeed? She just wanted to let it all go.

Avva was surprised by a sudden wail. It wasn't from her daughter. It was from her.

"I didn't have the strength," Avva said between sobs. "I'm sorry. I couldn't give you up or myself. Milda is right. I'm the worst queen of Azure. The absolute worst. Forgive me, Casey. I'm not strong like you. I couldn't do it. And because of that, the land is broken. Because of me. But it's not in me to give up. My mother could. She could sacrifice herself, and then turn from me, coldly imprison me … I can't do that. I love you more than anything in the world, but I'm scared. I'm so scared. It's not right that the gods force this on us."

They were interrupted by the sound of distant horses trotting. Then many more were falling down from the sky.

"They come," Avva said, holding Casey and patting her

back. Now her daughter was crying harder than she was. "I have to go."

Cassandra shook her head, still in tears.

They both looked toward the distant palace. They could not see the crowds, but they heard the sound of hundreds running and shouting through the woods. The sound of her people awoke Avva from her misery, and her tears stopped.

"Casey," she looked desperately into Cassandra's eyes. She kissed her forehead. "The gods force this. Like my mother, I won't sacrifice you. I understand now. I must do what must be done as queen." Her people were rushing through the forests, some on horseback, others on foot. One monokera swept down right beside them. It was Cambria. She jumped off, pulled out her sword, and stood in a fighter stance protecting them. "I need your strength, Casey. You've always been stronger than me. I'm not sure I have the strength for this."

"Then don't do it. Forget what I said, Mother. We'll find another way."

Avva grabbed her daughter tightly. "I love you."

They came by the hundreds. Her subjects and many men from throughout the empire who had heard of the rebellion.

Gavin approached on horseback first. He rode quickly and joined Cambria, ready to stave off the thousands of nymphs. It seemed the entire kingdom of Azure had amassed by the hole. Many more dropped from the sky above, while a great many more ran out of the forest.

"Ah, unlike my cold mother, at least I don't go alone," quipped Avva bitterly. "They have all come to say goodbye."

"No, mother," Cassandra said, shaking her head. "No. Why does anyone have to leave? Hades doesn't want you, he wants me. Let him have me."

"I know," Avva replied with a nod. "But you are not the only one, princess, who has violated Nefertiti's edict. And not the only one who can right this wrong."

"Mother, Hades asked for me!" Cassandra cried. "Me! He

will still want me whether you go or not. He wants me for Cora. Persephone wants my company. He doesn't want you."

Avva looked at the hole and felt determined. She shook her head. "You told me Cora helped you escape."

"She's a liar. A deceiver. Mother ... we ... you crossed Olympus. Father conquered all of Atala. We've done all this. Surely we can do something to stop this now?"

"I crossed the mountain for you. Father fought a war to protect you. We did these things because we love you. Were they so great?"

Avva leaned down and embraced her daughter one last time and then walked to Inghorn and mounted her. Then she rose in the air.

Once more, some of the traitors believed she intended to flee. Cassandra would not stop crying. It was her daughter's tears and her people's cold reaction to them that angered Avva the most. She shook her head violently, looking down at them, now not as a frightened princess, but as their queen.

Hanna ran below her in tears too. Then Avva spotted Cassandra's best friend, Lalaina, and Sandra running to her and helping her up. All three girls looked up at Avva. And Avva saw the terrible Milda. Milda had a nasty grin, for the wise witch had probably guessed Avva's terrible plans. Engel was there too, wiping tears and shouting something unheard among the murmurs of so many others.

Oh, husband, if only you were here now, my love. I regret not seeing you the most. I could take this step so much more easily with your strength.

The crowds became thick. Cambria and Gavin and many other guards pushed them back. But Hanna was permitted by the guards to run right under her.

"Must you do this?" Hanna asked, wiping tears with the sleeves of her dress.

"Goodbye, Hanna," Avva said. "You have known me like Engel ... And there ... there is Engel."

"Oh, Avva, I want you to know that you were right in passing beyond the Strait," Hanna said, choking on her words. "You were right when we were children. It was the right thing to do. It was your freedom that made me love you."

Engel was now crying.

"Did I pass the Strait?" Avva asked Hanna with a sad smile.

"Yes, my queen," Hanna replied with a curtsey. "Yes. Yes, you did. And you landed. You even fought on their lands like the great Harmonia Ambrosia. With her courage."

"Ah, I wish you had seen Gaia, Hanna. But instead, now you can help me keep the palace in order for the centuries to come."

"Oh Avva, I love you. I love you so."

Avva nodded sadly.

She turned to Engel.

But the crowds were too unruly for her to speak. Gavin, Falena, and other guards kept pushing the crowds away. Some were shouting for them to force their queen down. And some threw stones. Yet this time, the crowd was not only rebels but the queen's supporters, and any who attacked Avva fell into fist fights with her defenders below.

Cambria turned to Avva and tossed her the scepter. "For order, Queen Avivae," Cambria cried with a nod, while pushing her people back.

But Avva took the golden rod and threw it, in turn, to her daughter. Never had any coronation been faster than that. Then before the multitude, Avva bowed to her daughter on her flying unicorn. And at the sight of that, everyone in the crowd finally quieted. Even the rebels were affected.

"I am the only Azure queen who has ever attended her daughter's coronation," Avva shouted among the hubbub. People quieted more. "What a great honor."

"I love you, Mother," Cassandra said in tears, looking up from her friend's arms.

The multitude quieted more. How strange. The whole valley, with thousands of nymphs, turned completely silent as everyone, including all the usurpers, finally understood Avva's intentions. Only the flapping of Inghorn's wings could be heard.

Princess Cassandra took the staff and faced the crowds. She raised the scepter above her head. Then many nymphs bowed before their new queen.

Cassandra quelled her sorrow as best as she could and stood proudly before the multitude. Cheers and applause erupted from some. There were some dissenters, surely, but their dissent was now buried under the applause.

"Subjects!" Avva shouted. "Welcome your new queen. Be happy, for how fortunate for Azure to have Casey leading you. But, as for me, I'm afraid Imada's objections are sound. I've failed you. I renounce the crown."

There were some jeers, but many more objections. Avva raised her hand for quiet.

"This winter came from my selfishness. I … am afraid. The seasons turn. But our green lands have been frozen long enough. It is with sadness that I take my leave."

And then all that applauded cried out in protest, and the guards near the hole had to block a stampede, this time from Avva's supporters. Avva raised her hand yet again.

"Be proud, Amazon warriors. We've triumphed against those who would take our homes, and those who would enslave or defeat us. Be proud. From wood nymph to the strongest force in all of Atala, we remain supreme. It is for this reason that Demeter rages by sending this blizzard. It is because the gods fear us … I will miss you all."

She fought back her own tears. And struggled to maintain her courage again.

"I wish I could comfort you with the passing of time. But I'm not so wise. Some may ask, why do I leave? Remember the edict. The law of Olympus, forced on us by Hades and Queen Nefertiti: '*Any Outworlder who steps foot on Gaia will come to me.*'" She paused and nodded. Then she looked at them feeling fire in her eyes. "But don't take my leave as defeat. Do not be deceived. I urge you all, as your Amazon queen, to obey one order of mine after my departure. An answer to the gods' arrogance. Live with man. Not in festivals. Not in holidays. Go across the Strait and live with men. The gods fear us. Answer them with your defiance. I promise you, you won't regret it … For without my choice…" She turned and looked across the Strait, longing for her beloved husband once more. "I would not have met the greatest man in all the world, your lord king and my husband. His heart and his courage, I'm afraid, prove my mother was wrong about men. All my mothers, including even the great Queen Harmonia, were wrong.

"Your new queen, Cassandra, would never have been born had I listened to the gods, for I would not have fallen in love. So this is *my* edict, fellow nymphs, and my last wish before I leave. I, Queen Avivae, at the precipice of my fall, ask you to follow Avivae's edict: live with man and disobey the gods. Give up your immortality so that you may live. More so, disobey any law passed by Mount Olympus."

With her blasphemy came a sudden bitter rush of cold. Like a hurricane, freezing air made many fall to the ground. Snow flurried upon the crowd. The wind was so strong that it pushed people over in its wake, and some struggled not to fall into the hole themselves. Avva shifted on Inghorn, nearly falling off. But then there was a counter storm rising from the depths of the dark chasm below, and it kept Avva atop her. And inside Avva's heart, she rejoiced at the gods' fury, because she knew her words had hurt them.

Avva looked down into the pitch blackness below. And with the wind still raging, and all her friends fighting it to say goodbye, she flew directly over the center. Then she looked toward her palace, now frozen in the distance like a shard of ice. And then Mount Ambitus.

"*Let this sacrifice save my daughter!*" she shouted and raised a fist toward the Mount. "*Not for you, bastard Zeus, do I fall. I fall for her and my people!*" A thunderbolt came down, nearly knocking her from her unicorn. Then another. Then a third, but the third bolt of lightning changed direction and was diverted, exploding a tree many yards away. A rush of wind and rain, rushed forth from below, once more nearly knocked Avva off her unicorn, but Inghorn readjusted and remained aloft.

"I am afraid," she said quietly, mostly to herself. "Farewell, girl," Avva said, petting Inghorn's hide. "Do not—"

She stopped speaking. The violent wind rising from the hole changed the light from the green sun. For the first time in Napea, it burned a yellow-white like the sun in the Hinterlands. Avva glanced up in shock. And hovering in this bright white light, as Avva squinted, was a bird. And then, above the crowd, the bird burst aflame. The flame cut through the wind and rain like Zeus's thunderbolt under the yellow sun.

She looked down into the dark chasm. She could swear she heard Henri in the wind uttering words that comforted her soul: "*Neeteru Belok Dispin.*" It could have been imagined in her distress. But whatever it was, the words gave her great comfort.

"Oh, Henri," she said to herself. "Sol, it's Henri. Henri, if you're there, say goodbye to my love. Please. Say goodbye to Sol for me."

With those words, she leaped off her unicorn and jumped into the chasm.

The fall was sharp and she felt the rise in her chest and the wind rushing against her face and body. But then, strangely, she slowed. She was adrift midair, slowly descending. Perhaps she had already died and this was some strange illusion.

But the hole above was moving away at a very slow pace now. And she didn't have the sensation of falling.

A wind, now gentle, seemed to form below her again. A great multitude of faces, shadowed by a white sun, appeared over the hole. She guessed it was her people. She watched as their heads faded into darkness, and the hole soon faded.

She closed her eyes. She felt a calmness. Peace.

She would die now. She would let go and let this happen.

Then, upon her shoulder, she felt the flutter of a bird's wings touch her. Then a bird cooed.

"Oh, Mainax. Give me the strength. Please."

All grew dark.

A white light burst forth again through the opening far above. A bright white light. In the darkness, it appeared to be the brightest light Avva had ever seen.

45

RISE

Someone or something was near her. She even thought she heard a stranger's breath, but she could not see anything. Was this another illusion or was this death? Had she already hit the ground? And yet she continued to fall slowly. She fell forever, and she wondered if death was simply an eternal fall.

But Mainax, oddly, cooed by her shoulder. He was with her. She closed her eyes. Perhaps the phoenix had simply joined her on her way to Charon?

When her eyes opened, she found herself lying on a soft blanket under flickering torchlight. She turned her head and saw the torch was lit in a surrounding pitch blackness, as black as the chasm itself. And she heard breathing from horses, or monokera, and the flapping of wings. Then she saw a flicker of another flame. But this wasn't a unicorn. It was the breath of larger horses.

Her eyes slowly adjusted. She leaned on an elbow and found herself surrounded by dark hills and valleys for as far as the eye could see. The terrain was shadows in the far distance.

She sat up and red light shone on the cracks and craterlike surface in the distance. Then she jumped as she saw someone kneeling beside her, tending a lantern. At first, she thought it was

Cassandra. She seemed not much older. The lady had a youthful face with long flowing blond hair. Strikingly beautiful. The most beautiful girl Avva had ever seen. Yet she wore simple pants and a brown tunic. Her bright blue eyes flickered in the dim firelight.

"Am I dead?" Avva asked her. "Is this the Underworld?"

"You are alive, Ambrosia nymph." The girl said. Then she said very sternly, "But yes, this is the Underworld. We've never met before. My name is Cora."

THE END

Cora and the nymphs of Azure continue their Greek mythological mayhem in the epic fantasy "Azure Series":

- CORA: RISE OF THE FALLEN GODDESS
- AZURE BLUE
- CORAL RED
- HARMONIA (prequel)
- PRINCESS SOJOURN (prequel)

ALSO BY A. L. HAWKE

FANTASY: THE AZURE SERIES TRILOGY

- CORA: RISE OF THE FALLEN GODDESS
- AZURE BLUE
- CORAL RED
- HARMONIA (prequel)
- PRINCESS SOJOURN (prequel)

URBAN FANTASY ROMANCE

- MY EVIL EYE
- THE GUARDIAN
- NECTAR OF AMBROSIA
- CORA

PARANORMAL ROMANCE

- ALONDRA
- BROOMSTICK
- WINDSTORM
- THE HAWTHORNE WITCH

- SHADES
- HAUNTING JOY
- PHANTOM MASQUERADE

SCIENCE FICTION

- CANDY SAVANT
- MOTHER SAVANT

Books available at https://alhawke.com/books

PARTING WORDS

What did you think of *Azure Blue*? By placing a book review, you can inform others of your thoughts and help spread the word about my book.

Want more? Periodically I like to send news regarding current or new projects. If you'd like to be privy, I encourage you to sign up to my email newsletter. Your information will remain private and you can cancel any time.

Sign up at www.alhawke.com or scan the following QR code:

ACKNOWLEDGMENTS

The first draft of *Azure Blue* was written seven years ago. Before there was *Cora: Rise of the Fallen Goddess*, there was *Azure Blue*. Back then, when the novel was three hundred pages heavier, it was beta read and critiqued by John P. and Rob C. When I returned to the epic fantasy this year, I had the help of Monique S. and George B. It was polished through Stephanie Ward's copy edit and proofread by Alexa B. And, finally, I was fortunate to commission the artist Sean Counley to paint the cover and draw the maps. Thank you all for helping bring Azure Blue out into the world!

ABOUT THE AUTHOR

A.L. Hawke is the author of the bestselling Hawthorne University Witch series. The author lives in Southern California torching the midnight candle over lovers against a backdrop of machines, nymphs, magic, spice and mayhem. A.L. Hawke writes fantasy and romance spanning four thousand years, from pre-civilization to contemporary and beyond.

Visit A.L. Hawke at www.alhawke.com

Email: contact@alhawke.com

www.ingramcontent.com/pod-product-compliance
Lightning Source LLC
Chambersburg PA
CBHW060943190726
48286CB00005B/1402